The

HELICOPTER HEIST

The

HELICOPTER HEIST

A Novel Based on True Events

JONAS BONNIER

*Translated from the Swedish
by Alice Menzies*

Other Press
New York

Originally published in 2017 as *Helikopterrånet* by Albert Bonniers Förlag, Stockholm

Copyright © Jonas Bonnier 2017
Published by agreement with Salomonsson Agency

English translation copyright © Alice Menzies 2017

Production editor: Yvonne E. Cárdenas
This book was set in Arno Pro and Akzidenz Std.

10 9 8 7 6 5 4 3 2 1

Library of Congress Cataloging-in-Publication Data

Names: Bonnier, Jonas, 1963- author. | Menzies, Alice, translator.
Title: The helicopter heist : a novel based on true events / Jonas Bonnier ; translated from the Swedish by Alice Menzies.
Other titles: Helikopterrånet. English
Description: New York : Other Press, 2019.
Identifiers: LCCN 2018046495 (print) | LCCN 2018042714 (ebook) | ISBN 9781590519509 (pbk.) | ISBN 9781590519516 (ebook)
Classification: LCC PT9877.12.O66 H4513 2019 (ebook) | LCC PT9877.12.O66 (print) | DDC 839.73/8—dc23
LC record available at https://lccn.loc.gov/2018046495

Publisher's Note
This is a work of fiction. Names, characters, places, and incidents either are the product of the author's imagination or are used fictitiously.

Author's Note

This book is a novel based on true events. The author has, in other words, taken the real, the documented, the observed and the recounted as a starting point, and let his imagination take over, fill in, expand.

Certain locations and names have been changed, certain situations have been added, while others have been taken away, and in such cases, any similarities with reality are coincidental.

DECEMBER 2008

1

Hunched over his walking stick, the old man came out of the woods. The road was nothing more than a couple of overgrown tire tracks. He was wearing a pair of black rubber boots bought at Coop Forum in Handen a few weeks earlier, and a dark brown raincoat from Tempo in Fältöversten.

He wasn't much of a man for buying clothes, he never had been.

The ground was still free from snow, but the frost had the trees and bushes in its iron grip. It was a genuinely cold day at last, and perhaps the snow would arrive that evening.

In the icy woods, where the trees' dark green needles were the brightest color in an otherwise grayish-brown palette, a black dog appeared up ahead of the man. A Labrador retriever. The dog studied its owner, lowered its nose to the ground and ran off. A few yards later, three more black dogs came running, all the same breed and size. They crossed the track and vanished into the bushes on the other side. The old man followed them. He could hear the rest of the pack behind him, three bitches and a male, wandering back and forth over frozen sprigs of blueberries and thickets of ferns.

They were on their way home.

The man lived in a dark red cottage just south of Landfjärden, roughly halfway between Nynäshamn and Stockholm. Through the thick forest outside his kitchen window, he could see over to the island of Muskö during the winter. It was only a few hundred yards from his gate to the water's edge, and there were plenty of spots for his dogs to splash about during spring and summer. Labradors were a breed with webbed toes, after all, bred for retrieving things from the water.

The eight adult dogs lived with the man in the main cottage, and the two outhouses were for the litters of puppies. He had been breeding Labradors for almost twenty years, and preferred dogs to people. That was why he lived in the cottage in the woods. Since there was neither mains water nor reliable electricity in the area, he was left to his own devices. His neighbors kept their distance, the closest living in the urban development that started twelve or so miles to the south.

The man had gone to meet the buyers himself during the first few years, but he had always lost his temper when the fat old ladies asked whether the dogs needed a lot of exercise and when the spoiled young kids pulled on the puppies' ears. And when he lost his temper, he had always raised his voice and slapped away the children's snotty hands.

It had never been God's plan for him to be a salesman. These days, he had help. People from other kennels displayed the puppies and young dogs for him, they even looked after the business side of things. And took all the credit, not that the old man cared.

When he returned home from his morning walk, it was just before nine. His cottage consisted of three rooms and one kitchen. Since the dogs always brought half the forest back into the house with them, and the old man had been having back trouble for the past few years, there wasn't much point in cleaning. He didn't let the dogs into the kitchen, meaning it was the only room that had some kind of order to it. He turned on the coffee machine.

He was expecting company.

He knew them well enough to be sure they would turn up when he asked them to come. He assumed they were afraid of him, and they wouldn't be the only ones.

Sami Farhan was first to arrive.

The old man saw him approaching along the path from the main road. The bus from Västerhaninge to Nynäshamn stopped up on the 73, and the cottage wasn't much more than ten minutes into the woods.

It had been years since Sami had last sparred in the ring, but he still moved like a boxer. Despite his big, heavy body, he was quick and light on his feet, and it took him less than a minute to make his way from the gate up to the house. He was wearing a short gray woolen coat that seemed better suited to the trendy Nytorget on a warm spring day, and he had white sneakers on his feet.

The man let him in. The eight black dogs were so excited by his unexpected visit that they came close to flooring the boxer. Since the man's second guest clearly hadn't been on the same bus, they would have to wait another thirty-five minutes. That was the amount of time between departures. The old man grabbed the key to the outhouse from a hook behind the door, and they went out into the yard together.

"How are your brothers, Sami?" the old man asked.

"Why?"

"I saw your older brother Ali a while ago, but it's a long time since I saw the younger one, Adil, isn't it?"

"Yeah, that's his name."

"Everything OK with him?"

"You'll have to invite him over and ask him yourself if you're so interested."

The man nodded and looked down at the ground. An amused smile played on his lips. Sami's touchiness where his brothers were concerned was the same as ever.

In the yard between the two outhouses, the old man had a root cellar. It had been built during the fifties. Stone had been laid on stone in the old-fashioned way, and there was moss growing on the roof. After just a few decades, the building looked as old as the woods surrounding it.

Flanked by the eight dogs, the man and Sami stopped at the cellar to fetch food for the puppies. It was where he kept the dogs' food, the paper towels and toilet paper, and everything else that wouldn't fit into the larder in the main house. The cellar was much bigger than it looked, blasted into the rocks behind it.

At the very back, shrouded in darkness, the old man had fifty or so boxes stacked on top of one another. Each was filled with banknotes, sorted into plastic pouches. There were notes of all denominations, and the sum total exceeded 300 million kronor.

In all likelihood, the money was on the verge of rotting in the cool, damp cellar.

But the old man wasn't worried about that. There wasn't anything in particular he wanted to spend it on, after all.

He asked Sami to carry the dog food, and they went to feed the ever-hungry puppies in silence.

When they returned to the main house, the old man disappeared into his bedroom one floor up, and Sami sat in the kitchen, staring at the water running through the coffee filter for ten long minutes. He had always had trouble sitting still, and without even thinking about it, he impatiently began tapping his foot so vigorously that his entire leg shook. He stared out the window and eventually saw Michel Maloof approaching through the woods. Right then, he also heard footsteps on the stairs; the old man was on his way back down.

Michel Maloof was shorter than Sami. He walked with his shoulders gently hunched, though he also moved quickly and determinedly. He was wearing a pair of boots better suited to the forest, but it was obvious he was freezing. When the old man opened the door, Maloof's face cracked into its characteristic grin, revealing two rows of teeth that shone bright against his well-groomed black beard.

"All right," he said.

He held out his hand, forgetting that the old man never shook hands. Thanks to the dogs and the chaos of the situation, there was no time for embarrassment.

"Sami is already here," said the old man.

"Sami?" Maloof repeated. "That Sami?"

There was a barely perceptible sharpness to his tone. Other than that, it was impossible to determine what Maloof really meant by his question. His ability to hide what he was thinking and feeling was legendary; no one would voluntarily play poker with Michel Maloof. His expressions were imperturbable, the customary smile not affected by any external circumstances, and his movements were slow, as though well considered and thought out.

He ran a hand through his beard as Sami appeared in the kitchen doorway.

"What a surprise," the boxer said.

If you wanted to work with Michel Maloof or Sami Farhan, everyone knew that you couldn't be messing about with drugs at the same time.

Despite this, Maloof's and Farhan's paths had never crossed more than fleetingly.

Not before now.

They sat down at the worn kitchen table. Sami and Maloof both had their hands wrapped around their hot coffee cups, and Sami wondered how the man could live somewhere so cold. One of the dogs began to howl outside the kitchen, and it didn't take long for his relatives to join in. The old man silenced them with a brief command, without even needing to raise his voice.

Sami and Maloof glanced at one another.

They shared the dogs' respect for the old man, though they couldn't claim to know or like him. He wasn't the type of person you felt much affection for. Still, whenever he got in touch, they came. Why wouldn't they? The old man often had interesting ideas.

"You're not wearing enough layers," he said when Sami asked about turning the heat up.

Sami held back from telling him that you could buy battery-powered heaters these days, if the problem was the lack of electricity in the cottage.

"I've got a suggestion," the old man continued. "Or perhaps a question."

Sami and Maloof were listening. The difference between the two men was particularly clear when they sat next to one another. Sami's gaze was open and encouraging, it waited eagerly for the next sentence, it was urgent. Maloof sat with his face turned away, tense and seemingly uninterested, lost within himself. When he briefly met the old man's eye, it was with the cautious curiosity of a watcher.

"There's a building in Västberga," the old man said, "I know you're both familiar with it. A building containing a huge amount of cash. And an opportunity has arisen . . ."

The dogs growled. They started playing, and it soon sounded like they were tipping the furniture in the next room. But their game came to an end without the man having to say a word.

"I know of a woman," he continued, "who I think could be . . . of assistance. There's a chance, at the very least. She's looking for . . . company. She's registered on those sites? You know, the kind where you make dates?"

Sami and Maloof nodded. If it had been someone else talking, they would have laughed at his choice of words, about "making dates." But with this old man, there was no joking. With him, you kept your mouth shut and listened.

Instead, they drank the coffee, which was strong and bitter, and waited for him to go on.

"That's why I asked you here," he said after a short pause. "I thought it might be something for you. Maybe you'd like to meet the girl? She's your age. Go out and eat dinner with her. You can say you got her details from the ad."

Maloof and Sami glanced at one another. Neither of them had ever been lacking for women in their lives.

"I don't think I can, sadly," Sami eventually said. "You know we're having another baby, right?"

"I know." The old man nodded. "Pretty soon, isn't it? Your son can't even be one? What was his name? John? Has he been christened yet?"

"I can't date a girl," Sami said without answering his questions.

He stomped his feet in an attempt to warm them up, and explained:

"Not even pretending. You know what I mean? Plus, I'm not doing that kind of thing anymore. I've got something else on the go. You know?"

The man nodded, but his expression hadn't changed. It was as though he hadn't heard Sami's objections.

"And what do you say, Michel?" he asked.

"Yeah, I mean," said Maloof, "I can date anyone. I mean . . . this girl . . . there's a police station two hundred yards from that place in Västberga. She can't . . . change that, can she?"

The man didn't reply.

"No, no," Maloof continued, both cautious about disagreeing with the old man and keen to share his doubts, "and, yeah . . . they've got guards in reception twenty-four seven. A hundred cameras. One of the most secure vaults in northern Europe? But . . . maybe she knows all that?"

The man didn't seem to catch the irony.

"Meet up with her," he repeated, and turned to Sami. "Listen to her. She might happen to say something of interest."

Sami pulled at the neck of his sweatshirt as though he needed to get some air.

"No thanks, not for me," he politely replied, as though he had been offered another biscuit.

The man stared at him with no expression on his face, and then he turned to Maloof.

"Michel?"

"Yeah. Or"—he changed his mind—"I don't know?"

"If you take her out for dinner, I'll foot the bill," the old man said. "And if it leads anywhere, I could imagine helping out financially."

"Sure, sure." Maloof nodded. "No."

"No?"

Maloof made a gesture so vague it was impossible to interpret. He didn't want to seem negative. He looked at Sami, who shook his head

almost imperceptibly as he rubbed his hands to warm them up. Both had a huge amount of respect for the man with the dogs, but this time he seemed to be clutching at straws.

"That disappoints me," said the old man, getting up from the table. "That really disappoints me."

A dense silence spread through the kitchen, and both visitors felt uneasy.

The man took a piece of paper from his pocket and handed it to Maloof.

"You could at least take this? The girl's personal details. And the rest of her contact details. In case you change your mind?"

"Thanks," Maloof replied, taking the slip and shoving it into his jacket pocket. "You never know. You don't."

"I think that you and Sami could achieve something really . . . interesting if you worked together," the man added.

FEBRUARY–MAY 2009

2

Michel Maloof had decided to go for a walk through the newly built waterfront area along Hornsbergs Strand. He was wearing a thin black coat over his dark suit, and the smooth soles of his shoes hadn't been designed for the icy ground. Every now and then he slipped on the path. He was carrying a black briefcase in one hand. It acted as a kind of counterweight, helping him keep his balance when he turned onto the path down toward the canal on the other side of the Ekelund Bridge.

He was early. The meeting wasn't until two, meaning he still had twenty minutes to kill. He had parked his pale gray Seat Ibiza right outside the entrance to the G4S offices on Warfvinges Väg. The car was the most anonymous he had ever driven; if he left it in a big car park, he might even walk straight past it. But for Maloof, it was often important not to draw any attention to himself, and the Seat Ibiza seemed to have been designed with that very ambition in mind.

Even so, he didn't have the patience to sit and wait in it for almost half an hour.

He had never come this close before.

It wasn't nerves he was trying to shake off during his quick walk, it was excitement.

The cold weather was back after a warm January, but the narrow canal was still clear of ice. Maybe the city made sure to keep all its channels open? He didn't know anything about Stadshagen, it wasn't his neighborhood.

Michel Maloof had been born in Lebanon. When he was six, his family had fled the country's bloody civil war and made their way to Italy, via the coast, but for his father, the final destination had always been clear. They were going to Scandinavia, that paradise on earth. How or why his father had come to believe that the Nordic countries

were the solution to all their problems, young Michel hadn't known, but he hadn't been raised to question his father. Their journey from Italy continued north, and the bright colors and warm winters of the Mediterranean were replaced by cold Norrland seriousness. Maloof's lasting memory of that time in his life was that he had been freezing. Constantly.

After their first year in Åsele, in the north of the country, roughly halfway between Östersund and Arvidsjaur, even Maloof's father had decided that he was fed up with the silence, the darkness and the forests. He made the family pack up their few belongings once again. The dream of Sweden still lived on, but living so close to the Arctic Circle was too extreme. So the family set down roots in the Stockholm suburb of Fittja instead, a place many associated with criminality, poverty and social problems. But it was there that the family had finally found the security they had been searching for, where the positives were so great that the negatives could be ignored. It was where they lived to this day.

At the foot of the Essingeleden Bridge, Maloof turned to head back. A fine layer of powdery snow was covering the grass on either side of the path, making the gray afternoon seem a little brighter.

Of all the neighborhoods in Stockholm, Stadshagen, tucked away to one side of the city center, was one of the most anonymous. The district had been an industrial area since the fifties, with no other ambition than to offer cheap square footage and accessible docks. It was only recently that the politicians and town planners had realized that the location was far too good to be an industrial and business wasteland, and they were poised to transform the area into an attractive place to live.

As Maloof walked back up onto Hornsbergs Strand and saw the signs of the building work, which had been temporarily brought to a halt by the cold, he felt the familiar relief at not living in central Stockholm.

He liked Fittja and never felt the urge to come into town; in fact, he almost always wanted to get away from it.

He looked at his watch. Ten to two.

Maloof took a deep breath.

An older woman with blow-dried blond hair and glasses with black frames was sitting in reception. On the wall behind her, the G4S logo glowed like a religious icon for its employees to bow down to every time they came into the office.

The woman gave Maloof a stern look as he climbed the stairs from the street.

He unconsciously straightened the knot in his tie, quickly pushed his long hair behind his ears and ran a hand over his neat beard. Then he smiled broadly.

"I have a meeting with Anders Mild at two?"

The woman wasn't falling for his charms. She nodded reluctantly and told him to sit down to the right of reception while she called Mild's secretary.

The minimalist sofa was even less comfortable than it looked, and as Maloof sat down, he was reminded of just how much he disliked wearing a suit. The modern cut felt tight across his shoulders. He had bought a dark red tie the day before, and it had taken twenty minutes of increasing frustration to manage a nice knot. How was anyone supposed to feel successful with a noose around his neck?

Maloof leaned forward and peered down the corridor of offices. The man he was waiting for, Anders Mild, was the managing director and head of G4S in Sweden. Without Zoran Petrovic's help, Maloof would never have managed to arrange this meeting, and as Mild's secretary came down the corridor toward him, Maloof realized how Petrovic had managed it.

Mild's secretary was very young and very cute.

Maloof got to his feet. He realized he was clutching the handle of his black attaché case far too hard. He shook the girl's hand.

"Can I get you anything?" she asked as she showed him into a large

meeting room with a view out onto the roofs of the surrounding buildings and the treetops down by the canal. "Water? Coffee?"

"Sure," said Maloof. "That's fine, thanks."

He pulled out a chair in the middle of the long table and set down his briefcase on the one next to it.

"Do you need to use the projector?" the girl asked, still not sure whether her guest had said yes or no to the offer of coffee.

At first, he didn't know what she meant.

"For the presentation?" she explained. "You're giving a presentation to Anders, no?"

Maloof shook his head. "Right, right. Yes . . . no projector today," he said, patting his briefcase with a smile. "This is my presentation."

She nodded, not caring what he meant, and then left him with the door open while she went to fetch her boss.

Maloof was far too worked up to sit down.

Along with Zoran Petrovic, Maloof had done a lot of research. G4S was the world's biggest security company. Operating in 125 countries, it was also one of the largest private employers, with over 600,000 staff globally. The company's humble origins could be traced back to Copenhagen, where, around the same time as fireworks lit up the night sky to celebrate the dawn of the twentieth century, a small firm that hired out night guards had been born. A few decades later, the company was renamed Group 4 Falck, but it would be a while before its growth really took off.

"It's all about money," Petrovic had explained to Maloof. "You can chug away for year after year without anything really happening. I mean, who hasn't run a security company? But without resources, you're not going to get anywhere."

Some time after the dawn of the next century, the venture capitalists had suddenly turned their attention to the security industry. They opened their coffers, brandished their whips, changed the company's

name to Group 4 Securicor and launched an extensive takeover plan. In Sweden, the once state-owned ABAB fell victim to the growing firm, and Petrovic turned nostalgic and told a long, pointless story about how he used to trick ABAB guards in an industrial area.

Group 4 Securicor, or G4S, grew rapidly on the London Stock Exchange and eventually split into two distinct business areas: G4S Secure Solutions, which dealt with surveillance, and G4S Cash Solutions, which handled the secure transport of valuables.

Anders Mild was responsible for G4S Cash Solutions in Sweden, and he didn't leave Michel Maloof waiting for more than a moment or two in the meeting room. Mild was blue eyed and average height, with a neck that barely seemed able to support his head, and he was dressed in a shiny gray suit and an exclusive pale blue shirt that was unbuttoned at the collar. He moved energetically around the conference table, shook Maloof's hand and nodded toward the older man who had come in behind him, but who had chosen to remain on the other side of the table.

"This is Rick Almanza," Anders Mild said, introducing his colleague. "Rick here is responsible for our European activity, Michel. He's my boss. I told him about our meeting, and he thought it sounded so interesting that he flew over from London to join us. Is it OK if we continue in English?"

Maloof smiled and nodded.

Could it be true? What exactly had Zoran Petrovic said? Anders Mild didn't know a thing about Maloof, who hadn't even used his real surname when he booked the meeting, to avoid any problems with Google. Did people really fly over from London on such vague grounds? Was it a trap?

Suspicion was precisely what he needed. He felt his racing heart slow, his nerves give way to energy and this new challenge sharpen his focus. This was how he worked.

He was only ever nervous before the task itself, never while he was sorting it out. He nodded and enthusiastically shook Rick Almanza's hand over the table.

"English. No problem. I'm truly honored."

Anders Mild went back over to his boss's side of the table and sat down.

Maloof debated whether to move over to the whiteboard, but decided against it. It wasn't like he had anything to draw on it, anyway.

He glanced at the lapel on Mild's jacket, where there was a small G4S logo badge. Michel Maloof had been robbing secure transport vehicles bearing that same logo since his early teens. Did the two men opposite realize that they had just let one of Sweden's most notorious robbers into the boardroom of the world's biggest security firm?

3

Out in the hallway, Sami Farhan tied his boots, pulled on a thick, dark green down jacket over his polo shirt and was just about to step into the stairwell when he heard John wake.

He paused in the doorway, his fingers silently drumming the handle, listening tensely. The cot was in their bedroom, by the window. Since it was only six in the morning, he had pushed the door shut to avoid waking Karin or the boy. He stood completely still for a moment, and the babbling seemed to stop, but then he heard an expectant gurgle that gradually increased in volume.

The baby was definitely waking up.

Sami gently closed the front door and quickly made his way back down the hall and into the bedroom, still wearing his coat and boots. Karin was sleeping, but she turned anxiously in the big double bed. She had been up at least two or three times during the night, he wasn't exactly sure. Sami lifted the tiny body from the cot and held the boy against his soft down jacket, gently rocking and lulling the little bundle. But his efforts were doomed to fail. John was hungry, and no amount of rocking would fix that.

"What time is it?"

Karin mumbled into the pillow. Sami carefully lowered the baby onto the bed next to her. The scent of breast milk practically made John howl, and Karin pulled back the covers, revealing her round, pregnant belly as she uncovered her breast.

"Where are you off to so early?" she asked, still not knowing what time it was.

Sami was sweating under his thick coat. He stood there irresolutely, rocking nervously, as though he were still holding the baby. He couldn't tear his eyes from them. The pregnant woman breastfeeding

the tiny child. His family. The scent of bodies filled the room. Skin, closeness.

"Are you going to school?" she asked.

He grunted. It could be interpreted as a confirmation without actually being one.

"What's the time?"

The minute Karin opened her eyes and turned her head, she would see the digital clock on the bedside table. He told the truth.

"Five past six."

"Have they started doing dawn lectures or something?"

She smiled, but her eyes were still closed. The baby guzzled.

Sami was enrolled at the Kristineberg culinary school, in his second semester. He had always been good at cooking, but now he was going to learn the trade from scratch. He had promised her. When she got pregnant for the first time, she had given him an ultimatum. In her usual clear way, she had explained that if there was a risk that the father of her child would end up in prison, she would find a new one, one who had different ambitions in life. Either Sami stopped using his days to plan one spectacular robbery or break-in after another, or he could clear off right then, before he became emotionally attached to the baby. And vice versa.

There had been no question for Sami, it had been obvious. He was willing to do anything for Karin's sake.

That was why he had applied to Kristineberg. He had finally decided to get himself a real job.

"The whole class is going out to Frihamnen to meet the boats coming in with shellfish," he answered, bending the truth slightly.

Like always, he talked with the help of his arms and hands. He showed the direction of Frihamnen, mimicked the boats moving into the harbor and made a gesture that might have represented some kind of shellfish.

"Go," Karin whispered with a smile. "Get going. We might fall asleep again . . ."

He nodded. Tapped his foot like he was keeping time with a techno tune at double speed. But still, he couldn't move. John was feeding noisily. Karin could sense his hesitation. She opened her eyes and looked at him, standing fully dressed in front of her.

"You're so damn handsome." She smiled. "Don't just stand there being so ridiculously handsome, get going."

He smirked, nodded again and freed himself from the spell by turning abruptly and heading back out into the hall. He ran down the uneven stairs of their old building on Högbergsgatan. Those thousands of hours in the ring during his teenage years had left their mark; he practically flew down them.

As he stepped out into the cold February air, he allowed himself to fill with pride. During all their meetings and discussions last autumn, he had kept the feeling to himself. There had been so many loose ends that he hadn't wanted to talk about it in advance. But now he finally dared believe it was actually going to happen.

Sami jogged down the street. The snow that had fallen during the night would blow away as the day wore on. When he turned the corner onto Katarina Västra Kyrkogata, the bare trees in the churchyard were like black silhouettes against the dark gray sky. The sun wouldn't rise for hours yet.

The plan was to be back home with Karin by lunch, after a quick stop at Systembolaget to buy a magnum of Moët to celebrate.

When he reached the car, he sat down behind the wheel with a smile on his face. Without Karin and John, he reminded himself, he would never have made it this far. Without them, maybe he wouldn't have even tried.

He drove toward Katarinavägen, thinking about all the warnings he had been given over the years. Bitter former bachelors who missed their carefree lives. Those who knew enough to say that babies meant no sleep to begin with, then no sex, followed by no life. He would say

they were partly right. He was sleeping badly and his sex life was nothing to boast about.

But John was a miracle who outweighed it all.

Change was always difficult. People stayed in the same jobs for year after year because they didn't dare try anything else. They hung out with childhood friends they had long since grown apart from, who were easier to call up than finding anyone new. Sami's childhood had been one long journey of discovery through the southern Stockholm suburbs. If it had been twenty or forty different addresses in the end, he had no idea, but it didn't matter. In his day, the segregation hadn't been what it was today. Back then, people had just been lumped together, Muslims, Christians and Jews. Turks, Iraqis and Yugoslavians. He had learned to get along with everyone, had found it easy to talk and become friends with both Finnish migrants and African refugees. He had become a chameleon, been forced to learn how to quickly adapt to new situations.

It was something he made use of now. He had thought it before, but this time it was real. For Karin's and the kids' sake, both born and unborn, he would leave the criminal life behind him. He would shed his skin. Not delete any of the thousands of names in his contacts list, but add some new ones instead.

It wasn't the easiest way to go about it, but it was his way.

Sami Farhan drove across Skeppsbron and through Blasieholmen. It was Tuesday morning, and the traffic in central Stockholm was still sparse. Across the water, he could see *Af Chapman*, the ship that had been turned into a youth hostel. Its illuminated white hull lay quietly in the water, which was as black as a pool of ink.

He was out in good time. What he called being careful, others might call a need to be in control.

He really was going to Frihamnen. But he was going there alone, not with his classmates from Kristineberg. For him, the hours behind

a school desk were over, there wouldn't be any more lectures on cooking. He would never be able to give his family the life they deserved by slicing cucumber for cold buffets or pouring béarnaise sauce over filet mignon.

Today, that morning, was the first day of their new lives. And, like always, it was luck that had given him this chance. It hadn't been easy to find the money. He had gone in with everything he had, all the cash he'd been able to withdraw. Plus he had brought in other financiers. His brothers, first and foremost. They had mocked him, doubted him and called him "the fishmonger." But they had still made the investment, like so many of his other friends and acquaintances. Karin's uncle had even stepped up, and all without her knowing a thing. Clean money being placed into a lawful business.

By the time he reached Nybroplan, the city had clearly woken up. There were people walking from Strandvägen toward Hamngatan, and from Blasieholmen toward Östermalm. Stockholm's wealthiest neighborhood had never appealed to the Södermalm resident Sami. Besides, the suburbs felt more present in the city center than they did where he lived, and he had long since had enough of the suburbs. Karin Flodin was born and bred in the streets around Nytorget, and the schools there were some of the best in town. It was in Södermalm that his children would grow up.

Sami had loved Karin for as long as he could remember. He'd always believed that one true love awaited every person, and he had been lucky. He had met his while he was just a teenager.

The moment she transformed from his unattainable, youthful obsession into his actual lover, the love he felt for her had deepened in a way he would never have been able to predict. Vague dreams became a physical reality. Crumpled tubes of toothpaste, unwashed plates and scrunched-up underwear on the bathroom floor were all points of irritation that had never featured in his fantasies. But nor had he been able to imagine how the skin of her stomach would smell in the morning, how her eyes would glitter when she looked at him, or how she would grab his hands whenever he told a story, hold them still and gaze deep into his soul, revealing things about him that he hadn't even been aware of himself.

When she added the next role to those she had filled earlier and became the mother of his child, his love had undergone another transformation. It was most obvious when he thought about how he would feel if he lost her. That had always been his worry, but he could no longer imagine a life without Karin. The thought was too painful.

That was why Sami Farhan was in the car on that dark, early February morning. Driving along Strandvägen toward his new life.

4

"Here it is," Michel Maloof said in English.

He lifted the black briefcase from the chair next to him and placed it on the table.

Director Anders Mild and Chairman Rick Almanza stared suspiciously at the bag.

"Your briefcase?" Mild asked. "But . . . I think I must have misunderstood something. I thought this meeting was about streamlining our Swedish distribution activity."

"Exactly, exactly." Maloof smiled, flashing his white teeth, set off by his dark beard, at the two men. "There's no better way to put it. Streamlining. In Sweden."

"What do you mean?" Mild wondered.

"I mean that maybe . . . now that we're speaking in English anyway . . . this could be of interest elsewhere than just Sweden?"

The best way to deal with a bluff was to call it.

Maloof was still unsure whether the Englishman was who he claimed to be. The idea that the chairman had flown in to see him seemed absurd.

But the older man remained silent, and Maloof felt more like he was being observed than questioned.

"Let me . . . tell you about my briefcase," Maloof continued. He had told Anders Mild's secretary that he had flown up from Malmö for the meeting in Stockholm. "It was on the floor under the seat on the plane yesterday. And I had it next to me this morning when I drove over here. So . . . well . . . how many people do you think noticed it?"

It was a rhetorical question. The black briefcase on the table was as anonymous as the room they were sitting in. It looked neither cheap nor expensive, and it seemed to be utterly lacking in design. From a distance, it looked like leather, but a closer inspection would suggest it was some kind of tough plastic.

"Are you saying . . ." the Englishman began. He had worked out where Maloof was heading.

"Right, right." Maloof smiled, and his grin grew wider. "This brief-case isn't just the equivalent . . . it's more secure than any other security bag on the market. It holds much more."

He tried to prevent his pride from turning into self-conceit. But the truth was that Maloof himself was fascinated by the bag on the table in front of him.

Anders Mild seemed to have worked out what the day's meeting was about, what Maloof was doing there. The director twisted uncomfortably in his seat and gave a short sigh. Plenty of salesmen tried to sell new security bags to G4S. A Swedish company from the north of the country, SQS in Skellefteå, was already well into the development stage and had a number of customers on the continent. Maloof was sure that SQS, like everyone else, had also tried to get a meeting. But without a Zoran Petrovic to date the director's secretary, those doors remained closed.

It was too late now for Mild to do anything about it; Maloof's bag was already on the table.

"Is it really possible?" Mild asked. He sounded doubtful. "For it to be that big inside?"

Without further ado, and with an infectious enthusiasm, Maloof began his detailed demonstration of the inside of the briefcase.

For years now, G4S had been using blue security bags produced in southern Germany. One of Zoran Petrovic's Serbian contacts had been to the top-secret factory, and it was there that the idea had been born. The German bags were big and bulky, meaning the guards had to move them about using small dollies, and it was impossible to either pick up or drop off the cash without drawing attention to it. As a consequence, they had made a virtue of necessity and developed the big blue bags into portable spy centers. They contained, in addition to GPS devices capable of being tracked within a sixty-mile radius, built-in security cameras and hidden microphones. Which meant that they also registered and documented everything that a potential robber said or did. Many of Maloof's friends had learned that very fact during trials, as prosecutors presented the court with evidence that was impossible to deny.

According to Petrovic, the bag's greatest feature was its security-protected locking function. For one, it was impossible to pick with ordinary skeleton keys, but screwdrivers, crowbars and brute force wouldn't work either. A couple of inexperienced kids or an opportunistic junkie would never manage to crack the lock. Even professional robbers who took the blue bag to a workshop and laid into it with real tools would fail. The bag was booby-trapped and would detonate if opened incorrectly, causing dye ampoules to explode. The money, and sometimes even the robber's clothes, would be destroyed in the process.

The black bag Michel Maloof was demonstrating to the European division of G4S that Tuesday afternoon in February could boast all the same features as the blue bag. And since the company from Skellefteå still hadn't managed to take out patents on its products, Maloof's bag had also borrowed several functions from them.

But in addition to that, there were two crucial improvements. First of all, Maloof's black briefcase was roomier than the blue bags. The security and technology features had been condensed and stored in the lid and the bottom, leaving more space for the valuables requiring transport. The result was a light, discreet bag, when compared with the blue monsters currently being used.

"Incredible," Mild said once he had allowed himself to be convinced.

"Right, right," Maloof agreed. "We . . . that is . . . manufacture takes place in Slovenia. That's the reason . . . for the price."

He looked the two men straight in the eye. They still hadn't talked prices; the men hadn't asked and Maloof hadn't wanted to bring it up until he was sure they were convinced. But judging by how intensely they had been nodding during his presentation, he was cautiously optimistic. The Englishman was harder to read, but toward the end he had even allowed a quick smile.

Now the older of the two cleared his throat and spoke directly to Anders Mild.

"This was a surprise," he said. "Truly."

Almanza's English was the kind Maloof had grown up with on TV during the late seventies, from programs based in rural English castles and country manors, with men in green tweed clothing who hunted foxes at weekends and employed an army of servants.

The Englishman turned to Maloof.

"I'm in Sweden for a conference, not flying home until tomorrow evening," he explained. "Anders asked whether I would like to join him for this meeting, and I answered yes mostly because I had nothing urgent to attend to. I'm glad I did."

Maloof tried to hold back a satisfied smile, but he only half-managed it. He stroked his beard and looked proudly at his black security bag, as though it had performed particularly well.

"Naturally, there are a number of questions we will have to return to," Almanza continued. "Among them the security in the Slovenian factories."

"Of course," Maloof replied.

"And then there's the question of exclusivity."

Maloof nodded.

"Exclusivity. If G4S makes an order . . . then obviously none of your competitors would be able to buy our product."

He gave a wide smile. The Englishman nodded with satisfaction. Maloof realized that the price was clearly a minor detail in this context. They still hadn't asked about it. He had gone into the meeting with the intention of asking for 20,000 kronor per bag, but he now realized he could just as easily say 30,000. It would make absolutely no difference. He hardly dared think about how much money that would mean within the Swedish market, but imagine if they were talking about a Europe-wide deal?

According to Zoran Petrovic, each bag cost 5,000 kronor to produce. The number of security bags used in the Swedish market was somewhere around ten thousand.

The amount was dizzying.

"And there will have to be some discussion in London," Almanza added drily, "but I'm fairly sure my enthusiasm will rub off onto our colleagues there."

He raised a confident eyebrow to show that this was just a formality, and Anders Mild nodded in agreement.

"And you could fly over to London to repeat this presentation?"

Maloof smiled and sat down. "Of course, of course. Just give me a few hours . . . I'll be there."

Almanza looked pleased.

When Michel Maloof and his family had landed at Arlanda almost thirty years earlier, he had torn up his Lebanese passport and flushed it down the toilet before they even reached passport control. That was what you did back then, that was the advice they had been given from relatives already in Sweden. Without a passport, refugees were registered as stateless, which minimized the risk of being sent back. Where could they be sent back to? But that early morning in a toilet cubicle at the airport was something Maloof had come to regret over the years. He and his family had been permitted to stay in Sweden, but getting ahold of a Swedish passport without a foreign one to swap it for had proved almost impossible. And by the time Maloof had waited long enough for it to finally be a possibility, he had been arrested for the first time.

That meant he had ended up at the back of the line. The same thing would go on to happen again and again. Michel Maloof was now thirty-two, but he still didn't have a passport, neither Lebanese nor Swedish.

And since England was outside the Schengen zone, there was no way he could make the trip to London. He would have to send someone else. Petrovic could go. It wasn't a big problem.

Rick Almanza stood up, and Mild did the same.

"Thank you so much, Michel," the Englishman said. "It'll be a pleasure to do business with you."

Maloof got to his feet. He felt dazed and confused. He shook hands with the two men on the other side of the table.

He had just earned more money than he ever could have dreamed of. Millions. Tens of millions.

"Thank you. And as for the price . . . the quantity . . . and the delivery date . . . ?"

Almanza laughed.

"We'll have plenty of time to get back to you about that," the older of the men said. "The contract on our current security bags doesn't expire until 2024. That gives us fifteen years to negotiate."

Maloof's smile faded. Had he heard him right? Had he misunderstood?

"As I'm sure you can understand," Anders Mild explained in Swedish, "we can't do much as long as we're tied into our current contract. But we plan ahead within G4S, and I hope you can do the same."

2024?

Were they pulling his leg?

5

Sami Farhan turned left onto Tegeluddsvägen and drove across the train tracks toward the offices and warehouses in Frihamnen. It was six thirty in the morning, the sky was still dark and expectation made him drum the wheel with his fingers.

Compared with the sleepy inner city, the harbor was a hive of activity. Vans and trucks shuttled along Frihamnsgatan in the glare of the bright spotlights that replaced the streetlights out there, cranes lifted containers from ships and the thought that a metal box just like that would be the starting point for Sami's new life got him worked up.

Hassan Kaya's office was in Magasin 6, and Sami pulled up next to the loading dock.

In just under half an hour, the boat would be coming in.

He hadn't been able to stop himself from coming down to see it with his own eyes. He had agreed to meet Ibrahim Bulut, the one who had originally attracted him to the project, on the dock. It would be a moment to remember.

Four months earlier, Sami had stepped into Hassan Kaya's cramped, cluttered office off a narrow corridor with no windows on the second floor.

Ibrahim Bulut had taken care of the introductions.

Sami had boxed with Bulut at a club called Linnea during his teens. It hadn't been for more than a couple of months, but that was all it took for the two to strike up a friendship. They continued to see one another from time to time over the years, and had even done a couple of jobs together in the early 2000s. Since then, Bulut had been busy doing exactly what Sami was about to do. He had changed sides. The Turk had left his criminal life behind him and now ran a successful business importing flowers in Årsta. It was through his import work that he had come into contact with Hassan Kaya last autumn, just as Kaya was about to start a new company. That Sami had been invited to get involved was purely because he had been in the car with Bulut when Kaya called to talk about his plans.

A few days later, they met up in Kaya's office in Magasin 6. The room smelled damp and had been full of files and papers. Sami had sat down on a wooden chair and listened as Kaya explained the setup.

He had been in the game for a long time, he said, and had been importing fresh and frozen shellfish since the mid nineties. But now he was changing tack, giving up the fight against the big monopolies—ICA and Axfood. That was why he needed new partners. The majority of fishing for prawns and mussels was done in the North Sea, but if you went farther, up toward the Arctic Ocean, the quality of the shellfish was much better. The reason so few did it was that the journey back to Sweden often took a long time because the seas were so rough. But Hassan Kaya had managed to find a captain who froze the shellfish as soon as it was loaded onto the boat, and who also delivered superior-quality products at a reasonable price. With the kind of markup you could add as a wholesaler, they would be making money hand over fist.

On a paper napkin he grabbed out of an old takeout carton from a Chinese restaurant on Valhallavägen, Kaya had scrawled out the plan. Sami had taken the figures away with him. So he could work out for himself just how much money there was to be made in the import branch.

"We're starting a company," Kaya had explained. "You, me and Ibrahim. My captain needs to upgrade the freezers on board, and that needs capital. Ibrahim's promised to go in with ten million and I'm doing the same. How much were you thinking of investing?"

After the meeting, Sami had felt overwhelmed. He didn't have that kind of money. Once he had emptied his own bank account and his brothers had reluctantly agreed to loan him the majority of their savings, Sami had eventually managed to convince some of his friends and Karin's uncle to get involved. He managed to scrape together a total of five million. For that, he got 20 percent of the newly formed import company.

He told Karin about the project, but failed to mention just how much he was staking on it.

Still, risks were something he had lived with his entire life.

When Sami Farhan ran up the two flights of stairs in Magasin 6 to exchange a few words with Hassan Kaya that cold February morning, he wasn't surprised to find the door to the unassuming office locked. Kaya had advised Sami not to go out there to meet the boat; unloading a container full of frozen prawns was hardly a spectacular event for someone who had done it countless times before.

But Sami hadn't listened.

He rushed back down the stairs and out of the building. The water of the Baltic Sea was still a few degrees warmer than the chilly morning air. Fog lay over the bay and the docks, and his face grew damp as he crossed the street. It was ten to seven, and he smiled when he saw Ibrahim Bulut's white Mercedes parked at the end of the dock.

The successful wholesaler climbed out of his car as Sami approached, and they greeted one another.

"Time to make some damn money," Bulut said with a hoarse laugh. A cloud of condensation left his mouth, as though he were laughing in a speech bubble. "Where's the boat?" he asked, glancing around.

Sami shook his head and pointed randomly toward the harbor entrance. "You're the one who knows this stuff. I've got no idea. Are boats like planes? Do they dock at a set time, or how's it work?"

"When did a plane last land on time?" Bulut asked. "Have you seen the trucks?"

Hassan Kaya had shown them sketches of the trucks that would be emblazoned with the company's logo. They should have been there to take the cargo, but there was no sign of them. Sami was jumping up and down on the spot like a child who wanted immediate answers to his questions.

The clock struck seven, and the two friends talked about Årsta warehouses and how much money they were going to make on frozen shellfish, all while trying to keep warm as best they could. Sami was constantly glancing in the direction of the Baltic, hoping to catch sight of the boat.

But there was no boat anywhere to be seen, and no trucks either.

By seven thirty, Sami couldn't hide his frustration any longer. He told Bulut to wait by the Mercedes while he went away to talk to a couple of men busy unloading goods.

Sami Farhan wasn't someone who left things to chance. During the two months that had passed since he invested in the project, he had asked Hassan Kaya thousands of questions, and Kaya had patiently answered them all. Thanks to that, Sami not only knew that the boat they were waiting for sailed under an Estonian flag, but also what its designation was and where it would dock.

But no one working in the harbor that morning could give him the slightest idea as to what had happened.

At quarter to eight, Sami called Hassan Kaya. The phone rang, but there was no answer. For once, it also didn't go to voice mail.

"I don't like this," Sami said when he returned to Bulut and the car. "You know what I mean? This doesn't feel good."

He thumped his chest through his down jacket.

"You're just paranoid." Bulut smiled. He was leaning against his Mercedes, smoking a cigarette. "As usual."

"It's not just my money. Do you get that? People are expecting things. From all directions."

"You've mentioned that a few times," Bulut pointed out. "Like, a hundred."

"So where the hell's the boat?"

Sami's hand drummed against his thigh, and he shook his head.

"You want to sit down and wait?" Bulut suggested. His friend's behavior was starting to stress him out.

They climbed into the Mercedes and Bulut turned the ignition to get the heater going. They stared at the empty harbor entrance in silence, Sami still drumming his hands. On his thighs, on the dashboard, on the car door. After a few minutes, he couldn't bear it any longer.

"I'm going to see if he's in the office yet."

Ibrahim Bulut nodded.

When Sami Farhan returned to the corridor in Magasin 6, the majority of the doors were still closed. He knocked on Kaya's. Gently at first, then harder. Nothing happened.

He took out his phone and tried calling the number the shellfish importer had always answered in the past. It rang, but again, no one answered.

With the phone pressed to his ear, Sami studied the closed door. Some of the offices down the corridor had metal doors, but this one was wood. He shoved his phone back into his pocket and tried the door with his shoulder. It gave. Not much, but enough for him to know that it was worth another try, with more force this time.

On his fifth attempt, the door gave way. The frame broke with a crack and Sami suddenly found himself inside the tiny office he had visited so many times before.

It was empty. Even the desk had gone.

His blood was pounding in his temples.

There wouldn't be any boat. There wouldn't be any trucks.

Like a tiger in a small cage, Sami paced the room. The bastard had screwed them over.

Ibrahim Bulut was still waiting in the car. Sami tore open the door.

"He's gone! Do you understand what I'm saying? Gone! The office is empty, his phone's off. Shit! Shit, shit, shit. We're driving over to that asshole's place for a chat right now."

"What the hell are you saying?" The color had vanished from Bulut's face.

"We're screwed. There's no fucking boat. We're going over to that bastard's place now to get our money back."

"But . . ." said Bulut, "I don't know where he lives . . ."

"You don't know where he lives? What the hell are you saying?" Sami couldn't believe it.

"Somewhere in Gothenburg, I think," said Bulut. "Or Landskrona or somewhere on the fucking west coast."

"You said you knew him?"

"Yeah, but what the fuck, I do know him. We've fucking worked together. But not so much that I know where the hell he lives! He lives with his fucking prawns somewhere, that's all I know."

Sami was thinking about the money. He was thinking about Karin, about her big belly and the way she nursed John. He was thinking about his big brother, who had called him "Lord of the Prawns" and laughed.

He thought about how, in just a few moments, he had gone from being a successful businessman in the import branch to a debt-ridden trainee chef with a criminal past.

"Shit!" he shouted, hammering his hands against the solid paneling of the German car. "Shit, shit, shit!"

6

This wasn't where it was meant to happen.

Music was pounding from invisible speakers, so loud that she couldn't hear her own panting breaths.

You're hot then you're cold, Katy Perry sang. *You're yes then you're no.*

Why, Alexandra Svensson wondered as she mirrored the energetic instructor with a series of quick squat jumps, could her life be summed up by three short minutes of a pop song? She didn't want to be predictable. *You're in then you're out.* But it wasn't her fault. She had to remember that. For once, it wasn't her fault. Giving him an ultimatum had been the right thing to do. He couldn't have his cake and eat it too.

That Thursday afternoon, there were twenty or so people working out at her branch of Friskis & Svettis in Ringen. Alexandra had gone straight after work, and there were just two men in the room. One of them was gay. The other was desperate. Neither of them was a suitable candidate.

High knees.

Arms spinning.

Alexandra Svensson came to the gym twice a week and had learned all the moves, but it wasn't the place she would meet someone she could share her life with.

In the row in front of her, to the right, was Lena Hall.

Alexandra watched her friend in the mirror. Lena had an hourglass figure, and she always ordered a pastry of some kind when they stopped for a coffee afterward, scoffing it down in a couple of breathless bites and not thinking anything of it. But still, Lena's knees were higher than the instructor's, and she never seemed to sweat.

Life was deeply unfair, and Lena Hall was proof of that.

Lena and Alexandra were unlikely friends. They hadn't known one another particularly long, but Lena was the type of person people felt like they knew, even if they had just met her. When the women sat down in Espresso House for their usual coffee—and pastry—after class, Alexandra would talk about work and Lena about clothes. Those were the roles they had assigned to themselves. Alexandra told a new story about her boss, and Lena spent half an hour on a dress she had seen online, one she wanted to buy even though it was too expensive and she hadn't tried it on.

"I should do it though, right?" she asked.

"I don't buy many clothes," Alexandra replied.

She glanced at the time on her phone at regular intervals. She wasn't really in a hurry to get back to her apartment in Hammarby Sjöstad, all she had planned was to stop off at the supermarket in Hammarby Allé and buy dinner. Alexandra gazed longingly at Lena's pastry and decided she would add one of the mint dark chocolate bars from Lindt into her basket. She needed something to console herself with as she watched TV that evening.

Alexandra knew she shouldn't keep thinking about the man she would probably never see again, she knew he was no great loss, that he was just a placebo.

But she couldn't help it.

She had the ability to fall in love with the *hope*, she fell in love with love itself, and the actual object of her feelings wasn't always that important. Not to begin with. But sooner or later, reality always struck. And the man lying asleep in her bed would transform from a handsome magician who had made her loneliness disappear into a snoring pig who talked about himself with his mouth full while he ate breakfast.

All the same, she wasn't made for the single life.

She sighed.

"What?" Lena asked.

"No, nothing," said Alexandra.

"You know what I'm talking about though, right?"

The truth was that Alexandra hadn't been listening, so when she nodded she hoped there wouldn't be any follow-up questions.

Lena had finished her pastry and asked for the bill. "See you on Tuesday?" she asked.

Alexandra nodded. Going to the gym had become more fun with Lena there, but more than twice a week was too much.

"Maybe we could try the yoga class too?" said Lena. "Did you get the invite?"

"What invite?"

"Was it yesterday? No, over the weekend? No, hang on, it was through the Facebook group."

Alexandra shrugged. She had been on Facebook for a while now, but there were so many Alexandra Svenssons that everyone who ever contacted her seemed to be looking for someone else. It was easier not to take part.

"No," she replied. "I didn't see it."

"Seemed totally reasonable. Four classes for two hundred kronor, something like that. Shall we go?"

Lena began to talk enthusiastically about yoga groups, and Alexandra found her thoughts drifting again.

Life, her mother had said just before she died of cancer one overcast November day seven years earlier, was like any old party. If you want to, you can stay by the bar and drink until you're so drunk that you have to go to the toilet and throw up. Or else you can sneak home after dinner because you think everyone else is an idiot. Maybe you can try to have a deep conversation with some depressing guy who thinks he's an artist. Or maybe you'll dance the night away. Life is what you make of it, but it rarely gets better than that.

Alexandra had grown up with her mother. Just the two of them. Only four months had passed between diagnosis and death, and though it had now been seven years, Alexandra could still sometimes see her in her reflection.

She was home by seven, and an hour later she had eaten dinner. She washed up and then changed into a dressing gown and sat down on the sofa with her bar of chocolate. There was a film on TV about a female lawyer fighting the mafia. Being a lawyer was something Alexandra Svensson was still considering. She liked rules.

As anxious as she was about her loneliness, she was satisfied with her job. She worked at G4S out in Västberga, a huge multinational where she felt comfortable. She assumed she would find something else one day, maybe in the center of town, but she was in no rush. She was only twenty-four, she had her entire life ahead of her.

First, she needed to meet someone.

There were times when she could have gone home with absolutely anyone from work, cooked dinner and massaged his shoulders, just to avoid facing the loneliness awaiting her.

There were times when she woke at night, alone in her bed, curled up in the fetal position, and hugged a pillow.

There were times in the morning when she just wanted to scream to break the silence in her cramped, practical kitchen in Hammarby Sjöstad.

7

It was ten in the morning when Sami Farhan maneuvered the stroller into the elevator. For the first six months, they had just left it by the front door, but it had been stolen a few months ago. The new stroller Karin had bought with the insurance money had followed them up into the apartment ever since. What went on in the mind of someone who stole a stroller, Sami wondered, swearing to himself at the cramped elevator.

Out on the street, the light was unexpectedly bright. He slowly walked up Skånegatan, and the baby was asleep before he even reached the top of the hill.

Sami turned off into Vitabergsparken, pushing the stroller ahead of him up the slope toward the Sofia Church. He could see the silhouette of a man in a black jacket waiting for him outside the entrance to the house of God. His head was shaved, and there was a strikingly wide scar looping around it. As though his halo had fallen and branded him for life.

Toomas Mandel.

"Shitty business," was the first thing Mandel said as they greeted one another. "Real shitty."

Sami sighed. The whole city knew what had happened. He had no idea how the rumor had spread, he hadn't started it. But now it was too late to do anything about it. Everyone knew he had been screwed over by the Turk, who seemed to have gone up in smoke; everyone knew the whole frozen shellfish business had gone down the drain.

Sami shrugged. He was still pushing the stroller ahead of him like a plow, and Mandel fell in step with him. The two men walked through the park toward Nytorget.

"You thought about it?" Mandel asked.

Sami nodded. "I'm not sure. I'm really not sure, you know?" he said. "I've got thousands of questions. Or hundreds, at least."

"Ask away. I'm not sure I have all the answers yet," Mandel cautiously replied, "but I'm working on it."

"Tell me about the gates again. They shut when the alarm goes off, was that it? And there were how many guards . . . ?"

"Sixteen guards on site at night," Mandel replied.

"But that means sixteen people calling for backup. You know? If every guard calls in backup, and one car turns up per guard . . . That's like, a hundred pigs. How long do we have?"

It was a good question. Carrying out a raid on Täby Racecourse was all about speed. The money was kept waiting in a locked room for the guards to come and pick it up at midnight. Getting into that room wouldn't be the problem, it was getting out afterward that they still needed to solve.

While Mandel explained his plan, they turned right toward Malmgårdsvägen. Sami listened carefully and asked questions.

Ten days had passed since Sami stood on the dock in Frihamnen, waiting for the boat of prawns that would never arrive. When he got back home that morning, it had been without the champagne he had been planning, and with a despondency he couldn't hide.

Karin had been awake, eating dry, sticky prunes straight from the bag in the kitchen. The outer walls of their building on Högbergsgatan were cracked, and a cold draft rolled in across the floor. Karin had been wearing a long, white terry dressing gown that Sami had given her for Christmas, and she pulled it tight around her body.

"You think I'm gross now, right?" she asked.

He smirked and shook his head.

"I'm used to it," he replied. He still hadn't taken off his coat.

"What? Did I eat prunes last time?"

"Yeah."

She hadn't been able to control her craving for prunes then either. She was just over seven months into this new pregnancy; the baby was due in early April, meaning there would be just under a year between the two children.

"There should be a law against having kids this close together," she said.

She stared angrily at the prunes. After every bag, she was forced to spend an hour on the toilet. She had told him to stop her from eating too many of them, but when he saw her greedy eyes on the bag, he couldn't bring himself to say anything.

"Why can't I have cravings for something healthy?" she asked. "Some people just want broccoli."

Sami didn't reply, and it was only then that Karin looked up.

"What is it?" she asked. "What happened?"

The easygoing tone was gone, replaced by a concerned crease on her forehead and a look completely lacking in affection.

Sami had just turned fifteen when he first fell in love with Karin. She had been unobtainable, and he had no idea how they could have ended up in the same class. Karin was from the city and Sami the suburbs, she was from the middle class and he from somewhere below. Months had passed before he even dared to speak to her, much longer before he worked up the courage to actually ask her out. Sami and his brothers had always talked openly about girls, but he didn't dare say a word about Karin, terrified that his brothers would take an interest in her before he had time to get anywhere himself.

He was seventeen when they finally got together. For a couple of months, his experience was straight out of some predictable teenage American film, a time when every single song on the radio seemed to have been specially written for him and Karin. And then one evening he happened to tell her about something he had done, a break-in. Or happened to; he was boasting about it. He felt tough, grown up; it was something he had done with his big brother. Now he couldn't even remember what they stole. Karin had broken up with him a few minutes later. Just like that. He had caused the exact opposite of what he wanted. But her explanation had been clear. She didn't want to—ever—be with a criminal.

It had taken him a few years to win her back, but since then the pattern had repeated itself. Time and time again. Before she agreed that they should have a baby, he had promised once and for all that he was done with his old life. They had a future together, a life in which she wouldn't have to worry about the police turning up one day to take him away, lock him up and throw away the key. And the fact she was choosing to believe him, she had firmly explained, was proof of her love. But her belief had since been tested a number of times, and the frown on her forehead was a clear sign that this was another such occasion.

Sami explained what had happened, that he had been set up and the frozen prawns had been a lie, and Karin breathed out.

"Business can always be sorted out," she comforted him.

He didn't know where she got her strength from.

When he told his brothers what had happened later that evening, their reaction was very different. They shouted and swore, and spent an intense twenty-four hours searching for Hassan Kaya. But the Turk had gone underground, or else he was holed up with their money in the Taurus Mountains. There was no sign of him. Once his brothers realized that, they had sighed, sworn some more and told Sami that he didn't need to look so damn guilty. They had invested in the business together, and all three of them had been screwed over. That was that. It was no one's fault but Hassan Kaya's, and if that bastard ever turned up again . . .

To his friends who had invested money and who got in touch, one by one, as the rumors started to spread, Sami said the same thing over and over again. He would fix it. He would deliver. He had promised them a good investment, had promised them interest, and they would get it. Not in the form of earnings from frozen shellfish, but somehow.

He said the same to everyone he met, people who took his defeat as a sign of weakness and gullibility. The plan was still to go straight, to take on the role of a father. He would leave the life of crime behind him.

The difference was that he just needed to do one last big job to get back on his feet first. And the sooner it could happen, the better.

"I know how it sounds," Sami had said when he got in touch with Mandel. He'd heard that the Estonian had something in the pipeline. "You know what I mean? It's not that I don't know how it sounds, one 'last' job, but I mean it. I want to do one more job, and whether that's yours or someone else's depends on what turns up first."

Sami stopped dead.

What?" Toomas Mandel asked anxiously.

"Quiet."

Sami was completely motionless, listening intently. Mandel did the same. He couldn't hear a thing.

"Is it the pigs?"

Sami bent down to the stroller and lifted John from beneath the layers of blankets and covers. What had started as a quiet sniffle had turned into crying. It happened sometimes, when he woke from a deep sleep. Sami assumed it was his dreams that scared him.

"What the hell . . . is that a real baby?" Mandel blurted out in amazement.

"Are you stupid or what?"

"I just thought the stroller was a decoy."

"A decoy?"

"To fool the pigs!"

"You're sick," Sami told the Estonian, rocking the baby in his arms until the little one calmed down and dozed off again.

Mandel shook his head.

"Don't worry," Sami said, gently putting the baby back into the stroller. "He's not going to snitch."

Mandel rolled his eyes. They turned back into the park. As they

walked, Mandel went over the team and how he was planning on splitting the money.

"I need six million," Sami said. "You can split it any way you want, but
that's my minimum. Got that? If you can't guarantee me that, I'm out."

"There'll be more," Mandel reassured him. "Much more."

The majestic silhouette of the church was dark against the bright
blue sky as they struggled back up the hill.

"The point," Toomas Mandel explained, "is that it's only three minutes to the boat club. No one's going to believe we're on our way there.
We make it to the boat, we're practically home. The police are up in
Vaxholm and we'll be in Bergshamra in less than ten minutes. They'll
never make it down in time. By then, we'll be long gone, too much of a
head start."

"But does that mean you're saying," Sami asked, "that we have to
ride down to the boat club? I don't know . . . I've never even been on a
horse . . ."

He had a feeling that rather than this being an idea that would get
better the longer he sat on it, it was the opposite.

"It's a possibility," Mandel replied.

"But the whole of Täby fucking Racecourse is full of riders. You
know? We'll never manage to get away from them. They're professionals."

"All I'm saying is that it's a possibility," Mandel repeated. "It might
be a bad idea, but if you're on a horse, you can make it from the racecourse down to the boat club without getting caught up by any police
vans or response units."

Sami shook his head.

"I don't know," he said. "I buy the rest of it. Or I don't know, a lot
of it's good. But you need to come up with another way of getting out.
You know?"

"I'll work on it."

8

Michel Maloof was in the Hallunda McDonald's, waiting to pay for his large meal, when the inconspicuous and now crumpled scrap of paper bearing Alexandra Svensson's name and phone number followed a handful of change out of his pocket. To begin with, he didn't remember where it had come from; eight weeks had passed since he'd met the man with the dogs. Maloof waited for his cheeseburger, twisting and turning the piece of paper in his hands. And then he spotted the address for the dating site. That jogged his memory.

He took his tray and sat down in one of the window seats, looking out at a branch of Bauhaus. He had never used any dating sites himself, he'd never had trouble meeting women. But he assumed that it suited some people, and each to his own.

He held up the note and drank his Coke through the straw.

Should he call her?

After the meeting at G4S, Maloof had thrown the black bag into his car and dejectedly driven away, emotionally overwhelmed and exhausted. Going in just a few short minutes from believing he would earn millions to realizing that he had fifteen years of negotiation and discussions ahead of him had been a real blow.

It felt like he had been subjected to some kind of cheap joke, as though the two directors had deliberately allowed him to misunderstand the situation and then piled on the pressure with their "contractual agreements."

Maloof had driven straight from Stadshagen to Upplandsgatan to tell Zoran Petrovic what had happened. Maloof wasn't much of a car enthusiast, but driving a Seat was frustrating when you were angry. Any sudden braking became smooth, and his sharp accelerations had no bite. Though maybe it had a calming effect, because by the time he reached Café Stolen, the worst of his anger had abated.

Petrovic had been waiting for him in one of the booths. His long, slender upper body stuck up like a twig above the table. He had a glass of lukewarm water in front of him. It was three thirty in the afternoon, and other than the staff, the place was empty. A new waitress Maloof had never seen before came over and asked what he wanted.

"I gave her a job mostly to test my self-control," Petrovic had said once the girl in the tight skirt had gone back into the kitchen to fetch a cup of coffee.

It had been years since Maloof had stopped being surprised by Zoran Petrovic's attitude toward women. He ignored the comment and told him about the meeting he had just come from instead. Though Petrovic was one of Maloof's oldest friends, it was impossible for the Yugoslavian to detect any of the anger or frustration Maloof had just been feeling. Instead, he found himself faced with the always-smiling, calm and indifferent Maloof, who neutrally recounted the absurd conversation from the G4S conference room.

"That's perfect though," Petrovic had replied with his usual enthusiasm. "You've introduced yourself, they know who you are and what you have to offer. It couldn't have gone better."

"Right, right," Maloof had said, laughing. "But, I mean, no. They could've bought the bags."

"Forget about it," Petrovic said with a laugh. "This is just the beginning. Going forward, shit, there could be a lot of money in this."

After a few minutes, Maloof had reluctantly allowed himself to be infected by his friend's enthusiasm. Both men were fundamentally optimistic; if things had been any different, they never would have made it this far.

Maloof put the scrap of paper onto the tray, but his eyes didn't leave it as he lifted his cheeseburger out of the box.

Maybe Petrovic was right and everything would go to plan, but it was just as likely he was wrong. And what harm could calling her do?

Hadn't the man with the dogs said that this Alexandra Svensson was good-looking?

Maloof picked up his phone.

He invited her to a restaurant called Mandolin.

They agreed to meet at seven that Friday. Maloof made sure he was early, and he was waiting on the sidewalk on Upplandsgatan when the bells of Adolf Fredriks Church struck the hour. He had pulled up his hood to protect himself from the drizzle. The modern era's winter had the capital in its loose grip, and galoshes would probably have been the best kind of shoes for that time of year.

When he saw a woman coming toward him from Tegnérlunden Park ten minutes later, he immediately knew it was her.

Alexandra Svensson was wearing a pair of practical rubber boots with a slim fur trim at the top, and her long down coat was pale blue. In her description of herself, the one Maloof had found on Match.com, she had written that she was someone who wanted to "bring a little luxury to life." He was sure that the fur on her boots and the color of her coat were part of what she meant.

When she passed beneath the streetlight at the crossing with Kammakargatan, he could see her more clearly. She had written online that "biological age is meaningless," but Maloof would have guessed that Alexandra was around twenty-five. A blond-haired, blue-eyed woman with round cheeks, a distinct protruding chin and a small, pouting red mouth, as though she wanted to be kissed. Maloof waved. Alexandra took a few happy, skipping steps toward him and gave him an impulsive hug.

Maybe her experience was that men who got in touch online didn't always turn up?

They went into the restaurant together and were shown to a secluded table. They spent a moment reading the menus, but when the waiter came back to take their orders, he said that the chef wanted to surprise them instead.

"I promise you won't be disappointed."

Alexandra gave Maloof a questioning look, and with a smile and a quick laugh, he explained that he knew the owner.

Zoran Petrovic owned several places on Upplandsgatan.

They had a good night together. There was no other way to describe it. Maloof had decided in advance not to ask about either Västberga or G4S. If she wanted to talk about cash depots then he would listen. With interest. But if she decided not to, which had been the case for the majority of their dinner, he wasn't going to insist. He was convinced that he had to win her trust first, and only then could he approach the questions he was interested in. It was all about patience.

As it happened, Alexandra Svensson wasn't a particularly secretive person. Neither was she quiet. She talked openly about herself and her life. She had grown up in Nacka, studied economics at Stockholm University and dropped out to start working before she graduated. She liked having a regular income every month, it made her feel safe. She was subletting, or maybe she was subletting a sublet, a studio in Hammarby Sjöstad, and she said a few words about the secure transport company where she had worked for almost two years, and that she liked it.

"But basically half my wage goes to flowers," she confessed.

"Flowers?"

"I love flowers," said Alexandra Svensson. "When you get home and there are, like, flowers on the table, when it smells like roses and hyacinths . . . Is there anything better?"

"Yeah," said Maloof. "No."

"I've got a little herb garden in the kitchen, too. Nothing exotic. Basil, rosemary and, like, coriander. I think. Then there's my balcony. I don't know what I'd do without it."

"No," said Maloof.

"This time of year, all you can really do is plan ahead. But I've got all my geraniums in pots in the basement and as soon as it gets a bit warmer I'll bring them up and put them out on the balcony again. I had, like, no idea they could even survive over winter, but they can."

"Right, right." Maloof smiled with a laugh.

Alexandra suddenly grew serious, and looked straight into his brown eyes. "It's so easy to talk to you," she said. "Like, I really think that. Really."

"Right," he replied, flashing all his teeth in a wide smile. "It's . . . I think so too."

"Cheers, Michel."

She raised her glass and they sipped their red wine.

They were on their second bottle.

Alexandra Svensson continued. She hardly needed any encouragement; she took his opinions and thoughts for granted, and the evening passed without him having to give anything but his attention.

Something he was willing to give her.

They went back to Michel Maloof's apartment through a Stockholm that was damp, empty and dark, and he didn't even have time to take out the teacups before she had pushed him up against the wall with her tongue in his mouth. He was slightly shorter than she was, but he was surprised by her strength. She forced him to the floor in the living room and grabbed the blanket Maloof's mother had made, the one that had been on the sofa, so that they wouldn't be naked on the parquet floor.

After that unexpected and intense lovemaking session in which they had barely taken off their clothes, they sat down at the kitchen table and smoked—he had a pack of Marlboros stashed next to the spices in cupboard above the stove—before they went into the bedroom to make love again. This time more considerately.

Afterward, Maloof wanted to do nothing but sleep. It was four in the morning and he was tired from too much red wine and too many monologues. But it was right then, as he was on the verge of falling asleep on the soft down pillow, that she started talking about the building in Västberga.

He forced himself to wake up.

A few minutes later, he finally understood why the old man in the woods had suggested he meet Alexandra Svensson.

9

"Maybe it's best if the uniforms wait outside?" Kant said in the elevator on the way up through the third of the five Hötorget buildings in central Stockholm.

Björn Kant, director of the Regional Public Prosecution Authority, was in his sixties and was one of Sweden's most experienced criminal prosecutors. Seeing him walk the streets of the capital like an ordinary citizen, rather than sitting behind a desk, was an uncommon occurrence. The last time he had personally taken part in an arrest had to have been some time during the seventies, Caroline Thurn thought.

The prosecutor's crumpled, dark brown suit even seemed more creased than usual.

"You want them to stay outside?" she asked. "Why?"

"No, it's just . . ." Kant replied, "this isn't an ordinary . . . I mean, there's no need to embarrass the man. I don't know what kind of meeting he's in, and . . ."

"Embarrass?" Thurn repeated. She was surprised. "We're here to arrest him. Maybe that is something he should find embarrassing?"

She was genuinely surprised. Though she was only half Kant's age, she had worked as a task force leader with the Swedish Police Authority's Criminal Investigation Department for four years, and during that time she'd had plenty of dealings with the prosecutor. She had never thought of Kant as anything but efficient, objective and decisive.

She glanced at him now, standing next to her in the dark elevator in which one of the lights wasn't working. Thurn had a wiry, hard body, as tall as she was slim, with sharp features and blond hair tied up in a messy ponytail whose sole purpose was to cause as little bother as possible.

"Is that why you're here in person?" she asked. "To make sure I don't 'embarrass' our suspect?"

They had been working on the investigation with Interpol for almost two months now, and there was no doubt that Director Henrik Nilsson, with his thick, gray, combed-back hair and healthy tan, currently in a meeting on the eighteenth floor of the skyscraper, was much more than a simple tax evader. Thurn was convinced that the man had blood on his hands, even if he had made sure it was only flecks, splattered from a distance. He was a criminal and he would be brought to justice.

During the investigation, Björn Kant had been less convinced about the extent of Nilsson's activity than Thurn, but that he was guilty of a number of financial crimes was something they both agreed on.

"I know you think it's irrelevant, Caroline," Kant said. He was having trouble looking her in the eye. "But you know that he hunts pheasants with the minister for enterprise."

"That makes no difference!" Thurn blurted out.

With them in the elevator were the two uniformed police officers Thurn had more or less grabbed along the way. Both were staring at the floor, pretending they weren't hearing the conversation that was going on next to them.

"All I'm saying is that we should take it easy," Kant mumbled, knowing that his more pragmatic side wouldn't be appreciated by the young, and still shockingly naive, task force leader.

Certain police officers grew cynical after their first week on the job, but others were more resilient. The fact that Thurn had managed to retain her confidence in her fellow man year after year, despite everything she had been through, was an achievement in itself. Kant respected her highly for it, but he also knew that if the moral compass was working, it did no harm to act smoothly.

The elevator pinged and the doors opened.

The four public servants stepped out and moved quickly down the corridor toward the conference and meeting room on the south side of the building. The corridor was as tired-looking as those in police headquarters, Thurn thought. It even smelled of the same cleaning products.

"Do we know this is the right way?" she asked.

"I've been here before," Kant replied.

She didn't ask the obvious follow-up question. She was afraid that Björn Kant was yet another member of the minister's hunting team, and that if she asked he would be forced to admit it. Better, she thought, not to know.

They came to a door with a frosted glass panel. They could hear voices from the other side, and Kant knocked.

"You can wait by the elevator," he said to the two police officers, who nodded obediently.

Thurn sighed.

They stepped into the room.

It was smaller than Thurn had expected. The curtains were drawn, hiding what had to be a fantastic view of the capital, with City Hall and possibly even Riddarfjärden in the distance. There were five men sitting around the white conference table, all wearing dark suits, white shirts and ties. Director Henrik Nilsson, the man the police were looking for, had clearly been giving some kind of presentation. He was standing by a whiteboard and stopped to turn to them.

"Björn?" he exclaimed in surprise.

"Hello, Henrik," Kant replied.

Henrik Nilsson shook his head in confusion.

"What are you doing here? I'm . . . Björn, could you wait in my office, I'll come as soon as I'm done here? Fifteen, twenty minutes? I'm . . . a little busy, as you can see."

He gestured to the men sitting at the table, all of whom looked equally surprised and were staring at the prosecutor and the prosecutor's pretty companion.

Kant hesitated. "No, I'm afraid it's not quite that simple, Henrik. I can explain . . . If you give me a couple of minutes, I can . . . "

The prosecutor nodded toward the corridor.

"A couple of minutes? Now?" the suspect said with a forced laugh. "Like I said, Björn, I'm in the middle of an, er, let's say . . . a presentation of sorts. And I really need to finish it."

He turned to the men around the table for support, but they didn't say a word.

"I'm sorry, Henrik, but this can't wait," said Kant, trying to drum up some courage.

"Look," Nilsson said, this time with a note of sharpness and irritation in his voice, "I'll ask you for the last time, please go to my office and wait there, and I'll come as soon as I'm done here."

Caroline Thurn, who had been standing behind Prosecutor Kant until this point, had already lost her patience after their opening exchange. She had tried to help put the prosecutor on the right track using her body language, but now she stepped forward and said, loudly: "Henrik Nilsson, you're under arrest. You're going to come with us to police headquarters where we will conduct a preliminary interview."

Nilsson's jaw dropped.

"This is the most ridiculous damn . . ."

He shook his head. He didn't have the words.

"Henrik," said Kant, trying to soften Thurn's lack of tact, "we do actually have to . . ."

"Get out!" Nilsson shouted, suddenly finding his tongue. "My lawyers are going to—"

But Thurn couldn't bear to listen any longer.

Where the handcuffs had come from wasn't something the prosecutor would be able to explain afterward, but she stepped straight past him and snapped one of them around Henrik Nilsson's wrist. It all happened so quickly that the director barely had time to realize what was happening.

Caroline Thurn quickly fastened the second cuff around the wrist of prosecutor Björn Kant.

She looked at the two friends with a broad smile.

"I'm going back to police headquarters now," she said. "And wherever I go, the key goes too. Do stop by and see us."

With that, she left the room. She walked toward the elevators and the two waiting officers.

"The others are just coming," she said. "We might as well wait here."

10

Michel Maloof had chosen the soccer field in Fittja as their meeting place. Soccer fields were always a possibility, as were any other open spaces where you could be sure there was no one eavesdropping behind a bush. Maloof had said that he had followed up on the tip from the man with the dogs and that it was something Sami should hear with his own ears. But he hadn't said any more than that.

That was why Sami Farhan was waiting in a parking lot in Fittja, in the shadows behind a garage. One by one, the lights had gone out in the windows of the hulking tower on the hill, the enormous block of apartments that had been built during the fifties and sixties as part of the government's political experiment, an extensive public housing program known as the Million Project. Every time Sami went to places like Bredäng, Botkyrka or Flemingsberg, he was reminded of exactly why he now lived in Södermalm.

Out here was his past, not his future.

It was ten thirty in the evening. Though he was wearing two sweaters under his coat, his clothes were no protection against the cold. March had arrived, but the mercury was still hitting new lows.

Michel Maloof had said he would be there at quarter past ten, and, like always, Sami had arrived in good time. He had been waiting almost half an hour now. His impatience was worse than the cold. An inheritance from his father, his mother always said. A quick run around the park would warm him up and get rid of his restlessness, but who knew which eyes were on him in the tower block up there.

Another five minutes passed before a gray Seat pulled into the parking lot. Sami sighed gently. He wanted to be home before midnight,

Karin had already been suspicious when he said that he had to help out on the cold buffet for the second night in a row. It wasn't a lie that he worked extra shifts at his uncle's place in Liljeholmen, and the money it had brought in so far was proof of that. But his wages from the cold buffet were barely enough to cover the rent, diapers and gruel. It was Karin who kept the family together, both financially and socially. She was one of Stockholm's many struggling small-business owners, who, along with a friend, had opened a dressmaker's shop on Maria Präst-gårdsgata. They had been lucky and skilled enough to win a couple of big repeat customers, which helped them build up a certain level of stability and success. But things varied, of course, and some weeks were better than others. All the same, the majority of her months were considerably better than Sami's.

The nondescript Seat parked next to an Audi some way from the garage, and Sami immediately recognized the short, compact shape of Maloof as he moved around the car and opened the passenger's side door. The woman who climbed out was wearing a bulky blue down jacket and a white knitted hat. Sami couldn't make out much more than that from where he was standing.

He made himself visible by stepping forward out of the shadows. Maloof waved, and a few minutes later they were face-to-face.

"Alexandra, this is Sami. Sami, Alexandra Svensson," Maloof introduced them.

Sami took off a glove and shook Alexandra's hand. She looked away. If it had been light, Maloof was convinced he would have seen her blush.

"So . . . well . . . you can keep us company for a while?" Maloof suggested, as though they had only bumped into one another by chance.

Sami nodded and smirked. "What a coincidence," he said. "Bumping into you two here. You on the way back to your place, Michel?"

"Right, right. Some hot tea . . . with honey," Maloof replied, completely without irony.

Alexandra laughed as though he had told a joke, so that no one would believe she had gone along with the tea-and-honey idea.

Sami knew that Maloof's family had put down roots in Fittja and then let those roots grow wide in the suburban Swedish world. Sami didn't feel any such belonging to a place or neighborhood, not even to Södermalm.

They started walking. Maloof took them across the soccer field, which was currently bathed in darkness. The snow crunched beneath the soles of their shoes. Alexandra didn't say a word, and Sami waited for Maloof to start the conversation. Lights from the highway fell across the field in thin strips, and as they walked through one of them, Sami took the chance to get a better look at Alexandra Svensson.

He would have described her as more ordinary than cute. The shadows of her long lashes fell onto her round cheeks, which had turned red in the cold night air. She sensed his gaze and turned her head. The glimmer in her eye told him that she was slightly drunk, but she wasn't an idiot.

Sami made a mental note.

"Yeah, so," Maloof began, "we were in town for dinner. A place in Kungsholmen . . . well . . . yeah . . . Did you know Sami was a chef?"

"You're a chef?" Alexandra asked with interest. "I love food. And cooking. But I'm, like, not very good at it. I could never go on *Come Dine with Me* or anything like that. Or maybe I could? I'm good at chocolate mousse."

"Right," Maloof added, though it wasn't clear what he was referring to.

"I like baking," Sami confessed.

"Do you?" Alexandra sounded enthusiastic.

"Cookies, mostly."

She stopped and looked up at him in surprise.

"Yeah, raspberry caves, Finnish sticks . . ." Sami went on. "You know?"

He sounded serious, but the thought of this big, strong man

stooped over a baking tray, adding raspberry jam to his cookies, seemed so unlikely. She laughed briefly, as though to show that she understood.

"Where do you work?" she asked.

Sami told her the name of the restaurant in Liljeholmen.

"What about you? What do you do?" he asked.

"I count money," she said, giggling again.

Maloof was impressed. Sami had managed to get her to bring up the subject much quicker than he had. That was what he had expected, it was the reason he had wanted to let Sami hear it from her rather than recapping what she had said. Maloof would never be anywhere near as convincing.

"Count money?"

"I work for G4S," she explained, unnecessarily adding: "It's a company that does secure transports. We collect money from shops and stuff like that."

"Wow," Sami said tonelessly. "You like it?"

"It's OK, but like, I dunno . . . ? The hours are a bit . . . two days a week you have to work nights. Then the day after's ruined, you wake up late in the afternoon and can't sleep that night because you're not really tired. It's tough."

"A bit like being a chef," said Sami.

"I never thought of that."

Her voice sounded eager when she realized that she happened to have something in common with the stranger.

Maloof stopped by the far goalpost. A soft breeze was blowing across the open field, carrying with it the smell of exhaust fumes and an icy chill that stung their skin.

Without thinking about it, all three turned their backs to the wind and their faces to the ground. The sound of lone cars passing with a low whine on the highway was all they could hear. Sami stamped his feet hard against the snow, which was lying like a thin white blanket on the grass.

"Right, right," said Maloof. "And . . . didn't you say it felt like hard work . . . going out to Västberga every day?"

Maloof wanted her to get back to the main subject, and Alexandra was someone who quickly adapted to that kind of demand.

"Yeah, that's the thing," she willingly agreed. "Super hard. Väst-berga, I mean. What even is that place? I sublet in Hammarby Sjöstad, so you can go straight through Årsta, but . . . Especially in the evening and nights, it's like traveling abroad. Trains and metros and buses. I applied for a job at Lugnet, the school right next to where I live, but I didn't get it. There were like a thousand people who applied."

"You can just ask your new boyfriend for a lift," Sami joked, elbowing Maloof. "He works nights too, sometimes."

"My new boyfriend?" Alexandra blurted, surprised, realizing a moment later who Sami meant. "Yeah, I mean . . . I don't know . . ."

Maloof wasn't amused by the joke. He urged her on.

"And," he said gently, "you said you didn't have the best colleagues either?"

"Nope, that's true," Alexandra replied, though a note of hesitation had appeared in her voice.

Maloof was worried. Was she starting to realize how odd the situation was; that she had been brought out onto a cold soccer field in Fittja to talk with a complete stranger about her pointless job? But he was counting on her need to please being stronger than her anxiety.

"No, it's not exactly like I'd choose to socialize with them outside of work," she continued. "But I guess it's always like that? Plus, I'm not planning to stay there counting money for the rest of my life . . ."

"No," said Sami. "You seem smart, you could do whatever you want."

"Right, right." Maloof backed him up.

"I'm freezing, Michel," she said. "Can't we . . ."

"We're going," he promised. "But . . . I mean . . . while we're on the subject of your job . . ."

He turned to Sami. "When Alexandra told me about Västberga last time . . . you said . . . that it felt uncomfortable? Sometimes? 'Cause there are people who . . . you know, are planning to rob the place?"

"It's like, pretty hard to rob us." Alexandra nodded.

"Right, right," said Maloof. "But it's still possible?"

He was careful not to leave any pauses that might unintentionally increase the importance of what he wanted her to talk about.

"Because you had an idea . . . ?" he continued.

She laughed self-consciously and glanced around. As though someone was listening. But the soccer field was deserted that dark evening, and if anyone was approaching, they would notice them from a mile off.

"It's not exactly my idea," she said. "Everyone talks about that kind of thing during the breaks, you know. About how the people working in the vault think they're special because it's impossible to get in there. And then the rest of us, working up in Counting, we ask why someone would try to get in the vault. There are like a thousand doors and locks and cameras. But up in Cash, we've got hundreds of millions of kronor and nowhere near as much security stuff."

"I don't understand," said Sami.

"No, so," Alexandra explained, "if you were a thief, you shouldn't try to get into the vault. You should just go in through the roof. You'd just have to drill a hole and then you'd be in our section."

"A hole in the roof?"

"Right." Maloof nodded, trying to rein in his excitement. "Alexandra's department is on the top floor."

"So you'd go in through the roof?" Sami repeated in an attempt to understand.

"That easy." Alexandra nodded.

"Right?" Maloof laughed.

That was exactly what he thought. For years, more than he could remember, Michel Maloof had been trying to find out how to get into the cash depot in Västberga. Nowhere else in Sweden held as much cash as it did. But it had always seemed impossible, and the security was legendary.

And then it turned out to be this easy.

Right beneath the ceiling was an unguarded room full of hundreds of millions in cash.

The three stood in silence for a moment or two.

"My feet are freezing, Michel," Alexandra moaned.

"Right, right. Let's go now," he replied, putting an arm around her to share some of the warmth he felt inside.

They took a step toward the grass slope where you could take a shortcut straight to one of the foot tunnels.

"Through the roof?" Sami repeated, nodding to himself. "OK. See you later, Michel. Nice to meet you, Alexandra."

Maloof and his new girlfriend disappeared into the darkness.

11

Her water broke at home on Högbergsgatan on the second of April.

It wasn't anything like the first time.

Karin and Sami had gone to the hospital too early then. There hadn't been any free rooms, and they'd had to wait in the corridor of the maternity ward for six hours, from two in the morning until eight. When things finally got going, it took another twelve hours. Sami had fallen asleep in the bed in their room that afternoon, while Karin paced around him trying to manage her pain.

He knew that sleep was the body's way of managing a situation that couldn't be managed, but he had still felt ashamed when he woke up. Being so physically close to the person you loved and still being shut out and helpless was awful. He couldn't lessen or share Karin's pain, so his only escape had been to shut down.

The tension in the delivery room had grown the longer her labor went on, the nurses' eyes had started to wander, and by dinnertime, he'd heard them whispering about a cesarean. But then the time suddenly came, and John had been born that evening.

The second time was different.

When they arrived at the maternity ward, her contractions were so close together that the nurses and midwife immediately took them into a delivery room. Just under an hour later, John's little brother was born, and two hours after that, Sami was back home on Högbergsgatan.

During the month that followed, the Farhan family—Sami, Karin, John and the baby—lived life as though in a cocoon. They and the rest of Stockholm were trapped beneath a gray blanket of incessant rain. There were days when they didn't even get out of bed, days they never got dressed, with a newborn baby and his one-year-old brother both needing closeness, warmth, food and care. It didn't feel right to

leave either of the kids with a babysitter, not even with their grand-
mothers.

It was only as April was suddenly on the verge of May that the new
parents felt their isolation start to grate. They took turns leaving the
apartment, striking up contact with family and friends and regaining
their respective identities outside of being a parent.

Awaiting Karin was early spring, blue skies and mild winds, loyal
friends and a longing grandmother. Awaiting Sami were debts that
hadn't paid themselves during his monthlong paternity leave.

And on top of that, a large number of missed calls from Michel
Maloof.

The planning for different jobs went in phases, and you kept doors
open because you never knew what would happen. Things were leaning more and more toward the Västberga job, though Sami still didn't
want to rule out the Täby Racecourse plan.

The last thing he had done before he entered the new-baby haze
was to promise that he would try to verify Alexandra Svensson's story.
The idea of going straight through the roof into the room where they
counted money on the sixth floor sounded almost too good to be
true. Had she made it up because she wanted to impress them? Sami
thought he knew a way to check. And so, one day in early May, he
walked up to Pro Gym on Högbergsgatan to meet Ezra Ray.

"Here!"

Ezra shouted across the entire gym. It was just after ten on Saturday
morning, but despite the relatively early hour, the place was full. As
ever, interest in working out always peaked once spring was on its way;
the thought of swimming trunks and bikinis terrified people back onto
exercise bikes and StairMasters.

Sami waved and made his way over to the corner with the free
weights, where Ezra was busy. He recognized that familiar gym scent:
sweat and metal, deodorant and cleaning products.

"Jesus!" Ezra Ray shouted across the room. "You look like shit!"

Everyone within hearing distance automatically turned to see exactly who it was who looked like shit. Sami Farhan felt their eyes mercilessly boring through his thin sweater, revealing the excess fat he had gained around his stomach over the winter.

He'd had trouble getting back into working out for the past few years; he associated that sort of discipline with the routine in prison, and ever since he'd gotten out, lifting weights was the last thing he wanted to be doing.

"What about you, then?" he said to his friend. "You're so weedy you look like a stickleback. You need to be able to put some weight behind those punches."

Ezra had been using the dumbbells, but he dropped them onto the mat with a rattling thud. With his shaved head, high cheekbones, sunken cheeks, broken nose and wiry, overly muscular frame, Ezra Ray didn't have trouble looking intimidating.

"You what?!" he shouted. "You what?"

The entire room fell silent.

Ezra clenched his fists and got into the classic boxing position. All around them, people's mouths were open, they were staring. Sami lost no time in mirroring his friend's pose.

"Right, you bastard," said Ezra, "I'll show you how weedy I am!"

A second later, he burst into laughter. Disappointed, the drama-thirsty gym rats had no choice but to turn their attention back to themselves.

"Seriously though, Sami," Ezra said once he picked up the dumbbells to finish his last few repetitions, "you look like you've lost some of your edge."

Sami nodded. There was no denying it.

The two men had first met during their teens. They had worked out together from time to time, but for Ezra Ray, boxing had been too traditional, too regulated. He had started with karate and jiujitsu, but he'd had trouble taking all the bowing and meditating seriously. When

Ultimate Fighting broke through, it was as though the sport had been made for him. He was probably too old for it now, but so long as he won matches, his age wasn't a problem. During the last ten years, Ezra Ray had constantly been in training for one championship or another, and that Saturday in May was no exception.

These days, he rarely ended up on the podium, but he never came last either.

"I'm just going to finish up," he said, "then we can have a delicious protein drink and talk seriously."

"I spoke to my sis," Ezra Ray said a few minutes later when he joined Sami at the makeshift bar on the other side of the room. A strawberry white-chocolate protein shake was waiting for him. "I didn't tell her exactly what it was about, but I asked how you could get hold of the plans for different buildings, if she could sort that kind of thing out. She said you just have to go to the town planning office."

Ezra Ray's sister Katinka worked for an architecture firm. She was the one Sami had been thinking of when he promised Maloof to double-check Alexandra Svensson's story.

"The town planning office?"

"I checked. Anyone can go there. You don't even have to be an architect. It's on Fleminggatan. That's your patch, Sami." Ezra laughed. "Next to the police station and the jail."

"Cool," Sami said, though he didn't smile.

"That's that anyway."

Ezra sipped his shake and was left with a pale pink protein mustache. Somehow, it suited his wild appearance. "Shit, that's good!"

"I don't know," Sami replied. "Just going into the town planning office and asking for the drawings for the city's biggest cash depot doesn't exactly seem smart. You know what I mean?"

Though he was sitting on a bar stool, he managed to keep his ankle moving so that his leg bobbed up and down.

"Katinka said that was how it worked. Can't you sit still?"

"But it's a cash depot," Sami replied, his foot keeping the same rhythm.

"Yeah."

"She must've been joking. Course they won't give out the drawings. You know? Maybe you can get the drawings for an ordinary house, but a bank? Of course you can't."

Ezra shrugged.

"She said all the drawings were at the town planning office. I've got no idea. Guess we can try."

"You're insane," Sami declared.

"You know it," Ezra laughed, downing the last of the liquid in his glass and getting strawberry on his nose. "I can test it out if you want?"

Sami smirked. Ezra Ray had been kicked in the head one too many times.

On Monday morning, they parked up on Scheelegatan. Sami waited in the car as some kind of moral support while Ezra walked down the hill toward the town planning office.

He crossed Fleminggatan in his typically inimitable way. His arms didn't just swing by his sides, they were like small propellers. Ezra had been severely bow-legged since childhood, meaning that every step forward looked more like a lurch to the right or the left.

He jogged up the stairs to the huge brick building, and used the information board at the entrance to work out where the town planning offices were located. It was just before eleven, and he didn't see another soul on his way through the long corridors, which eventually came to an end by a pretty glass door.

He rang the buzzer. A whirring sound opened the door and Ezra stepped inside.

Without hesitating, not even for a fraction of a second, he walked over to the elderly man sitting behind the reception desk.

"Hi," he said cheerily, "I'd like to look at the drawings for a building in Västberga? Västberga Allé Eleven?"

The man behind the desk studied the relatively young fighter wearing a pair of ripped jeans, a black leather jacket and a broad smile. He nodded and then typed the address into his computer.

"Aha," he said without looking up. "Vreten Seventeen, you mean? By Georg Scherman. On the corner of Västberga Allé Eleven and Vretensborgsvägen Thirty-Two?"

"Exactly," Ezra replied, not having a clue what the old man was talking about.

The man was reading the screen.

"The last time someone requested these drawings was October 1979," he said. Ezra shrugged. The man seemed to be reading aloud from the archival notes.

"If you go in there," he continued, nodding toward a small room full of desks and chairs, "I'll bring you everything we've got. Are you familiar with the rules?"

Ezra didn't dare answer yes to that question. His hesitation caused the old man to explain.

"You can study the plans on site, you can take photographs if you want, but the originals don't leave this building. Understood?"

Ezra Ray nodded.

"Right then," the old man said, waving his visitor away to the adjoining room and leaving Reception in order, Ezra assumed, to go down to some dark basement archive and dig out the drawings.

Ezra Ray wasn't the least bit surprised. His big sister Katinka had said it would be this way, and she was never wrong.

It took twenty minutes for the old man to return with a huge stack of papers, which he dumped onto the table in front of his young visitor.

"This is everything we had," he said. "Enjoy."

Ezra looked down at the pile of papers and leafed through them at random. Understanding these lines and numbers required knowledge he himself lacked.

"Thanks," he said, pretending to be absorbed by one of the blueish originals.

But the old man was already on his way back to Reception, with zero interest in what Ezra Ray was doing with the documents.

Ezra stayed in that small room for almost an hour. That was how long it took for the next visitor to turn up. This time, again, there was a short discussion at Reception and then the old man got up to disappear into his archive.

Sami, waiting patiently in the car and, becoming more and more anxious about not making it back to Karin by twelve as promised, suddenly saw a madman running down Scheelegatan with his arms full of papers. Through the open window, he heard Ezra's triumphant voice:

"I did it! See, you fuck! I did it!"

12

The first modern bridge to the Stockholm suburb of Lidingö was completed after the end of the First World War, and by the time the next one ended, the country's politicians had decided to transform the villa enclave into a modern community. They planned and built new neighborhoods, with functionalist blocks of apartments in Rudboda, Käppala and Larsberg. These were the finishing touches to a suburb that would reflect the big city. Traces of the older rural society's farms and fields remained, as did the beautiful merchants' villas from the nineteenth century. A handful of the island's industrial areas and magnificent brick factories even managed to survive the later vogue for tearing things down, all while the Swedish welfare state's 1950s aspirations for solidarity were abandoned on the island, just as they were everywhere else.

Today, Lidingö is far from a homogeneous rich enclave, but the middle-class majority in the municipal council remains unchanged.

Hersby was one of a handful of areas on Lidingö mentioned as early as the Viking age, but the scrapyard next to Vasavägen isn't named on any rune stones. For a couple of twenty-kronor notes, or maybe a hundred, Svenne Gustafsson offered a solution to busy city dwellers who didn't know what to do with a car that was no longer worth repairing.

He towed the rusty vehicles around the corner, behind the little wooden building that also served as his office. He had blocked off the scrapyard with a high fence topped with barbed wire, and, using a stationary crane, stacked the car skeletons on top of one another while he waited to sell their unique spare parts, each of which was worth more than he had paid for the car itself.

The stacks of cars formed narrow alleyways, and at the very end of one of these was a large container, tucked halfway into the woods. From the outside, its green corrugated metal looked unassuming and rusty, but when Zoran Petrovic opened the door at one side, he stepped straight into a modern workshop. The walls had been clad with aluminum foil beneath an interior wall of steel, and the ceiling was soundproofed.

Petrovic was Svenne Gustafsson's business partner and financier, but no one knew that. It was how Petrovic wanted it. He was involved in a number of other businesses in the same way: a cleaning firm, a couple of restaurants, a handful of beauty salons, a building firm in Tallinn and one in Montenegro.

Among others.

The tall, slim Yugoslavian, who had been born in the southern Swedish city of Lund almost forty years earlier, closed the container door behind him, and the six people working inside looked up from their workstations. On top of their clothes, each was wearing a bulletproof vest, and they all had on helmets with visors. It was like being on the set of a science fiction film where the props had been bought from Bauhaus.

"No, no, just keep working, keep working," Petrovic instructed them.

On each of the six workbenches was a blue security bag that had recently been stolen from a secure transport vehicle or a guard. Without the right code and key, a dye ampoule would explode if they tried to open the bags using force. Petrovic was paying the six amateur engineers to find a way of opening the bags without setting off the explosives. The youngsters—and all six were young—had divided the methods of attack among themselves. One was using a welding flame to try to open the bag, another a small circular saw. One was trying to pick the lock, and another was trying to tackle the bag from the bottom. Each had a digital camera mounted on a tripod just behind them, filming his or her every move. What all six had in common was that none had made any progress in weeks.

Zoran Petrovic had lost count of how many bags he had sacrificed so far in his quest to open them without setting off the explosives.

He slowly went over to each of the young workers and exchanged a few words with them. Petrovic found talking to a nineteen-year-old emo kid as easy as talking to the infrastructure minister of Montenegro. That was how it had always been.

"Good, good," he said to a girl in her twenties. She was busy using the welding flame to burn a hole in the bottom right-hand corner of the bag.

Petrovic stretched out a long arm and, with a lazy elegance, drew a pattern in the air above the metal of the bag.

"That's how to do it, that's right. It's like painting a picture, you move the flame back and forward, like Monet. Or Manet. I have an acquaintance, he's the head of a museum in Lyon, obsessed with brush-strokes, he's filled his yard with sand and bought a special rake that's finer than a normal rake, so he can drag it across the sand and . . ."

"Zoran?"

It was Svenne Gustafsson's assistant who had stuck his head around the door. The Yugoslavian turned around, annoyed.

"What?"

"You've got a visitor. Maloof's here."

"OK." Petrovic nodded. "OK. I'll finish the story later. Just keep going. And remember, we're not in a hurry. We're never in a hurry, nothing good will come of that."

His statement was met with a certain gratitude, but Zoran Petrovic had made it only halfway back through the scrapyard labyrinth to Gustafsson's office when he heard a dull thud, a sound so familiar that he didn't even jump. Yet another bag had been triggered, and they would be forced to burn yet another stack of dyed notes. They had tried cleaning the dye from the notes in every way possible, but not even boiling them, putting them into the washing machine with chlorine or scrubbing them by hand had brought the color out. It simply couldn't be done.

Petrovic stooped to avoid hitting his head as he stepped into the building through the back door. Michel Maloof was waiting on a chair in the kitchen behind Svenne Gustafsson's office. Gustafsson was currently out, something he always made sure to be whenever Maloof stopped by.

"Just a glass of lukewarm water," said Petrovic.

"What?"

"I don't want anything else."

Maloof stared at his tall friend in amazement as he sat down at the table. "Water? You want me to get your water?" he asked.

Petrovic made a gesture that showed it was clear that Maloof should be serving him the water. Maloof laughed and shook his head.

"Right, right," he said, getting up. "Yeah, well, it is your . . . lukewarm water."

Maloof went over to the counter and filled a glass from the tap. Overly casually, he returned to the table and placed it in front of Zoran Petrovic, who nodded indulgently.

The two men had known one another a long time, but their relationship would always be shaped by the fact that Petrovic had been leader of the playground where Maloof had hung out during his school years. Zoran Petrovic became the only role model that Maloof had who didn't play soccer. And since Petrovic had known how to spend money even back then—his wardrobe had been full of nothing but Armani, and he had never left home on a Friday evening without his American Express card—that had helped Maloof define his own life goals.

"I'm going to be a millionaire," the young Maloof had said, and Petrovic had laughed.

"A million's what I make in a month," he had replied.

*   *   *

"Through the roof?"

"Right, right," Maloof explained with a smile, "through the roof."

It was two thirty in the afternoon. The stack of plates and mugs in the sink had been there for months. Svenne Gustafsson wasn't the pedantic type, and both Maloof and Petrovic did their best to pretend that the broken drain in the toilet didn't stink. They never usually had this type of conversation unless they were out walking somewhere, but the heavens had suddenly opened and neither of them wanted to get wet. They had been talking about all the money they would earn from the black security bags when Maloof mentioned Alexandra Svensson.

"Talk about an old dream," said Petrovic. "You've been going on about Västberga for years."

Maloof smiled and nodded.

"OK," said Petrovic, "But how the hell do you get onto the roof?"

"There must be a way."

"Jumping shoes?" Petrovic sneered. "Or what's it called . . . a jet pack? With a jet pack, like in the opening ceremony of the Olympics. Is that what you've got planned?"

"Right, right." Maloof smiled. "Like the Olympics. Exactly. No."

"Maybe you could use a cherry picker? I've got a friend with a company in Monaco. He cleans windows, you know, thirty floors up. Monaco's one great big window. He sends people up in a box. It's big enough for five, six people. I sat in one of his cherry pickers once during the Formula One. You know, fifteen floors up, right above the track. The cars were driving past under our feet. We were drinking fizz and the girl dropped a sandal. I thought I'd shit myself. You know? A sandal straight onto the track. Jesus."

"A cherry picker?" Maloof asked. "Is it on a flatbed?"

Petrovic nodded. "He has them mounted on cars."

"Right," Maloof replied, thinking aloud. "A crane? On the front? A building crane. One you could drive up at night."

Petrovic reached for the glass of water on the table and took a sip.

"Could work," he said thoughtfully. "Could work. Getting hold of a crane's not exactly hard . . ."

"Or . . . a hot air balloon."

"Are you serious?"

"A helicopter?"

"Is there room for a helicopter to land on the roof? Have you ever flown a helicopter, Michel? Damn noisy."

"No . . . But you'd be able to get away in a helicopter too."

"I prefer the crane," said Petrovic.

Maloof nodded and grinned.

"Exactly. Sounds most plausible, maybe? But . . . how would you get away then?"

They heard the outer door open and close. Gustafsson had returned from his made-up errand, and Maloof got to his feet. It was time to leave.

"OK. Well . . . think about it," he said.

"A crane," said Petrovic. "I'll think about it."

"How's it going in the container out there? Getting anywhere soon? Or not?"

Petrovic twisted self-consciously.

"Just take it easy," he said in a superior tone. "It'll work out."

"You think?"

"You don't want to wait fifteen years, I don't want to wait fifteen years. So it'll work out because it has to work out."

"Right, right." Maloof nodded.

"I've got something on the go," said Petrovic. "I ordered something from France. It's coming next week. A crazy thing, but it'll solve the problem. I'm not even going to tell you how much it cost."

They heard yet another faint boom from out in the container. Petrovic got up.

"I'm going to tell them to stop," he said, sounding annoyed. "I don't want to have to find more bags. It'll work out. Next week. Finally."

Maloof grinned. "What kind of thing?" he asked as Petrovic was on his way out.

The rain had eased up, but it was still coming down.

"You'll see," the Yugoslavian said over his shoulder. "All you need to know for now is that it's going to make you a rich man."

13

Jack Kluger was sitting in the Wasahof restaurant on Dalagatan, waiting for Basir Balik. It was twelve thirty, and though they had agreed to
meet at twelve, Balik was always late for lunch. Kluger didn't mind, he
wasn't in a hurry.

At the table next to him, two women were eating shrimp salads.
Kluger would have guessed they were in their thirties, and that they
might have worked at the hospital farther down the street. Both were
blond and well dressed, and Jack couldn't stop himself from smiling
and giving one of them a friendly nod. The one sitting closest to him
said something in Swedish that Kluger couldn't understand, but her
expression was crystal clear.

She wasn't amused.

"I'm sorry," he said, "but in my part of Texas, nobody speaks
Swedish."

Then he smiled again, showing off the white dental veneers the
American army had paid for.

It worked every time. His American accent was like a skeleton key,
it could unlock any door. The woman's irritated expression was replaced by an embarrassed smile, and just a few minutes later the three
of them were sitting together, making small talk. There was nothing
people in this city liked more than speaking English with a man from
Texas. Kluger had even started dressing like a cowboy, with rough
checked shirts and traditional boots. Clothes he had never worn when
he lived in Texas.

"So if I only have a couple of days in the city, what would you suggest I do?" he asked.

*   *   *

Jack Kluger wasn't a city person, but the minute he opened his mouth and said anything in his broad Southern accent, he was immediately identified as "American" and therefore someone who thought that Sweden and Stockholm were small and provincial.

Nothing could be further from the truth.

Compared with Goldsboro, Texas, Stockholm was an exotic metropolis, full of dangers and temptations. Temptations in particular. There were beautiful women everywhere. They were in the parks, on the streets, sitting in restaurants. And the real miracle was that they all seemed to want to talk to him, of all people. Back home in Texas, he had been just one of many well-built boys who played American football and had a jaw as square as a cake tin. But in Scandinavia, he became exotic and unique.

In the past, he'd had low self-confidence when it came to the opposite sex, not least because he wasn't much of a talker. It had been easier to fight for his opinions than to defend them with words. That was something he had inherited from his father; none of his siblings were particularly quick thinking.

But in Europe, and Sweden in particular, no one called Jack Kluger an idiot. There, the language barrier became a natural defense. Though everyone watched American films, no one realized that his vocabulary was as limited as his education.

"Gamla-stan?" he said, pronouncing the area of the city in his heavily accented way. "From what you're saying, I'd need a guide. Would either of you ladies be interested?"

They laughed, but he could see that both were willing to lead him through the narrow streets of the capital's main tourist thoroughfare.

Kluger glanced at his watch. Quarter to one. Where was Balik?

Goldsboro was a town of a few hundred people just south of Abilene, itself home to a hundred thousand inhabitants and a few hours west of Dallas. Kruger had been on his way back there for years now, but he was constantly finding new excuses not to get on the plane.

The detour to Stockholm hadn't been planned, but he had managed to stay put there. He had always thought that Sweden was the country where they made chocolate and cuckoo clocks, but he now knew he had mistaken it for Switzerland. Geography had never been one of his favorite subjects at school. In fact, he hadn't had any favorite subjects at all.

He was the third of five children. He had no contact with his brothers, but he thought that his older and only sister was still living at home. Kruger himself had dropped out of high school and enlisted in the army, back when the war in Afghanistan had recently begun, and since that day he hadn't seen either of his parents.

Joining the military hadn't been a patriotic decision, even if his sense of patriotism had grown during his service. It was just a way of getting away from home, of getting a job and health insurance and being able to avoid thinking about what he was going to do with his life.

Jack Kluger wasn't much of a thinker.

He didn't want to think about the war or about Afghanistan. He was tired of all the films about Rambo and war veterans coming home full of regret and with shot nerves; men who couldn't sleep at night and started drinking or smoking crack, who lost their jobs if they'd even had one to begin with. Jack Kluger was better than that. He wasn't helpless, he wasn't a victim, he wouldn't go crazy and kill himself or be haunted by memories of people blown to pieces or children losing their legs. He was strong. He could control his thoughts. He could shut out everything he needed to, and turn his mind to beautiful, easy and fun things instead.

But sometimes, whenever he lowered his defenses for a moment or two, the doubt reared its head. It was as though he got confused, and it always happened without warning. In the middle of a conversation, at the checkout when he went to the supermarket, or during a lunch when he was meant to be talking work.

Or, like now, when he was trying to charm two women in a restaurant.

He lost focus, suddenly didn't know where he was or what he was doing there.

And as long as these moments of confusion continued to affect him, he held off on buying that ticket back home to Goldsboro, Texas.

He wanted to be completely back to normal before he returned.

He was just about to ask one of the women, the one with the bigger lips, what she was doing that evening and whether she wanted to go to a restaurant he had been recommended, when Balik came in through the door.

The sight of him made Kluger quickly end his conversation, and he got up to greet his friend. When the women left a few minutes later, the one with the bigger lips left her phone number on a napkin on the table. Kluger let it lie. There were plenty of other phone numbers in Stockholm.

14

Michel Maloof had been surprised at how unfazed Alexandra Svensson was by her own nakedness. Not wearing a thread, she climbed out of bed, went into the bathroom and left the door open. Once she was done, she flushed and continued, still naked, into the kitchen, where she first switched on the coffee machine and then began to slice oranges.

It was an early Sunday morning in early May. Alexandra had slept at Maloof's place again; it was almost becoming a habit, the third time in two weeks. Compared with the way she lived, with someone else's furniture in a tiny studio apartment, staying at his place was like visiting a castle. The roller blind wasn't fully down, and he could feel the warmth of the sun on his skin. He lay in the soft bed, slowly waking to the sound of Alexandra in the kitchen. There was a growing knot of anxiety in his stomach, and he knew exactly why.

He was enjoying this far too much.

Maloof slowly turned onto his back, his head on the pillow. He opened his eyes. The sun glittered on the mirror on the wall. Why did his bedroom suddenly feel so much more comfortable? He glanced around and realized it was because of all the new feminine touches; the cushions she had brought over from her place, the new striped sheets she had bought, the pots of creams and perfumes on the counter, all the clothes she had strewn about and that smelled like a woman.

Maloof's phone was on the bedside table, but he didn't reach for it. That was one of the privileges of Sunday mornings.

He would have to watch out, he realized, though he was already longing to get back into bed after breakfast. Ideally with Alexandra. He smiled at the thought. He wasn't in a proper relationship right now, though he did know a couple of women who wanted just that. If he didn't actively fight it, he might easily end up in one with Alexandra

Svensson. Just because it felt nice to know whom you would be spending the night with, and it was better than giving out keys to several women at once. He was well aware that that wasn't a good enough reason to move in with someone, which meant he had to try to keep Alexandra Svensson at arm's length. He was letting her sleep over for professional reasons, and he had to bear that in mind.

He climbed out of bed. After the obligatory visit to the bathroom, he pulled on his T-shirt and underwear from the day before. He was far from as comfortable with his own naked body as she was with hers.

He found her by the counter in the kitchen. She was standing with her back to the door, squeezing oranges against the juice press with both hands. Her round bottom trembled with the vibrations it was sending through her body. He laughed quietly.

"Can I help?" he asked.

"Very manly of you, Michel," she replied without turning around. "But I think I can manage to make some orange juice without your help? You could, like, take out the coffee cups? Do you want anything else? Should I toast some bread?"

"No, don't worry," he said. Coffee and juice was a perfect breakfast.

She moved around his kitchen as though she was at home; she had even rearranged the furniture. He took out two cups and two glasses and put them down on the counter. He couldn't help but glance at her small breasts as he did it.

"Stop it," she said with a smile when she realized.

He tried, but he couldn't help himself.

"Are you working tonight?" he asked.

They were sitting at the kitchen table. Alexandra had pulled on a dressing gown so as not to distract her lover, one made of silk that seemed to have taken up permanent residence in Maloof's wardrobe.

"Yep," she replied with a nod. "I tried to put together a time sheet for May where I wouldn't have to see Claude, but no matter what I do he just turns up anyway. I mean, it doesn't matter. He'd never dare do anything. But, I don't know, he's creepy."

Maloof nodded. The kitchen smelled of cinnamon, something it only ever did when Alexandra was there. He didn't know why, maybe it was her perfume.

"You get it, right?" she asked, continuing without waiting for an answer. "He thinks he's, like, the world's best boss. He's been through management courses. And he's basically promising me a career. I mean, what does he think? There are fourteen of us working nights, when we're all in, which only happens on Tuesdays and Thursdays. What kind of career is that going to be, exactly?"

"Right, right. Is there . . . more to do on Tuesdays and . . . Thursdays, or something?" Maloof wondered.

"Mmm. We take the most money then. But, I mean, day shift on Fridays, there's never more than maybe seven, eight people? So what's he thinking? Am I meant to be the boss of three people and him the other four?"

She laughed. Maloof did too.

"It's like," she said, "get it together, you know?"

"Right, right."

"I don't want to go straight home," Alexandra said with a sigh, changing the subject. "It's going to be a nice day. If you wanted, we could have a picnic."

This was how Maloof's knowledge of the cash depot in Västberga grew. Each time he saw Alexandra, she revealed something else that could prove useful. That morning alone, he had learned that it was the morning after a Tuesday or Thursday that they should strike.

It was a long-winded way of planning a job, but this was how he worked. Thoroughly.

Alexandra's dressing gown slipped open when she twisted to close the window. He couldn't resist the urge, and reached forward to move his fingertips gently over her small nipple, which immediately hardened at his touch.

"Or," she said with a shiver, "we could blow off the picnic and do something else?"

It was Alexandra Svensson's description of the counting department that eventually convinced Maloof that Ezra Ray had stolen the right documents from the town planning office. She had described the big room on the sixth floor as being "banana shaped" several times now. What she was trying to say was that the open-plan office where she worked was constructed in some kind of arc, a gentle curve, across the top of the building.

Maloof had been in the café by the bowling alley in Heron City on the afternoon when Sami had given him the drawings. The thundering of the balls and the crash of the occasional strike had drowned out the canned music. Each had ordered a cup of black coffee, and Maloof had leafed through the stack of papers that Sami had brought in a plastic bag from H&M.

"But the fact he stole them," Maloof had asked, "isn't that basically like . . . announcing we're planning something?"

"Do you know when someone last requested these documents?"

Maloof had shaken his head. Sami's leg bounced impatiently beneath the table.

"October 1979. That was the last time. And before that, it was 1970. Said so on a note that came with them. Like some kind of library card."

"Right, right," Maloof had said, though he had never taken out a library book in his life.

"If someone only asks to see these drawings every thirty years, there's not much risk in borrowing them for a few months, right?"

"No, no, of course," Maloof replied, searching through the pile of papers and realizing why no one was interested.

The drawings were indecipherable. It was impossible even to tell whether the Vreten 17 building really was the G4S cash depot.

When Maloof got home from Heron City that day, he had spread out the drawings on the floor and started to methodically go through them. What made them particularly difficult to interpret was the large, open atrium that cut straight through the building. There was a glass dome on the roof, in the shape of a sharp pyramid, and beneath that, the huge space opened out. The various floors were built around that square void in the center.

After an hour or so, he managed to find the room Alexandra had been talking about. Its curved form was the only one like it in the entire building, and the key to understanding the drawings. Using that room as his starting point, Maloof was able to work out far more over the days that followed.

It didn't worry him that he still wasn't sure what the lower floors of the building were like. He found what he assumed was the vault, split between two levels, but knew there was no point attempting to break in there. Not just because Alexandra had talked about the legendary security system, but also because he had been hearing stories about officials from the Swedish Central Bank going there to study the setup before updating their own security systems for years.

The vault was one of Scandinavia's most expensive. If you had access to a small army, you could probably get in, but otherwise it was better not to even try.

Every night, Maloof called Sami and gave him an update on his progress. The exhausted father was enthusiastic rather than helpful.

"OK," he said to Maloof, "but is it going to work? What do you think?"

"Yeah," he told Sami. "Just like she said. You blow a hole through the roof, and that takes you straight to place we're aiming for. It . . . should take five, ten minutes. No more."

There was a general rule that if it took more than fifteen minutes to get in and out of a bank or post office, the police would have time to arrive. But five to ten minutes felt good.

"OK," said Sami. "But how the hell do you get onto the roof to begin with? And how do you get down again?"

15

It wasn't like in the movies.

Sami Farhan had never been to a racecourse before, but he felt like he had seen hundreds of Hollywood films full of people doing dodgy deals as they walked around the trotting tracks, or cheering on their favorites from the stands.

The atmosphere at Täby Racecourse was nothing like that.

On the way in, there had been far more horse paddocks and stalls than he had expected, but once they reached the main building, he couldn't hide his disappointment. There was barely anyone around, and the whole place was in disrepair. It was a gloomy, abandoned scene.

"Where is everyone?" Sami asked.

"At home in front of their computers," Toomas Mandel replied. "They built these grandstands before you could gamble online. They thought thousands of people would come to the races. Tens of thousands. But now you'd be lucky to see a few hundred."

It seemed incredible. If you watched daytime TV in Sweden, harness and traditional racing seemed to be two of the country's great interests. How many times had Sami seen cute girls with huge microphones asking short men in colorful clothes whether the track was heavy or not? Where were all the TV cameras today?

They went into the restaurant. It took Sami a moment to realize that the restaurant *was* Täby Racecourse. There was nothing else for the spectators.

"I don't know," he said as they each ordered a tomato salad from an old, bored waiter. "If it's this empty, surely there can't be any money here? You know what I mean?"

"No," Mandel said. "There isn't. Three hundred and sixty-four days a year, you'd get no more than small change. That's why they reduced the number of security guards and got rid of the police. These days, they only have surveillance around the tracks and the stalls. They're not worried about anyone stealing money, they're just worried someone's going to . . . mess with the horses."

Sami nodded. He knew people who had made money on harness racing. People he had grown up with, but others too. People from the pub. Half celebrities. Mafia.

"OK," Sami said. "So tell me the plan again?"

"The Diana Race is the exception. It's the same day as the Jockey Club's Jubilee Race. Always in early summer. I'd guess there'd be up to ten million in cash here then. Maybe more? Still no police or guards though."

"Ten million?" Sami repeated.

He was disappointed. Like always when you were planning a job, people had a tendency to overexaggerate. Toomas Mandel was trying to sell this opportunity, and it was clear he was exaggerating. Meaning the ten million was probably more like five. Which would be split among several people.

"It's not that much," Mandel agreed, "but it's relative to the risk. It's a small amount of money, but it's low risk."

"Riding down to the boat club afterward? Low risk? That's not low risk."

"I told you, the riding thing is just one of several ideas," Mandel replied, sounding annoyed. "Forget that. I'll think of something else."

Their salads arrived. Sami could say with confidence that the restaurant kitchen at Täby Racecourse wouldn't be the future of racing. And that, despite having had several weeks, Mandel still hadn't come up with anything better than riding off with the money. Like a couple of cowboys.

Sami called Michel Maloof that same afternoon, and they agreed to meet in Skärholmen the next day. He had thought he would be able to sneak off for a few hours around lunch, but Karin woke with a migraine and he had no other option than to take the baby with him. They hadn't decided on a name yet, but it had taken a while last time too. Karin was relieved when he left. It meant she could pull down the blinds in the bedroom and wrap herself in darkness; the only way to dull the pain. Her mother was taking care of John.

Sami left the stroller at home, as it was impossible to get around with one on the subway. And so, with a warmly dressed baby in his arms—though it was the second week in May, the temperature still hadn't made it above 50 degrees—he walked down to Slussen and took the red line out to Skärholmen. Sami didn't know what the baby could see through the dark windows in the tunnels, but it must have been fascinating enough to keep him captivated the entire way. When they finally arrived, he was so tired that he had fallen asleep.

They met outside a Foot Locker.

The baby lay like a bundle over his father's shoulder, and Sami effortlessly greeted Maloof with his right hand.

Maloof laughed and nodded. "That alive . . . or what?"

"You bet your ass," said Sami.

Maloof laughed again. "Right, right. But you know . . . Pacino probably wouldn't—"

"I'm not Al Pacino," Sami interrupted him.

"No, no, not even Al Pacino is these days," Maloof agreed.

They started walking. It was just before lunch on a Thursday, and the shopping center wouldn't be setting any new sales records that day. But there were still enough people around for no one to pay any attention to the ill-matched pair, the short Lebanese man and the big Iraqi with a baby on his shoulder.

Sami had peeled back the baby's outer layers of clothing like a banana skin. They were now hanging from his feet.

"I've been thinking," he said.

Maloof nodded. He had too. He didn't know if he wanted to call it a plan. It was more like jigsaw pieces scattered around his head, waiting to be put together.

"Yeah?"

"What kind of money are we talking about? Do you know?" Sami asked.

"Yeah, yeah. More than any individual bank in Sweden. You want the exact amount?"

"Roughly?"

"Half a billion?" Maloof suggested.

Sami nodded. He absentmindedly patted the baby's diaper through his trousers. It was as he had thought. There was no comparing it with the Täby Racecourse job.

"How do we move forward?" he asked.

"The first step . . ." said Maloof, "is to find a helicopter."

Because if they were going to pull off the job in Västberga, they were going to need a helicopter.

There were a number of different ways of getting onto the roof, but only one realistic way to get off it. Since his conversation with Petrovic, Maloof had looked into how fast a crane could drive, and then banished the thought. He had even learned about using climbing equipment, bolts and ropes, on mortar. It was too complicated. Elegant solutions like hot air balloons and gliders looked exciting on film, but they were unthinkable in reality. Jet packs, on the other hand, those small flying motors you wore on your back, were a possibility. But if you could afford to buy a couple of jet packs, you didn't need to rob a cash depot.

No, it had to be a helicopter, or else they could forget the whole idea.

"OK," said Sami. "A helicopter."

They continued through the shopping arcade. Over the years, the men had perfected the art of strolling. They knew how to walk slowly, without drawing attention to themselves. They stopped at every third shop window and absentmindedly looked in at the spring coats, head-phones, bikes and sofas.

Thanks to this way of meeting, they could talk freely without wor-rying about being overheard.

"I don't know," Sami continued, "who do we know with a helicop-ter? Who has a helicopter just sitting in the garage?"

"There's . . ." Maloof replied. "It's no harder than getting hold of a boat."

"It's harder," Sami argued. "Plus, anyone can drive a boat. I can drive a boat. You can drive a boat. You know what I mean? Neither of us can fly a helicopter. Maybe we can steal one, but we won't be able to get it to lift off."

The baby on his shoulder was slowly waking up. Sami assumed that Maloof wouldn't appreciate sitting down with a bottle, so they started walking again, Sami in a bobbing motion he hoped would send the baby back to sleep.

"Right, right," said Maloof. "We'll have to . . . find someone. A pilot."

"I don't know," Sami said again. "Do you know anyone?"

"I don't know anyone," Maloof said with unexpected firmness. He laughed briefly. "Or actually . . . I know someone who can sort some-thing out."

"Your friend? Tall? Petrovic?"

"Right, right." Maloof smiled.

"Seems difficult. And her, the girl . . ."

"Alexandra."

"You're completely sure about her now?"

"Definitely."

"I don't know. Why would she tell you so much? You know? She must be wondering."

"Nope," Maloof replied. "We talk . . . you know. I'm not the one ask-ing. She just talks."

"OK . . . Maybe . . ." Sami said hesitantly. "So what do we do once we've landed the helicopter on the roof?"

Maloof nodded and smiled. "We'll have five minutes . . . There's a police station two blocks away. Maybe ten minutes? Max. We blow a hole in the roof . . . we find someone who can blow a hole in the roof. Below that's the room where Alexandra works. Cash. Counting. She calls it different things. On Tuesdays and Thursdays they take in . . . a few hundred million in cash."

They were standing outside a secondhand shop, studying the strange objects in the window. Sami was rocking gently to keep the baby asleep.

"Money into bags . . ." Maloof continued, "back up onto the roof . . . using a ladder? And then we fly off."

"And the police helicopters?" Sami asked. "Where are they? You know what I mean? If we're on the roof and there's a swarm of police helicopters just waiting for us above?"

"Right, right," said Maloof. "No. We'll have to make sure the police helicopters never get airborne."

"How do we do that?"

"We'll work something out." Maloof laughed confidently.

Sami nodded. Then he shook his head. He felt the tiny body on his shoulder wake and stretch, the prelude to a loud protest that could be stopped only by giving him something to suck on.

"What you're saying is," Sami quickly tried to sum up, "that we need to find a helicopter. And a pilot. Then we're going to blow our way in through the roof and climb down a ladder to grab the money. And that all this can take ten minutes max. And at the same time we need to make sure the police helicopters can't take off."

"Exactly, exactly." Maloof nodded. That was roughly what he had envisioned.

"It sounds . . . you know how it sounds, right?" Sami asked. "You know what I mean?"

Maloof laughed, but it was with pride. He thought the plan was full of possibility, challenges, grandeur.

People were mad, Sami thought. Horses and helicopters.

He quickly said goodbye to his friend and headed into an Espresso House, where he could ask the staff to warm a bottle of breast milk for him.

It sounds crazy, he thought with a wry smile.

Hundreds of millions?

JUNE–JULY 2009

16

Zoran Petrovic, sometimes called Tall by his friends, was sitting in Café Stolen on Upplandsgatan. The restaurant was only a powerful stone's throw from the building where he lived. He had ordered a glass of lukewarm water, and it stood on the table in front of him. The place was almost empty, but he had still chosen a table far enough toward the rear that he wouldn't be visible from the street.

He was speaking on the phone, in Montenegrin.

It was an agitated conversation, and he used his left hand to paint a wide arc through the air as the words poured out of him. His right hand had a tight grip on the glass of water. Zoran Petrovic was a storyteller. He spoke both as he inhaled and exhaled; he wasn't going to let language, objections or reality get in his way. It was that which had taken him to the top.

Over the years, Petrovic had bought up all the places he liked to visit on Upplandsgatan, from his building down to Norra Bantorget. That had left him with a handful of restaurants, Café Stolen and Mandolin among them, and a beauty salon, where he liked to sit down in the comfortable chairs for manicures and pedicures—he flashed his vanity, it was the best way to avoid being accused of it—and he had also stepped in as a financier for a framing shop and a secondhand-clothes boutique.

Zoran Petrovic had been born in Lund, but he'd barely had time to learn to walk before a moving van brought the family up to the capital. Once in Stockholm, the Petrovics bought Benny Andersson's old house in Tumba. This was a few years into the seventies, and the former owner naturally became more and more interesting to mention as the popularity of his band grew. A few years after ABBA's success with "Waterloo," Petrovic's parents divorced. He and his brother moved with their mother to Hallunda, and later to Norsborg; by the time Petrovic began school, he had lived at six different addresses.

After he'd been thrown out of his first school just in time for Christmas, and the second during second grade, Petrovic's parents decided to send him to Montenegro, where discipline and respect for adults were built in to the system. However, their hopes that a tougher school system would tame him turned out to be futile.

In the playground on the very first day, Petrovic had been given a taste of the forbidden fruits that he would never be able to get enough of going forward: the power of manipulation and the force of provocation. He had realized that he could make people do what he wanted, sometimes in exchange for nothing but flattery, praise or a smile. Other times, using threats of violence as persuasion. People reacted in different ways, and discovering what worked for each individual in his class was a challenge he could spend days, weeks and months on.

Until he had learned to control them all.

Unfortunately, this was at roughly the same time that the school decided to expel him. Norsborg or Podgorica, it made no difference.

The best thing about the two years he spent with his maternal grandparents in Montenegro was that he had learned a new language. Plus, he'd made friends for life. He returned to Sweden and continued his education in Fittja, but by then it was more like the school had adapted to Zoran Petrovic than the other way around.

His mother would often blame the school system for the career her son later chose. But what made his parents most bitter, both of them dyed-in-the-wool Communists, was to see their son grow up to be a full-fledged capitalist.

Money was Zoran Petrovic's first great love.

And it was a love that would never fade.

The new waitress changed the radio station and carefully turned up the volume. Petrovic gestured for her to turn it down again. He was working. It was just after lunch, and the afternoon clientele who usually sat playing with their beer coasters still hadn't turned up.

Petrovic had barely finished the call with Montenegro when his phone rang again. A typical day for him. A never-ending stream of phone calls.

"Yes?" he said into the phone.

"It's Svenne," said Gustafsson from the scrapyard in Lidingö. "Something's arrived for you. Damn dodgy thing. Big as hell. Should we try to set it up? There are drawings and stuff with it."

A powerful feeling of joy filled Petrovic. Finally.

"Yeah, yeah," he said breathlessly down the phone. "Set it up! Put it in the container. Drop everything else and assemble the bastard. I'll be there in fifteen!"

Without another word, he got to his feet, bumping the table and knocking over his glass. The water ran across the tablecloth and dripped to the floor, but he didn't notice.

He was finally about to defeat those damn secure bags.

Zoran Petrovic could smell the money.

The idea was neither original nor difficult, and it was, as usual, the implementation that had caused him problems. Petrovic took a right up by Tegnérlunden Park and crossed Sveavägen just as the lights turned red. He was driving a BMW he had borrowed from a friend who owed him money, a fast car built for Germans with long legs. Neither Ferrari nor Maserati seemed to realize that people could be taller than six and a half feet.

The plan was to film how to break into one of the G4S bags without causing the dye ampoules to explode. A bit of basic editing, some cool music, and then the film would be uploaded to YouTube. Would-be robbers across Europe—and the rest of the world—would be able to watch it, meaning that G4S would have to scrap the blue bags within a few hours, binding contract or not. That was when Maloof would return to the security firm's head office and remind them that there was another, better bag that they could order now that the secrets of the blue bag had been revealed.

If Petrovic had calculated the production and distribution costs and the business tax correctly, a company with an exclusive contract to sell security bags to G4S could make a profit of a million or so during the very first year. After that, you could probably maintain a sustainable level of earnings of a few million in Sweden alone.

The BMW flew over the Lidingö Bridge.

He parked badly outside the scrapyard and ran on his long legs through the building, out the back and across the labyrinthine car cemetery to the container. There were three men inside, all studying the master-piece that had been sent over from France, and which they had just managed set up in line with the instructions.

"Move, move!" Petrovic demanded.

The machine was worth veneration.

It was a guillotine.

What could be more French? A guillotine with huge titanium blades, so sharp that they could cut a strand of hair. Or a brick.

Or a steel bag.

But not just that. The blades—there were two of them—weren't reliant only on gravity. The manufacturers had helped nature along by installing them onto two steel posts with a chemical rocket engine on each bracket. The blades' short journey toward their goal was an explosive one. Petrovic had seen the machine in action a couple of times, and the force was incredible.

Zoran Petrovic had asked the manufacturers of the magnificent rocket guillotine to construct two titanium blades that came down onto a rectangular plate. The measurements of the plate were the same as the blue security bags' minus seven millimeters on the short sides.

In other words, the guillotine would be able to cut the dye ampoules straight off the bag in one fantastic clean sweep.

"It's beautiful," he said with a sigh, happy as a small child, staring at the unlikely machine.

"What the hell is it?" asked Svenne Gustafsson.

Petrovic sent Gustafsson and his men out. His own amateur engineers would be arriving soon, two of the kids who usually worked in the container and in whom Petrovic had developed a special confidence over the past few months.

He moved around the guillotine, admiring its razor-sharp blades and brilliant steel construction. Basking in his own genius.

During the afternoon, it transpired that they would need more cables and connections before everything worked like it should. It wasn't until nine that evening, under the glow of the bright ceiling lights in the container, that they were finally ready to put one of the blue bags onto the guillotine for the first real test.

The six video cameras that had previously been on tripods facing each of the workstations had now been turned to face the guillotine. From six different angles, they would capture the moment the blue security bag from G4S was freed of its edges and Petrovic's financial future was secured.

The idea of selling the black bags to the security firm through a new company, a legitimate tax-paying company that submitted annual reports registered with the Patent and Registration Office, seemed particularly appealing to Petrovic. The profits would be big enough that he and Maloof might as well share it with the state. As only wealthy people could afford to do.

Petrovic switched on each of the six cameras himself. Then he took a few steps toward the door. He nodded gravely, and one of the two assistants placed a bag on the plate. Petrovic nodded again, and the other assistant pressed the button.

The guillotine motors exploded into life.

The razor-sharp titanium blades fell at rocket speed toward the security bag, but in Petrovic's eyes, everything happened in slow motion. He saw the blades gliding down the two poles, and the cameras captured every tenth of a second.

The titanium forced itself into the edge of the bag and ate its way into the steel. Petrovic grinned.

Then it stopped.

Everything stopped.

Something was putting up a fight.

And just a second later, they heard the sound of the dye ampoule exploding inside the bag.

Petrovic and his engineers jumped at the familiar noise.

Their disappointment was mute, and time seemed to come to a standstill.

"WHAT THE HELL?"

The young men were on their way out of the container before Petrovic even had time to say another word. They knew that the easygoing nonchalance the tall man radiated, those streams of words that usually entertained them, was masking something else.

Something hard and black.

And they had no intention of staying to witness that.

"Shit," Petrovic mumbled quietly, without even noticing that he was alone beneath the bright strip lights.

The expensive, wrecked machine stood in front of him, a hope that had cost months of his time and hundreds of thousands of his kronor, and which had proved to have no value at all.

It was over.

The idea of replacing the blue security bags with the black briefcase from Slovenia had lived for almost five years. But that night, it died. He tried to calculate how much it had cost him, but the figures quickly grew so large that he gave up. It was far too depressing.

Maybe he could sell the container to Gustafsson and the scrapyard?

Maybe the titanium in the blades would be worth something if he took it apart?

Petrovic slumped onto a stool by one of the six workstations. He fished his phone from his inner pocket and dialed Michel Maloof's number.

Maloof answered immediately.

"Did you say you needed help?" Petrovic asked.

"Right, right," Maloof's voice came down the line. "It was that thing we talked about last time . . . getting off the ground?"

Petrovic thought for a moment. He was used to riddles of this kind, you could never talk plainly over the phone. After a few seconds, he remembered what Maloof meant. The cash depot in Västberga, the helicopter.

"Sure," he said. "I remember."

"Do you know anyone with . . . one of those machines?" Maloof asked.

"Consider it done," Petrovic replied.

He shoved the phone back into his pocket. He had found himself a new project. But how did you get hold of a helicopter?

17

"You locking up, Niklas?"

Carsten Hansen was standing by the open door, and without waiting for Niklas Nordgren's answer, he let it swing shut behind him.

Nordgren continued his soldering. He was used to locking up and setting the alarm, and he usually got more done once the others had left. The working hours at the electricians' were flexible. Carsten, who owned the business, preferred to arrive and leave early. Nordgren thought that was good, better than staying on and surfing the tabloids' websites instead of going home to the family.

The reason Nordgren often stayed longest in the evening was that his partner, Annika Skott, rarely got home from work before seven. That meant he might as well work a few extra hours before leaving for the day. He fully accepted that the overtime might not always be reflected in his monthly paycheck. In a way, he had a permanent job, but the company had only four employees, and if there wasn't much work around, you couldn't expect any extra pay, no matter how many hours you worked.

It had started as a simple repair job on a couple of electrical circuits in a food processor from the sixties, but Nordgren had soon taken the entire device apart. He couldn't help it. People brought in all kinds of strange objects to be fixed, and nine times out of ten it would have been better to say no from the outset. But Nordgren liked fixing old things. Modern mixers couldn't compete with the quality of the past; these days, a particularly thick dough could blow the fuses, a tough nut could knock out the power in an entire house. But the bulky food processor lying in pieces in front of him had once been able to knead stoneware clay without overheating.

It was obvious that Nordgren would stay behind a few extra hours to fix a machine like that.

At six thirty, he took the bus home. He had stopped off at the supermarket on the way, to buy food for dinner. The gray sky seemed not to be taking into account the fact that the calendar claimed it was June, and Nordgren stepped beneath the bus shelter to get out of the rain, which had been drizzling down since yesterday morning. He was wearing a quilted navy jacket he had bought from H&M the previous autumn, some boots he had found on sale at Naturkompaniet, and he was holding the carrier bag from ICA in one hand. He had pulled his blue-black cap low on his head, and no one who saw him on the bus would remember him afterward.

In the public sphere, Niklas Nordgren was the anonymous man who crossed the shot as the evening news was setting up a camera in Sergels Torg, randomly filming people on their way down to the subway. He was ordinary personified, a statistician's wet dream.

Niklas Nordgren's mother and father had been married for almost forty years, and their love story was one of the family's most repeated legends. The way Lars Nordgren, working for PEAB construction at the time, had traveled to Poland to build apartments, and while he was there met Ewa—who would later become Niklas's mother. After a year living not far from Crakow, the pair had moved to Sweden, where they bought a small house in Vårby Gård.

Just in time for Niklas to start high school, the family moved to Skärholmen, somewhere Nordgren's three-years-older sister had never learned to feel comfortable. He had suffered through school in silent protest. The way the teachers and the curriculum managed to drain such a curious young man of his thirst for knowledge was a miracle, Niklas thought today. He had barely had time to start school in Botkyrka when his parents moved again, this time north, to Solna. His sister moved with them and found an apartment in Sundbyberg, where she lived to this day, but he had taken the opportunity to fly the nest.

Like so many other people of his age, he had ventured out into the world. Today, the years he spent in Asia and Europe seemed like a dream someone else had dreamed. And when he returned to Sweden, he ended up in Lidingö. It had been down to chance, like so much else in his life.

Niklas Nordgren stepped off the bus at the stop in Larsberg and trudged eastward along empty sidewalks. The anonymous blocks of apartments that rose up from the rocks had been built in the late sixties, with an aesthetic, ambition and thrift similar to that of the infamous suburbs of Tensta and Akalla. But that evening, almost all the windows glowed cozily, and the views across Norra Djurgården were spectacularly pretty in the early sunset. To Nordgren, the large, anonymous tower block area was perfect. He wasn't someone who liked being the center of attention. He wasn't someone who thought that life was about collecting friends and acquaintances.

There had been a time, immediately after he returned from Asia, when he had tried to take on the role of someone who was both seen and heard. He had made an effort to become someone people pointed out, talked about.

No good had come of it.

At the entrance to his building, Nordgren entered the security code and pushed the door open with his shoulder. The empty street and anonymous buildings, the silhouettes of the industrial area: this was exactly how he wanted it.

When Annika got home, just after seven, Nordgren had already started to prepare dinner. He wasn't a particularly remarkable cook. When men cooked, they often had trouble not spicing up their performance with testosterone, but Nordgren cooked everyday food. Today, it was pasta with Bolognese sauce. He fried grated carrots, onion and garlic, and then added half a jar of ready-made tomato sauce to make his Bolognese more juicy.

He was stirring the sauce when he heard the front door open. Annika took off her coat in the hallway, went into the bedroom and changed. The gray dress she wore during the day at the accountancy firm where she worked was put back onto its hanger, and she pulled on some jeans and a sweater instead. She came into the kitchen, gave him a quick hug and then got to work grating parmesan as Nordgren drained the boiling water from the pasta.

"Good day?" she asked.

"Yeah," he replied. "You?"

She shrugged. "*Scent of a Woman*'s on tonight," she said.

"Which channel?"

"Four."

"Mmm," he replied without enthusiasm.

He didn't know whether he could bear to watch Bengt Magnusson deliver a half-hour news report midway through the film.

"I think I'll watch it," Annika said.

He nodded. To keep the peace, he would sit down next to her and start watching the film, but they both knew that he would disappear into his hobby room as soon as the news started, probably not returning when the film came back on.

Things had been worse than usual these past few days.

"Are you working on anything special?" she asked suspiciously when they sat down at the kitchen table and started to eat.

"Yeah," he said.

It wasn't as a conversationalist that Niklas Nordgren had built his reputation.

The evening unfolded as usual. Annika used the news interlude to get herself ready for bed, and by the time she returned to the living room to watch the rest of the film in her dressing gown, he had vanished. She slumped onto the sofa with a resigned sigh, but as her eyelids started to droop during the first ad break, she realized she wouldn't manage to make it through the film tonight either.

The attractiveness Nordgren had radiated when he first met Annika had been linked to his mysteriousness. Like many others, she had been struck by the contrast between his criminal past and his down-to-earth honesty. But the things that had once attracted her now left her cold. He was no more than he pretended to be. It had come as a surprise to her, even if it shouldn't have.

In a grand gesture, Annika had let him take over the room next to the living room, turning it into a space for his hobbies. How he had managed to collect so many things was beyond her. He was essentially an orderly person, but it was impossible to organize chaos when it was constantly growing in scope. It was as though things were drawn to him, tools of all kinds, wood and plastic tubes, old cell phones, broken food processors, mountains of nuts and bolts, copper wire and deto-nators. Within their group of friends, everyone knew that rather than throwing away their worn-out stereo or old showerhead, they could just give it to Nordgren. He would appreciate it.

And so, the piles of junk in his hobby room grew.

It was almost twelve thirty when Nordgren realized he would need the screwdriver with the short handle to finish the night's self-appointed task: installing a clock in a radio-controlled car. But he had stored the screwdriver and some other tools down in the basement last week.

Was that a sign he should finish up for the night?

He looked at the car on the table. An Opel, perhaps? It was battered and blue, and he didn't know how it had come into his possession. But he nodded to himself. He would sleep better if he finished it off rather than leaving it until tomorrow. And so he got up, opened the door to the living room and padded silently into the hallway, past Annika, who had fallen asleep in front of the TV.

*   *   *

He found the screwdriver where he had left it, in the toolbox. Just as Nordgren was about to turn off the light, he caught sight of something black on the floor beneath the shelves. For a moment, he thought it was a rat, but then he realized what it was. The lava rock. He went back, bent down and picked it up. It was dry and porous. The reason he had once shoved it into his backpack was that it weighed almost nothing.

His eyes searched for the dark brown packing box where the stone should be. It was closest to the wall, of course, beneath a couple of other boxes. That was why, he now remembered, he had never put the stone back.

Nordgren glanced at his watch.

He decided to overcome his laziness. It wouldn't take more than a couple of minutes to move the other boxes to one side. But it wasn't the physical effort that was the problem. He knew what would happen when he opened the door to his past, and on that particular night he let it happen.

In the brown box where the black lava stone was meant to be, there were four photo albums. There was also a skateboard, a bag of extra wheels and a couple of trucks that had never been used. There were two BMX pedals he had once ordered in from Germany, and a bottle of special lacquer for treating the wood on surfboards. Another small box, containing gloves, glasses and the climbing harness he had used in Thailand, lay beside it.

He stared at these hidden remnants of a forgotten life and found himself frozen to the spot, the open box on the floor in front of him.

What had happened?

Why had he given up on the skateboard, the surfboard and the bike?

Why had he swapped that kind of adrenaline for a darker, more destructive kind?

He sat down on the cold stone floor and lowered his head between his knees. Life, he reminded himself, was what went on while he fixed radio-controlled cars and food processors from the sixties. The days went by. They turned into weeks and months.

It was six months now since he had been released from prison. What had he done with his freedom? Wake up beneath a pitch-black sky, get dressed, eat breakfast, go to work and then come home as the darkness was once again descending over Lidingö. But that wasn't living, it was just a way of passing the time.

Nordgren peered into the box and closed his eyes. These were the memories of the life he had once begun.

The waves foaming and thundering onto the beaches in Bali, the way his body had tensed completely as the water reached his chest, hand on surfboard, looking out to the horizon to spot the waves it was worth paddling toward.

The silhouette of the Matterhorn's dramatic peak; the thin, clear Alpine air, and the way his eyes had sought out the best way up the mountain as he stretched his aching muscles by bending his fingers backward after the morning's stages.

The pain in his tailbone when a 360 failed on the half-pipe, and the board that had rolled away, leaving him with a friction burn stretching from his knee halfway down his leg. He still had the thin white scar today.

He could no longer explain why he had abandoned that life.

He had loved it.

But something had gotten in the way, he had found a kind of excitement that was even more intense. His criminality had been an addiction. Could he break free of it by searching for his future through his past, by following in the tracks of what was in the brown cardboard box?

He put the black lava rock into the box and folded the flaps down. Then he pushed the box back toward the wall and stacked the two others on top of it so that everything looked just like it had before.

18

"What . . . I mean . . . what is this place?"

Michel Maloof glanced around. He was in one of the nightclubs near Stureplan in central Stockholm, it was three thirty in the morning and the beautiful people had been even more beautiful a few hours earlier. Pounding house music washed over the low clusters of sofas where men bragged about their achievements to women who gave fake laughs and flashed their teeth. Lips glistened, drinks were drunk, skin sweated, hands waved and Maloof was in agony.

"Let loose, Michel!" Zoran Petrovic said, laughing at how uncomfortable Maloof looked. "You should get out more. Widen your horizons. There's nothing wrong with Fittja, but, you know, there are people in other places too?"

The tall Yugoslavian set off toward the bar, and Maloof made sure he was hot on his heels. The nightclubs had been Petrovic's playground since the late 1990s and early 2000s. Dressed in an Armani suit and with a pistol in a holster beneath his arm, he had been king of these places. His jacket pockets had been full of wads of notes tied with elastic bands, just like in the movies. Some months, he had probably spent more money in the restaurants and bars around Stureplan than Montenegro had in GDP.

They pushed their way over to the long, white bar where people were crowded together, trying to talk over the music with short, confidence-inspiring phrases. As Petrovic approached, a space suddenly seemed to open up for them, something that never would have happened if Maloof had been alone.

"What do you want?" the tall Yugoslavian asked.

"Mineral water."

Petrovic nodded, but a second later his eyes moved diagonally across Maloof's shoulder. Maloof turned and found himself staring straight into a blond woman's décolletage. When he looked up and caught sight of her bright red lips, he understood why Petrovic had temporarily lost interest in their drink order; those lips were precisely the type of attribute he was interested in.

"Can I get you a drink?" Petrovic asked.

The tall blonde was wearing a white dress that she definitely wore only in the summer. June had just arrived, though the air felt more like March.

"Champagne," she replied.

"In that case, a 1988," said Petrovic. "Don't drink any other vintage, they're not worth the trouble."

And with that, he had caught her interest.

"Have you ever been hunting with hawks?" he asked.

Equally confused and impressed, she shook her head.

Petrovic told a short story about how, in the vineyards of the Champagne region of France, they trained hawks to wipe out any pests that might damage the vines, and then he leaned his long body over the bar. In doing so, he crossed the invisible but absolute line between the paying guests and the hardworking staff on the other side. The bartender immediately came running. Petrovic ordered two glasses of champagne. He even remembered Maloof's mineral water.

While they waited for their drinks and Petrovic entertained the blond with the story of why the grape harvest in 1988 had been so good, Maloof noticed a short, wide-eyed man, somewhere in his early middle age, heading straight toward them through the crowd. He was wearing a pair of well-worn jeans and a checked shirt with huge sweat patches beneath the arms.

Maloof elbowed his tall friend. "Is that him?

Petrovic turned and instantly lost interest in the blonde.

"Manne!" he shouted. "Come, come."

The invitation was unnecessary. Manne Lagerström was already next to them. He smelled awful.

"Are we going?" Manne asked.

He stared at Petrovic without acknowledging either Maloof or the blonde.

"Sure," said Petrovic. "Behave now, Manne. This is Michel. I don't think you've met before."

Maloof held out a hand. Manne had a limp, wet handshake.

"I hate this fucking place," he mumbled.

Then he leaned forward to say something else, but the music was too loud and Maloof heard only every other word.

"What's he saying?" asked Petrovic.

"He's asking for money."

Petrovic shook his head and rolled his eyes. "Let's go," he said.

The pretty blonde seemed to have completely vanished from his consciousness.

"Right, right," Maloof agreed.

The bartender had just returned with two glasses of champagne and a bottle of sparkling water. Petrovic dug around in his pocket and fished out a couple of 500 kronor notes. He threw them onto the bar, put a hand on Manne's shoulder and steered him toward the exit.

"Next time," he shouted over his shoulder to the blond woman. "Next time."

She picked up her champagne and turned her back to them.

When they came out onto the street, Manne started protesting again.

"It's payment in advance, you know?" he said. "Money. Now."

His voice was weak and shrill. It was as though Lagerström's sweaty body contained too much energy, and part of it had found an outlet through his mouth.

Petrovic shook his head. They were walking west, along Birger

Jarlsgatan, and there seemed to be as many drunk people out on the sidewalk as there were inside the clubs. The taxis were parked up in rows three deep, waiting for customers to stagger into their backseats; the police had positioned a patrol car on Biblioteksgatan as a reminder of their existence; and techno music was leaking out through doors and windows.

"Shut it, Manne. You promised to show us what you had. Then I'll show you what I've got."

"It's four in the damn morning," Manne whined. "I'm not going all the way up there for fun. Because it's not fun."

They had reached the car, and Petrovic opened the door for the skinny man, whose entire body seemed to be trembling. But he shook his head and refused to get in.

"I swear," he said, and his weak voice reached a falsetto. "I don't work for the Red Cross. I'm not some free app."

Petrovic sighed, shoved a hand into his pocket and pulled out a roll of banknotes held in place with a rubber band. He threw the money into the backseat, and Manne jumped in after it. Petrovic closed the door behind him.

"He's like a dog," Petrovic said to Maloof, glancing at the man in the backseat with a look of disgust. "Just easier to train."

Petrovic was driving toward Roslagstull. He had changed 500-kronor notes into twenties to make the roll seem thicker, and Manne was deep in concentration in the backseat, counting them. When he finished, he started counting from the beginning again. That kept him busy until they reached the Stocksund Bridge. By then, he was satisfied that the roll contained the amount they had agreed on, and he shoved it into his pocket and stuck his head between the two front seats. The energy that had made him shake with anxiety earlier seemed to have undergone a transformation, and it was now directed at the two men sitting in front of him.

"OK, guys," he said. "Since we're on this little trip together, we need to make the most of the situation. Will one of you sing me a song?"

Manne Lagerström laughed at his own joke as though it were the funniest thing he had ever heard. His laugh was bright and piercing, and it barely stopped before he continued:

"No, no, serious now, no singing tonight. But, Jesus, when I was little, that was all my mom and dad used to do when we went on car trips. Sang all those old songs and smoked menthol cigarettes. But you two aren't singers. Or smokers. Right, lads?"

The roar of laughter that followed was like a minor explosion, though neither Petrovic nor Maloof knew which part of his monologue was meant to be funny. But Manne Lagerström wasn't a performer who relied on the reactions of his audience; just having an audience was enough. He talked without break all the way to Norrtälje. He laughed uncontrollably at his own jokes, was moved to tears by his admissions, and told them his entire life story—everything from the early years in Sollentuna to the lonely man he was today.

Manne worked as a caretaker at the helicopter hangar in Roslagen. He had been in the job almost ten years now, and he hated it. He almost never saw the owners of the helicopters, other than when they turned up and shouted at him for doing something wrong. The pilots were invariably bullies who thought they were better than everyone else just because they could pull on a lever and step on a pedal at the same time.

"It isn't fucking difficult to fly a helicopter," Manne explained. And having a stupid certificate didn't give anyone the right to act like an utter shithead. Not bothering to say hello, stubbing out cigarettes on the floor or putting chewing gum under the seats.

"You know how to fly?" Maloof asked.

"Course I fucking do!" Manne replied.

He was like a child in the back of the car, shifting back and forth on his seat and pulling at the dials for the air-conditioning before he realized that the backseats could be raised and lowered. That kept him busy for a long time, but he kept talking all the while.

"Can you?" Petrovic repeated. "Do you really know how?"

"Of course I can!" Manne yelled. "But who the hell can afford doing the cert? Who the hell has access to a helicopter?"

This was yet another joke that seemed to surprise him with its finesse. He laughed loudly.

"Right, right," Maloof agreed, and in an attempt to bring some clarity to the matter, he asked, "But you've . . . never actually flown?"

"No, I've never flown a helicopter," Manne Lagerström shouted. "I can, but I never have. Forget that now. Forget it. Did I tell you about when my dad chased the bloody badger that lived in the earth cellar?"

"Shut up, Manne," Petrovic ordered as the forest on the sides of the road seemed to grow darker. "We don't care about your dad. Just shut up."

The story about the badger lasted almost all the way to Östhamra.

When they arrived, Manne jumped out of the car and ran around the hood to open the door for Petrovic. Then he ran across the parking lot to make it to the helicopter hangar first.

"So . . . Manne," said Maloof, "seems . . . pretty special?"

"There aren't enough letters in the alphabet to describe his combination," Petrovic said with a sigh. "But beggars can't be choosers."

To the sides of the open landing site in front of the building were a number of tall pines. They formed a wide alley down toward Lake Limmaren. The office park on the other side of the main road was quiet and deserted, but the breeze carried with it the smell of burned rubber and wood.

On the way over to the hangar, Petrovic told Maloof what was what.

There were fifteen or so helicopters based in Roslagen. They were either owned directly by multinational corporations or else by private individuals who recouped the costs by renting out their expensive investments to the multinationals. Manne was the caretaker and the helicopter club's only employee. His job was to make sure the hangar always looked clean and tidy. If management groups were going out on shorter day trips, the machines had to be ready, tanks full, all the paperwork in order. Manne could even carry out a basic service on them, if necessary.

When the managing directors' secretaries called to book a helicopter for their bosses, Manne was the one who looked after the calendar. Zoran Petrovic knew many secretaries at that level.

The overexcited caretaker was waiting impatiently next to the unlocked hangar doors.

"Come on, come on!" he shouted.

There was a strong smell of gasoline and metal inside the hangar. The helicopters were lined up in rows in the darkness. Like sleeping horses, Maloof thought, not that he had ever seen a sleeping horse. There was something solemn about the scene. Powerful. Excessive. Rich. And the fact that Manne was running back and forth, babbling constantly, was extremely annoying.

"Here it is," he shouted, waving them over. "Here it is, this is the one I thought you could take? A Bell 206 JetRanger. Nice, right?"

The distinguishing feature was that the helicopter was white, but otherwise Maloof thought that it looked just like all of the others.

Manne moved around it, pointing out features and telling them stories that seemed increasingly incoherent.

"You borrow it, you bring it back. I'll take payment in advance. You know that, Zoran, I always take the money in advance. That's how it goes. Money first."

"Feels like you've already been paid," Petrovic replied.

"Right, right," Maloof agreed.

"No joking, boys, no joking," Manne begged them. He looked like he had been wronged. "I'll get my money. And I'll make sure she's ready with a full tank whenever you need her. You just make sure it looks like you've stolen her. Everyone's happy. OK?"

Maloof didn't answer, but he nodded.

They had found themselves a helicopter. Now they just needed to find someone who could fly it.

19

Blood had been spilled.

The knife, whose razor-sharp blade had cut the entrecôte into strips, was still lying next to the chopping board on the kitchen counter. Sami Farhan never tidied up while he was cooking. The browned meat had been simmering away in the stew for over an hour now, but there was still blood on the counter. There were dirty bowls on the kitchen table, pots stacked up in the sink; knives, wooden spoons and whisks were everywhere, dripping onto the floor and the counter. If he had been asked to re-create the whole process again afterward, explaining what he had used each of the tools for, he would have found it impossible. He cooked the same way he did everything else in his life: with a restless, physical energy.

The aromas of his cooking filled the kitchen. Sami had started the day by making a vegetable stock. There was nothing wrong with cubes, but if you had the time, then real bouillon was better.

He added some finely chopped fresh red chili, cinnamon and *sambal oelek* to the stock in the stew. Onions and garlic were frying in the pan next to that. He would later mix the softened onion into the couscous with some apricots and orange.

Karin had taken the kids to her mother's house a few blocks away on Sankt Paulsgatan. The idea was to give Sami an afternoon to himself and his stew, and it was the best present she could give him. There were people who emptied their minds by running mile after mile on the treadmill. Others had sex or got drunk. But Sami's preferred method of soothing his soul and bringing new ideas to life was cooking.

When he tasted the bouillon with a teaspoon, he didn't give a single thought to the recurrent anxiety he had been feeling at nights lately. Rumors about how he had been screwed over with the frozen prawns seemed to be growing, and soon there wouldn't be anyone in the whole of Stockholm—suburbs included—who didn't already know the story. Whenever he bumped into people he hadn't seen for years in the supermarket, they would lower their voices and sympathetically ask how much money he had really borrowed from his brothers. Then there were the young men from the suburbs who, just a few months earlier, would have barely dared look him in the eye. Now they laughed behind his back.

There were no more clean knives in the drawer, but he found one on the windowsill, with no idea what it was doing there. He gave it a rinse and then chopped the apricots into smaller pieces. That took all his concentration, which meant he could avoid torturing himself with all the questions he still needed answers for, even if Maloof and his friend said they had sorted out a helicopter.

Sami peeled the skin from the oranges with a knife as sharp as the one he had used on the meat and continued to work at the same high tempo. Karin and the boys would be back at five, but Sami finished preparing the food by two. The stew could bubble away under the lid for a while. He didn't plan to mix in the couscous until the last minute.

He glanced around the kitchen.

He needed to tidy up, but this was about using his own time for something more valuable than washing bowls. He took off his apron, threw it onto the kitchen table and went out into the living room.

Several years earlier, Sami Farhan had read a long article about online footprints, and ever since he had been worried about what Google and Facebook could reveal about him. The less he used computers and phones, the better. Being called a technophobe was a low price to pay.

He went over to the bookshelf and took down a trusty old telephone book. His children, he knew, would never understand why someone had printed these enormous stacks of paper and delivered one to every home in Sweden, much less why anyone had ever opened them.

The first pages of the yellow section contained maps of Stockholm's suburbs, Västberga included.

Sami leafed forward to the right spread and studied the map. He put his finger on the building at the crossing of Västberga Allé and Vretensborgsvägen. Vreten 17, the G4S cash depot. He used a pencil to mark a thin line on each of the access routes.

The plan was to spend less than ten minutes inside the building.

In other words, they needed to hold the police off for the same amount of time.

The usual approach was to scatter so-called caltrops across the road, sharp steel spikes that puncture car tires by embedding themselves in the rubber. The problem with that method was that once they had been discovered, they could simply be swept away. They would provide a few minutes' distraction, but no more.

Michel Maloof had told Sami that the Serbs did things differently. They soldered the caltrops onto a chain that they then pulled tight across the road, fastening it on both sides. Car tires would be ripped to shreds without taking the tacks with them, which meant that the following car's tires would also be punctured. You couldn't just sweep them away, you had to cut the chain with pliers instead.

Rather than delaying the police for two to three minutes, the chains would add roughly the same amount of time. Assuming it would take a few minutes once the alarm went off, and another couple before the police reached wherever the chains had been stretched, that was all they needed.

Sami marked the access route from the north, from the highway and via Västberga Allé. Then he drew another line over Elektravägen, since that was the road the local police would take from their station. Just to be on the safe side, he drew a third line across Västberga Allé by Drivhjuls-vägen, in case anyone tried to approach from the south. The question was then whether they also needed chains across Karusellvägen and Vretensborgsvägen. The likelihood was pretty small, Sami decided, plus those were both detours that, in themselves, would take more time.

Next, he tried to work out exactly how wide the roads he had marked out were. Since neither he nor Maloof dared go out to the Västberga industrial park and risk being seen in the vicinity of the cash depot, he had no choice but to estimate.

He decided that they would need three, maybe four, fifty-foot chains with caltrops soldered onto them. It seemed like a lot, but though he calculated again and again, he kept coming to the same conclusion.

Two hundred feet of chain would cost money.

Exactly where they would be able to fix the chains on either side of the road would be down to the creativity of the person setting them out. Doing any kind of reconnaissance in advance was far too risky.

It was three o'clock when Sami finally felt happy with his afternoon's work. He pushed the phone book back onto the shelf, confident that no one would see the pencil lines that, just to be on the safe side, he had rubbed out. He returned to the kitchen and was met by fantastic aromas and chaotic mess.

He took a deep breath and turned on the radio on the windowsill. It was playing nonstop music he didn't recognize, and he started cleaning. He had just managed to wipe the table and most of the counter when the local news came on. It made him stop in his tracks.

"Just before midnight yesterday, thieves struck Täby Racecourse in a robbery linked to the Diana Race . . ." said the news reporter.

Sami's jaw dropped.

That madman. He had done it.

". . . but after a failed escape attempt on horseback, the thieves were apprehended before they reached the gates. We head now to our reporter at the scene . . ."

And failed.

20

Zoran Petrovic was early.

He moved on foot through the streets of Podgorica as dusk fell over the valley and the lights of the city replaced the overcast day with a warm, yellow glow in the sky. Petrovic was heading west. He turned right onto the wide Svetog Petra Cetinjskog Boulevard, which skirted the edge of Kraljev Park. The trees were in full bloom, as though they didn't dare believe in a long summer and thought it would be best to give everything they had before June was out. Spring and early summer had been unusually cold in Montenegro, and the short, thin navy coat Petrovic had had tailor-made at Götrich in Stockholm wasn't enough to keep out the chill. As a result, his long stride was even longer than usual.

Podgorica was a city that had been given many names over the years. It was somewhere that had always attracted settlers, the point at which two great rivers met on their way through Europe toward the Mediterranean.

Petrovic walked over the ugly new highway bridge spanning the Moraça River. From there, he could see the remains of the old stone bridge over the Ribnica, one of the few historic structures that had survived the bombs of the Second World War. The Hotel Podgorica, where he was now heading, was on the other side. In the bar, just beyond the front desk, one of the capital's best bartenders was hard at work.

Petrovic took a table by a window that looked out onto the lush riverbed, and he ordered olives and glass of lukewarm water.

It was only a quarter to eight, and he was fifteen minutes early. He took out the phone he used whenever he was in Montenegro. It was two weeks since he had last been there, and he had forty-three new messages. He scrolled through all of them before going back to the top of the list to reply to those worth replying to. His more important business contacts would use his Swedish number if they needed to get ahold of him, so these were really the dregs of his acquaintances.

Though he came down to Montenegro no more than once or twice a month, he felt as comfortable there as he did in Sweden. Generations of Petrovics had left their mark in Podgorica, making him part of their shared history. Those relatives who had survived centuries of war and ruin had done so thanks to their deep roots. You could always find a family connection if you looked far enough back in time.

He had created his own universe in Stockholm. Everyone seemed to be a new arrival there, whether from the north of Sweden, Finland or Istanbul. The suburbs buzzed with energy, a suspicious nervousness that stemmed from efforts to fit in or stay on the outside.

He didn't want to live without either of his two cities.

The bar and restaurant slowly started to fill with guests. Compared with Stockholm, things were done late in Podgorica; the rhythm of daily life in the countries around the Mediterranean was suited to a different climate. Through the huge windows out onto the river, he watched as the deep gray sky turned dark above the line of mountains. He usually waited like this only for beautiful women or rich men.

Filip Zivic belonged to neither category.

This was all for Michel Maloof's sake.

Petrovic felt like he was both Maloof's protector and admirer. It had been an oddly mixed feeling to see little Michel grow up and take the blows that had made him into the man he was. Petrovic no longer had any reason to take such a protective attitude, but after so many years it was hard not to.

In this particular case, there were two reasons he thought it was especially important to help out his younger friend. Partly because he knew how long Maloof had been eyeing the cash depot in Västberga.

This was a chance for him to realize a lifelong dream. And also because Petrovic felt guilty for having wasted Maloof's time on the blue security bags.

It had taken him a while to find Manne Lagerström, but that there would be helicopter pilots in Montenegro had seemed obvious from the outset.

The ugly civil war in the Balkans had raged for the whole of the nineties. Historical injustices had been atoned for or deepened, and the wider world had been taken by surprise by the hate that these former neighbors held for one another. Early on, one of Zoran Petrovic's uncles had advised him to "ignore the politics as long as you live," and that was precisely how Petrovic had handled the war. For as long as possible, he had tried to avoid taking any side in questions that had no answers. He continued to refer to himself as "Yugoslavian" and with time became a skilled diplomat in a conflict that demanded that everyone pick a side.

It was during the war in the nineties that he had come into contact with those people who now held high office in both Serbia and Montenegro. People who, back then, had run wild in Bosnian forests were now in charge of infrastructure spending, approving construction permits and dealing out taxes. Back then, dressed in ragged uniforms, they had mined bridge abutments against the enemy. Today, they wore suits and ties, surrounded themselves with lawyers and economists, and set political traps for their opponents.

Zoran Petrovic had called several of these people to ask for help, which was how he had come to hear about Filip Zivic—a man who, at that moment, at the very stroke of eight, had just entered the room.

Petrovic immediately knew it was him.

Zivic was a short man with thick hair and a dense, dark beard. He was wearing a well-made suit, and nothing about him screamed pilot or former soldier. Petrovic's uncle had known Zivic's father, and Petrovic thought that he had a childhood friend who had married one of Zivic's sisters.

There was a calm presence to the man as he took a few steps toward the bar and glanced around. Petrovic raised a hand, Zivic nodded, came over to the table and sat down. He looked at Petrovic's glass.

"Water or vodka?" he asked.

"Water," Petrovic replied. "Lukewarm."

Zivic laughed. "Your trademark, so I hear."

"You've been checking me out?" Petrovic asked.

"Of course." Zivic nodded with a smile. "And I'm assuming you've done the same for me."

Petrovic nodded.

"I got the brief," Zivic continued, "and I think it sounds exciting. You can count on me."

Petrovic felt an immediate trust for the helicopter pilot, who also ordered a glass of water, this time carbonated, with ice and lime.

"But I do have a couple of questions," Zivic continued.

It ended up being a long night, and Zoran Petrovic reluctantly said more than he had been planning to. Filip Zivic had survived the Balkan wars by not leaving anything to chance. He asked questions and then follow-up questions—both expected and unexpected. Petrovic answered as best he could.

Landing on the roof of a building in the middle of the night was, according to Zivic, no problem. It might seem difficult, but even in normal cases, helicopters landed on something called a "dolly," a metal plate on wheels that wasn't much bigger than the helicopter itself, and considerably smaller than the roof of a cash depot.

No, Zivic was more concerned about other things. Could Petrovic be sure that the Swedish police wouldn't get into their own helicopters? Could the robbery really be carried out in ten minutes? And wasn't there a risk that the police would open fire?

Zivic wasn't happy until Petrovic had given him long, detailed answers.

By midnight, the two men had finally managed to talk everything through, and Zivic knew exactly what was expected of him.

"OK," he said. "And when am I meant to be doing this?"

"We were talking about the fifteenth of September at the latest," Petrovic replied.

"Why then?"

"Partly"—Petrovic sighed at the pilot's inquisitiveness—"because of the day of the week. It has to be a particular weekday. And partly to give us enough time to prepare everything. Sweden comes to a standstill during July and half of August . . ."

"It's a long time until September. Can I be sure you won't change your minds?"

"This is going to happen," Petrovic reassured him.

"Do I have your word?"

"You can have something better than that."

Petrovic took out his Montenegrin checkbook. He found a pen in his inner pocket and wrote out a check for 20,000 kronor. He tore it out and handed it to Zivic, who stared at the slip of paper in surprise.

"I don't need this if I have your word," said the pilot.

"One doesn't cancel out the other," Petrovic replied with a smile.

They got up and shook hands.

21

The antenna on top of the Kaknäs radio tower blinked lazily in the distance. Its diffuse white glow vanished into the night, fading against the pale sky. The deer that hid among the trees on Djurgården during the day roamed across the dry fields at night, confident of remaining undiscovered by either dogs or people out for a stroll. And along the beaches around Hundudden, the swans rested at the edge of the water and the white-breasted Canada geese dozed by the footpaths.

The explosion ripped through the tranquil air.

The car was in the parking area hidden away behind the old riding school by Djurgårdsbrunn. During the winter, it was mostly used as a dumping ground for snowplows, and in summer by only the occasional taxi driver needing to attend to a sudden urge.

The windshield flew out of its frame, and tens of thousands of shards of glass rained down like crystals onto the concrete and into the woods. A red-and-yellow blaze flared up when the oil in the engine caught fire, ripping the hood from its hinges and sending it in a wide arc over the parking lot. It landed with a pitiful clatter a few yards away.

"Shit," Michel Maloof said, running his hand over his beard.

"Wait," said Niklas Nordgren.

They were standing at the edge of the woods, fifty or so yards away, watching the burning oil trickle beneath the car, a line of flame heating the gas in the tank. The flames from the engine compartment died out as suddenly as they flared up, and the wrecked car looked dark and burned out.

"Wait," Nordgren repeated.

His words were followed by a second, more powerful explosion, as the flames finally made their way into the gas tank, possibly through the exhaust pipe or from beneath.

Maloof instinctively fell to his knees. Car parts flew through the air and landed on the ground all around them: window frames, electronics, plates and metal. Once it was all over and the silence had returned, the foam filling from the seats was still floating slowly through the air.

"Shit," Maloof said again.

Nordgren took out his phone.

"The interesting thing about using a phone," he explained, "is that you can be absolutely anywhere. On the other side of the world, if you wanted to be. All you need is for someone to put the other phone by the accelerator, or even better in the engine cavity, then you can call that phone's number from the other phone and detonate it."

He held up the phone he still had in his hand. "And then it explodes."

"Shit," Maloof said for a third time. He was genuinely impressed.

"Was it something like this you had in mind?" Nordgren asked.

He still didn't know exactly what Maloof was planning. He was starting to suspect it was something big, something meaningful, but he had learned not to ask any questions, not even of his close friends. All Maloof had asked him so far was how they could use cell phones to detonate bombs from a distance. That was the reason for their trip to Djurgården.

From Maloof's perspective, the secrecy wasn't even about mistrust. It was more about respect. The robbery in Västberga was still in the planning stages, and raising Niklas Nordgren's expectations would have been doing him a disservice. There were few people Maloof trusted as fully.

"This is better," Maloof replied. "Much better."

Nordgren smiled.

The two men stared at the wrecked car. It looked more like a burning skeleton.

"Should we . . . go?"

"Just need to put it out first," said Nordgren.

He went to fetch a fire extinguisher from the car that Maloof had parked over by the old stables.

As they crossed the Lidingö Bridge, both the sun and the moon were visible in the pale summer sky. Maloof felt satisfied. Their quick trip out to Djurgården had shown once again that Niklas Nordgren's know-how was exceptional. The man always lived up to expectations. He kept a low profile, but he knew more about almost everything than most other people. Maloof had never regretted saving Nordgren as "100%" in his contacts list. They had met five years earlier when they were both arrested for instigating the same robbery.

By then, Maloof had already lost count of how many times he had been thrown into a claustrophobic cell inside Kronoberg remand prison. For Nordgren, it had been the first time. They arrested him at work. Drove him to Kungsholmen in cuffs, booked him in, took DNA samples and fingerprints and then left him to spend a few nights on a rickety pallet bed before they unlocked him and sent him home. It turned out that Nordgren hadn't had anything to do with the robbery that Michel Maloof would be convicted of just a few months later.

And so, when two uniformed police officers knocked on Niklas Nordgren's door in Lidingö a few days later, he had assumed it was a simple misunderstanding.

"No," he protested. "I've already been cleared in that investigation. You must have old information."

The police grinned.

"You bet we do," they replied, and while Nordgren said a few words to Annika about being back in time for the late news, the officers waited for him in the hallway.

It would be five years before Nordgren next sat down on the sofa in front of the TV.

Any DNA found at crime scenes across Sweden is registered and archived, and, as a matter of routine, this DNA is also checked against the country's master database. As it happened, Niklas Nordgren's genetic evidence had caused the computers in the police station to flash like one-armed bandits, spitting out one jackpot after another.

It transpired that Nordgren was a match for DNA found at the scene of a four-year-old bank robbery in Sollentuna. He was also matched to a two-year-old robbery in Mörby. And to a raid on a post office in Sundbyberg in 2001. As well as a robbery at a jewelry shop in Östermalm the year after that.

By chance, Niklas Nordgren was sentenced to the same amount of time in prison as Michel Maloof. When they got out, it was almost like they had gone down together. They started meeting more and more often.

Maloof's infectious positive attitude toward life, his good nature and clear loyalty were a good match for Nordgren's thoughtful curiosity. On top of that, they shared a fundamental character trait: both always looked forward, never back.

Maloof turned right after the bridge and continued along Södra Kungsvägen toward Larsberg. He parked two blocks from the building where Nordgren lived, and together they walked along the empty sidewalks through the warm summer night. It was just before midnight.

"You know . . . if you want," Maloof said, "you can get in on it? There'd be four of us. Split everything by four?"

"OK?" Nordgren asked. "How big is it?"

"Well . . ." Maloof replied. He knew that not even paraphrasing it could make the plan seem less mad. "We're planning to . . . land a helicopter on a cash depot right next to a police station and then grab a few hundred million." He laughed.

"Seriously?" asked Nordgren.

"Yep, yep." Maloof nodded.

Nordgren looked his friend in the eye.

"I'm in," he said.

"That's why we need your phone bombs," Maloof continued. "To stop the police helicopters from taking off."

22

At around nine in the morning, Sami gently pushed the door to the bedroom open. Karin had been up since five.

"We'll go out for a while," he whispered, referring to himself and John.

The baby had fallen asleep during his feed and Karin's breast was still in his mouth. She gently pulled herself free.

"That's not a problem, is it?" she wondered.

There was no mistaking the relief in her voice.

"Get a few hours' sleep," Sami said gently.

"So the milk has time to thicken and put him to sleep this afternoon," she whispered with a sigh without opening her eyes.

"Kids are great," he replied with a wry smile.

He gently closed the door again.

John was waiting on the floor in the hallway. When Sami picked him up, he laughed. He was a happy baby. According to his parents, the boy was already talking, though not even his grandmother could understand the noises Sami heard as "Mom," "Dad," "car" and "bird."

In truth, he was a little too heavy to be carried around now, but he liked it, and Sami felt freer without the stroller. In the bag he swung over his shoulder, he had packed gruel and extra diapers, and he added a blanket. Summer had spread its warm embrace over Stockholm the day before, but the weather report that morning had said that the warm front would be taking a temporary break for a few days. They wouldn't be needing the overalls, at least, and for that Sami was grateful.

He carried John on his arm as he walked down Högbergsgatan, but as he turned the corner onto Götgatan, the feeling of being followed struck him unexpectedly.

*   *   *

The sidewalks were crowded. One week into July, and people still hadn't started their summer holidays. Or maybe that was the reason everyone seemed so stressed, Sami thought. Over the course of four drizzle-filled summer weeks, passions were meant to be rekindled, relationships with children restored, books read, friends met and the fence scraped before being repainted. When it was finally time to go back to work in August, it felt like crawling back onto land after swimming through the stormy waters of time off.

They reached Medborgarplatsen. Sami quickly headed for the subway station and ran down the escalator. Once he was almost at the bottom, he turned around. At least a handful of people farther up seemed to be in as much of a rush as he was.

On the platform, he boarded the train toward Hagsätra that had just pulled into the station. But just before the doors closed, he jumped back off again. John, still resting on Sami's arm, laughed happily. The leap onto the platform had given him butterflies in his stomach.

No one else seemed to follow Sami's example.

He crossed the platform. According to the screens, the train toward Åkeshov was two minutes away. When it pulled into the station, he repeated the maneuver. Stepped on board, waited a few seconds and then jumped back out onto the platform. When he didn't see anyone else do the same, he climbed back on board. John gave a big, gurgling laugh.

They took a train to the central station, where Sami ran up to street level only to take the escalator right back down to the blue line.

By this point, he was pretty sure he had been wrong.

No one was following him.

Still, to his son's amusement, he repeated his platform-hopping trick on the train toward Hjulsta.

Sami Farhan had moved around Stockholm's southern suburbs while he was growing up, but he was less familiar with those to the north.

When he finally emerged aboveground in Rissne, between Sundbyberg and Rinkeby, he initially went in the wrong direction. He was
heading for the Shurgard building, a warehouse where private individuals could rent a dark storeroom to lock up whatever they didn't want
to use, throw away or sell.

The one-year-old had almost fallen asleep during the subway ride,
but as they came out into fresh air, he opened his eyes and seemed to
be on the verge of protesting. As long as he was being carried, however,
things could be worse, and so he remained in a good mood.

The walk should have taken five minutes, but it took Sami fifteen.
Eventually, he managed to find the place. He spotted the Albanian sitting on a stool outside the entrance to the new building from a way
off. He was the sort of beefy man who, beneath all the fat, was more
muscular than the majority of people. The man's hands and arms were
covered in tattoos, and on his neck, above the collar of his T-shirt, dark
green flames licked at his earlobes.

The Albanian struggled to get up from the stool as Sami approached. He didn't give the baby a single glance.

"You can go in," he said.

The building was dark, but there was some light coming from an open
door farther ahead. Sami saw two more people inside the office. They
looked exactly like the man who had been left on guard duty outside,
and he remembered that they were all brothers. He had never done business with them before, but that was the whole point. Not using any of his
normal contacts. The room was crowded and dirty, and the computers
looked like something IBM had thrown together during the nineties.

"This way," one of them said, laboring to get up from a dark green
velvet armchair that was leaking stuffing.

Sami followed the man into the corridor, up a dark staircase and
past a long line of locked doors. They didn't pass anyone else along the
way. Maybe the brothers were renting out the entire building?

The Albanian stopped in front of the second-to-last door, unlocked
it, reached inside and switched on the light.

"Have a look round," he said. "And tell me what you want."

Sami stepped into the room. It was both an exhibition room and a storage area. Machine guns and smaller firearms were displayed on top of wooden boxes in the same way you would see sneakers on sale at ICA Maxi. Sami absentmindedly touched some of the pieces with his left hand; he was still carrying John with his right arm.

The Albanian followed him.

"We've got a few new pieces over here," he said. "If you want . . . But . . . what the hell's that smell?"

"What do you mean?" Sami asked, unconcerned.

"You can't smell it?" the Albanian said. "Smells like shit?"

Sami had felt it against his arm as they climbed the stairs: the pattering fart and subsequent warmth. He had thought it could wait.

"Can you give me a minute?" he said. "I just need to do something. It'll be quick."

Before the Albanian had a chance to reply, Sami was on the way out. He ran down the stairs, out of the building and around the corner. He lay John on his back on the grass next to the parking lot, took out the blanket and wet wipes from the bag and put a clean, dry diaper on his son. On the way back to the Albanian and the automatic weapons, he found a trash can by the ticket machine and threw away the old diaper.

The boy laughed as his father ran up the stairs two at a time.

Sami chose a traditional Kalashnikov that he knew he could handle. He pointed to a couple of pistols and read from the list he had been given by Maloof. It detailed the things Niklas Nordgren had asked for.

"Let's do it like this," said the Albanian. "Next time you come here, you bring the dough. We give you a key to one of the stores. The things you've asked for'll be inside. You can pick them up whenever you want, then just leave the key in the lock when you're done. OK?"

AUGUST 2009

23

One Monday in early August, Niklas Nordgren installed an air-conditioning unit in a shop in Sigtuna and then headed up to Arlanda airport, which was just a fifteen-minute drive away.

Airports were always sensitive targets, classified as high security and guarded around the clock. The police were based in one of the buildings adjacent to the main terminals, but the signs and the building itself were more impressive than the actual staff. The representatives of the law at Arlanda were neither the best educated nor the most heavily armed; their work usually just involved apprehending or ejecting disorderly vacationers who had been trying to drown out their fear of flying with alcohol. Terrorist threats and tips about drug smugglers were handled by other, more suitable units than the Arlanda police.

Nordgren parked his car inside the round multistory parking garage by Terminal 5 and took the glass bridge over the taxi stand to the terminal buildings. He turned left into SkyCity, which linked the international terminal to the domestic ones. It was here that he found the information desk.

A young woman chewing gum looked irritatedly up from her book. Her hair was dyed red and she had a piercing in one eyebrow.

"Excuse me," Nordgren said, looking at her from beneath the shadow of his cap. "Just a quick question. Where do I find the police helicopter base?"

"Helicopter base?" the woman mumbled, using her middle finger to search the directory she had on the screen in front of her.

Both Michel Maloof and Niklas Nordgren had, each in their own way, used the Internet, police websites, Flashback and other chat forums to try to find out where the police helicopters were based.

They hadn't had any success, they hadn't found a single straw to clutch at.

Nordgren was well aware that audacity was something you should use sparingly if you were in the robbery business. But sometimes that method was best, and he was prepared to go further than usual right now.

"Nope, can't find it," the woman eventually said. "Give me a second and I'll call over to the police and ask."

Nordgren nodded gratefully.

"Hi," she said once she was connected. "This is Sophie from the information desk in SkyCity. I've had a question about the police helicopters. Are they based here somewhere? Terminal Three?"

She continued chewing her gum as she listened to the answer. Then she thanked the person on the other end of the line and hung up.

"Nope," she said, "the police have never had any helicopters here. We actually have very few helicopters at Arlanda. They said they weren't sure but that you should try Tullinge."

"Tullinge? The police said that?"

"That's what they said," the woman confirmed, losing interest in him and returning to her book.

Three days later, Michel Maloof was in the passenger seat of Niklas Nordgren's car, watching the rain fall over Tumba. The nonstop music on the radio provided a perfect accompaniment.

"I still can't believe it," Maloof said.

"It was a surprise," Nordgren agreed. "But a good one."

"I can't believe it though. You're really sure? Completely sure?"

Nordgren was as sure as he could be. He had several contacts within the police force in Stockholm, and none of them had been able to say where a police helicopter depot might be based. But the one thing they did all claim was that there was only one helicopter stationed in the capital.

"They've got a helicopter in Norrland," Nordgren said to Maloof. "One in Malmö, one in Gothenburg and one in Stockholm. It sounds strange, but . . . when it flies over the city, everyone can see it, and they take it for a couple of spins a day so we think there are more. Apparently they sometimes borrow the one from Gothenburg. If they need it for any particular reason. If we're unlucky."

Maloof nodded. If Nordgren said it was so, then that was that.

"Just one helicopter . . . it's still so strange."

They reached Tullinge and turned off toward the old airfield's only landing strip to take a look around.

"But you don't . . . think it's here?" Maloof asked.

"No," said Nordgren. "I'm pretty sure. But you never know. The police have apparently been moving the helicopter around for years. Not to be clever, but because no one seems to want it."

"No." Maloof nodded. "Why doesn't anyone want it?"

"No idea," said Nordgren. "But it doesn't help."

In appearance, the two men were very different: the outgoing, always-smiling Lebanese man with thick, glossy hair and a perfectly groomed beard, and the introverted and sullen Swede with no hair at all. They had grown up close to one another—it was no farther than a good goal kick between Nordgren's Vårby Gård and the Maloof family's Fittja—and neither had been particularly interested in school. But where Nordgren had discovered a love for extreme sports, Maloof had stuck to the position of center back on the soccer team, something that reflected their personalities well.

Niklas Nordgren's need for company was limited. He was more interested in electronic circuits than human relationships, and the questioning look with which he studied the world around him from beneath his cap was constant. He didn't want to label himself a brooder, but the concept of happiness had never seemed definite to him. At times, he struggled with his self-image, and there was no denying the fact that there was a hint of destructiveness in his choice of work.

Michel Maloof was different. He liked sun more than rain, soccer more than hockey; he preferred the solution to the problem. He wasn't someone who made life difficult for himself. Maloof's parents were both Christians, and they had forced their children to traipse off to church at regular intervals. But the Christian faith had never managed to take hold in Maloof's heart, and his siblings were convinced that it was down to his Buddhist orientation. Maloof's ability to tolerate injustice, to remain indifferent to provocation, to smile at stupidity rather than get worked up, to sit still and listen while someone told the same story for the hundredth time—that was nothing but miraculous. The Dalai Lama claimed that the road to happiness was achieved by replacing every bitter or negative thought with one that was positive and beautiful. That was precisely how Maloof lived his life.

His only problem was money.

He didn't have enough of it.

But what that word—"enough"—meant, he couldn't say.

Michel Maloof's family, his four siblings and happily married parents, were the bedrock of his life. Thanks to the combined strength of the family, the children had made it through the Swedish school system with only superficial bruises and established themselves in the society their parents still frequently misunderstood. All but him. And the reason was that he had never been able to define the word "enough."

Even Niklas Nordgren's parents' near forty-year marriage had survived the strains that many of their friends' relationships had collapsed beneath. Niklas didn't have the same feeling of belonging to a flock as Maloof, he had only one sister, but neither she nor his parents had ever come close to the kind of life he ended up living.

Their sons' criminality had come as shock to both Nordgren's and Maloof's families. All the same, they had done nothing but be supportive, both when the two men made their pathetic calls for help from prison that very first time, and when they broke their promises never to do it again and ended up calling a second, third and fourth time. Their crushed mothers and brooding fathers had loyally waited outside the prison on leave days, and furious siblings had angrily had a go at them when they came home.

And worse than the thought of the isolation cells in prison was the thought of being a disappointment in the eyes of their families when the blue lights of the police appeared in the rearview mirror.

Unlike the majority of other people Nordgren and Maloof met in their line of work, they were both exceptions in their respective families.

And the fact that their friendship, once it had been established, grew strong was because they could both see themselves in the other person's self-appointed isolation.

The rain was still falling when they arrived, and it would have been difficult to find a more abandoned and gloomy place. The idea that planes had ever taken off and landed on this tiny strip of ground was hard to imagine. They drove a few loops around the area to make sure there was neither a living soul nor a threadbare helicopter hangar in sight.

Maloof sighed and ran his hand over his beard.

"This is . . . different."

Nordgren laughed. "Some people go fishing in the archipelago. We're on a helicopter safari in the Stockholm suburbs."

But there was no police helicopter to be found in Tullinge.

Before they parted ways, they divided Google Earth between themselves. Nordgren had printed out and drawn a line right through Stockholm County. He would take the eastern half, Maloof the western.

"What is it we're . . . looking for?" Maloof asked.

"A hangar. In a forest. Big enough for a helicopter or two. With asphalt in front of it. It doesn't need to be as big as a landing strip for planes."

"Right, right." Maloof nodded with a smile. "It's . . . it sounds . . . more like a hangar in a haystack."

"We don't have any other option, do we?" Nordgren said firmly.

The rain had grown heavier again, and was now hammering against the windshield as he drove along Hågelbyvägen, back toward Fittja.

24

It was three thirty in the morning, and no one would be coming out of the door they had been watching since midnight. Caroline Thurn, task force leader with the National Police Authority's Criminal Investigation Department, had already given up hope an hour earlier. Still, she had chosen to stay.

They were parked on Karlavägen, almost at Karlaplan. The building on the other side of the road functioned as a covert brothel for foreign ambassadors stationed in Stockholm, but it seemed like the diplomats' testosterone levels must be low that night.

Thurn glanced at Detective Chief Inspector Mats Berggren, her colleague for the past three weeks. He was asleep in the passenger seat. The whistling noise coming from his throat, along with the sound of his fleshy cheeks vibrating, would be difficult to get used to. But so far, Thurn had managed to work well with every colleague she had ever been subjected to, and she had no intention of failing with Berggren. The secret was respect and distance.

Thurn didn't become friends with anyone, or enemies. It was about being professional. Her job wasn't to make friends, it was to maintain and defend their democratic society.

"Mats," she whispered, and he jerked awake. "Let's give up for tonight."

She had never met anyone as big as Berggren before. He had to weigh around 300 pounds, and she had heard that he was always struggling with one diet or another. Clearly it was an unequal struggle. She herself weighed only 135 pounds, despite being five foot nine. She had denied herself sweet things and white bread since her teens, though she no longer thought about pushing her food around her plate rather than eating it, to avoid any questions about why she wasn't eating.

Thurn wasn't the missionizing type. Everyone could do as he or she liked, and if her new colleague didn't manage to lose any weight, that wasn't something she had any opinions on.

"Maybe we just got the wrong night?" Berggren said.

He had a rough voice, which definitely wasn't improved by only just having woken up.

"Wrong night," she agreed. "Or day, or date, or time? Or maybe they've just managed to move somewhere else."

Berggren mumbled something inaudible, and then added,

"Jesus Christ, I'm tired. Just the thought of making my way home . . ."

He was the whining type, she had realized that the very first day.

"I live around the corner," she replied. "If you want, you can get a few hours' sleep on my sofa before you go back to Hägersten."

In Caroline Thurn's world, not making the suggestion wasn't even an option. That kind of good-mannered consideration had been drummed into her from a young age; it was a reflex, like breathing. Being kind was also risk free, because the answer was always no.

"Yeah, sure," said Berggren, who hadn't grown up in the same kind of social environment.

They drove into a garage on Väpnargatan, around the corner from Strandvägen, and took the elevator straight up to the top floor, where Caroline Thurn lived. As Mats Berggren stepped into the hallway and looked around, he had to fight to hide his surprise.

The words that popped into his head were straight out of an estate agent's ad: "Grand apartment at the city's most exclusive address."

The dawn light cast a warm glow through the windows, and the fishbone parquet flooring in the suite of rooms seemed never to end. But as Berggren peered around, he saw that the apartment was in need of renovation. There were cracks in the ceiling, though hopefully just in the paint. Someone had started to take down the yellowed wallpaper in the hallway and given up before he or she finished the job, and the parquet was almost black in places. But what made the greatest impression on Berggren was that the place was almost completely empty.

"Nice place you've got here," he mumbled, not knowing what else to say.

Berggren had been working for the National Criminal Police for only a week when he was asked if he wanted to be Thurn's new partner. He had been equal parts terrified and curious. Thurn had a reputation. She kept her distance. She was respected because she rarely failed, she was approachable and obliging, and yet none of her colleagues could be counted among her friends.

Mats Berggren had done some research on his new partner before their first meeting. He hadn't needed to go any further than the details in the police's own database.

Caroline Thurn was born on February 16, 1977, meaning she was thirty-two years old. Berggren couldn't see where she had grown up or gone to school, but she must have enrolled in the police training academy straight after high school, because she had been given a position with the Stockholm police force as early as autumn 1998. After that first year on the beat, she was recruited to a group that had been given a good deal of media coverage back then, part of an international exchange. Berggren remembered it well; his own application to the program had been unsuccessful.

That initial year abroad had turned into several for Caroline Thurn, but in 2005, she had moved back to the National Criminal Police, and after that there was no information about exactly what she had been doing. Berggren had needed only to ask a couple of his new colleagues in the department for the picture to emerge: Caroline Thurn was someone who worked day in and day out, and who couldn't handle failure. Still, Berggren was congratulated by everyone he asked. Thurn was the kind of person you wanted on your side.

The first time they met, Mats Berggren had been shocked. After everything he had heard and read about her, the tall, slim woman wasn't at all what he had been expecting. Her profile, with that narrow, beaklike nose and those high cheekbones, was certainly razor sharp, but Thurn turned out to be both warm and empathetic. Berggren would even go as far as to say soft.

He took a step into the room off the hallway.

"Have you just moved in?" he asked.

The suite of five rooms stretched along Strandvägen, a street that was home to Stockholm's rich and powerful, with views out onto the whole of Nybroviken and Blasieholmen on the other side of the water. There was no furniture, no rugs, pictures or curtains, just creaking wooden floors.

"Mmm," she eventually said, "my parents bought this place just after the war. I . . . haven't got round to dealing with the decoration yet."

"Haven't got round to it?" Berggren said, going over to the window. "Which war are we talking about?"

"I have a sofa where you can sleep," she replied, waving him away from the view out onto the calm waters.

They passed through another couple of empty rooms on the way into a smaller room with a door. Inside, there was a deep, worn sofa.

"Do you live alone?" Berggren asked.

Men had long since fulfilled their role in Caroline Thurn's life. That wasn't a bitter fact, she assumed her experience of relationships was no different from other people's. Still, she had made the decision to live on her own. She didn't like talking about it. In other people's eyes, choosing to live alone took on political or philosophical dimensions.

Instead of replying to Berggren's question, she said,

"Get a few hours' sleep. You need it."

"Looks comfy." Berggren nodded toward the sofa, suddenly remembering how tired he was.

She smiled. "You can make coffee in the kitchen when you wake up," she said. "I don't have much china, but if you can't find anything you can wash one of the cups in the dishwasher."

If I can find the kitchen, Berggren thought.

He had grown up with his parents in a small apartment on Hant-verkargatan in fifties and sixties Stockholm, back when the city had been full of hope for the future and what would later come to be called "honest hard work." His childhood had been a struggle. Being fat had meant he was always an outsider. He hadn't played sports, never got invited to parties. His ambitions had always been bigger than his abilities, which meant that his schoolwork had been one long torment. He had inherited his pathos, his passion for solidarity and justice, from his father, a metalworker who had moved to Stockholm from Falun. From his mother, the academic from Kungsholmen, he had learned that a just, democratic society had to be built on the principle of equality in the eyes of the law. From both of them, he had learned not to believe that he was better than anyone else. He had always known he would be a police officer, and the one time in his life he had managed to shed some of his excess weight for a few months was ahead of his entrance examination to the National Police Academy.

But he had never lived anywhere bigger than that childhood apartment.

"How many square feet is this place?" he couldn't stop himself from asking.

"More than I need," Thurn replied. "You'll be OK?"

"What?" he asked. "Are you . . . leaving?"

"I just remembered something," she said. "I wanted to check if there was some other way into that building on Karlavägen. Through the building next door, or the garage. We never checked."

"Now?" Berggren was taken aback.

"I don't need much sleep. You get some though."

Berggren knew he should protest, but he didn't have the energy. Instead, he nodded and lay down on the sofa, which was even more comfortable than he could have imagined. He fell asleep immediately.

25

During the Second World War, Montenegro's capital had been flattened by the sixty or more bombing raids the city was subjected to. It sounds absurd, some kind of gross overexaggeration of Podgorica's importance, but that was how many times the bombers had swept into the beautiful valley and unloaded their cargo, an evil rain, onto the once pretty town where the two rivers met.

By the end of the war, there was nothing left.

When the Communist Party got to work rebuilding the city during the fifties and sixties, it did so following the same model as everywhere else in the new Eastern Europe: it created a kind of budget variant of brutalist modernism. Like Stockholm, Podgorica became a city where the buildings were never allowed to be taller than five or six stories. But unlike Stockholm, Podgorica became homogeneous, planned, cheap and soulless.

Filip Zivic, the helicopter pilot, loved Podgorica, but not because of the city's beauty. Lots of positive things had happened to the overall look of the town over the past twenty years, but Zivic would play no part in how it continued to develop over the next few decades.

It was with sorrow in his heart that he loaded his bags into the trunk of his car.

"Shall we go?" his wife asked. She was already sitting in the passenger's seat.

Their son was in the back, focused on some kind of game on his phone. As far as the boy was concerned, there was no real difference between Montenegro and Serbia, and the thought made Filip Zivic all the more depressed.

"Yes," he said. "Let's go."

*   *   *

The Serbian justice minister, Nebojsa Have, assumed that the meeting straight after lunch would involve a new negotiation of some kind. But unlike the other meetings he suffered through during his long days in the government offices at Nemanjina 11, a beautiful corner building, he wouldn't have to conceal it. He was a minister in a Serbian government that, beneath the surface, sprawled in all directions and built on compromises.

He heard a knock at the door, and a moment later one of his secretaries appeared, a young man with a straight back and ambition in his eyes.

"Filip Zivic is here to see you," he said.

"Good," said Have. "Ask him to come in."

Have knew what kind of impression his office gave to someone visiting for the first time. Ceilings almost thirteen feet high, with decorative stucco, tall windows out onto the street and heavy, pale velvet curtains. He had a cluster of antique armchairs and a glittering crystal chandelier above a coffee table, and the walls were covered in oil paintings of famous Serbian men. It was impossible not to be impressed.

Filip Zivic stepped into the room. The two men's friendship was so old that golden pen holders and Persian rugs should have had no impact on it, but Zivic still reacted to the elegance of the place.

"We can sit here," the minister suggested, pointing to a more modern cluster of chairs near one of the windows.

They sat down opposite each other.

"I was slightly surprised by your call, Filip," Have began. "I didn't even know you were in Belgrade."

"No," Zivic replied, "that's deliberate. No one knows I'm here. But I think I have something which might finally bring our negotiations to a close."

The justice minister nodded, but he said nothing.

Have was sure his room had been bugged, and he assumed that whoever was listening wished him well. All the same, he had made it a habit not to say anything on tape that could be turned against him in future. Regimes toppled one another, after all; it was practically a national tradition.

"I have information," Zivic said, "about a robbery. The people involved are from Montenegro. And the whole thing is ... spectacular ..."

Nebojsa Have continued to nod.

"I can't use information based on rumors," he explained. "We've already talked about this, haven't we, Filip?"

"This is more than just rumor."

"And this robbery is going to take place here in Belgrade?"

"No."

"In Montenegro?"

"No, it's going to happen in Sweden," said Zivic.

"Really?"

"Wasn't it an EU country you wanted?"

"Sweden is good," Have confirmed. "Sweden is very good."

The justice minister was keen for his country to be involved in Europe-wide police cooperation, but it was always a case of give and take. The last time he had talked to Zivic about it was over a year ago. Back then, he had been careful to stress that any agreement must be based on mutual benefit.

"I can give you detailed information," Zivic continued. "I don't have many names, but I have everything else. Using that, the Swedish police should be able to work out where, when and how the robbery is going to take place. Judging by the plan, this would be the biggest robbery in Swedish history."

Have sighed.

"Everyone's planning to carry out the biggest robbery in history," he said. "It's practically par for the course."

"But I need reassurances that you can keep your promise."

Have had made the promise to his childhood friend a year earlier. It was the sole reason the pilot was sitting in his office today.

During the war, Filip Zivic had taken part in events that had earned him enemies for life. For a few years, it had seemed as though all had been forgotten, but then these old injustices had suddenly blown up again. He didn't know why, but for eighteen months now, he and his family had been living under constant threats of death. Zivic forced his wife and son to move at least once a week, and he slept with a weapon on the bedside table. He had also cut off all contact with the majority of his friends and family. It was a way of protecting them, rather than himself.

But that kind of existence was unsustainable in the long run.

In parallel to this, Serbia's justice minister—in an attempt to achieve real change in a country saturated with corruption and organized crime—had created the first credible witness-protection program. A program people could trust. In exchange for information, the state could provide a new identity, a new life under a new name, and it did seem as though all government leaks had, for the moment, been stopped.

Because Filip Zivic had followed Nebojsa Have's career since his friend first entered politics, he knew that this was his chance. Have's ambitions and morals were greater than any other politician's.

"I can't guarantee anything," he now said, being deliberately cautious. "Especially since people know that we have been friends for years."

"Let me say this," said the pilot. "If I had information which was so unique and relevant that it could be used as currency in conversation with the Swedish and European police, would that get me into your program?"

"Of course," said the minister. "You wouldn't be treated differently to anyone else."

"OK then," said Filip Zivic. "The man planning the robbery I mentioned is called Zoran Petrovic and he lives in Stockholm. Should I save the details for the Swedish police?"

26

It was ten thirty when the national police commissioner's name flashed up on Caroline Thurn's phone. Thurn was having a coffee at Villa Källhagen on Djurgården at the time. Earlier that morning, she had discovered a door leading from the garage into the property on Karlavägen, but it didn't matter, because the location of the garage meant that she and Berggren had—unwittingly—also had it under surveillance that night.

Thurn had returned home to find Berggren still snoring away on her sofa. She had pulled on her running clothes and decided to do a lap around Djurgården. It was on the way back that she had stopped for a black, liquid breakfast.

National Police Commissioner Therese Olsson sounded agitated.

"We've had a tip-off," she said down the line. "We're considering it extremely interesting. Meet me outside the Ministry for Foreign Affairs in half an hour."

Thurn confirmed and hung up.

After that, she called Berggren. He sounded like he had just woken up. She passed on the National Police Commissioner's orders.

"See you there," said Berggren. "And thanks for letting me use the sofa."

She could hear cars in the background and assumed that Berggren was no longer in her apartment.

It wasn't unusual for Caroline Thurn to be called in to meetings at the Ministry for Foreign Affairs, which was based in one of the oldest buildings on Gustav Adolfs Torg in the very heart of Stockholm. One of the reasons the National Criminal Police had been formed was to facilitate cooperation with foreign police authorities, and as a result there was a natural connection between the two institutions.

As Thurn parked her new-smelling service Volvo in one of the reserved spaces immediately outside the entrance to the building, she saw both Berggren and the commissioner waiting on the sidewalk.

Olsson was in uniform, and Berggren in the same clothes he had been wearing that morning.

It was the twentieth of August, and the summer heat had returned to the east coast a few days earlier. The sky was pale blue beneath a faint haze of cloud, and families wearing ugly sneakers were leaning against the railings by the water, using their phones to take photos of themselves with Norrbron in the background. It was only eleven o'clock. Late-summer Stockholm was a tourist's paradise of hesitant cars on the roads, backpacks on the subway and pickpockets in every crowd.

Thurn climbed out of the car.

"You beat me," she said to Berggren with a smile.

"I was just around the corner," he said apologetically, as though he felt disloyal at having arrived before her.

Berggren wanted to ask about her bedroom, but he realized it wasn't the moment.

When he woke that morning, he had searched the apartment for Thurn and realized that there wasn't a bed in any of the rooms. Other than behind a locked door in the kitchen, he had looked everywhere. There was no bedroom.

They showed their IDs at reception and the state secretary to the minister for foreign affairs appeared a few minutes later.

"To what do we owe the minister's interest?" Thurn asked as they climbed the wide stone staircase to the second floor.

Olsson made some kind of dismissive gesture that indicated that she would like to explain, but not right now. Therese Olsson was consumed by her professional role, and she would rather be accused of being boring than unclear. Climbing your way to the top of the envious ranks of the police hierarchy wasn't something you did with straightforwardness and a cheerful temperament.

The police officers were ushered into the minister's room behind the secretary, and they sat down on a sofa and waited in silence. When the minister appeared, they got to their feet.

The energetic minister greeted each of them with a firm handshake and asked them to sit down.

"I understand," he said, and Thurn wondered whether it was his coarse dialect that made the Swedish language sound forced coming from his mouth, "that we are continuing our cooperation with Belgrade?"

"That is correct," Olsson replied.

"As you know," the minister continued, "I still have good relationships with the majority of decision makers in the Balkans. I just wanted to point out that if you need any help, I'm at your service."

"That's very kind, Minister," Olsson replied, "but I think we have the situation under control. While the initial contact was at the ministerial level, our Serbian colleagues have also provided our liaison office in Belgrade with extremely detailed information that they seem to have stumbled on by chance."

"Well, stumbling is rarely deliberate, is it?" said the minister.

Berggren laughed, and the minister flashed him an appreciative glance. Caroline Thurn smiled reflexively. She wasn't much of a fan of jokey word games. A wave of weariness washed over her, and she closed her eyes and fell into a microsleep. She opened her eyes a few seconds later, without anyone else in the room having noticed what had happened.

Sleep was Thurn's greatest enemy and challenge. She had always slept badly, but she couldn't remember exactly when her nights had turned into drawn-out nightmares. At some point during her late teens, she would guess. It had begun as a sleeplessness, an inability to get any rest. The nights had become one long torment, the days a hazy fight to stay awake until it was time to repeat the whole process again.

She had experimented with everything she could think of. Eaten a lot or very little in the evenings, worked out or avoided working out after a certain time of day. She had bought mattresses of varying firmness, humidifiers and sound effects—rain and wind. She had started meditating and taken a long list of concoctions and drugs that both ordinary doctors and therapists had prescribed to her. Things had become more and more dramatic.

It was after only a few years, once she stopped fighting it and managed to find the right dose of medication, that her days became tolerable again; when she decided to stop trying, and didn't even bother going to bed at night. Instead, she would sit in the dark and allow her thoughts to come and go, without any resistance and with the aim of saving as much energy as she could for the day ahead, before it was time to function in a social context once again.

The microsleep she had hated in the past—because it made promises and always broke them—became her best friend.

But she also knew she was different and that different wasn't good. When Mats Berggren later asked where her bedroom was, she would lie like she always did and mention a fold-down bed hidden in the wall.

When Caroline Thurn and Mats Berggren left the office of the minister for foreign affairs thirty minutes later, they weren't much the wiser. Commissioner Olsson had repeated over and over again that they had received a tip of great importance. She had even used the word "unique," which was why Serbia's foreign minister had contacted his Swedish counterpart. To win political points at the highest level.

The crime being planned would be the biggest robbery in Swedish criminal history. And thanks to their foreign colleagues, the Swedish police suddenly had a real lead, Olsson said.

But when Caroline Thurn tried to find out exactly what that lead was, the commissioner failed to answer. She didn't know the details, she said. But she knew that this was a unique chance to show organized crime in the Balkans what the Swedish Criminal Police could do, what international cooperation could achieve. For the minister for foreign affairs and the government, it meant a debt of gratitude to the Serbians.

"I'll call Björn Kant when I get back," Thurn said as they were leaving the building. "He can fill me in."

She hadn't seen Kant since Henrik Nilsson's arrest in one of the Hötorget buildings a few months earlier. Nilsson had barely made it into police headquarters before his lawyers and contacts had seen to his leaving again. When Thurn heard about that, she had gone out to Djurgården and run three loops of the canal to work out her anger. Men like Nilsson always got off, despite Sweden's best prosecutor having been involved in the case. If Henrik Nilsson ever crossed her path again, she swore she would send him down.

"Björn Kant wasn't available," the police commissioner said in a neutral tone. "The International Public Prosecution Office appointed someone else to this case. Lars Hertz."

"Lars Hertz?" Thurn repeated, racking her memory. "Is he from Gothenburg? I don't think I know who . . ."

"This will be Hertz's first criminal case," Therese Olsson replied.

Caroline Thurn stopped dead.

"I'm sorry, but I don't think I understand. We're meant to be working with a prosecutor who's never tried a criminal case before?"

"I've heard he's very competent," said the commissioner.

A black car pulled up to the sidewalk. Olsson opened the back door and climbed in without another word. Thurn and Berggren were left standing outside the Ministry for Foreign Affairs.

Thurn was furious, but she managed to force a mild smile.

"I guess it's up to us to give Lars Hertz a crash course in international criminality," she said.

27

Through the half-drawn curtains, Michel Maloof could see down to the soccer field, the high and, farther in the distance, the dense forest. There always seemed to be an open box of pizza from the night before within reach, and he grabbed one of the leftover slices he had been managing to resist since lunch.

He didn't know how long he had been staring at his computer screen. He hated Google Earth. The afternoon was slowly drawing to a close, and this was what he was spending his time doing. Searching for something he would never find. On the table beneath the pizza box, he had the printout of the map Niklas Nordgren had given him. Maloof had methodically split it up into squares, and he still had as much of it left to go over as he had already checked.

His one consolation was knowing that to the north of the city, in Lidingö, Niklas Nordgren was doing the exact same thing.

It was six thirty in the evening when, as he was staring three days later at the pixelated version of reality provided by Google, Michel Maloof found the dolly. Over the past week, the light from the screen and the terrible resolution of the images had given him headaches, so when he first spotted it next to the two small buildings in the middle of the forest on Värmdö, he was sure he was imagining things.

He leaned back and stared and stared, but he couldn't come to any other conclusion: the picture, taken by chance by an American satellite, really was what he had been looking for.

Helicopters had no wheels, and that was why they landed on a metal plate that did—a so-called dolly—meaning they could be pulled, either by hand or using a vehicle, in and out of the hangar.

What Maloof was staring at in the fuzzy image in front of him looked just like one.

He opened a new tab, found a picture of a dolly and brought it up alongside Google Earth.

Staring at the two images, he called Nordgren.

"Hey. Listen . . . you can probably turn off the computer."

The line was silent. Maloof could hear Nordgren breathing.

"Are you telling me you've . . . have you found it?"

"Right, right."

"You're kidding."

"Nope. Yeah. Ninety-nine percent."

"Unbelievable."

"I'll double-check tomorrow. OK. Sleep well."

"Finally," Nordgren declared.

Myttinge was to the north of Värmdö.

Maloof picked up Sami Farhan at Slussen just before lunch, and they drove out toward Gustavsberg in Maloof's silvery-gray Seat. Thanks to the highway, it didn't take much more than half an hour to reach Värmdö, but then the road past Ängsvik and Siggesta Gård was narrow and curving. There was no other traffic, but it was still hard to get up to the speed limit.

And then, suddenly, they saw it.

The hangar.

It was to one side of the road, unassuming and without any kind of surveillance. The fence surrounding it was made of ordinary chicken wire. They found a small forest trail around a bend in the road and parked the car, walking back to the hangar to make sure they really had found the right place.

The police had put up stickers on both the buildings functioning as the helicopter depot and on the gates. There were two small hangars, and through the window on the side of one, they could see a helicopter.

On the way back into town, Sami was in high spirits.

"It's like they're keeping it in a child's house."

"Right, right," said Maloof.

"Getting in there with Nick's mobile bombs'll be a piece of cake."

They drove over Danvikstull and then continued along Stadsgård-sleden where the huge ferries lay in wait for their paying conference attendees.

"I can give you a ride home," said Maloof. "I don't have to be any-where until two."

"Could you drop me off by Sergels Torg instead?" Sami asked. "I promised Karin I'd swing by that stroller shop to see if they have any spare wheels."

While Sami went into great detail about the stubborn locking feature on the wheel of the stroller, Maloof drove along Skeppsbron, passing the king's ugly castle and heading straight after the bridge. Kungsträdgården Park was lush and green, beautiful even without any elms, and there were people sitting on the grass around the statue of Karl XII, enjoying the heat. The schools had gone back already, but you couldn't tell; summer vacation still seemed to be ongoing.

"God, that looks nice," Sami remarked at the lightly dressed sun worshippers sitting with their picnics. He lowered the window on his side of the car.

Maloof slowed to a halt as the bus ahead of them pulled into a stop.

"What the HELL!"

It was Sami who had shouted. It came completely out of the blue, and Maloof, who had been just about to pull away, slammed on the brakes.

"Look! What the hell, LOOK!"

"What the hell is it?"

Maloof felt a cold wave course through his body. It was quickly fol-lowed by a rush of adrenaline.

"It's him!" Sami shouted, pointing out the window. "The Turk! Has-san Kaya! That's the fucking prawn thief!"

And before Maloof had time to process what was happening, Sami had opened the door and was sprinting across the road. A red Porsche screeched to a halt and the people who had just left the bus had stopped and were pointing, but Sami continued to run.

"YOU BASTARD!" he shouted.

"STOP!" shouted Maloof.

28

Early the next morning, after their meeting at the Ministry for Foreign Affairs, Thurn and Berggren were called into the prosecutor's office on Östermalmsgatan. They met at a 7-Eleven not far from there at quarter to nine. Each bought a coffee, and Berggren couldn't resist paying another five kronor for a sweet bun to go with it. To make the defeat less painful, he had eaten it by the time he left the shop. Thurn had trouble not looking away as he made a mess of himself. He was ashamed and could completely understand her.

"Want a napkin?" she asked.

He shook his head and licked his sticky fingers. "Let's go now," he said. "I'm curious. I heard it was something really impressive. You know, same level as the National Museum."

Berggren was referring to one of the most audacious heists in Swedish criminal history. The robbers had struck two days before Christmas Eve, on a Friday just before closing, when the museum had been virtually empty. They had grabbed three priceless paintings no bigger than postcards, two Renoirs and a Rembrandt, and shoved them inside their coats. And then the robbers had run twenty yards to a waiting boat, which had disappeared into the pitch-black darkness of Stockholm's open waters.

Caroline Thurn mumbled something inaudible.

"You worked on that, right?" Berggren asked. He didn't want to sound too curious.

"Yeah," Thurn replied. "Ali Farhan sent his younger brothers in to steal the paintings. There were loads of us on that case. We never would've managed it without the FBI. But we got them in the end. Not just the Farhan brothers either, there were plenty of others involved. They ended up being convicted of receiving stolen goods."

"Right," Berggren said, pretending to recall the information that he and every other police officer already knew in detail; almost as much had been written about the subsequent investigation as the robbery itself. "No, it's one thing to wave an automatic weapon in the air, but it's trickier to do business afterward."

Caroline Thurn didn't reply. She wasn't sure she agreed. Doing business required different skills, of course, but did that have anything to do with the level of difficulty? And how were you meant to assess the risks being taken? When criminals put their lives on the line, it was often for a fraction of the amount of tax that director Henrik Nilsson withheld from the Swedish state. And the only risk Nilsson was taking was a few petty fines. In the traditional world of crime, the risk was no longer relative to the reward; it was in the newer criminal sphere, the world of banking and finance, that the big money was up for grabs.

Still, a crime was a crime, Thurn thought, regardless of whether it happened behind a desk or out on the street.

Prosecutor Lars Hertz was sitting in one of the impersonally decorated rooms along the long, dark corridor in the Swedish Prosecution Authority's offices.

He leaped to his feet and greeted the two police officers with a firm, enthusiastic handshake when they came into his room. Hertz was a man in his prime, seemingly fit and fashion conscious in a slim-fitting, well-ironed white shirt. He looked kind, the furrows on his brow suggesting a troubled thoughtfulness, the thick mop of blond hair and blue eyes screaming energy and youth.

Berggren, who had begun panting as he made his way up the stairs, pulled out a tissue from his pocket and wiped his forehead as he sat down on the austere wooden chair in front of the prosecutor's desk. Thurn sat down next to him.

"So," Hertz began, "as I understand it, this is something of a sensational story?"

Berggren took out a notepad and pen. It was a habit of his; he could think more clearly with a pen and paper in hand, even if he rarely read through his notes afterward.

"What's sensational?" Thurn asked. She hated the word, it sounded like a vulgar tabloid headline and had no place in serious police work.

"Well, I mean, the sensational aspect is in the level of detail in the information we've been given," Hertz replied uncertainly.

"We were only given this case yesterday," said Mats Berggren, "so we're obviously curious about the details."

"Of course," said Hertz. "Of course. I understand. Well . . . as you might have heard, this will be my first criminal case?"

"I'm sure it'll be fine," Thurn said encouragingly.

"I need your help," the prosecutor replied. "You have the experience I'm lacking. I'm well aware of my limitations."

He looked from Thurn to Berggren and back again. During his career, he had learned not to waste time on pessimists and prophets of doom. The corridors and halls of the country's courts and prosecutors' offices were full of bleak professionals who barricaded themselves in their dark rooms and dismissed every possibility as meaningless.

The two police officers in front of him seemed difficult to place in a particular category. They seemed to be opposites; the tall woman, who was more beautiful than she pretended to be, was still smiling encouragingly. He had never come across such charming condescension before. And by her side, the fat, sweaty man no one would ever call beautiful, jotting down every word and seeming so at ease in his subordinate role.

"The information came from the Serbian police," Hertz began. "We don't have the name of their source, but it's someone who has sought and been granted witness protection in Serbia."

Hertz pushed his fringe, a serious tangle of hair, to one side.

"Witness protection?" Thurn repeated. "In Serbia? That's a bit like hiding behind a lamppost."

"No, it's not," Hertz objected, wounded on behalf of the law-abiding

European state. "We're talking about our colleagues here, correct, Detective Chief Inspector. Besides, it's in Europe's interests that our witness protection systems really do work."

"You said the original source was granted witness protection," Berggren interjected. "Does that mean there are others?"

The prosecutor nodded. "After the original tip, the Serbs tapped several phones. One of them, the most active, has been in regular contact with an individual in Sweden."

"Who? Do we have a name?" asked Berggren. "You need to tell us what we know."

"We know that they are planning a robbery on a cash depot in Stockholm," said Hertz. "Not a secure transport vehicle, not a courier, the depot itself. The original source was one of the people who would be carrying out the robbery. He's considered entirely trustworthy, an experienced helicopter pilot from the civil war down there."

"A helicopter pilot?" Berggren repeated, looking up from his notebook. "The robbers are going to fly helicopters?"

Berggren laughed as though he had told a joke, but he fell silent when he saw the prosecutor's face.

"Yes," Hertz said. "According to the information we have, the robbers are planning to fly a helicopter to a cash depot in the Stockholm area. The depot is apparently in a four-story building. They're going to blow a hole in the roof. They're also planning to sabotage and neutralize the police helicopter so that they can make their getaway undisturbed."

The room was silent. Not even Caroline Thurn knew what to say. This kind of detailed information from a reliable source wasn't something they often had access to.

Hertz smiled. He knew he had won a partial victory. He pushed his fringe to one side again.

"Which cash depots in Stockholm—" Berggren began, but he didn't have time to finish his sentence before Hertz started speaking again.

The prosecutor knew how to ration information. He had more to reveal.

"Through our unique channels," he continued, sounding more like he was talking to a large audience than two police officers, "we have also been able to confirm the informant's information. As a result, we know that the robbery will take place on the fifteenth of September."

"That's just over three weeks away!" Berggren panted.

"Yes, correct. Slightly over three weeks. This information is fresh, but it also leaves us with time to prepare."

"Incredible," said Thurn.

She was willing to admit that this tip really could be described as sensational. But Hertz wasn't done yet. He continued, amazing the officers further:

"We know that the helicopter the robbers will use to get to and from the cash depot is likely to be a Bell 206 JetRanger—"

"Surely it can't be that hard to find one of those?" Thurn interrupted. "What do you think, Mats? There must be some kind of register of helicopters in Sweden?"

But before Berggren had time to reply, Hertz raised his voice a few notches to answer the question and finish off his monologue:

"The register won't help. That type of helicopter is very common, and buying a helicopter for private use has never required any particular license. Plus, the helicopter they're planning to use could just as easily have been brought over from one of our neighboring countries, or flown in from Germany. Because this robbery is big. We believe that there are already around twenty people involved in the preparations, and the haul is estimated to be at least ten million euros."

Thurn and Berggren stared at the prosecutor.

"OK, that's all." Hertz nodded.

A new silence descended over the anonymous office of prosecutor Lars Hertz. Mats Berggren's mouth was open. Thurn was grinning.

"You're in luck, Lars," she said.

"Yes. Or rather, what do you mean?"

"The chances of you succeeding in your first criminal case seem pretty good."

She got up, and Berggren followed her lead.

"We know *what* the robbers are going to do," she summed up. "We know *when* they're going to do it. So all that's left is to find out *where* they're going to do it. There aren't all that many options. How long have you been sitting on this information?"

"Since the evening before last," Hertz replied. "The Serbian police approached us in Belgrade, but there was some delay after the ministers' meeting."

"We've lost several days?" asked Thurn.

"The Serbian police have been keeping the pressure on," Hertz reassured her.

"And our Swedish suspect?" said Berggren. "You said the Serbs had been listening to a Swede?"

"Correct," Hertz confirmed.

"Do we have a name?" asked Thurn.

"Zoran Petrovic. He's the one who will carry out the robbery," Prosecutor Lars Hertz replied.

"We'll have eyes on Petrovic within the hour," Thurn said, speaking clearly as she stood in front of the prosecutor's huge desk. "Twenty-four seven. I'd like to bug him too. I want to be able to hear everything he says. I want microphones in his car, wherever he works, in his bedroom. Do you understand, Lars? I want to know who he's calling, where his mother is from, who he went to school with. Everything. OK, Lars?"

Lars Hertz nodded. He understood. What he didn't mention was that he had already requested the relevant background information, but that Zoran Petrovic wasn't in the police crime database, or in any other register. He didn't say that. He was keen for their first meeting to end on a positive note.

"I'll sort it out," he said. "You can have everything I've got."

29

Michel Maloof pulled over to the side of the road and, from his seat behind the wheel, watched the disturbance unfolding on the southern edge of Kungsträdgården.

Sami ran straight across the road. Cars slammed on their brakes, sounded their horns, people raised their fists. But the boxer saw none of this, he was running as though his life were at stake.

Sitting at a table outside one of the park's busy cafés was Hassan Kaya, the Turk who had conned Sami out of his money in the shellfish business. The man who had gone underground without a trace. He was here. In the flesh.

Sami wasn't thinking, couldn't think; how many nights had he dreamed about finding Hassan Kaya? And finally, here he was.

"YOU BASTARD!" he shouted, running straight toward him with his fists clenched and his eyes black with hate.

As he reached the line of tables closest to the road, Kaya finally realized what was happening. He stared in terror at the furious, sprinting Sami Farhan, and got to his feet with a start. The table he had been sitting at tipped and fell, his plate of food shattering on the gravel, and then Kaya fled, as fast as he could, knocking over several other tables on the way. He ran toward Hamngatan, away from the danger.

Sami's bulky frame plowed its way between the tables. Rather than taking a detour on the paved footpath where he would have had no trouble running past the office workers, he transformed into a homing missile. He shoved tables to the side, pushed people who got up to protest out of the way. It was like watching a huge combine harvester make its way across an unplowed field, leaving a path of overturned tables and chairs, crying children and confused diners in his wake.

Kaya ran faster than his heavy old body could really manage.

"Stop, you bastard!" Sami shouted.

But his words only made the Turk change gear. He turned right, around the corner of the café with the outdoor seating area, and crossed the road.

Maloof was still waiting by the sidewalk with his engine running. Kaya came charging past. He was only five, six yards away, and if Maloof had wanted to, he could have put the car into gear and rammed straight into the Turk.

But that was the last thing he wanted.

No.

After weeks of searching, he had finally found the police helicopter. Drawing attention to himself was the last thing he needed. And Sami should be thinking the same thing. But as Maloof saw the furious boxer come running after the Turk, who had continued down Arsenalsgatan, he realized it wasn't consideration controlling the big man's movements.

Hassan Kaya had reached the entrance to Kungsträdgården subway station, and Sami was hot on his heels. He had realized that the Turk was getting tired. That the burst of explosive energy awoken by his fear had been used up.

Sami was gaining on him.

Inside the subway station, there were a number of short escalators down to the ticket hall. Kaya took the stairs to the right instead, and then leaped over the high ticket barrier. He almost managed to clear it, but one of his feet got caught, and he stumbled and fell to the floor on the other side. He scrambled back up and hurried toward the escalators down to the platforms. It was clear that his strength was failing him.

That gave Sami a renewed burst of energy. The station was the last stop on the blue line, and in the middle of the day it was practically deserted. Sami had time to use his card to get through the barriers, and then he continued to run.

Now, you bastard.

Kaya had already reached the escalators, but if there was one thing Sami was good at, it was running down stairs. Kungsträdgården was the city's deepest metro station, almost one hundred feet belowground, and the escalators were endlessly long and steep. Sami felt his confidence grow. The prawn bastard was screwed. Sami ran as though he were a bull and Kaya his red flag, and the distance between them grew smaller.

To Sami's surprise, Kaya passed the first set of escalators and continued toward the one farthest away. He was so close now that Sami could almost touch him.

Kaya awkwardly reached the top of the escalator. Along the far wall, which was made of red mesh, there were a number of advertising boards, and Kaya desperately tore one of them loose, a poster encouraging people to drink juice.

Sami couldn't work out what the Turk was playing at. He didn't care. He lunged at him just as Kaya threw himself forward, the sign beneath him like some kind of sled, and started to slide downward on the metal surface between the escalators. Not even the ridges, which stuck up at regular intervals, could stop him; they made distinct clicking sounds as he passed, but the Turk quickly gained speed.

"What the hell . . . ?"

Sami rushed down the escalator without letting the Turk out of his sight. The metal sled picked up speed as though it had been shot from a catapult. Kaya flew toward the platform. Soon enough, there would be no way for the Turk to slow down. He was going too fast.

"Shit," Sami swore, not knowing exactly what he meant. "Shit!"

His legs pumped away like two sewing machine needles as he raced down the escalator.

"Shit!"

And below him, at the very bottom, Kaya disappeared from view.

Had Sami lost him again?

*   *   *

But when he made it down to the empty platform a minute or two later, he found Hassan Kaya in a bloody heap on the concrete floor. He was several yards away from the escalator, beneath a replica of an ancient Greek statue. There was no sign of the metal sled, which spoke volumes about the journey through the air that must have ended his ride.

Sami stopped. Glanced around. There was no one else about. Slowly, he walked forward, squatted down and carefully turned over the Turk.

"I don't have it," Kaya mumbled.

Those were his first words. His face was covered in blood, his eyes closed. When he opened his mouth, blood trickled down his chin.

"You lost five, but I lost ten mill," he groaned. "The fucking captain bought his fucking freezers and then vanished. He screwed us all."

The Turk's voice grew fainter and fainter. Sami leaned in so that he could hear his final words, which came out as a faint whisper.

"I didn't dare . . . I thought you'd kill me . . . I'm sorry . . ."

And then he lost consciousness.

As Sami took the escalator back upstairs, he could still see Kaya's chest rising and falling. He would live.

Up on Kungsträdgården, Maloof was waiting in the car. Sami jumped in.

"And that was really necessary, was it?" Maloof asked. "Today, of all days?"

30

"You look worried," Zoran Petrovic said mockingly.

Michel Maloof's smile was as wide as usual, but Petrovic had detected a rare flash of uncertainty in the eye of his short friend.

"Right, right," Maloof replied, quickly running his hand over his beard. "No . . . it's just . . . don't worry. Course we're going to do this. And your pilot . . ."

"Zivic."

"Zivic. He's good. Right?"

Petrovic smiled.

They were standing next to the launchpad at the helicopter hangar in Roslagen, just south of Norrtälje. Maloof hadn't told Petrovic about Sami and the way he chased Hassan Kaya. The impulsivity of it still bothered him; it wasn't something Petrovic needed to know.

It was a beautiful Sunday. The breeze was making the waters of Lake Limmaren glitter temptingly, the sky was pale blue and the bank of white clouds was keeping to a reasonable distance, far out over the Baltic. Still, the difference between today and when they had last been there at night, with Manne Lagerström, was smaller than you might imagine. There was an entire summer between the two occasions, but there was still a beauty and tranquility to the place.

As long as you stood with your back to the industrial area on the other side of the road.

"We could fly over to a couple of my friends on Blidö," Petrovic suggested. "I know a guy who owns a mink farm on the island. I think he's started with polecats too. Makes forty thousand an animal. I helped him take the first pair over there. Long time ago now. We hid them in the rubber hoses we used when we built the wet rooms for that area in Nacka, you know? They can be thin as worms, mink. Polecats too, I guess."

Maloof nodded, and Petrovic got lost in a long story about what had happened when the load of building materials had crossed the border between the Soviet Union and Finland and one of the animals had started squealing. Without listening too closely, Maloof flashed an extra-wide smile whenever it seemed appropriate.

A certain amount of activity was going on in front of them. After a few blustery weeks in early August, the meteorologists had finally been able to promise a calm, beautiful weekend. Several of the owners of the private helicopters parked in the hangar had taken that as an opportunity to finally get up in the air after a long summer break.

Petrovic and Maloof had made sure they weren't in the way. They were standing a few yards away from the opening in the hangar, at the edge of the woods, watching the simple tractor reversing the huge flying machines out of the hangar. The helicopters looked like angry bees, their antennae drooping toward the ground.

"Toys for people who already have everything," said Petrovic.

"Right, right," Maloof agreed.

"I'd rather buy a Bentley, you know?"

"Right." Maloof nodded, though he had absolutely no interest in cars.

Michel Maloof had never been in a helicopter before, and he had figured that he needed to get up in the air at least once before the big day. How big was the inside of a helicopter? What was the storage space like? Navigating at night didn't seem to be a problem, but with the normal communications systems shut off to reduce the risk of being spotted on radar, how well would an ordinary GPS system work up in the air?

Maloof wasn't the only one who had thought that the day's trip was necessary. Filip Zivic, the Serbian combat pilot Petrovic had already paid, had also insisted that they carry out a few test flights over the summer. There was nothing strange about that. Every aircraft had its quirks, Zivic had explained, and both Maloof and Petrovic had appreciated what they saw as dedication and diligence on the part of the pilot.

Petrovic had contacted Manne, who promised they would be able to borrow the white helicopter for a few hours without any trouble. Manne could write the usual pilot's name in the logbook, and, if anyone asked—which was unlikely—he could just say he had made a mistake. That kind of thing had happened before.

Maloof was also looking forward to meeting the pilot and looking him straight in the eye. This job would succeed or fail on the helicopter pilot's skill, and that was why Maloof had been eager.

"If you can drive ninety miles an hour under the bridges in Croatia, and I mean *under* the bridges, I promise you can also land a helicopter on a roof in Västberga," Petrovic had said.

"Right, right," Maloof had replied. "But . . . no . . . you don't actually know that?"

He glanced at his watch.

"It's twenty past two."

He gave a quick laugh, almost like he was apologizing for pointing it out, but then he scratched his beard nervously.

"It is strange," Petrovic admitted. "When we met in Montenegro, he came dead on time."

"OK," said Maloof.

"I'll call and check."

Petrovic had saved Zivic's number under "P" for "Pilot" in his phone. But it didn't ring, Zivic's phone was switched off.

Petrovic hadn't just bought the plane ticket to Sweden, he had also arranged a room for Zivic at the August Strindberg Hotel on Tegnérgatan. Petrovic knew the night porter, and in exchange for certain services he could have one of the rooms for free whenever he wanted.

He called the hotel.

"What was the name?" the receptionist asked.

"Filip Zivic," Petrovic replied, speaking excessively clearly. "He checked in yesterday, late afternoon."

There was a moment's silence on the other end of the line, and then the receptionist's voice returned.

"I'm sorry, but that particular guest never checked in."

"What?"

Petrovic instinctively turned away from Maloof to hide his reaction.

"I can see that we were expecting a guest by that name," the receptionist continued, "but no one named Zivic ever checked in. I . . . don't know any more."

Michel Maloof didn't get his helicopter ride that afternoon.

Instead, the two men returned to Stockholm in the Seat. On the way Zoran Petrovic came up with at least a dozen reasonable explanations as to what might have happened. Maybe Filip Zivic was ill. A stomach bug from the food on the plane from Croatia, one so bad that he couldn't even make it out of bed to call and cancel their meeting. Or maybe something had happened on the way to the airport in Dubrovnik. Petrovic had booked a plane from there because he wanted a direct flight. He might've been ambushed on the way, struck down and robbed of his phone, passport and money. He could be lying in a rock crevice somewhere along the Croatian coast, with no way of getting in touch.

"Right, right," Maloof agreed. "Or . . . anything?"

"When I get home, it'll take me five minutes to check," Petrovic swore. "Five minutes."

"Right, right. Five minutes."

Maloof dropped off the tall Yugoslavian on Upplandsgatan. Petrovic nonchalantly crossed the street, trying to use his body language to show that he had the situation under control, but the minute the door swung shut behind him he ran up the stairs.

He found his Montenegrin phone on the desk in his office and called his uncle in Podgorica. He got straight to the point, setting out the situation for him.

It was his uncle's responsibility to track down Filip Zivic, since it was through his contacts that the pilot had been signed up in the first place.

The uncle promised to look into it. When Petrovic said he needed answers that same evening, his uncle laughed and explained that it wasn't going to happen. He was going to a soccer match and then planned to go out for a beer. It was Sunday.

Petrovic didn't have the energy to argue. Instead, he made a few more calls to Montenegro, and by evening he had five different people trying to find out what had happened to Filip Zivic.

But no one he put on the job managed to get ahold of Zivic that night. Petrovic grew more and more anxious. It wasn't a feeling he was used to.

He fell asleep around dawn and was woken by the sound of his Montenegrin phone ringing the next morning.

Without getting out of bed, he fumbled for his phone and answered without opening his eyes.

"Mmm?"

"He's gone."

It was his uncle on the line.

Petrovic sat up in bed. He was wide awake.

"Did you hear me?"

"Yeah."

"He's gone. Filip's missing. Him, his family, wife and boy, the lot of them are gone."

Rage rose up inside him. He stared straight ahead, the blood pounding in his temples.

"What do you mean, gone?"

"Their place is empty. No one saw them leave. No one knows where they are. It's a few weeks since anyone saw them."

Zoran Petrovic threw the phone across the room. It broke into a thousand pieces against the radiator beneath the window. His shout woke the people living in the apartment above his.

31

It was five in the morning when Niklas Nordgren and Sami Farhan climbed out of the car Michel Maloof had parked on Malmskillnadsgatan, just around the corner from Mäster Samuelsgatan. They were only a stone's throw from the absolute center of Stockholm, but it was so quiet that they could hear their own breathing.

Maloof hadn't told Nordgren and Sami about the missing helicopter pilot yet. Petrovic had said there was still a chance he would turn up, and without definitive answers, Maloof didn't want to worry the others.

The city center was deserted. Other than the odd summer temp, the office buildings around Sergels Torg would be empty all day. Sweden had slowly adapted to European practice, and August was now one long, drawn-out run-up to autumn. During summer, native Stockholmers fled the inner city; if you could afford to live in the center of town, you could also afford a summer house in the archipelago or one last charter holiday to Greece. Behind them, they left closed, dug-up streets that the authorities took the opportunity to repair when there was no one but German trailer campers, American cruise passengers and families with small children from the south of Sweden to annoy with the traffic jams and chaos. In a week's time, normality would resume, the roadwork would end and the summer temps would be sent home, but so far the summer calm was still holding sway over the capital.

Nordgren went to fetch his huge rucksack from the trunk.

The bag was full of plastic explosives, batteries and detonation cables. Like always, he kept the detonators themselves inside his vest.

Together, the three robbers walked toward Jakobsbergsgatan. The sun had risen, but it was hidden behind a haze of white cloud. The smell of chlorine and old beer lingered in the air, and a confused gull was flying between the buildings up by Oxtorget, but they couldn't hear any of the nightlife that probably was still going on around Stureplan. A street sweeper passed by with its brushes spinning, and the sound of its industrious swishing faded as it turned the corner.

They spotted the police car at the same moment.

It was driving straight toward them, no faster than five miles an hour.

The police were looking for someone or something.

Without having discussed how they would handle a situation like this, Niklas Nordgren stopped, squatted down on the sidewalk and pretended to tie his shoelaces. Sami Farhan sped up and sneaked around the corner onto Jakobsbergsgatan, and Michel Maloof continued heading straight for the police car.

Rather than being three men in a group on Malmskillnadsgatan at five in the morning, they now looked like three strangers with different agendas. They seemed less threatening.

The reason Maloof, Nordgren and Sami were on Malmskillnadsgatan that early August morning was that Nordgren was worried. The plan was to blow a hole straight through the roof of the cash depot where Alexandra Svensson worked. They would have ten minutes in total, and Nordgren had promised that the explosion wouldn't take more than a couple of those precious minutes.

But earlier that week, he had learned from Ezra's sister Katinka that the roof of the cash depot in Västberga consisted of three layers. Concrete on the very top, joists beneath that and then the sheet metal protecting the inner ceiling. Blowing a hole in the sheet metal with a U-channel was possible. The joist layer was nothing but wood and insulation, and he could manage that with a saw and a crowbar.

The question was how thick the concrete was.

To avoid any surprises on the day, Nordgren had started looking for buildings that had been built in the same way, so that he could carry out a test. The partially completed building on the corner of Jakobs-bergsgatan and Regeringsgatan in central Stockholm was the result of his search.

Its roof was constructed in the exact same way as Västberga's. Over the summer, the builders had managed to lay the foundations, con-struct the load-bearing outer and inner walls and build the floors and ceilings on each of the eight floors. There was an entire skeleton for Nordgren to practice on, with no risk of anyone getting hurt. But since the building was still under construction, they had been forced to get up at dawn to beat the builders to the site.

Maloof was just a few steps from being able to turn the corner onto Ja-kobsbergsgatan, a pedestrian street, when the police car rolled up next to him. Nordgren was ten yards away, still busy tying his shoelaces. He heard how close the police car was, but managed to stop himself from looking up. It was the most careful knot he had ever tied.

A moment later, out of the corner of his eye he saw the blue-and-white car roll on. He made sure not to get up. As Maloof disappeared around the corner, out of sight, Nordgren took the opportunity to tie his other shoe, and then he got up.

He resisted the urge to turn and check whether the police car had stopped at the crossroads of Mäster Samuelsgatan. Instead, he rushed to catch up with his friends, who were already some way down the steep slope of the pedestrian street.

"Puts you on edge," Sami said.

"With a bag full of explosives in the middle of town, we've got rea-son to be," Nordgren added.

They reached Regeringsgatan without meeting anyone else. Farther down the street they could see a young couple making out furiously;

the girl was pushed up against the wall and was practically climbing the man's leg. They could hear the sound of the street sweeper in the distance.

The iron gate outside the building was locked with a chain and padlock. Nordgren pulled out some clippers. That was all he needed to cut the chain. He opened the gate and they sneaked inside. Nordgren put the chain back in place, with the cut-off section hanging inward. To a passerby, everything would look normal.

"Should we use the elevator?"

Just the thought that the three of them might get stuck in the slow, creaking, rickety building elevator, fully visible from all directions and with a rucksack full of explosives, was completely idiotic.

And it felt no better a minute or so later when they actually stepped inside it.

"This is insane," Sami said.

"Right, right," Maloof agreed.

Nordgren didn't say a word. In just a few minutes' time, he would be trying to blow a hole in a concrete roof in the heart of Stockholm. He didn't want to admit it, but the idea was starting to seem doubtful to him. Though at the same time, the alternative was worse: not having done his homework and being forced to realize that it was impossible at a more critical moment.

The elevator seemed to take forever, and when they finally made it up to the roof, the view wasn't what they had expected. They had been talking about it in the car, how they would be able to look out across the entire city, but the neighboring buildings blocked their line of sight. The haze in the sky suggested it would be a warm day.

Nordgren glanced around. He pointed to a big pile of timber.

"We can use that to shield ourselves," he said.

And with that, he started to prepare the explosives. Like always, he would try a small charge to begin with.

Sami read his thoughts.

"We can't do that now," he said. "You know what I mean? We're on a roof. In the middle of town. The police are driving around right below us. You know? We can't be testing and testing and testing. We're not out in the woods anymore."

"No . . ." Nordgren began hesitantly.

Caution was a virtue he was reluctant to give up.

"Right, right," said Maloof. "One time only. No more. One charge to . . . see if it works. Then we run."

Nordgren heard what they were saying.

"OK," he mumbled, bending down to dig deeper into his rucksack.

They were right, of course. In a few weeks' time, when they were standing on the roof of the cash depot, they wouldn't need to be discreet or precise, it would be a simple matter of blowing a big enough hole to be able to get down to the joist level. And that was the morning's task. To see whether it was possible.

Niklas Nordgren took a small yellow plastic cone from his bag. It was the type soccer teams used when they practiced moving laterally. The shape of the cone was perfect, given that the aim was to aim the explosion directly downward.

Nordgren filled the cone with explosives. He was using red plastic explosives with a detonation velocity of twenty-five thousand feet a second. He wanted to create a concentrated explosion so that he could guarantee a hole. Semtex would have managed the same task, but the explosives used by the military were both more expensive and more difficult to get ahold of. He pressed a detonator into one edge.

"OK," he said. "One try. No more, no less."

He clipped the detonation cable onto the loose wires of the detonator, and the three ran behind the pile of wood and squatted down.

"It's going to be a hell of a bang," Nordgren said matter-of-factly.

Maloof and Sami got onto their knees. They had their hands over their heads, and Nordgren touched the exposed metal of the detonation cable to the poles of the motorbike battery.

The explosion was deafening.

But what came next was worse.

The entire building shook. Nordgren got to his feet, and a second later it was as though the ground had been snatched from beneath them. He hadn't been prepared for that. The pile of timber they were behind fell to one side, and again the noise was incredible, even louder than the initial explosion. Maloof fell over.

"Shit!" Sami shouted.

In a compact cloud of dust, the floor where they had been crouching collapsed onto the one below. Two or three different alarms started ringing simultaneously.

"Sami!" Maloof shouted.

He couldn't see a thing.

"I'm here. Where's Nick?"

"Here!" a voice shouted from the cloud of dust.

They could hear one another, but a few seconds passed before they could see anything.

"We need to get out!"

Nordgren started running toward the elevator, which, unbelievably, seemed to have survived the blast unscathed. Sami and Maloof followed him. As the dust started to settle, they studied the damage around them.

Sirens from emergency vehicles could be heard in the distance.

They ran into the elevator and Nordgren pushed the button. The motor started with a jolt, slowly winching them toward the ground. Down on the street, a crowd of people had already gathered.

"What the fuck happened?" asked Sami.

His forehead was damp, his eyes bright. He shook his sweater. Flapped it here and there.

"Bad workmanship," Nordgren replied. "We took down the entire roof."

"Shit!"

Maloof started to laugh. Sami's mouth twitched.

"You two are insane," Nordgren snapped. "It's not funny. The place'll be crawling with cops any minute."

After what seemed like an eternity, they reached the ground. The alarms on the building site sounded even louder down there. A TV van pulled up by the sidewalk at roughly the same time as the first fire engine from the station on Malmskillnadsgatan arrived. The explosion had even set off three or four car alarms.

People were pouring in from all directions.

The three men responsible for the chaos discreetly left the former eight-story building as the firemen stormed inside. Nordgren, Sami and Maloof sneaked quietly past the spectators on the sidewalk, all of whom were desperate to get a glimpse of what was going on.

"This is insane," Sami said as they moved quickly down Jakobs-bergsgatan.

None of the three turned as the police cars began to arrive, their sirens blaring. They headed back to the car without saying a word, and only once they had climbed inside and shut the doors did Nordgren break the silence.

"Fuck," he said. "It didn't even make a hole. We're not going to be able to get in through the roof."

32

On Karlavägen, just around the corner from Skeppargatan, there was an elegant candy store called Karla Frukt. It had been there since the midsixties, supplying the neighborhood's praline-eating residents and sugar-starved students with sweet treats. Its pretty neon sign, shaped like a peeled orange, lit up the front of the building. The front windows of the shop angled into the building, giving Caroline Thurn space to stand in the shadow of the overhanging roof by the entrance. Tucked away there, she could be completely invisible, despite the streetlight illuminating the sidewalk just a few yards away. It was two thirty in the morning, a clear summer's night, and Karlavägen was quiet.

Karla Frukt was diagonally opposite the door Thurn and Berggren had been keeping under surveillance, the door to the supposed brothel. Thurn knew she should drop the case, but she didn't want to. The National Criminal Police had been brought in because the case involved ambassadors, foreign citizens committing crimes on Swedish soil. The information they had was from a reliable source, and the vice squad also supported their theory of a brothel.

The traffic along Karlavägen was separated by a wide footpath in the middle of the road. Lawns, leafy trees and thick bushes had been planted along the gravel path on which dogs were exercised in the evenings and children walked to school in the mornings. Thurn had been standing in the entrance to Karla Frukt since midnight, and nothing had happened. No one had either entered or left the building opposite.

She hadn't bothered to ask Berggren whether he wanted to come with her. Right now, he was completely focused on the cash depot robbery, and he would have just told her to hand the case over to their colleagues in vice. In all likelihood, the supposed brothel probably had as many visits from Swedish dignitaries as it did foreign ones, and her colleagues at Stockholm Police also needed something to do.

Thurn smiled to herself. She could just hear Berggren's argument.

And then she saw him.

On the other side of Karlavägen, a lone man was walking along the street. Thurn had noticed him as he passed Artillerigatan, he was on his way toward Karlaplan. Almost immediately, she had taken in his unusual walking style. He limped, as though one leg was shorter than the other, and every step he took involved pushing his right hip forward with a slight twist.

It took Thurn a few seconds to retrieve the relevant information from the rich archive of her subconscious. She knew exactly who the man with the limp was.

On the opposite sidewalk, at two thirty in the morning, in the middle of one of Stockholm's sleepiest neighborhoods, a recently retired headmaster from the deepest forests of Värmland was out for a walk. Jan Löwenheim.

And given everything Caroline Thurn knew about Headmaster Löwenheim, the chances that he was heading for the brothel the police had long been trying to uncover were good.

Thurn was halfway over the road when Löwenheim reached the building she had been watching. But rather than stopping, the limping man continued past the door and turned the corner onto Grevgatan, just before the roundabout by Karlaplan's fountains. Thurn started to run.

The fact that Löwenheim had passed the brothel both surprised and relieved her.

She rounded the corner at high speed, and found herself about to run straight into the older man. He was standing outside the entrance to Grevgatan 63 with one hand on the door handle, and he turned around in panic.

"I, what?" he exclaimed.

His shock was understandable. He hadn't seen another living soul in several minutes, only to find himself being almost mowed down.

Thurn stopped dead. Her pulse was racing, her breathing heavy, and she had no idea what to say.

In the next instant, he recognized her.

"Caroline?" he said. "Is that you, Caroline? My . . . what a coincidence!"

She tried to compose herself.

"Headmaster Löwenheim," she replied. "It's . . . been a while."

He held out a hand and she took it automatically, shaking it as though she was thanking him for a diploma at a graduation ceremony. His handshake was limp and damp, she remembered it well. But it wasn't his handshake that the girls at school had gossiped about, it was the hugs that quickly became too intimate, the glances that lingered for far too long before they reached your eyes. The scandal with the matron in one of the boardinghouses was something Löwenheim could never shake off.

"I saw your father only last week, at a dinner in Nääs," Löwenheim now said. "He seemed to be in good spirits."

"Yes," Thurn replied evasively. "I'm sure he is."

"We spoke about your brother for quite some time, but we never got round to you . . ."

"No," she said, "these things happen."

Caroline von Thurn hadn't used her noble "von" since she realized that Grefvelsta Gård in Närke, the place where she and her father, her grandfather and great-grandfather had all grown up, would be taken away from her.

She was fifteen at the time, and had recently enrolled at Lundsberg boarding school, where her classmates had explained what would happen. She wouldn't get a thing. Thanks to laws dating back to the seventeenth century, the farm and its land would be inherited by her younger brother. Fifty years earlier, the Swedish parliament had agreed to phase out the so-called *fideicommissum*, the rule that decreed that the oldest son was the heir of his ancestors, but an exception had been made for Grefvelsta, among other places.

To begin with, she hadn't believed her friends. Thurn had called her mother that evening, but all she had been able to do was refer her to her father. She explained that she had nothing to do with "all that"; it was something her father had decided.

And when her father came to her school a few weeks later, it wasn't for Thurn's sake, it was because he sat on the governing board. He was more irritated by her questions than anything else. He didn't need to justify a thing, he couldn't be held accountable. It was just how it was, the way it had always been, it wasn't about fairness. People were born into a certain context, in a certain place, some were born men and others were born women. The girls in the family would never be running farms or inheriting land.

When her father left that day, the betrayal had burned in Thurn's throat and heart. By evening, she could barely breathe. It was as though a thin, beautiful rug on which her entire childhood was depicted had been pulled out from beneath her feet, leaving her standing on an earth floor that stunk of old prejudices and was steeped in small-mindedness.

Over the week that followed, her initial shock was replaced by a deep sense of injustice. It was something she would nourish and develop during the three years she spent at that boarding school in the forests of Värmland. When she graduated from high school, it had long been too late for her to return to her family home.

The day she left school was the last time she saw her father, mother and brother. There were no dramatic farewells, she was far too well raised for that kind of drama; causing scenes was something that the boarding school drummed out of its pupils, if they hadn't already learned it earlier. She would see her mother and father again if it was necessary. If not, she wouldn't bother.

And so, Caroline von Thurn became Caroline Thurn, and she sought out a different life for herself.

She became a police officer.

"Well," said Headmaster Löwenheim, "running into one another like this, in the middle of the night? But I'm afraid I must hurry off."

"Aha?" said Thurn. "Where are you heading?"

In the moment he recognized her, he had let go of the door handle as though it had burned him. He now mumbled a vague reply.

"I have a sister whose sister-in-law lives around the corner. I sometimes help . . . it was urgent . . . she has trouble with her hip . . . living alone isn't easy."

He was already on his way, backing up a few steps.

"Say hello to your parents, Caroline," he added before turning around.

She stood there, watching as he limped away. She let him leave.

Then she turned to the door he had been about to go through.

This address on Grevgatan, this entrance, led into the same building they had been watching on Karlavägen. And she realized it was the reason she had never seen anyone go in or out of the brothel.

The ambassadors and members of society who frequented the establishment would enter through this considerably more discreet entrance around the corner.

Sometimes, the answer was simpler than you wanted to believe, Thurn thought.

She slowly walked back out onto Karlavägen. As she did, she called for backup. The uniformed officers could go up into the building and catch the men there in the act.

There was no doubt about where Löwenheim had been heading, and when he failed to follow through on his plans, he had inadvertently revealed them.

Caroline Thurn no longer had any interest in going in to make the arrests herself. If the headmaster knew about the brothel, there was a risk that other men from her father's circles might be up there in its bedrooms. And she was happy to avoid that discovery.

33

When Maloof pulled into the parking garage at Skärholmen Centrum on Tuesday, August 25, it wasn't particularly busy. For once. He had planned for them to keep moving along the long, shop-lined corridors of the shopping center, but he changed his mind when he saw how quiet it was. Zoran Petrovic was a head taller than everyone else, and it took a real crowd to hide him.

Better to go for a walk in the woods around the shopping center, Maloof thought, pulling in between two dirty gray cars—it was impossible to determine their make, an Asian variant of some old car.

The parking garage smelled of exhaust fumes and greenery. Maloof took a deep breath and shivered in the cool breeze. On the backseat, he found a scarf that must have been lying there since spring. He wasn't ready for autumn yet.

He also hated problems. Petrovic was suddenly having to find a new pilot. Nordgren hadn't managed to blow a hole in the concrete roof, meaning they had to come up with another way of getting in. If that was even possible. Everything seemed to be going against them all of a sudden.

Maloof saw Petrovic's blue BMW approaching from the north entrance. He also noticed the car that pulled in after it, a silvery-gray Saab. It was no more than a brief observation, however; the car rolled on and he soon forgot about it.

Petrovic parked and then the tall Yugoslavian came loping across the garage in his short, pale summer coat. He waved cheerily.

Maloof replied by pointing toward the woods.

Petrovic turned and started to walk in the other direction, away from the shopping center. Maloof followed him.

Rather than parking, the silvery-gray Saab continued to creep along at a safe distance behind Maloof and Petrovic.

The first stage of their walk took them down a winding path deep into the forest, over hills and past small fields. The ground was dry, the deep furrows the summer rain had dug into the gravel on the slopes had vanished without a trace, and Maloof's new sneakers survived without getting dirty.

They were talking about helicopter pilots.

"I might have a guy," the ever-hopeful Petrovic said. "When I was down in Cannes last time, I met an American who . . . he was in the import and transport branch. Sold American chemicals that made potatoes grow bigger. Or maybe it was less grainy? Anyway, he'd been in . . . the transport branch . . . a long time. And when he was working over in the West Indies, he'd had a helicopter pilot who flew stuff between the islands. That guy, Kluger, he's been in Sweden for a few years now."

The path led them out into an open field, and they passed an abandoned farm. Maloof had never seen a single sign of life in there. As they reached the middle of the open field, approaching the next wooded area, something made him turn around and look back.

The silvery-gray Saab was parked by a broken fence, almost out of sight. This time, Maloof paid attention to it. He waited until they were back among the trees before he said anything.

"We've got company."

"What?"

"We've got company," he repeated. "Look."

They walked back on themselves. Maloof pointed between the thinning trunks and Petrovic saw the silvery-gray car.

"It followed you into the parking lot."

"Me?" said Petrovic. "Are you sure?"

Maloof smiled and shrugged. "Yeah, yeah," he said. "No."

"No?"

"Let's check."

Rather than continue into the woods, Maloof turned back and cut across the grass to the narrow paved road that passed the abandoned farm, the way the Saab must have driven. Petrovic followed him. After walking for a few minutes, Maloof took out his phone and held it in front of him. In the reflection of the screen, they saw the car start up and slowly begin to follow them.

"Shit," Petrovic swore.

They continued toward the shopping center parking garage. Maloof's intention was to shake off the tail by heading down into the subway. An increasingly irritated Petrovic, however, seemed to have different plans.

"Jesus Christ," the Yugoslavian swore. "This is so fucking low. We'll show that bastard. He's got no damn right to follow us. We haven't done anything."

"Well, I mean . . ."

"Today. We haven't done anything today."

They had reached the parking garage, and while the silvery-gray car continued to creep along the small road, Petrovic ran to his BMW and jumped in. He leaned across the passenger seat and opened the door for Maloof.

"Come on!" he shouted.

Hesitantly, Maloof climbed inside. In the rearview mirror, he saw the Saab approach the entrance to the parking garage and then come to a halt. After that, everything happened very quickly. Petrovic reversed out of the space so quickly that the tires screeched. He threw the car into first gear, revved the engine and drove straight at the exit. To make his intentions even clearer, he sounded the horn madly.

"What are you doing?" Maloof shouted in surprise.

Petrovic didn't reply, he just continued to drive straight forward. The driver of the Saab realized that he would end up on the wrong side of the exit unless he did something, and so he picked up speed and made it just before Petrovic, who turned the corner on two wheels.

"What are you doing?!" Maloof shouted again.

The sudden turn had thrown him against the door, and he crawled back upright and put on his seat belt.

"We'll get him. I want to ask why that bastard is following us!" Petrovic snapped irritatedly, attempting to talk over the engine, which was approaching 4,500 revs.

"Right, right," Maloof mumbled. "We'll get him. We'll get him?"

The German car roared. The Saab was a hundred or so yards ahead of them, on its way up the exit to the highway.

"We'll force him off the road!"

Maloof didn't reply. It was the worst idea he had ever heard. He glanced over to the speedometer. They were already doing a hundred, but the Saab seemed determined not to let them catch it.

"Why isn't he stopping?!" Petrovic yelled.

The Saab was heading toward Södertälje, and Petrovic kept after it. They were almost bumper to bumper, but whenever the traffic thickened, the tall Yugoslavian changed his mind and focused on survival.

"We're chasing a cop," Maloof pointed out.

"That's the way it should be," Petrovic said, laughing.

"Right, right," Maloof agreed. "But if he's police, why doesn't he just pull over, stop us and give us a ticket for speeding?"

After passing the exit for Fittja and Botkyrka at 120 miles per hour, they approached Södertälje.

"To hell with this now," Maloof pleaded.

He looked indifferent, as usual, but inside, the panic was rising. However this ended, it couldn't be good. But Petrovic seemed to have no intention of giving up.

On the straight stretch to the south of Salem, they saw the roadblock. Right in the middle of the highway.

To begin with, it seemed to be nothing but a single patrol car with its blue lights flashing, but the closer they came, the clearer it became that this was something else. Maloof could count five police cars parked across the road, waiting for them.

"Shit," Maloof mumbled, sinking into his seat as though he were trying to make himself invisible.

Up ahead, the silvery-gray Saab slowed down. The cars blocking the road moved to the side, and it passed them. The gap closed again behind it.

Petrovic braked. He slowly pulled up and came to a halt a few yards from the patrol cars, he wound down his window. A female police officer came over and nonchalantly greeted him, as though she were helping a tourist with directions.

Maloof was expecting the worst, but nothing happened.

"That was a bit fast, wasn't it?" she said kindly.

Maloof couldn't believe it. Why did she sound so friendly?

"We want to report that car," Petrovic said, pointing to the Saab which was vanishing into the distance. "He's been harassing us."

"In what way has he been harassing you?"

"He was following us."

"Really?" the officer replied, giving Petrovic a few seconds to think.

"Not right now," Petrovic said when he realized why she had paused. "That was me following him. But only to ask him to stop following us."

"I suggest we draw a line under this," the police officer said. "You've clearly been following one another. I think we can leave it like that?"

Maloof continued to stare through the window, but the situation was just getting stranger and stranger. Why weren't they asking for driver's licenses, ID, how could she not point out that they had been driving at 120 miles an hour?

The police directed Petrovic onto the other side of the highway, where he could drive back to Stockholm.

SEPTEMBER 2009

34

"Seems like an uphill struggle," said Ali Farhan.

"Tricky," Adil Farhan agreed.

Sami Farhan shrugged. His brothers were, of course, right.

They were eating dinner at their uncle's restaurant in Liljeholmen, and the fact that they were three brothers sitting around a table wasn't something anyone could have missed. Big brother Ali looked oldest, tougher than the others, with furrows on his forehead and around his eyes. Still, his eyes and nose were identical to Sami's. Their younger brother, Adil, had considerably more hair and smaller eyes. There was also a sense of calm about him, whereas both Sami and Ali gestured intensely as they spoke, and radiated the same kind of impatience.

"I mean, sometimes it's just like that," Sami defended himself. "Things are a bit up and down?"

"Yeah, but there are uphill struggles and uphill struggles. You lot seem to be stuck," Ali determined.

Coming to the restaurant as a guest was a very different experience from working in its cramped kitchen. In the kitchen, you toiled away and were proud of your work. The equipment wasn't new, but it was well cared for; the fresh ingredients weren't exclusive, but they were carefully chosen. Ambitions were always high in the kitchen, and the food they prepared was worthy of a better fate than ending up in the hands of the weary serving staff who carried the plates out into the tired, dark restaurant that looked like any other drinking hole.

Being a guest should have been better than working on the cold buffet, but to Sami it was the exact opposite. He had just gone through the situation. Not in detail, but he had given his brothers the bigger picture. There was no doubt they were right. Right now, everything was going in the wrong direction.

"We've got something on the go," said Ali. "Maybe you could hang with us instead?"

"Yeah," Adil agreed. "It would be cool. Like back in the day."

Sami squirmed.

"I need to pay people back first," he said. "You know what I mean? You get your interest first, then we can talk about the future."

"Take it easy, little brother," said Ali.

"The hell with that. We'll get the money when you get the money. No more complicated than that," Adil backed him up.

Sami knew they wanted to be kind, that they wanted to play down the fact he had burned their money and allowed himself to be screwed over by the captain of some fucking ship. But neither the fact that Hassan Kaya had also been burned nor his brothers' consideration made it feel any better. He owed them, and he had to repay that debt. As well as the promised interest.

"No, it doesn't work like that," Sami said, pulling at the neck of his T-shirt. "I made you a promise. You know?"

They understood, but they took no notice of him. Ali changed the subject and started talking about soccer instead. Adil joined in. Sami had nothing to add to a conversation about Chelsea and Arsenal, and he quickly retreated to the silence that his brothers always reduced him to.

They ordered coffee and tiramisu.

It was his older brother, Ali, who had dealt out the roles in their family, in the much the same way as you would deal a pack of cards. It was him the siblings had looked up to during their teens, when they first started trying to find their own identities; he was the one they had feared and admired. But once the others had taken their cards and defined themselves, the pack was dealt, and Sami's position between his protective older brother and explosive younger sibling was still something he struggled to define. There had been days, moments, when he thought he had finally managed to find an image of himself, but then the outline had quickly lost its sharpness and vanished. All that had been left for Sami was the Joker.

"It has to be over for United now," Ali said, as though it were a question. "Everything has its time, and Manchester United's is over. Finished. Done. From now on, it's all about Arsenal."

"Arsenal!" Adil shouted, pretending to look shocked. "How the hell can you say that? Arsenal? Did I miss Drogba being transferred?

They laughed at the joke, and Sami laughed with them, though he didn't know why. He didn't care about soccer, never had, he was the middle brother who didn't quite fit in. For a long time during his teens, the solution had been to wrap his hands tight, pull on the boxing gloves and punch his knuckles bloody on sandbags and balls. He had feinted and jabbed at the shadows of a father he could barely remember and who had left behind the mystery of why he disappeared. Then, damp with sweat, his brow split and his rib broken, Sami had been able to slump into the changing room after the fight and, for an hour or two, while his body recovered, experience a peace he never usually felt.

Now, in the restaurant, Sami found himself getting lost in his thoughts. No one, neither his brothers nor the friends who had invested in his plan, had pressured him to repay the money. But he had made each of them a solemn vow that he would get it by autumn. The Stockholm underworld had been his witness. Everyone had heard him say it, and now it was already September.

"Listen to me now, Sami," Ali said, tasting the dessert that had been more or less dumped onto their table. "I still think you should stick with us. Screw whatever you've got planned, it doesn't seem to be working anyway."

"We've come too far to drop it now," Sami mumbled.

"Sometimes you've got to spend a bit of time on something before you see the truth," Ali said wisely, giving Adil an encouraging look. The younger brother nodded in agreement.

Sami left his brothers in Liljeholmen at eleven and took the subway back to Södermalm. He had been away for most of the past few weeks.

There were moments when Karin let him know that, but then there were evenings like tonight.

When he got back to the apartment, both kids were asleep and Karin was sitting on the sofa. She smiled when she saw him.

"What?" he asked suspiciously, taking a few steps into the room.

"I watched a romantic comedy," she said. "It put me in a good mood and I remembered why I let you convince me."

"Convince you? How did I convince you?"

"I could've kept my clothes on, you know?" she said. "Or at least my underwear. But I didn't. You convinced me."

"I've got the gift of the gab," he smirked.

"Maybe. But you'd also poured a lot of vodka down my throat."

"The two aren't mutually exclusive."

He peeled off his coat and threw it onto an armchair. Then he moved over and sat down next to her on the sofa, but he was still on his guard. Over the past few days, he had been worried that she knew what he was planning. On a few occasions, both yesterday and the day before, she had repeated her mantra: that their relationship was built on him not doing anything stupid. And by that, she didn't mean other women; she wasn't worried about that. Sami had loved Karin since high school and there would never be anyone else for him. She knew that.

"Why're you saying that?" he had asked. "I haven't done anything I shouldn't."

"Just a reminder," she replied.

He hated female intuition.

But now, he put an arm around her and pulled her close.

"I seem to remember," he said, his face so close to hers that he could smell her lipstick, "that you took off your bra before I even suggested it."

Karin smiled, wormed her way out of his grip and got up.

"Not the first time," she replied. "It's every other time you're thinking of."

She pulled her top up, over her head.

35

On the morning of Wednesday, September 9, Detective Chief Inspector Caroline Thurn left the offices of a business called Panaxia on Linta Gårdsväg 5 in Bromma. There were six days to go until the biggest heist in Swedish criminal history.

Without letting on that the situation was critical, she had spent over an hour in the Panaxia meeting room on the third floor, going over every conceivable scenario with the management team. The room was bright and airy, and low-flying planes passed overhead at regular intervals on their descent into Bromma airport.

For Thurn, the conversation had walked a fine line between revealing too much and making sure she wouldn't regret anything in a week's time. If she told them everything she knew, there was a risk the information would be leaked, which could result in the robbers changing their plans. But if she didn't prepare Panaxia for what might happen and one of the company's employees ended up getting hurt, she would bitterly regret her secrecy.

Panaxia was on the verge of moving some of its business activity away from Bromma. In exactly one week's time, on Wednesday, September 16, the move was scheduled to finish, but until then, the company would be more vulnerable than usual, from a security point of view. As a result, it was "positive that the police are showing an appropriate level of interest," as Panaxia's security chief put it.

Thurn, who hadn't known about the move in advance, nodded in agreement.

They had gone over the flow of the building in detail, and when Thurn eventually got up on her long legs to shake hands with everyone in the room, she thought she had found the answer to the question they had been searching for.

She knew where the helicopter robbery would take place.

The car was parked directly outside the entrance. As Thurn sat down behind the wheel and fastened her seat belt, the feeling that Panaxia was some kind of provincial cousin to the international G4S welled up. On the one hand, its staff did their best, but on the other, their best wasn't enough. There was something that didn't seem right about the country's second-biggest secure transport company, but Thurn couldn't put her finger on exactly what that was.

Maybe the robbers had made the same observation?

She started the Volvo and pulled out into the road.

The figure the Serbian informant had mentioned to the police, a haul of up to €10 million, could be found in only three places in Stockholm. The central bank and the two cash depots, Panaxia in Bromma and G4S in Västberga.

It was unlikely that anyone would attempt to rob the central bank. It was one of the few buildings in Sweden that even Caroline Thurn dared call secure, and there was no way you could land a helicopter on the roof.

Of the two remaining depots, only Panaxia in Bromma matched the description of a four-story building with a flat roof.

Today, Thurn had learned that the company had been planning to move parts of its business for some time, and that the move was scheduled to begin on the fourteenth of September. The robbers had chosen the fifteenth, which had to be seen as the optimal time, given that the company would be particularly vulnerable then.

Whoever was planning the robbery had to have someone on the inside of Panaxia, Thurn thought; otherwise, they would never have found such a perfect opportunity. She wondered whether she could ask for lists of employees now, without raising suspicions. She turned left onto Drottningholmsvägen and headed back toward Alvik and Kungsholmen.

On the way up to her department in police HQ, Thurn passed the colleagues responsible for listening in on Zoran Petrovic.

They had microphones hidden in Petrovic's restaurants on Upplandsgatan, in the bedroom and living room of his apartment and in the headrest of his BMW. The resources that had been put at the disposal of the investigation were wastefully large, and Thurn knew that this was partly because of the personal involvement of the minister for foreign affairs in the case.

But she also knew that the national police commissioner's plan was to defend the increased costs at the end of the year by going public with the international success their efforts had led to.

And that success was something she held Caroline Thurn responsible for.

Thurn stuck her head around the door into a room full of electronics. "Nothing?" she asked.

Two technicians wearing headphones turned to the doorway and stared at her like they had just woken up. Their eyes were red and they didn't look like they had changed their clothes in weeks. A couple of empty white cartons on the desk made the place stink of Chinese food.

"You kidding?" one of them said.

"You've always been a real joker, Caroline," said the other.

"No," the inspector said with a friendly smile. "Not joking at all."

The technicians sighed.

Bugging Zoran Petrovic was a bit like pointing a microphone toward a soccer stadium during a derby and then hoping to hear someone whisper. Words poured into the ears of the police officers who, in increasing confusion, allowed hard drive after hard drive to fill up with talk of great deals and boasts about conquests of impossibly beautiful women.

Though Petrovic didn't appear in any of the police databases, the officers listening to him were certain that someone had taught him to speak like a seasoned criminal. He never named names, and whatever he did say usually lacked a time and a place.

The police now knew that Zoran Petrovic was active in the building trade, but he also seemed to have a finger in the cleaning and restaurant trade, the beauty world, the import and export branches. Exactly what he did, owned or spent his time doing in any of these areas remained unclear, however. It was possible that he was just a silent partner, some kind of adviser, or maybe the businesses were run by dummies and Petrovic himself was ultimately in control. In all likelihood, it was a combination of all those things, but since Petrovic's phone conversations were vague and elusive, never naming names or exact amounts, this was all guesswork on the part of the police.

During an ordinary day, he might have upward of twenty meetings, and they took place all over Stockholm. He could send fifty text messages and make a similar number of calls, half of them in Montenegrin, a language closely related to Serbian. Since the police interpreters weren't always available, there was a chance they would find something more useful in the conversations that weren't in Swedish, but judging by the conversations they'd had translated so far, the content seemed to be exactly the same.

They weren't getting anywhere. The only reference to the helicopter robbery came when Petrovic uttered that he was planning something on September 15. But that was something the Serbs had known from the beginning.

Caroline Thurn struggled on up the stairs and down the corridors of police headquarters. She was just passing Mats Berggren's room, heading for her own office farther down the corridor, when he saw her and shouted.

Thurn stopped. The sun was so low in the sky during the morning that she was no more than a silhouette in his doorway.

"How did it go?" he asked.

"It's going to be Panaxia," she said.

The information about their upcoming move had convinced her.

She had her left hand high on the doorframe, meaning that the sleeve of her blouse had slipped down her arm. If the light had been different, he never would have noticed it. But the smooth skin of the scar shone straight across Thurn's wrist, and Berggren immediately recognized the type of wound.

He had been on the verge of asking something else about the cash depot in Bromma, but he lost his train of thought. If it had been anyone else, the discovery wouldn't have hit him nearly as hard.

"What are you thinking, Mats?" Thurn asked. She had noticed something had happened to her colleague.

"No, no . . . nothing," he mumbled.

She shrugged and left his doorway.

36

Zoran Petrovic was sitting in Café Stolen, and he felt restless. It made him a bad listener. He glanced down at his watch. He was meeting the potential new helicopter pilot in an hour, but until then he was stuck listening to a vegetable grower from Poland who was trying to establish himself in Årsta. The Pole needed help with both contacts and cash, and he was bragging about his biodynamically grown carrots and beetroot. Petrovic, who was relatively familiar with the vegetable trade after a few attempts to break into the market himself, knew that the care the farmer put into the quality of his produce would never be compensated for in price. He hated meetings that ended on a bad note.

After escorting the Pole to the door, Petrovic took a moment to glance up and down the street. To begin with, he didn't spot anyone, but then he saw them. They were standing on Upplandsgatan. Over the past week, they had been everywhere. It might be the badly dressed, early middle-aged man who turned around when he left the pub late one night. Or the neutrally dressed woman pretending to stare into an uninteresting window opposite the door of his building.

The police always seemed to be able to catch the scent whenever anything particular was on the go, once the vague talk turned into concrete plans, and the stroll along the water's edge in Gröndal was now about a security company's routines rather than last night's girl. Petrovic had long since stopped being surprised by the sharp nose of the police force, and he now accepted it as a fact.

Besides, that refined sense of smell had reached the same level of sophistication on both sides of the law.

Someone within the police force or prosecution authority must have suddenly decided it was worth keeping Petrovic under tabs, and he felt a reluctant sense of flattery. His relationship with his self-image was split. Just over a year earlier, his face had accidentally flashed up in a TV4 report on criminality in Farsta. He had barely been involved, but he was still the one the camera crew had caught on film. As a result, he had ended up in custody. Petrovic had sued the TV channel and been awarded a symbolic figure as some kind of sticking plaster over the wound. All the same, other than that film, the police didn't have anything on him.

Which meant that their newfound interest both worried and amused him.

Just before twelve, Café Stolen started to fill up with lunch guests, meaning it was time for Zoran Petrovic to leave. He had to get out to Saltsjöbaden to meet the American pilot Jack Kluger, but his new followers left him with no choice but to perform an evasive maneuver first.

Petrovic left the restaurant, crossed Tegnérlunden, walked down the hill toward Sveavägen and then continued straight ahead. His two tails did the same. When the Yugoslavian reached Birger Jarlsgatan, he turned right and paused outside a food shop. His followers slowed down and stopped ten yards away, pretending to be interested in the way a garage door had been constructed.

Using the reflection in the shop window, Petrovic decided that Jason, who worked in a computer shop farther down the street, had followed his instructions. He glanced in the direction of the plainclothes police officers, smiled and waved.

Everything happened very quickly after that.

Petrovic ran straight across Birger Jarlsgatan. He jumped over the barriers at the bus stop and continued toward the motorbikes parked on the other side. He leaped onto a Honda whose engine was already running and, with a roar, tore off in the direction of Roslagstull.

He left the two disconcerted police officers in his wake.

Petrovic drove at high speed for a few minutes, passing Odengatan, and then turned right onto Surbrunnsgatan and parked the bike outside the building where Jason lived. He hung the keys on a forked branch on the cherry tree by the door and then walked up Valhallavägen to find a taxi out to Saltsjöbaden.

37

"You seem a bit low, Michel?"

Alexandra Svensson was looking at him with concern. It was just before lunch on a Tuesday as overcast as Maloof's mood, and they were walking across the bridge toward Skeppsholmen, trying to ignore the fact that they were freezing. Summer was definitely over, and autumn's arrival had been abrupt. Despite that, Alexandra was dressed for summer, in a skirt and blouse with a thin cardigan on top. It hadn't been a good choice.

She had been nagging Maloof to go to the Moderna Museet with her for several weeks now, and he had finally given in.

He deeply regretted that decision.

He had experienced setbacks before. Without making any claim to be scientific about it, he would say that nine plans out of ten never came off. The criminal life was, just like all other ways of living, based on hopes and dreams. The wildest ideas were barely ever meant to come true; they were more like a box of chocolates—something sweet to savor for a moment.

He would even say that it was quite unusual to get as far as they had with the Västberga plan. Being forced to call it off now, with just days to go, when they'd thought they had everything in place, was out of the question.

They had met two days earlier, at the Kvarnen pub in Södermalm. Sami, Maloof and Nordgren. They had arrived early, before it filled up, and sat at one of the tables behind the bar, at the very back.

When you were planning a job, the first rule was that you never allowed the group to be seen together so close to the deed. But they hadn't had any choice.

"You're sure?" Sami had asked.

"I'm sure." Maloof nodded. "Absolutely."

"I trust you," Sami swore. "I trust you. It's your friend I don't know. I've never even met him. You know what I'm saying? You can't trust someone you don't know. And the fact he has a tail . . ."

"And it's definitely him with the tail?" asked Nordgren. "Not you?"

Maloof nodded. After the incident in Skärholmen, he had spent the rest of the week reassuring himself that no one was after him. He had hunted for bugs, searched for shadows, but nothing. He'd had no contact with Petrovic, so he had no idea how things were on that front.

"I'm clean," he said. "So that thing with the car . . . it's not something else. It isn't the first time they've tried the scare tactics."

"Easier to cut him out than risk it, maybe?" Sami suggested. "Maybe? You know? I don't know if—"

"No. We need him," Maloof interrupted. "He's in."

Sami didn't reply. He pulled at the neck of his T-shirt, trying to make it looser; maybe he needed more space to breathe.

"That's not the issue anyway," said Nordgren.

He met their eyes from beneath his cap.

"It's the roof," he explained.

"But we need to work something out?" said Sami. "You know? After plan A, there has to be a plan B. That's how it works. Something happens, we move on to plan C. Then D, then E, then F?"

They nodded. But what was plan F?

Maloof had gone home after that, and taken out the drawings of the building in Västberga. He had spread them out on the living room floor. The answer had to be there somewhere. If you couldn't go through the roof, if that wasn't possible, maybe they didn't need a helicopter and a pilot after all?

But how could you get up onto the sixth floor any other way?

On Saturday, he had sent a message saying he couldn't play in the soccer match that had been planned for that afternoon. On Sunday, he had called his mother and said he felt lousy, and rather than going for Sunday lunch with his parents and siblings, he'd gone up to Kungens Kurva, bought food from McDonald's and then returned to the drawings, which had to contain the key. Breaking the glass skylight would be easy enough, but what would they do then? There was nothing beneath the dome, just six floors of free fall.

"No, no," he now replied to Alexandra Svensson, not looking her in the eye. "I think I'm just getting a cold, that's all."

She shook her head. Women were always complaining that Maloof was hard to understand, that he was hard to read. He didn't react the way they expected him to, he remained calm until the day he ended things. He rarely got angry, never showed any weakness, and that was why Alexandra's intuition confused him. He hadn't behaved any differently with her than he had with the others.

The waves were foaming beneath the bridge. The wind was strong, and they hurried over to the island on the other side.

"A cold? Really? You never said anything about that yesterday?"

Alexandra had called early on Monday morning. By then he had already decided that his strategy of staying locked up in his apartment in Fittja wasn't sustainable. Maloof wasn't really the giving up type, and setbacks tended to make him more determined to prove the opposite. But he did admit that it felt tough.

"Sometimes," she said as they continued up the hill on the other side of the bridge, "things can feel, like, hopeless."

"Yeah, yeah, that's true."

"So let's say something's happened," she continued.

"I think it's just the start of a cold," Maloof insisted.

"But say it's not that," she said firmly. "Say it's like I said, something tough's happened, and that's why you look like you want to hang your-self or something?"

Maloof didn't reply. He was staring straight ahead and continued to plod up the hill toward the museum building that the original Spanish architect, after all the political modifications, no longer wanted to be associated with.

"That's when you've got to find that extra bit of strength, Michel," Alexandra continued. "That power we've got, the thing that's made us come this far. You know?"

He couldn't help but smile and run his hand over his beard. Every time things felt too much, she was there to support him. But as nice as it was to have her support, he also felt a pang of guilt.

Maloof was used to living a double life. During all the years he'd worked at the youth center in Fittja, his family and friends had thought that was how he earned his money. As a youth leader. No one knew that at night, he pulled a balaclava over his head, or that in parallel with his law-abiding life, he'd also found himself another career, a profitable kind of moonlighting. But that was how he had wanted it, and it wasn't something that had bothered him.

But now, with Alexandra, things felt different.

He felt less and less comfortable lying to her.

They had reached the open space by the museum entrance, and Maloof stopped.

"Right, right," he agreed. "You've got to be strong. But you've gotta be a realist too. Being an optimist can't mean that . . . you're a dreamer?"

"Find a new solution," Alexandra said firmly. "That's why I like you, Michel. You're like, the happiest person I've ever met. It's like there are no barriers for you, you know? Like, you fix them."

"No," said Maloof. "Well . . ."

"Come on, Mickey," she said, laughing, using the nickname he hated.

"Yeah, yeah," he said with a smile. "I'll sort it out."

He looked at her big, pale pink lips, shiny with gloss; lips that never wanted to stop talking. He raised his gaze and met her blue eyes.

"Cheer up now," she said. "Is there anything I can do to help?"

He laughed again. At how easy he was to read, and at how right she was.

"Yeah, yeah," he said. "You can help."

"So tell me how?"

"You can let me off going to the museum today."

"I can help in any way. Other than that, I guess," she replied with a laugh, pulling him toward the entrance.

38

Jack Kluger parked his Jeep in the Royal Swedish Yacht Club parking lot and crossed the bridge onto Restaurantholmen on foot. Tucked into the cove behind him was Saltsjöbaden's magnificent Grand Hotel Stora. Not that big, white houses impressed a man from Texas. To him, the natural world of Stockholm's inner archipelago was far more exotic. The moss-covered rocks, the trails lined with last year's needles and fallen leaves, the pines and spruce trees whose dense foliage created a green grotto all around him. The smell of the brackish water of Baggensfjärden blowing in over the islet.

Kluger had never been there before, but he immediately knew that the tall wooden building that rose up by the rocks at the water's edge was the place he was looking for. Stockholm's only open-air baths, hidden away and grand in their decay. When building work had started on the baths over a century earlier, there had been plans for an amphitheater on the slope down to the water; it would be somewhere people could sit in high galleries, watching the swimmers jump from the protruding jetties below. But the money ran out before the building was finished, meaning the jetties and high wooden walls with their narrow balconies looked less Grecian and more archipelago.

By September, the tired old outdoor baths, with their three sections for men, women and communal bathing, were abandoned for the season. Kluger found a way in and immediately spotted his contact, who was on his phone up in one of the balconies. The American climbed the narrow spiral staircase, his colorful boots echoing in the stairwell.

"Jesus, you make a lot of noise," Zoran Petrovic shouted from a distance.

Kluger worked his way forward along the balcony. Fifty or so feet below, the waves from the bay rolled in onto the rocks. The sky was gray, and the day cold, but the closer the American got, the clearer it became that the tall, slim Yugoslavian waiting for him on the balcony was wearing a white bathrobe.

"Where the hell are your swimming trunks?" Petrovic asked when Kluger was only a few steps away. "This place is for swimming."

Jack Kluger stared at the Yugoslavian, not knowing whether he was joking. The two men had never met before. In fact, just three days earlier, Jack Kluger had never even heard of Petrovic.

"Go and get changed first," Petrovic now said in English. "I brought an extra bathrobe. It's hanging in the changing room."

"Are you kidding?" The American was genuinely shocked.

"You don't know me, I don't know you. What better way to build friendship than a little shared nudity?" Petrovic smiled.

Kluger stared at him, red in the face. They were the only two people there, and the weather wasn't exactly made for bathing.

"You think I'm bugged?" he eventually asked.

"I don't think anything," Petrovic replied. "Just go and get changed."

Kluger shrugged in irritation, but he went back down the spiral staircase and found the changing room. Sure enough, there was a white bathrobe hanging up inside. He took off everything but his underwear, pulled on the bathrobe and went back up the stairs. He demonstratively opened the robe to show the Yugoslavian that he had neither a weapon nor any listening devices on his nearly naked body.

"Sit, sit," said Petrovic said, and Kluger sat down on the bench diagonally above. "You sure you're alone?"

"Do you think I'm some fucking amateur?" the American asked.

Petrovic didn't answer. Jason, who had helped him with the motorbike just a few hours earlier, had found five bugs in his apartment on Upplandsgatan the day before yesterday. Later that day, they also found a further two beneath the table in Petrovic's usual booth at Café Stolen. For some reason, the police were suddenly obsessed with listening to his every word and following his every movement. He couldn't be careful enough.

Petrovic had left all the bugs where they were. Better to let the police think he had no idea they were listening to him. There was a challenge in doing so that he couldn't help but enjoy.

"OK," he said with a nod. "OK. I'm Zoran Petrovic, nice to meet you."

In the American's eyes, Zoran Petrovic looked like a typical European. There was, Kluger thought, a certain kind of appearance that looked neither Scandinavian nor French, not English or Italian, just *European*. Maybe it had something to do with their heads being so small.

"I'm supposed to pass on greetings from Basir Balik," said Petrovic. "I hear you've done a few jobs together?"

If Jack Kluger had worked for Balik, that decided things for Petrovic; the man could be trusted.

"The job involves flying at night, at a low altitude," the Yugoslavian said.

"Heard that. I've done it before." Kluger nodded with a wide smile, showing off his white teeth. "Thousands of hours in the Afghan mountains and ravines. I can do it."

"Shit, the entire meaning of life has to be flying low and landing softly," Petrovic said, looking out over the bay.

The waves foamed as they rolled in toward the building and broke against the jetties.

"Could be," Kluger admitted. "Could be."

This was the reason he was still in Sweden. One job kept leading to another. Nothing big or well paid, but he had enough money to get by.

It was a long time since he had last been behind the controls of a helicopter, and he was longing to get up in the air again.

"It's also about being able to keep your mouth shut and be loyal," Petrovic added.

Kluger's face turned red again. "Who the hell do you think you're talking to?" he asked.

The broad-shouldered man leaned forward and, in a single breath, reeled off a list of qualifications including far more than just the jobs he had done for Basir Balik. Some of what he said would be easy enough to check out. If what he said was true, there was no doubt that Jack Kluger had the experience.

They agreed on the terms of payment, and since there was so little time left, there was no point setting out smoke screens. Petrovic was straight with him, told him everything, and Kluger said he would be ready.

What the pilot failed to mention was the moments of confusion that struck him several times a week, and which had so far stopped him from setting foot in a helicopter ever since he left Afghanistan. Because he couldn't predict or ward off these periods of confusion, he hadn't been sure he could trust himself. But it had been so long now.

And from a purely technical point of view, the job was simple.

"I want half the payment up front," he said.

Petrovic nodded. "No problem."

They shook hands. Petrovic swayed as he got to his feet.

"Christ, this is high," he said, trying not to look down toward the water.

"It's not you I'm flying, right?" Kluger said.

Petrovic laughed. "You get changed first," he said. "I'll wait till you're done and gone."

Kluger nodded and headed down the stairs in his white bathrobe. Petrovic allowed fifteen minutes to pass before he went to get dressed himself. On the way back to Upplandsgatan, to his police tail and bugs, he felt lighter than he had in a long while.

Michel Maloof had a pilot once more.

39

National Police Commissioner Therese Olsson was sitting in a big, beautifully decorated office with views out onto the park. As yet, there was still no sign of any red or yellow in the dense green treetops outside her window. She looked up from her desk as Thurn and Berggren came into the room.

"Caroline. Mats. Come in. Sit down. Lars is on his way."

One of Olsson's many qualities was her surprising capacity for remembering names. She was a politician, a careerist. At some point, Thurn thought, she must have been a good police officer. But that was a long time ago, and being a good boss was now enough.

It was down to Thurn's initiative that Hertz would be involved in the meeting. The prosecutor may have been inexperienced, but he had shown a certain sharpness. Thurn knew that he wouldn't show any initiative himself, but she was no longer afraid he would sabotage the operation.

While they waited for the prosecutor, they made small talk about the ambassadors, the brothel on Karlavägen and how the minister for foreign affairs would react when the time for prosecution finally came around. Hertz appeared ten minutes later, and breathlessly sat down on one of the chairs in front of the desk.

"Well," said the police commissioner, "now I'm obviously curious what you have to say."

Thurn concisely summed up what they had found out about Panaxia in Bromma. When she finished, the prosecutor made his first request, as Thurn had instructed him to do that morning.

"We would like to move the police helicopter from the base in Myttinge," Hertz said.

"Move it?"

"It's cheaper to move it than to increase our surveillance out there," Mats Berggren explained.

He knew which arguments would be most effective.

"But do you really think—" Olsson began.

"The robbery is going to take place on the fifteenth," said Thurn, "and we have information suggesting the robbers will try to destroy the only active helicopter in the Stockholm area. Why wouldn't we move it?"

"And where should it go?"

"Our suggestion," Hertz took over, "is that we leave it with the National Task Force in Sörentorp until further notice."

It wasn't a big decision, but the police commissioner had learned to gain points whenever she could. As a result, she looked hesitant at first, and jotted down a few words on a pad of paper on her desk. Then she nodded her approval.

"We had a similar thought," she eventually said, studying Thurn thoughtfully. "I was planning to talk to you about the National Task Force."

No one replied, despite the fact that Olsson had left a clear pause for them to say something.

"Yes, well," she continued, "as you know, the preliminary investigation has, as of lunchtime, been upgraded to an extraordinary event."

Berggren nodded.

"On my initiative," Prosecutor Hertz pointed out, annoyed not to have been given credit. "It was my suggestion to upgrade it to an extraordinary event."

Within the National Criminal Police, an "extraordinary event" meant that the case was now being given highest priority, with increased preparedness a result. An "extraordinary event" could be anything from the attempted murder of a high-ranking politician to an acute terror threat.

"And so," Therese Olsson said, not paying any attention to the pros- ecutor's territorial thinking, "we have come to the conclusion that we should call in the Task Force."

A silence settled over the room. Thurn looked down at her hand, seemingly studying her nails. Mats Berggren had more difficulty being quite so subtle.

"What the hell do you mean by that?" he said. "Why bring in that pretend army to mess about in this? Don't you think we can handle the situation?"

"It's a decision we came to jointly," the police commissioner said deliberately.

"Jointly?" asked Berggren.

"Within command," Olsson clarified. "Even Carlbrink was in- volved."

"Command?" asked Thurn. "Because that's not good. The more who know about this, the greater the chance of leaks."

"Are you suggesting that Carlbrink . . . that the head of the National Task Force can't keep a secret?" Olsson snapped.

"I don't mean anything other than that the more people who know, the greater the chance of leaks," Caroline repeated.

She could no longer hide her irritation. She looked up, straight into the commissioner's eyes.

"This is our case, Therese. We have it under control. Don't you think we can manage without their army boots and rocket launchers? You're our boss. Don't you have any faith in your own staff?"

"Are we talking about the entire Task Force?" asked Berggren.

"Fully armed," Olsson confirmed. "And with orders to shoot down a helicopter, if necessary."

"This is a robbery we're talking about," Thurn pointed out. "It might be spectacular, possibly better planned than anything we've ever seen on Swedish soil. But it's still just a robbery, not a coup. The police force has the resources to be able to handle this. We don't need help from—"

"The Serbian police aren't the only ones following this case," Olsson interrupted. "Interpol is being updated continually. And the minister for foreign affairs has a personal interest in it too. If we let him down, then the minister for justice won't have a leg to stand on when it comes to discussing resources at the next budget."

Politics. There were few things that interested Caroline Thurn so little that could also make her quite so agitated. But she could see that this wasn't a simple matter of police work, that it was about the ministers' egos and the way the state distributed resources.

She got up.

"Fine," she said. "So let the National Task Force handle it."

The prosecutor got to his feet too. He nodded stiffly, and Thurn got the sense that somehow he had also been involved in the decision.

"We know where and when they're going to strike," said Berggren, who also got up from his chair with a labored groan. "By this stage, with everything handed to them on a silver plate, even the Task Force should be able to manage this."

"They will be ready outside the Panaxia premises in Bromma from twenty-three hundred hours on the fourteenth of September," Olsson replied. "But let us be clear about one thing. Until then, it's you who are responsible."

40

There was a balcony on the fifth floor.

Michel Maloof spotted it after his deathly boring visit to the Moderna Museet. He had parted ways with Alexandra Svensson outside the Grand Hotel and headed straight home to his drawings. He hadn't given the fifth floor the same manic attention as the sixth, where Counting was located, but he spotted it among the drawings on the floor by his dining table. One sheet had been covering another, and when he pushed it to one side, there it was.

A small balcony sticking out from the fifth floor above the open atrium.

It meant they could go in through the glass ceiling.

If they smashed the glass and used a long ladder, maybe they would be able to reach all the way to the balcony.

Alexandra had been right, he thought. He wasn't someone who gave up. He found new ways forward.

Maloof pulled out his phone and called Sami.

"There's a balcony," he said. "Looks like a little ledge. We could use ladders. One to get down and one to get back up to the sixth floor."

"You sure?" asked Sami. "About the balcony?"

"Definitely, definitely," Maloof replied. "I'll check with Nick."

"This is Plan F, I can feel it," Sami said defiantly, adding, "Is Nick any good with ladders?"

"He's good with everything," Maloof mumbled.

"Maybe he can work out how long the ladder needs to be?" Sami continued. "It's gonna take a damn long ladder. You know what I mean?"

"I'll talk to Nick."

Maloof hung up. He could feel his heart pounding in his chest, feel himself literally sitting taller. He was himself again.

*   *   *

That evening, Niklas Nordgren spent hours in his hobby room, studying the drawings from Vreten 17. Once he knew what he was looking for, it didn't take long for him to find the balcony on the fifth floor.

All night, and long into the early hours, Maloof, Sami and Nordgren called one another from different phones with different SIM cards. They spoke without mentioning any key words, using broken sentences and repeated euphemisms, just to make sure that if anyone happened to be listening to their conversation, they wouldn't understand a thing.

Nordgren agreed that it shouldn't be impossible to smash the glass on the roof and lower a ladder down to the balcony.

The wall out onto the atrium on the sixth floor was made of bulletproof glass. It was there to let light into what would otherwise be an entirely dark floor.

"What the hell do we do about that?" Sami asked.

Nordgren reassured him. The words "bulletproof glass" implied something more impressive than the reality. Using a shorter ladder to climb up from the balcony on the fifth floor and blow a hole in the glass on the sixth wouldn't be a problem. But the explosion would cause glass to rain down onto the balcony, meaning that the only place they could take cover would be up on the roof.

They would have to climb down to the balcony, apply their explosives to the strengthened glass, and then climb back up to the roof. They would also have to make sure the detonation cable was long enough to reach up to the roof with them.

All of this meant a hell of a lot of climbing, Sami declared.

"We'll manage it," Nordgren said drily. "The doors'll be worse."

Once they made it through the armored glass on the sixth floor, they would end up in the room directly next to Counting. All that divided the two rooms was some kind of fire door and a security door.

"What the hell's a security door?"

"Made of steel. Thicker kind. Fire doors are easy. Security doors are . . . worse."

"Worse? But, can you do it?"

"It's fine," Nordgren was firm. "It'll be fine."

"We only have ten minutes," Maloof reminded him.

"Impossible," Nordgren replied. "Ten minutes won't be enough. Maybe if we had fifteen? We'll have to count."

"No longer," said Maloof.

"OK, let's say fifteen," Nordgren said.

Sami was happy.

The question now was how long the ladder from the ceiling to the balcony would need to be. Judging by the plans, the fifth and sixth floors looked like they were a normal height, and according to Maloof, Alexandra Svensson had suggested that the ceiling height definitely wasn't any more than ten feet.

"How the hell could you ask her about that?" Nordgren wondered.

"She talks more than Zoran," Maloof said. "I don't ask, I just listen."

"Ouch. How d'you manage that?"

"Exactly, exactly. That's a better question."

All of this meant that in total, there were nineteen or twenty feet between the floor of the balcony on the fifth floor and the ceiling on the sixth. A thirty-six-foot ladder would leave them with sixteen feet to spare once it was through the skylight.

Those weren't huge margins, but they would be enough.

When Maloof eventually fell into bed at dawn that morning, it was with a wide grin on his lips. He was convinced things were about to turn around now, that they were overcoming their problems.

Late the next afternoon, when he woke, he realized Petrovic had been trying to get in touch with him several times, to tell him both the good and the bad news. The good news was that they had a new pilot.

"But I've got half the police force on me." Petrovic sighed. "It's not a mistake, they haven't got me mixed up with someone else. It's me they're after, but the one thing I don't know is why."

41

Caroline Thurn wasn't the type of police officer to leave things to chance. On Wednesday afternoon, the decision had been made to allow the National Task Force to keep the Panaxia cash depot in Bromma under surveillance during the night of the fourteenth of September.

But by Friday afternoon, Thurn had started to have doubts.

Most of what they knew pointed to Panaxia, but she suddenly felt unsure.

What exactly suggested that the G4S depot in Västberga wouldn't be the target of the helicopter robbery?

Thurn was at the gym, and with every mile that passed on the rowing machine, the feeling grew. Eventually, she had to get off, go into the changing room and call Berggren.

He was still at the office in Kungsholmen, and he sighed loudly when she told him about her hunch.

"And you're aware that it's three thirty on a Friday?" he said.

"Meaning what?"

"People are heading home, Caroline," Berggren explained. "It's the weekend. They want to spend time with their families, eat chips and watch some TV show with an overexcited host who laughs at their own jokes."

Thurn didn't watch TV, she wasn't even sure whether there *was* one in the apartment on Strandvägen.

Before she moved into the nine-room apartment with views over the water, she had instructed the auction firm Bukowski's to sell everything that might be of value. Anything left behind had been stashed in one of the rooms looking out onto the courtyard. That was almost six years ago now, and Thurn still hadn't opened the door. She would deal with it one day, but not quite yet.

"Plus," Berggren continued, "G4S doesn't fit the information we have. The building in Västberga has six floors. And we know that Panaxia's starting a big move the day before, meaning there'll be people running all over the place and that security'll be lower."

"That's what the tip we have said," Thurn replied. "Which isn't the same thing as knowing it. I just want to check one last time."

Berggren was careful not to sigh audibly again.

Thurn's need to be in control was about as big as Berggren's appetite.

"Do you want me to do anything?" he asked.

"No need," Thurn replied. She wanted to add that it was Friday afternoon and that he should prioritize his family, but then she realized that she didn't even know if Mats Berggren had a family.

Caroline Thurn never asked her colleagues personal questions. It meant she could avoid being asked the same kind of thing in return.

On that overcast Friday afternoon, the task force leader drove through town toward Västberga. Like always, there was a lot of traffic heading south, and she had to join a long convoy of trucks. But Västberga Allé, the street that cut straight through the industrial area, was deserted.

Work at the loading docks often finished early in the afternoon ahead of the weekend, and the offices there were already empty. Thurn drove slowly past the deserted buildings and then slowed down further as she approached the G4S building at the corner of Vretensborgsvägen. Work there went on seven days a week, but even cash depots were quiet on Friday afternoons.

Thurn glanced out of the side window. The six-story building was like a fortress on the inside, and the cash depot's vault was in a completely different league from the Panaxia safe in Bromma.

No, Thurn thought, it was reasonable to assume that this wasn't the building the robbers were planning to attack. Besides, Thurn could practically see all the way to the police station on Västbergavägen. Given the choice, Panaxia was better in every respect.

She drove on.

Rather than doing a U-turn, she turned right at Vretensborgsvägen. She sped up and was just about to take another right onto Drivhjulsvägen, looping the block and continuing north, back toward the highway, when she glanced in her rearview mirror.

She slammed on the brakes.

It was sheer luck that there were no cars behind her.

From where she was sitting, she could see the G4S building from behind. It had to be built into a hillside, or at least a steep slope.

From this side, it looked like the building had four stories.

42

Hans Carlbrink, the head of the National Task Force, was the type of officer who made the general population hesitate before calling the police. His career path had been through the military, which was also where his references and attitude toward the world came from. His sense of discipline was stronger than his sense of justice, and if you wanted to emphasize his positive sides, you might say that he radiated some kind of equality. He was equally arrogant toward victims and perpetrators, civilians and police officers, men and women.

Caroline Thurn and Mats Berggren drove out to Solna, where Carlbrink's men were stationed and the police helicopter was now safe behind walls and barbed wire. It was late in the afternoon on Saturday, September 12. Carlbrink gave the tall, fit Thurn an appreciative glance and then turned to Berggren and stared at his considerable stomach with a look of disgust. He showed his visitors into a windowless room to one side of the canteen, a room that gave Thurn the feeling that it was being used in an attempt to demonstrate how tough the conditions were for the Task Force.

"Three more days," said Carlbrink.

They were in agreement that it was a frustrating and unusual experience to be counting down the days. The reason for not just bringing Petrovic in, thereby preventing the robbery, was that the information they had was already a month old. Plenty could have changed, and Thurn spared a thought for the technicians who spent all day, every day listening to the slippery Montenegrin refuse to give himself away. What exactly did they have on him?

All the same, Thurn couldn't deny that the excitement rose with every day that passed. Her colleagues from National Crime nodded in understanding whenever they passed her office, and with just three days to go, all those involved could feel their hearts beating that little bit quicker. Even the minister for foreign affairs had been in touch for an update.

They sat down at a tired old conference table.

Thurn got straight to the point and explained what she had discovered the previous evening. That the G4S depot in Västberga was also, if you chose to look at it from a certain angle, a four-story building.

"But G4S isn't planning a move on Tuesday," Berggren butted in.

His usual whininess had increased in this new environment. He felt uncomfortable under Carlbrink's elitist gaze, and he hated the uncertainty that Thurn had introduced into the equation.

"We don't know that," said Thurn. "I haven't asked them."

"Come on, it'd be pretty unlikely?"

Thurn agreed.

"My point is that we can't rule out Västberga. And my question, Hans, is whether we should station some of your men out in Västberga and some out in Bromma?"

Carlbrink nodded. That was perfectly doable.

"I've heard there'll be around twenty people?" he said.

"Involved in the preparations," Thurn replied. "I doubt there'll be twenty people there during the actual robbery."

"It's not a problem," Carlbrink said, smiling as though he were eating something tasty. "Let them come. Twenty or thirty. We could probably handle it. My suggestion is that we make sure to have enough men and equipment to be able to take down a helicopter in both Västberga and Bromma. But that we leave the majority wherever you feel it's more likely to happen."

"Which is Bromma anyway, right Caroline?" asked Berggren.

Thurn looked unsure.

"If you'd asked me yesterday," she said, "I would've been sure. But now I don't know anymore."

43

Niklas Nordgren was struggling to concentrate. He was sitting on the stool by his desk in the hobby room, and through the wall, he could hear the TV news from the living room. Rather than soldering the phone case in front of him, he was listening to the host's serious voice reporting on the death of the American actor Patrick Swayze.

He wasn't worried about Annika coming in and seeing what he was doing. The wall between their worlds, between a normal and a criminal life, may have been thin, but it was thick enough. Annika would never open the door to his hobby room without knocking first. And if her thoughts were elsewhere and she did happen to come in without warning, she wouldn't understand what he was doing. She wouldn't recognize the explosive putty he was pushing into the cell phones he was busy priming.

How many times had she threatened him? She would leave him the minute he broke their agreement. She had waited long enough, their relationship wouldn't survive another stint in prison. Sometimes, he still got the feeling—and it happened increasingly often—that she was actually just looking for an excuse.

But it wasn't the fear of her leaving him that was making it hard for Nordgren to concentrate that evening.

Eventually, he put down the soldering iron and unplugged it at the wall. He went over to the window. The light on top of the Kaknäs tower was blinking away on the other side of the water. He stood there, the dark night in front of him, and allowed himself to get lost in the moment.

From the minute the helicopter landed on the roof, no more than fifteen minutes could pass before it took off again. That was how long it would take for the G4S security staff to mobilize, for the police to organize themselves and make rational decisions.

Considering how close the police station was, he would have preferred it if they had been able to do it in ten minutes.

Getting out of the helicopter, smashing the skylight, putting the ladders into place and climbing into the building would take at least two to three minutes.

Breaking through the bulletproof glass would take two to three minutes.

Getting through the security door would take two to three minutes.

Filling the bags with money wouldn't take any less than two to three minutes.

Hauling the bags of money back onto the roof wouldn't take any less than two to three minutes.

And then their time would be up.

There was no room for error; they would have to work quickly and without any surprises. Their biggest problem would be if the staff in Counting caused any trouble. Obviously it would be best if the premises were emptied before the security door was blown open, but that type of thing was hard to take for granted.

If the staff were still inside when they made it in, their plans would fall apart. Gathering them together and making sure they stayed calm wouldn't be a problem; Nordgren was sure of that, it wasn't a risk. But it would take time.

The Kaknäs tower flashed away in the distance.

A large boat covered in colorful lanterns was on its way through the channel between Lilla Värtan and Saltsjön.

But the fact they might run out of time wasn't the thing worrying him most.

He went back to his desk and plugged in the soldering iron. The plan was to prepare four phone bombs. Two would be placed in the police helicopter on Värmdö and two would be kept as backups. The risk of the Stockholm police's other helicopter turning up, the one currently on loan to Gothenburg, wasn't particularly high, but neither was it impossible. Meaning they would also need to be able to place two phones in that one, if necessary.

But as Nordgren moved the tip of the iron to solder the casing together, he realized that it was this that was causing him to hesitate.

The idea of putting the phones in the police helicopter and then, while they were heading toward Västberga, blowing the thing to pieces by activating the charge.

Would there be a pilot behind the controls?

Would there be anyone else in the hangar?

Would this plan, meant to prevent anyone from following them, turn into a bloody massacre?

There was no way to ensure it didn't happen.

Through the living room wall, he heard "The Time of My Life" from *Dirty Dancing*, probably being used as the soundtrack to Patrick Swayze's life for the customary retrospective of his career.

Nordgren nodded to himself. In the documentary of his life, no one would be able to say that he had killed anyone. That line was as clear as it was unwavering. He was a criminal, he was a robber, but he wasn't a killer.

He looked down at his explosive phones.

44

Hjorthagen sports complex was just behind the gas tanks in the neighborhood tucked away beyond Östermalm and Lidingö, built at one time to give guest laborers somewhere to live. It was thanks to soccer that Michel Maloof had first gone there, and he had realized just how perfect Hjorthagen was for meetings that needed to stay secret. Though the area had its own subway station, it was still one of the city's most forgotten neighborhoods. A professional soccer team used the sports complex to train, but at one in the morning, it was guaranteed to be empty.

On his way to the meeting, Maloof had changed trains several times before he felt confident enough to sit down on the red line toward Ropsten.

Walking toward Hjorthagen from the station, he thought about how quickly the bright summer nights had turned into something more like autumn. Though the trees were still green and the lawns looked as though they thought it was midsummer, the darkness had returned at night. It wouldn't be long before it was time to dig out the hats and gloves, he thought.

Or maybe six months in Thailand would be preferable to winter in Sweden.

If everything went according to plan, that wouldn't be unthinkable, and he was sure Alexandra Svensson wouldn't have anything against going with him.

Maloof crossed the parking lot and kept to the edge of the woods as he moved around the fence surrounding the soccer field. Someone had cut a hole near the very middle, and it had gone ten years without being fixed. He pushed the fence to one side, squatted down and sneaked in, then he hid in the shadow of the changing rooms, right next to the entrance.

Sami Farhan appeared on Artemisgatan five minutes later. Maloof saw him from a distance and shouted gently. Sami took the same route via the woods and the hole in the fence.

"Tell me everything's sorted," was the first thing he said.

Maloof recognized the tone of voice.

That aggressive and expectant tone.

"I don't give a shit what this is all about," Sami said. "Let's go. I can't wait any longer."

"Wait till Nick gets here."

Nordgren appeared from the long shadows of the trees. Maloof saw the movement before he saw the person, and he jumped.

"Sorry," said Nordgren. "Didn't mean to scare you. I got here a bit early. Just wanted to make sure you weren't being followed."

Maloof nodded. He liked Nordgren's caution, he always had. Sami, on the other hand, was annoyed.

"What the hell is this?"

"Can't be too careful," said Nordgren.

They walked toward the northern end of the field, by Gasverks-vägen. The trees were tight around them. All three men were wearing dark clothes and talking quietly. It would be impossible to see them unless you got very close.

"I don't get why we always have to meet on soccer fields," Sami muttered grumpily, gesturing to the eerie, empty field.

Maloof laughed. "Soccer's . . . a team sport, Sami," he said. "Maybe you could try it sometime."

They stopped on the goal line. It was a cool, clear night, and Maloof knew that it was one he would remember.

It was time to make a decision.

"We've got a pilot," he said.

The relief of the others was greater than their joy. Sami did a quick pirouette.

"Finally!" he shouted. "Let's do this!"

Maloof told them what he knew about the American, what his qualifications and references were. He added, "But it was Zoran they were tailing, not me, and not by mistake. They're on him twenty-four seven. They put microphones in his apartment, in the restaurants. And a couple in the car."

His words dampened the mood.

"OK," Sami eventually said. "So they suspect your friend? What's that got to do with us? You know? Nothing."

"Lay off," Nordgren mumbled.

"I'm serious," Sami continued. "It's his business."

"Right, right," said Maloof. "Except . . . Zoran knows everything. Him and us . . . we're doing this together."

"Yeah, I know," Sami said, unable to stand still any longer. "But he hasn't been involved in any of the details. You know what I mean? He must have a tail for some other reason. We've been working round the clock for months. He's . . . done a load of other stuff. You know? He's got his business, we've got ours."

"You think he's said anything?" Nordgren asked. "That they've heard?"

It was the question they had to consider. The reason Petrovic was being watched and listened to so intently had to be because of something else, or had the police heard something about Västberga on one of their microphones over these past few weeks?

Maloof shook his head.

"Don't worry. He'd never name names. Never say anything which . . . "

"So why's he got a tail?" asked Nordgren. "That kind of surveillance. Sounds really fucking weird."

Maloof shook his head again. He didn't know.

"Can't be a leak," said Sami, "because no one knows. No one. It's us four and only us."

"The pilot knows now too," said Maloof. "Zoran had to tell him. There's no time left."

"But when did that happen?" Sami asked. "Yesterday? A few days ago? It's not him."

Maloof shook his head. He didn't know any more than that.

"So . . . what do we do?" he asked, his calm smile making his face impossible to read, like always.

No one replied. Nordgren's cap was casting a dark shadow over his face. Sami was digging the toe of his shoe into the grass. His mind was on his brothers, his investors. But above all, he was thinking about Karin. And the boys. He wasn't planning to let them grow up with a dad who was away every night, doing the occasional job and being sent away at regular intervals. A dad they would be embarrassed of, one they would never get to know. He needed this to work.

"What do you mean?" he asked. "What do we do? We do it."

His words were followed by a long silence.

"I agree it sounds weird," Nordgren said when Maloof didn't reply. "We're going to steal a helicopter and fly it to a cash depot where there's a police station just down the road. We climb down ladders and blow open doors and carry out the biggest robbery in Swedish history. And all while we know the police have unlimited resources, that they've been listening to Petrovic for a month while we've been working on the details."

"This is a job everyone will hear about," Sami tried to convince his friends. "You know? Across the whole world."

"Right, right," said Maloof. "Or . . . at least the whole of Sweden."

"I guarantee you," Sami said, "this is bigger than Sweden."

His gesture was directed out into space, as though their fame would reach far out into the universe.

"Are we really doing it?" Nordgren wondered.

Silence again. This time, it was Sami who broke it.

"I'll say it again. It's a go. We're doing it. What do you think, Michel? You in?"

Maloof laughed. He glanced at Sami, standing there with a wry smile and drumming his hand against his leg while he waited for an answer. He thought about the months of planning, the drawings spread across the floor in his dark apartment in Fittja, and about Alexandra. Could a life with her be awaiting him? Would it be enough money? In his head, he turned over the question: If this wasn't enough, what would be? His serious face cracked into a wide smile.

"Definitely," he said. "Yeah, definitely. I'm in. We're doing it."

"OK," said Nordgren. "Then we're doing it."

45

Prosecutor Lars Hertz and Detective Chief Inspector Caroline Thurn were sitting in the front seats of Thurn's newly washed, dark blue Volvo. It was parked in the shadows between a couple of wheelless wrecks outside a tire-fitting company at Linta Gårdsväg 25. Hertz looked unashamedly alert, his blond fringe bobbing like a thick cloud above his forehead, and he seemed tangibly excited to be involved in a huge police operation. The difficult scent of Mats Berggren's aftershave enveloped them both, and it was something Hertz would forever associate with that night in the car.

Berggren was in the back. He leaned forward between the seats and said that memories of family car trips in Europe were coming back to him. Were they nearly there yet?

In the front seat, the reaction to his joke differed. Thurn smiled kindly. The idea that her parents might have ever taken her on car trips when she was younger was about as unlikely as it was bizarre. Herz blushed in the darkness, thinking that he wouldn't have anything against starting a family with Caroline Thurn.

Since the moment she had stepped into his room a few weeks earlier, the prosecutor had found it difficult to look her in the eye. She had the kind of appearance that made him shy. He assumed it was her lack of flattery and her clear unwillingness to please that appealed to him.

And embarrassed him.

They sat and waited in the darkness. The fourteenth of September had crossed over into the fifteenth a few hours earlier. The anticipation they had felt as they drove out to Bromma had passed, but the minutes still felt endless. Thurn's breathing was heavy and regular. She had fallen into a microsleep a couple of times, but for no more than ten minutes in total. She had also wound down one of the side windows to prevent them from fogging up with condensation. The crickets were all that broke the silence, and the clouds that had rolled in an hour earlier filtered the moonlight into narrow stripes on the flat land on the other side of the road.

"It's two o'clock," Berggren informed them.

"That's correct, Mats," Thurn replied.

"We've been sitting here for three hours."

Thurn didn't reply. She wasn't impressed by her colleague's mathematical abilities.

They had spent the first hour in whispered, uninspired conversation about the latest in a line of internal investigations into the organizational structure of the Swedish police force. There had been a presentation of the findings in one of the conference rooms a few days earlier, and both Thurn and Berggren had felt obliged to attend. Hertz hadn't been there, of course; he worked for the prosecution authority and had no strong opinions on where the county police's responsibilities started and ended. Berggren, on the other hand, had formed a whole range of opinions that he was more than happy to share with his colleagues in the front seats. Thurn knew that the conclusions of the internal reports would be compromised down to nothing, which meant that her level of interest was negligible.

Since then, they had been sitting in silence.

Thurn had made the decision to place the majority of the Task Force outside the Panaxia building in Bromma the day before, but Carlbrink had enough men lying in wait outside G4S to stop a small army all the same.

There were two walkie-talkies in Thurn's lap. One to contact Carlbrink in Bromma, and the other to be able to quickly get in touch with the team in Västberga.

So far, both had remained silent.

The minutes passed reluctantly.

The Panaxia depot rose up like a huge dark block, high above the surrounding buildings. A few hours earlier, the contracted moving team had left the building. They had been working since the morning before, right up until midnight.

As the movers drove away in their vans, Thurn breathed out. Money was money, colorful pictures printed onto paper that could be exchanged for valuable things, services and experiences. But human lives couldn't be swapped for anything at all.

What had been worrying Thurn most was that they would end up with a hostage situation that the National Task Force, under the leadership of the insensitive Carlbrink, would fail to handle. But now that the moving staff had gone, that risk had vanished.

Thurn and Berggren had taken a trip out to Solna to brief Carlbrink before his men set out at around ten thirty that evening.

The two officers from the National Criminal Police had watched the elite unit's preparations. The amount of weapons, shields and safety equipment they packed into their vans was striking. Their arsenal even included a couple of rocket launchers, presumably in case they had to open fire on a helicopter.

"It's like being back in Israel," Thurn had commented, mostly to herself.

"Never been," Berggren replied.

Thurn had given Carlbrink a good head start before she and Berggren drove back into town. She went via Fleminggatan, where she picked up Hertz, and then they headed out to the area behind Bromma airport. She had found the parking lot outside the tire fitter during an obligatory reconnaissance mission on Sunday.

Berggren suddenly jumped in the backseat.

"What was that?" he said.

They sat perfectly still, straining to hear. Even the crickets had fallen silent. After a few minutes, they started breathing normally again. False alarm.

"Still pretty impressive that Carlbrink can get his soldiers not to mess about with their weapons," Berggren said quietly. "I thought we'd be able to hear them rattling the bolts all night."

"Where are they?" Hertz asked.

Thurn pointed out the rear window, and the prosecutor thought he could discern the outlines of the vans.

"How many?"

"Not sure," Thurn replied. "Was it twenty men?"

"Don't know either," Berggren piped up from the backseat. "Felt like a small army. They must be packed like sardines inside those vans."

"Maybe that makes it easier to sleep against one another?" Hertz joked.

The image of those elite police officers leaning their heads on one another in the back of the vans made Berggren laugh.

Thurn hushed him.

"Are you scared they'll hear me from the helicopter?" he snapped.

"They might arrive in a helicopter," said Thurn, "but they could just as easily turn up in a couple of cars. Maybe the helicopter's just their escape plan. We have no idea."

Berggren was about to argue, but he resisted the urge.

They knew considerably more than that, they knew an incredible amount, that was why they were sitting in this car, waiting for one of Sweden's biggest robberies to take place.

But the minutes passed, and Mats Berggren grew more and more restless.

"Isn't this exciting, Lars?" he said to the prosecutor in the front seat. "Finally getting to see what real police work's like?"

Hertz gave a brief laugh and the conversation died out. The two men fell asleep, and Thurn stared out into the darkness as the hours ticked by.

*   *   *

At three in the morning, the police helicopter took off from Solna. Just like the National Task Force, it had been put at the operation's disposal. Rather than allowing the pilots to sleep in the nearby barracks, it had been decided that the helicopter should be in the air once an hour during the night. That way, it would not only be able to help with the surveillance work, it would also be much quicker onto the scene when the time came.

There had been discussions as to whether they should try to move it to Bromma airport, meaning they would be able to get to Panaxia even more quickly, but a decision against the idea had eventually been made. The airport's rates were, in the eyes of the government, hair-raising, and the distance between the area in Solna and the airfield was only three or four minutes as the crow flies.

The agreement was that the helicopter wouldn't fly anywhere close to Bromma until it was called in. They didn't want to scare the robbers away.

"That was definitely something!"

Berggren was whispering loudly. The sound had come from some distance away, though not too far.

"Did you hear that?"

He hissed, his voice reaching a falsetto. Thurn had thought that Berggren was asleep. But she had heard it too. It wasn't his imagination this time. The clear sound of movement in the grass not far from the road.

Thurn glanced at her watch. Five past four.

"It's not far away. Should we let Carlbrink know?" Berggren whispered from the backseat.

Thurn nodded. She didn't know where Carlbrink had positioned his men, but there was a risk that none of them were stationed along the road.

The detective silently closed the window, picked up one of the walkie-talkies and pressed the button.

"We can hear something," she whispered into it.

"Understood," came the immediate reply, followed by silence.

Thurn gently placed the radio in her lap and lowered the side window again. The three of them listened carefully. Hertz and Berggren nodded almost simultaneously. Someone, or perhaps several people, was out there in the darkness.

Movement. Silence. Movement. Silence.

It was heading straight for them.

"Are they moving away?" Hertz whispered.

His observation was correct. The sound was heading away from the Panaxia building.

"But that's impossible," Berggren said, equally quietly. "Carlbrink has a ring around the building. No one could've made it inside and back out again already."

A few seconds later, they spotted the dog.

It was big and black, a cross of several breeds, and it wasn't wearing a collar. It was thin and hungry; its ribs were clearly visible.

"Stay here," Thurn instructed, possibly to stop Berggren from getting out of the car.

She picked up the walkie-talkie.

"False alarm," she whispered.

They heard a crackling on the other end, which Thurn took as a confirmation.

The realization that nothing would happen, that the robbery wouldn't be taking place, didn't dawn on them until Berggren informed the others that it was quarter past six in the morning and that the sun was coming up.

It began as a joke.

"The Serbs said it would be a night flight," said Berggren, "but I think it's getting a bit late."

Thurn muttered something incomprehensible. Her body was stiff. Her mouth as dry as paper.

"The one thing I'm worried about," Berggren continued when neither of his colleagues replied, "is that if Carlbrink doesn't get to set his army on the robbers, he'll take his disappointment out on us."

Hertz had dozed off in the front seat. He was sleeping deeply, his breathing calm, and neither Thurn nor Berggren wanted to wake him.

For some reason, the robbers had changed their plans.

Suddenly, Thurn jumped. One of the radios in her lap buzzed.

Was it Västberga?

Was G4S the target?

She picked up the walkie-talkie and held it to her ear, but it wasn't Västberga. It was Carlbrink trying to get ahold of her.

"Nothing," his tired voice said down the line. "And nothing in Västberga either. Over there?"

"Nothing," she replied.

Caroline knew it was over.

She thought about the commissioner, about the minister for foreign affairs. Then she thought about all the police officers who had been involved in the investigation; those hundreds of hours of Zoran Petrovic's inane chatter they'd had to listen to.

She sighed.

Had there been a leak at police HQ? It wasn't impossible, the leaks there sometimes resembled a Chinese river delta. Maybe the robbers knew it had been a trap, and that was why they had canceled.

But it was equally likely that some part of their plan had failed at the last minute. With so many people involved, anything could have happened.

When the clock struck six thirty, Caroline Thurn was sure.

It wasn't her job to dismiss Carlbrink, and so she called the commissioner instead, on her direct line.

"Hi, it's Caroline," she said, using her normal voice rather than whispering for the first time in hours. "It's a nonstarter," she continued.

Hertz woke in the passenger seat.

Thurn listened in silence for a moment while Berggren and Hertz looked searchingly at her.

She put down her phone and started the engine.

"They're sending Carlbrink home," she said. "They're moving the helicopter back to Myttinge. The political version will be that with the help of our Serbian colleagues, we managed to prevent one of the biggest robberies in history."

"Did we?" Hertz asked, newly woken. "Did we stop the robbery?"

"What do you think, Lars?" said Thurn. "What do you think?"

46

"I feel pretty crappy," Niklas Nordgren said to Carsten Hansen.

"Yeah? But you hardly ever get sick."

"I guess it was something I ate yesterday. My stomach's kind of churning."

"Shouldn't you go home then?"

"I just got here," Nordgren protested.

It was nine in the morning on Friday, September 18.

"But," he added, "I really don't feel right. Shit. You sure you'll cope?"

"Go home and rest," said Hansen. "It's more important you're OK than that the locksmith's microwave works."

"Yeah," Nordgren agreed. "Yeah, I guess. Thanks, Carsten. It's good of you."

Nordgren packed up his things, thanked Carsten again and pulled on his coat. But as he turned the corner, he didn't head for home. He headed for the station instead. He took the Lidingö line to Ropsten, the subway to Slussen, and from there a bus to Stavsnäs. When the Waxholm ferry docked at the quay and Nordgren stepped on board, he calculated that it had been five years since he last made this journey.

It was lunchtime when he stepped off the boat on the island of Sandhamn. The season was short in the archipelago, and by that time of year, mid-September, the only people to get off ahead of Nordgren were a couple of handymen in overalls. No more than a hundred or so people lived permanently on the island, and for that reason seeing strangers was unusual. Nordgren passed the hotel with determined steps, and then headed up the hill toward Trouville. He too was wearing overalls and was carrying a tool bag. If anyone noticed him, they would just assume he was on his way to repair something in one of the houses that lay empty at this time of year, along the road toward the island's southern cape.

In summer, the beach in Trouville offered seclusion to any tourists wanting to swim, at least if they moved away from the more built-up area. But by September, the area was completely deserted.

Nordgren turned right when he reached the water, and walked along the narrow beach. He clambered over piles of damp seaweed that had washed ashore. It didn't take long for his shoes to be soaked through.

He was looking for the rowboat he had dragged onto land five years earlier. He had pulled it up to the edge of the trees and tied it to a trunk. You couldn't see the boat from the water, and barely even from land unless you got lost in the woods and tripped over it. It belonged to an old childhood friend of Nordgren's parents, who had sold their place on Sandhamn and bought another on Runmarö. But the little boat had been left behind, and it wasn't in anyone's way.

He went too far at first, but Nordgren eventually found the little plastic boat exactly where he had left it. The oars were still inside, as was the bailer. He couldn't manage to undo the knot he had tied around a tall pine, and he had to cut the rope with a knife instead. He pulled the boat down to the water, pushed it out and jumped in. His shoes were already soaked anyway.

Thanks to the southerly wind, it took him no more than two hours to row over the strait to the edge of Runmarö. That was where his parents' friends had bought their new house, and there was a playhouse with a bed in their yard. Nordgren had slept there before.

47

Just as Niklas Nordgren was rowing ashore on Runmarö, the referee blew his whistle to start the match at Råsunda Stadium in Solna. The arena had been built as the national stadium for the Swedish soccer team, and it could hold almost forty thousand fans. Tonight, with AIK playing Trelleborgs FF at home, roughly half that number of paying spectators were in the seats. It was AIK's year, the team was heading for victory in the Allsvenskan league, and that fact made Michel Maloof neither happy nor sad. He didn't have a favorite team in the Allsvenskan; he thought English league soccer was far superior to Swedish, and was much more interested in the Premier League. On top of that, Trelleborg were one of AIK's least entertaining rivals, sitting midtable and with a game that could sympathetically be described as defensive.

But there was no denying that the nearly twenty thousand spectators that evening were giving the boring match a relatively grand feeling. The terraces were lively, and though the score was 0–0 at halftime, it was going to be the home side's night; you could feel it in the air. Maloof bought a hot dog and a Coke Zero in a soft plastic cup that was difficult to hold, and he went back to watch the second half, still not feeling particularly engaged.

Sure enough, the home team sent a ball into the back of the net at seventy-five minutes, and a quarter of an hour after that, Maloof got up and pushed his way out of his row. He was carrying a sports bag in one hand. It wasn't unthinkable that the lukewarm cola had forced him to go to the toilet with just injury time to go.

Next to the enormous men's restroom and its many cubicles and urinals, there was a separate disabled restroom with a door you could lock behind you. That was where Maloof headed.

With just a few minutes of the game left to play, the corridors of the stadium were practically deserted. This was when everything would be decided out on the field, it wasn't something you wanted to miss.

Still, Maloof was careful to make sure no one saw him open the door to the restroom.

He locked it carefully, hung the bag on a hook on the back of the door and pulled out a sleeping mat and pillow. The room reeked of urine, but he had seen worse. He put everything on the floor in the corner opposite the toilet and sat down on the mat. He had a book with him, a thick Stephen King paperback, but he wouldn't read any of it. It was more a ritual; he always brought a thick book that he wouldn't read.

It took almost ten minutes before the noise outside the restroom door gradually increased to a roar. Desperate soccer fans who didn't want to wait in the long lines for the normal toilets started pulling at Maloof's door.

But the lock held, and Maloof remained sitting on the floor.

After fifteen, possibly twenty minutes, the stadium fell quiet again. All that remained now was to wait. The cleaning staff wouldn't arrive until the next morning, it was a way for the company to avoid paying overtime. Zoran Petrovic had been running a successful cleaning company for ten years, and he knew how things worked at Råsunda.

But not even Petrovic knew where Michel Maloof was at that moment.

Maloof slept in intervals of fifteen minutes, the floor was too hard and the mat too thin for any longer than that. When he eventually got up at four thirty in the morning, he was stiff and in a bad mood.

He opened the door to the disabled restroom and found Råsunda Stadium quiet and deserted.

Maloof walked slowly down its dark corridors, past the shutters on all the food stalls. It was impossible to think that just last night, tens of thousands of people had been shouting, cheering, drinking and laughing on the now-empty terraces; right then, it felt more like the day after a nuclear holocaust.

There were turnstiles at the exits. They turned only one way, so there were no locks. Maloof left Råsunda in the early-morning darkness, taking the train out to Kårsta. From there, he would take a bus to Norrtälje.

The likelihood of him bumping into anyone he knew in any of those places was tiny.

48

Sami Farhan waited another day, until Saturday, September 19. If Michel Maloof had found it easy to disappear and Niklas Nordgren slightly harder, the task was by far the most difficult for Sami.

He did what he usually did. He booked a flight leaving late in the afternoon. This time, he had chosen Hamburg as his destination. The return journey was booked for a month's time, but the seat back to Arlanda would be empty. When he landed, there would be a car waiting for him at the airport, and he would drive it back to Stockholm that evening and night.

He was doing someone a service, the car had been bought in Germany and would later have to pay duty in Sweden. But that wasn't his problem. He would leave it in a parking garage in Östermalm and then make his way through the city unnoticed, heading for an apartment in Södermalm where no one would either think to look for or be able to trace him.

Abracadabra, and Sami Farhan would have disappeared.

No, that wasn't the problem.

It was the farewells that were impossible.

That Saturday morning had followed its usual, chaotic pattern. The baby had woken and started screaming at four, and before he had been fed and gone back to sleep, he had managed to wake his older brother. Sami had walked around and around the kitchen table with John in his arms, loop after loop after loop, listening to his sniffles eventually grow quieter and cross over into sleep.

But the minute he put the boy down in his bed, a mattress on the floor in the room Karin had previously used as her office, Sami himself had felt wide awake. He had sat down on the sofa in the living room and tried to work out what he was going to say. It was impossible.

By five, he had dozed off again, and he slept through until seven. He woke to the sound of Karin trying to make coffee as she prepared the gruel for the one-year-old. She had been up since six, and she handed Sami a bottle and pointed to the baby, who was sleeping in the stroller in the hallway. After that, she staggered into the bedroom, pulled the door shut and slumped onto the bed with the hope that a few hours' uninterrupted sleep would allow her milk to thicken enough for the next feed.

This isn't right, he thought.

I can't leave her like this.

Not now, not for a week, not even for a day.

But he had no choice.

Going underground and disappearing from the system was his way of protecting Karin and the kids. Both in the long and the short term.

Sami wasn't planning to be sent away again. He couldn't, not now that he had created all of this. A home. A family.

His plan was to stay away for almost three weeks, but he was doing that to avoid being sent away for three years.

Or even longer.

It wasn't that prison scared him. If you got into the game, you had to accept the rules. But for his family, things were different.

Sami made lunch and gently woke Karin by taking her a tray of food, a ham-and-cheese omelet and a large glass of milk. For once, both boys were sleeping.

He put the tray on the bed and sat down by her feet. He watched as she wearily sat up. She was so incredibly beautiful. Like always when he watched her without her knowledge, he knew that he could never be with anyone else.

"I have to go away," he said.

The words came suddenly, and he surprised himself. However he had been imagining their conversation would start, it wasn't like this.

She had just picked up the cutlery to start eating, but she put it back down.

"No," she said firmly.

Her eyes were serious.

"Honestly, love, it's got to wait. Whatever it is. I need all the help I can get right now."

"I know," he said. "I know."

He sat perfectly still. Karin could count on one hand the times she had seen him sit motionless like he was right now. She allowed the silence to grow before she asked the question.

"Where are you going?"

"I have to go away," he repeated.

"Where?"

He couldn't meet her eye. He turned to look out of the window. He pulled at his sweater, which suddenly felt tight.

"I can't say."

"Don't do it," she said. "You promised."

She spoke quietly, so as not to wake the boys. There was no anger in her voice, just sadness. That made everything worse.

"I know," he said. "I'll keep my promise."

He meant it. He wasn't going to live a criminal life. He truly believed that.

"So you can tell me where you're going then," she said. "Is it overnight?"

"It's for a few weeks," he said.

That made her explode.

"You can't!" she shouted.

The tray tipped. Milk sloshed out of the glass.

"You can't just go away for a few weeks! Not without telling me where you're going. Not when we've just had a baby!"

And at that very moment, the baby started crying in the hallway. Sami took it as an excuse to get up.

"Did you hear what I said!" she shouted after him.

SEPTEMBER 22–23

49

It's a few minutes before five. His shift ends then, when the evening and night staff take over. But it's been quiet all afternoon, so he goes out to get changed a couple of minutes early.

He has been working at the Statoil gas station on Magelungsvägen in Bandhagen for almost two years now, and he likes his job. There's a small gang of them that usually work shifts together, three guys and two girls, and they've also started hanging out after work. When he first arrived from the north five years earlier, he had trouble finding a job and making new friends. He got by, lived in sublet sublets like everyone else, and the days passed. He heard about the job at the Statoil station by chance while he was working overtime for a pizzeria in Högdalen, delivering pizzas on a moped he'd stolen from outside the Globe Arena. He had happened to stop there for gas and heard the manager complaining about how they were one man short that night.

He started immediately, eating the pizza he had been carrying rather than delivering it.

They gave him more and more night shifts, and after a year or so he started working during the day.

That was what everyone there wanted; no one feels like sabotaging their circadian rhythms.

Like always, they pause outside the gas station for a while, chatting before they head home. His gym bag is on the floor between his feet. It's pretty big, an overnight bag, but he often has it with him, so no one thinks anything of it.

It's Tuesday evening and nothing much is going on, there's nothing worth watching on TV. Someone invites the others over to watch a film; *The Girl Who Played with Fire* came out in theaters on Friday, but it's already up on Pirate Bay.

Ordinarily, he likes their film nights, but this time he says no.

The others laugh and make fun of him. Does he have something secret on the go? Someone secret?

He laughs with them and says there's no secret at all, he's going to work out. He gestures to his bag.

As a joke, one of the other guys bends down to grab it and remove the obstacle to their film evening.

But when he takes the handles and tries to lift the bag from the ground, he's completely unprepared for the weight of it. He can't even make it budge.

"What the hell?"

Inside the spacious gym bag is a long, thick chain. One that has metal barbs soldered onto it and which will be stretched across Elektravägen at the crossroads with Västbergavägen in a few hours' time.

He swings the bag up onto his shoulder.

He's keen for it to look like a simple motion.

Then he laughs at how heavy it is and starts making his way toward the bus stop.

He has a job to do. He takes out his phone and makes a call.

50

The minute the phone rings, everything gets under way. Months of planning, years of dreaming about the building in Västberga.

It's time.

Michel Maloof gets up from his chair and goes over to the kitchen counter. He picks up and hears his chain man say that he's on the way. His task for the night is to stretch the string of caltrops across Elektravägen at the crossroads with Västbergavägen, and also across Västberga Allé by Drivhjulsvägen, to put a stop to any police cars which might come racing out of the station on Västberga Gårdsväg.

Maloof quickly confirms and then hangs up.

He returns to his chair by the window. It has rapidly become his favorite spot in the newly built, sparsely decorated apartment in Norrtälje that Zoran Petrovic swore no one would be able to link to them. Petrovic knows the guy who installed the HVAC when the apartment were built a few years earlier, who's the one who got them the key.

Maloof has been staring out that kitchen window for four days now, and there's one thing he's sure of: He'll never move to Norrtälje.

His mind turns to Alexandra Svensson. He hasn't missed anything more than her soft body over these past few days. The scent of her skin has filled his dreams. He can't remember that ever having happened before.

Soon, he'll be able to look her in the eye without having to worry that she can see straight through his pupils and into his soul, finding him out. Over the past few weeks, he was worried she would be working tonight, that for some reason he would bump into her in Västberga in the middle of it all. But a week or so ago, he learned that Alexandra's night shifts didn't start until Thursday, meaning she would be at home in Hammarby Sjöstad tomorrow morning. That was an enormous relief.

Soon, everything will be different.

Soon, he won't have to lie to her about what he's doing anymore. Never telling her what he did won't be a problem for him; it's the basis for every relationship Maloof has ever had.

He sinks into daydreams and mentally ticks off the list of things that could go wrong tonight and tomorrow morning. There are so many that he no longer has the energy to care. He hears Sami talking about his "plan F" and smiles. When reality gets its teeth into their plans—as it always does—it's the ability to improvise that separates the pros from the amateurs. That's why he's working with Sami Farhan and Niklas Nordgren: they both know how to improvise.

All three set up filters earlier that week. Went underground. Nordgren calls it "ducking." A week or so before a big job, you vanish from the radar. Then you find somewhere to lie low, alone, for a few days.

It's not just because of the police, it's also because of their own families and friends. If no one knows where they are, no one can give them away or accidentally reveal anything important.

Maloof sighs. It's as much a sigh of satisfaction as it is of fear. He hates these last few hours of passive waiting ahead of a job. During the planning phase, he's always calm and methodical. He makes lists in his head and ticks off the points one by one. And once things get started, it's as though he transforms. With a mask covering his face, it's like he rediscovers his true identity. His senses are heightened, he breathes more calmly and thinks more clearly.

But this period of limbo between planning and action is unbearable.

He throws his phone onto a cloth on top of the dishwasher, tips the last of the cold coffee out of the pot and refills it with water to brew a fresh batch.

Petrovic isn't coming until one. Maloof smiles at the thought of his tall friend and the way he made the Swedish police think the robbery would be taking place on the fifteenth.

Petrovic enjoyed doing that, and he spoke extensively about how he did it. He said it's hints that are reliable, not loud statements.

And he was right.

51

10:50 p.m.

The old man in the hat walking northward toward Karusellplan in Västberga could, without doubt, have lived in one of the three-story buildings in the area, and though it was approaching eleven at night, he wasn't drawing any attention to himself.

Nor had he done so earlier that day, when he spent just over an hour tending to his car at the gas station overlooking the G4S cash depot. Or when he sat down on the grass behind the depot reading a book in the still-warm sunshine. He just looked like an old man taking care of his old car, someone who liked to read old books.

He turns off into the Västberga industrial park, a place people don't tend to go for a late-night stroll.

He isn't worried about being seen. He isn't doing anything illegal, he has no criminal record, and tomorrow morning he'll head back to Åkersberga, where he lives.

In his jacket pocket, he has two cell phones. One of them is his, and the other has been loaned to him. Only one number has been saved in that phone, and his job is to call it and report on the situation.

If he sees anything out of the ordinary.

Police officers out on patrol, guards that don't seem to belong in the area. Or any unusual activity around the building itself.

He's even meant to call if everything seems fine.

Just to report that.

52

The phone rings.

Though he has been waiting for the call, the sound still surprises Sami. He jumps up from the sofa and runs into the kitchen. He has four phones, lined up in a perfect row on the table, each loaded with a brand-new SIM card. The vibration from the ringing phone makes the others tremble in anticipation. He had programmed the numbers he would need that night and early morning the previous Sunday.

TEAM 1, he reads on the screen. That's how he's labeled them, with different numbers, and that's what he's planning on calling them. Nordgren had pointed out that a "team" needs more than one member. Sami explained that this isn't some grammar exercise.

He picks up the phone and answers.

"Still quiet," says Team 1.

"Good."

That's all.

The afternoon has been a long one. It felt endless. Sami Farhan has been in the apartment on Kocksgatan in Södermalm for three days now, two floors up, facing the courtyard. This is where he has been lying low ever since driving back from Hamburg.

He hasn't been out during the day. Instead, he has watched TV, slept and eaten. His sister had left food for him in the fridge and the freezer; the apartment belongs to one of her friends, currently traveling around Asia. The friend has no idea that her place is currently being used by a robber who, for the past few days, has turned his sleeping patterns on their head in order to be able to perform at his best during a night that has been six months in the planning.

Three days have passed since Sami went underground and vanished from the police and his friends' radars, heading for Arlanda. He hasn't spoken to Karin since, he hasn't been in touch with his mother, Michel Maloof or Niklas Nordgren; he hadn't touched a cell phone in a week.

Throughout his thirty-year life, Sami has involuntarily had plenty of experience of loneliness and inactivity, both in custody and in prison. But lying low means that the boredom is self-inflicted, which makes things only slightly better. The closer to the finishing line he comes, the harder it is to keep his cool.

His lift won't arrive until twelve thirty. He has, in other words, just over an hour to kill.

He thaws a couple of square chunks of fried chicken in the microwave and then stares at them on his plate, completely uninterested. Ketchup won't make them any more appealing. Even food requires planning. He knows how much he can drink every hour without having to go to the toilet. After having spent days and weeks planning the helicopter route and the strength of the explosives, it would have been idiotic not to chart his own body's processes. He knows he shouldn't eat any more solids after a quarter past eleven.

He leaves the kitchen after throwing away the remains of his meal, turns off the light in the living room and sits down in an armchair. He tries to focus.

After catching the connecting bus directly to Danvikstull, he kills a few hours in an Espresso House before arriving at Kettola's place at midnight, as agreed. He had been fantasizing about a cup of hot coffee and a muffin during his time in the playhouse, when his only sustenance came from warmed-up cans.

53

11:15 p.m.

Niklas Nordgren takes the last boat to Stavsnäs at dinnertime. He is the only person waiting on the jetty on Runmarö, but it doesn't matter if the captain can point him out at a later date. Having been on Runmarö isn't incriminating evidence.

With each day that has passed, he has become increasingly stiff from sleeping in the slightly too-short bed in the playhouse on Runmarö. He has flipped his normal routine upside down, and spent his days asleep. Though the house is on the east of the island, and dangerous reefs off the coast prevent any boats from getting too close, he didn't want to move around on the plot of land during the day. At this time of year, there are barely any tourists left in the archipelago, and the boats that do pass belong to the year-round residents, people who keep an eye on where there are guests and where there should be empty houses in the middle of September. Instead, he took quick runs in the woods after midnight, constantly afraid of stepping on a snake or coming face-to-face with a badger. But he knew that he needed to keep moving, otherwise he wouldn't be ready when the time came.

On Tuesday afternoon, when he woke and realized that his short vacation in the archipelago was over, he felt great all the same. His back wasn't aching in the slightest, and the cold he thought he could feel developing when he went to bed at dawn seemed to have vanished.

*　　*　　*

54

11:30 p.m.

She gets a fare out to Bromma and has to wait only half an hour before she gets another back into town. That's the good thing about working for one of the big taxi firms, there are always plenty of new customers. This time, it's a businessman with flushed red cheeks who probably couldn't have said no to an extra bottle of cognac on the plane.

If they still served alcohol on domestic flights?

She doesn't know, it's been years since she last flew anywhere.

The businessman is headed for Östermalm, he gives her the address. The man stares out the window the whole way there, he's too good to talk to her. Just a few minutes into the drive, she already knows that he won't leave a tip. That type never does.

She drops him off and checks the time. She makes trips to Östermalm often enough to have become hooked on the specialty hot dog kiosk on Nybrogatan. Does she have time to try out one of his Turkish lamb sausages and then squeeze in one more fare? But before her conscience has time to give an answer, her stomach directs her onto Kommendörsgatan, down to the old post office where the kiosk is. There's a parking space right next to it, which she takes as a sign.

The sausage is just as spicy as she hoped.

When she gets back behind the wheel, it's already a little past twelve, and she has two, three hours before it's time. She isn't really meant to clock off before morning, but she will shut down the system at three, making herself both unavailable and invisible. In the trunk, she has the chain with the caltrops welded onto it, the one she is meant to stretch across Västberga Allé. She assumes it will take her a while; according to Niklas Nordgren, the chain needs to be fastened on either side, but he couldn't explain how to do it, he just gave her two padlocks.

She's an imaginative woman, she'll work something out.

She drives downtown and passes the long line for taxis outside the restaurants there. In a way, it feels good to be avoiding the fight for yet another fare that night, even though her job of stretching the chain across the road won't pay much more than a few trips to and from Arlanda.

She takes out her phone.

55

Niklas Nordgren feels the buzz of his phone in the inner pocket of his jacket. He fishes it out and answers with a grunt.

It's his chain woman. She has no idea that she's part of a bigger plan. She has no idea that she's one of many. She's calling to say that she knows what she has to do. Nordgren answers monosyllabically and then hangs up. He hopes she finds somewhere solid to fix the chain at either side of the road.

He reaches the doorway on Rosenlundsgatan at ten past twelve, five minutes earlier than planned. The building is where Jan Kettola lives. Kettola sometimes helps out at the electricians' where Nordgren works, and he's the one who has promised to drive Nordgren out to the meeting place in Stora Skuggan Park. The two men aren't close friends. They've done a couple of jobs together, a few years ago now, but there's a certain loyalty between them. Nordgren isn't worried. All Kettola knows is that they're driving out to Stora Skuggan. Even when he hears the news about what happened on the radio tomorrow morning, there's no way he'll join the dots.

Rather than ringing the buzzer, Niklas Nordgren starts to worry. He thinks about the huge rock at the gravel pit in Norsborg where they'll land once it's all over. Without the patience or the sense to use pulleys, the rock is impossible to shift, it weighs almost a ton. But it should work, he instructed the team in Norsborg himself.

Then his thoughts turn to the police helicopter.

When he told the others what he had eventually worked out, how he was planning to keep the helicopter—or helicopters—on the ground, he did it with a certainty that immediately convinced both Maloof and Sami. They asked questions afterward, particularly Sami, since it's one of his teams who will do the job there in a couple of hours. But neither of them had doubted the idea itself.

But now Niklas Nordgren has second thoughts.

Would it really work?

56

Claude Tavernier's mother had always said that he was a natural leader.

It wasn't something he quoted, he wasn't stupid, he knew how it sounded when a man in his thirties referred to his mother's opinions. But for Tavernier, those words had taken on lifelong meaning. His mother had given him the self-confidence, which had given him the conviction, which had given him the courage. He wasn't much of a scholar and he definitely wasn't an athlete; he had studied economics at college in Lyon, but he still had his dissertation to write. He had moved to Sweden and learned the language because of a love that had turned out to be more fragile than he had imagined, but since he had already organized both a job and a place to live, he remained in Stockholm when it all fell apart. He still wasn't sure whether that was just a temporary detour, or whether it was the path he would take in life.

Deep down, he knew he was the kind of person other people followed. He was a leader. That was what his mother had predicted, and that was how he had always thought of himself. Despite the setbacks and limitations.

He usually ate out when he worked nights. Then he would hang around in a bar somewhere until it was time to go. The alternative was spending the evening at home, checking his watch every five minutes. Night shifts started at midnight and ended at eight the next morning. They worked to a rolling schedule, two nights in a row, one day off, and then three day shifts from nine till five.

Just over four years after he was first hired, he had been called to the top boss and asked whether he was ready to take the next step in his career. It hadn't come as a surprise. On the contrary. Tavernier had calmly asked about the pension terms, taken the weekend to make it seem like he was thinking about it and then signed the contract.

He was in his third year in a leadership role now, and felt like it would soon be time to move on. Remaining an anonymous middle manager among hundreds of others wasn't what his mother had meant when she saw the leader in him.

All the same, he was in no hurry to leave. The work itself might have been monotonous, and it was a struggle to convince himself he was doing something meaningful. But whenever he scrolled through the job listings in either Stockholm or Paris, he felt certain that things would be no different anywhere else. Neither in terms of working conditions nor career prospects, neither in Lyon nor in Malmö.

When it came to colleagues, Tavernier assumed that in any group, there would always be those that people liked, and those that people liked less.

In his current workplace, there was an older woman, Ann-Marie Olausson, who drove him mad. She was sixty-one, had worked for the company her entire life, and acted as though she owned it. She was the type of person who, without an ounce of irony, would say, "But that's how we've always done it." Tavernier assumed that his youth must antagonize her, but there wasn't much he could do about that.

On Tuesdays, Claude Tavernier liked to go to the middle bar at Sturehof, waiting for midnight and the start of his shift. The middle bar was small and intimate, at once both a passageway and a cozy corner. He liked to exchange a few comradely words with the hardworking barman and then just stand around with his cold beer, watching all the beautiful people come and go in the mirror. In the taxi on the way to work, he would then chew some menthol gum so that no one would notice that he stunk of alcohol and decide that he had a drinking problem.

There was no real need for him to take a taxi out to the suburbs. Tavernier had bought a used Nissan a year earlier, a car he liked more than he cared to admit. But since the number of parking spots the company had out in Västberga was limited, Tavernier would have to wait for someone else to quit or die before he managed to get ahold of one.

He sighs, pays the bill and heads out onto Stureplan. He finds an empty TaxiKurir, the company he feels loyal to for some unclear reason, and then jumps in the backseat.

"Västberga Allé," he says.

The driver nods and steps on the gas.

When Claude Tavernier climbs out of the taxi outside the G4S cash depot on the night of September 22, it's ten to twelve. And there, just as he is making his way into the building, he loses all confidence for a very brief moment.

It's something that happens a few times a week.

It's like when you're on a plane and the weather is good, and then it suddenly, unexpectedly, drops a few feet due to turbulence. Or like when you're sprawled over the toilet and have been throwing up and up and up, so much that it feels like there's nothing left to throw up, but still you know that the next stomach cramp is on the way.

I'm no one, he has time to think. I can't be in charge of a load of people. I can't make decisions for others.

Claude Tavernier takes a deep breath. He fills his lungs with the cool night air, raises his face to the sky and then the moment passes.

He's the night manager for Counting on the sixth floor of G4S once again.

A young career man.

He finds his ID card in his pocket and holds it up to Valter Jansson, the security guard in Reception that night. Tavernier and Jansson have worked plenty of nights together in Västberga; they feel comfortable with one another.

57

11:52 p.m.

On the top floor of one of Stockholm's few skyscrapers, a building where the newsrooms of Sweden's biggest morning paper, *Dagens Nyheter*, and the country's second-biggest evening paper, *Expressen*, were once based, is an internal dining room available only to the businesses in the building. Turning the room into a commercial restaurant has been discussed on a number of occasions; the views are spectacular and it's not like there has been a lack of interested restaurateurs. But one of *Dagens Nyheter*'s historic boardrooms is on the other side of the wall to the kitchen, and though it's been decades since the paper moved downstairs, the top floor is still thought of as its executive floor. And, naturally, it doesn't want any outsiders up there.

It's approaching twelve when the kitchen staff leave the restaurant kitchen on the twenty-third floor that evening. Food has been cooked and served to a working group from *Expressen*. Top-level management must have been present, because less alcohol has been consumed than usual, and the evening was quickly wound up. The kitchen and service staff are glad for the early finish, and they laugh on their way down to street level on Rålambsvägen.

No one notices that someone who has been working on the cold buffet all night is missing from the cramped elevator. If they had, they might just assume that he had already left or that he was sorting out one last thing in the kitchen before heading home.

Both assumptions would have been wrong.

The missing man waits on the twenty-third floor until he sees on the display that the elevator carrying his colleagues has reached ground level. He holds back until he's sure that none of the elevators are coming back up again. Then he takes out his electronic pass and opens the door to the stairwell. He climbs the stairs to the roof and opens the door, which is locked from the inside. Before he steps out into the night, he pushes a cork into the doorway so that the door won't lock behind him.

During a shift a few days earlier, he had gone up to the roof to take a leak and hidden a pair of night-vision goggles behind one of the chimney stacks. This time, he's carrying a black gym bag from SATS, inside it a warm sweater, a thermos full of coffee, four bananas and a bar of Marabou chocolate. It's going to be a long night, and he'll need the extra energy.

The man from the cold buffet breathes in the cool night air and looks out over the beautiful capital. Right below him, Riddarfjärden glitters in the glow of the streetlamps, the water curling like an autostrada from Rålambshovsparken to city hall. In the other direction, to the west, the Traneberg Bridge rises up across the narrow sound, and to the south, he can see red and white dots of light moving along the winding bridges of the Essingeleden highway.

It's because of the view that the man is on the roof. From the highest building in Marieberg, he'll be able to see anyone approaching Västberga from the air. He'll be able to blow their cover in good time, whether they're on the way from Berga or Uppsala.

He takes out a brand-new cell phone and dials the only number saved in the contact list.

Sami Farhan answers.

"Team Four. I'm in position," the man from the cold buffet says.

58

11:55 p.m.

Ezra Ray is sitting in a gray 1999 Volvo V70, with all the registration and tax documents in the glove compartment. He doesn't know who owns the car, but he assumes it belongs to the scrapyard in Lidingö where he picked it up an hour or so earlier. He drives across Lidingö Bridge and decides not to take the route through Lill-Jansskogen Park. It's the middle of the night, and he imagines that the risk of being pulled over by the police will be greater if he chooses a dark forest road. Instead, he takes Valhallavägen, wide and well lit, full of heavy trucks delivering or picking up goods from the harbors beyond Gärdet.

Ezra Ray doesn't know exactly what is happening tonight, but by putting together the pieces he has been involved in, the drawings he stole from the town planning office and the ladders he bought from Bauhaus, he could work some of it out. Studying the items beneath the blankets in the roomy trunk of the Volvo, he could probably work out the rest. There's a circular saw and some mailbags. Ropes and frame charges. Detonators, cables and explosives. Face masks, body armor and headlamps. Two crowbars, an enormous sledgehammer and a smaller toolbox. The ladders. The longer of the two is twelve feet long when folded, Ezra had to push it between the front seats and let it rest on the dashboard. He still couldn't close the trunk lid properly.

But he doesn't put the pieces together, he doesn't draw any conclusions. If he never thinks it, it'll be easier to deny knowledge later. If he has to deny anything.

*   *   *

It's not the ladders preventing him from closing the trunk that will be his biggest problem if the police pull him over. If they've set up a drunk-driving checkpoint by Roslagstull, if the car's registration number is in a database of people who haven't paid parking fines, or the traffic police happen to stop him, it's all over. Possession of explosives is an offense in Sweden. Ezra knows that he's aware of only a fraction of the planning that must have gone into this evening. He knows how this type of project is built on hopes and dreams.

And right now, the entire thing hinges on him.

Ezra smiles. He glances at the speedometer. The risk isn't that he's driving too fast, it's that he's driving too slowly in his attempts to seem law abiding.

The lights are green all the way to Roslagstull, and he drives straight on toward the university and Frescati. They had scoped out the place a few weeks earlier, and since then Ezra has swung by a few times at this time of night. He'd never seen another living soul there, not a single dog owner or taxi driver stopping for a piss.

He passes the turnoff to the university and drives on, via Svante Arrhenius Väg, so that he's approaching Stora Skuggans Väg from the north. After a thousand feet, he turns onto a small forest road he would never have noticed in the dark. He parks. Kills the engine and immediately starts unloading the car. He runs the items from his trunk into the woods in batches. It's quite a long way from the car to the meeting place, but that's how it has to be. Discovering the car can't be the same as discovering them.

It's a few minutes after midnight.

Ezra Ray takes out his phone and dials the number saved on it.

Sami answers immediately.

"I'm here," Ezra says.

59

11:58 p.m.

The phone rings again. It's the fourth call in an hour.

This time, TEAM 2 flashes on the display.

Team 2 is responsible for moving the huge rock used to block the entrance to the gravel pit in Norsborg. It's there that the getaway cars will be waiting once it's all over. It'll still be dark then, so Team 2 also has to make sure that the helicopter pilot can see where he's landing.

"Yeah?" Sami answers.

"We're here," says the voice on the other end.

"Thanks," Sami replies, hanging up.

It's time to get changed.

He goes into the bedroom and takes off his sweatpants and T-shirt. He shoves these, along with his toiletries, into the small bag his sister will pick up tomorrow afternoon. She's also promised to tidy up after him.

Sami picks up the waist pouch he bought. He fastens it around himself after checking the documents for the tenth time that evening. Inside the small pouch, his passport and a plane ticket to Punta Cana. His plan is to head straight to Arlanda from the gravel pit in Norsborg and then kill some time in one of the cafés in SkyCity. The plane takes off seven hours later, which might seem like a long time, but it's considerably less than he's waited already today.

On top of the waist pouch, he pulls on a thin black sweater. Over that, he'll be wearing a tight black windbreaker. His trousers are a pair of black jeans. They've agreed to wear black, all three of them, with one exception. Sami has to be wearing his white sneakers. Adidas. They bring him luck.

Once he's ready, he goes back out into the living room and waits for the next call. It should have already come in, but maybe they rang at the exact same time as Team 2, maybe they got the busy signal?

The minutes tick away.

By the time the display reaches 12:05, Sami can't sit still in the armchair any longer. He gets up, grabs the phone and goes into the bedroom. He moves around his bag, which he placed on the floor by the bed, and then goes back out into the living room. He repeats this twice. It's 12:09, and his phone still hasn't rung.

Team 3's number is saved in his phone, but he knows he isn't meant to make any calls from this SIM card. If they've run into trouble, a vibrating phone in their pocket isn't going to help.

Sami composes himself. Moves behind the armchair and peers out the window. When the living room is dark, the glow from the streetlights on Kocksgatan seems even brighter.

His phone rings. It's 12:18.

Team 3. They're in Myttinge on Värmdö. It's Team 3 that is responsible for keeping the police helicopters on the ground, a prerequisite for being able to carry out the job in Västberga tonight. If any of the chain teams fail, it's unlucky, but it's not critical.

Team 3, on the other hand, has to succeed.

Sami answers.

"Hello?" he hears a voice say on the line.

"Yeah?" Sami replies.

"It's not here," says the voice.

"What do you mean?"

"The hangar's empty. The helicopter's not here."

60

Michel Maloof sees the car approaching through the kitchen window. It's the first one to drive down Billborgsgatan, in the heart of Norrtälje, in over half an hour. The nightlife in the town could hardly be called pulsing. The car slows down and finds an empty parking space right outside his door.

Zoran Petrovic unfolds himself from the driver's seat. It's a new BMW, it looks black from Maloof's window, but it could just as easily be dark blue. The passenger's side door opens. It's the American, Jack Kluger. This is the first time Maloof has seen him. The man on the sidewalk reminds him of a quarterback from an American football team, he's knock-kneed and his upper body is oversized in relation to his lower half. In all likelihood, he has no real idea where he is right now.

Petrovic and the American step into the building, and a few seconds later the buzzer rings. Maloof opens the door.

"Been a while," Petrovic says, stepping into the apartment.

Maloof grins. "Right," he says. "Been a while. Hi, hi."

He shakes the American's hand. Kluger's grip is strong and dry. Reassuring.

"Where's the food?" Maloof asks.

"Shit," says Petrovic. "I forgot it."

"You forgot it?" Maloof repeats, unable to hide the disappointment in his voice. He scratches his cheek. "But, I can't . . . you can't have forgotten it?"

They're speaking Swedish. The American doesn't seem to care what they're talking about. Or maybe he understands Swedish but isn't letting on. According to Petrovic, Kluger has been living and working in Sweden for a few years now.

"Sorry," Petrovic says again.

Maloof struggles to seem indifferent. He smiles and shrugs. All the same, he can't understand how Petrovic can have forgotten to drive by McDonald's. They've been working together for so long now that he should know better.

"No, no," Maloof says. "No, it's OK. No problem. We can go now instead."

He glances at the helicopter pilot and adds, in English: "We need some food."

Maloof doesn't wait for a reply. He goes out into the hall and pulls on his shoes and coat.

"You're not serious?" Petrovic says.

"He's coming. The weapons are in the bedroom. We can't leave him alone with the weapons . . ."

When Maloof took the bus up to Norrtälje a few days earlier, he had walked past a McDonald's on Stockholmsvägen. It was one of the few places that stayed open until one in the morning. They didn't have much time.

"Come on, come on," he says when he notices that the American is hesitating.

Maloof wouldn't call himself superstitious. He's not even religious. But there is also no point tempting fate.

He always eats a large meal from McDonald's before a job.

It's nonnegotiable.

61

In the end room in the apartment on Strandvägen, there is a deep alcove, and it is in this alcove that Caroline Thurn has placed an enormous armchair. It isn't visible unless you actually step into the room. The soft embrace of this armchair is where Thurn sometimes spends her nights, her legs on the matching footstool or her knees drawn up to her chin, staring out across Nybroviken. She can either turn to face the roof and masts of the Vasa Museum, next to the silhouettes of the roller coasters of Gröna Lund, or else the other way, toward the center of town and the heavy stone facades of Nybrokajen leading up to Raoul Wallenbergs Torg.

Over the past week, she has found it unusually easy to banish certain thoughts and keep her worries at bay.

She's wearing a pair of big, white headphones, and the incessant chatter saved on the hard drives she copied and brought home with her, hard drives that are now piled up on the kitchen counter next to her Nespresso machine, is fascinating her. Listening to Zoran Petrovic's monologues is like watching waves roll ashore; there's a kind of uniformity to them which has her spellbound.

Despite the hundreds of hours they have recorded, they still haven't found a single clue relating to the aborted helicopter robbery.

Their surveillance has now stopped, but Thurn had wondered whether they should go back to the beginning and listen to the tapes without specifically trying to spot anything linked to the aborted raid on Panaxia. If they listened with an open mind, without any preconceptions, what might those hours of phone calls reveal? Petrovic's address book was overflowing with criminal contacts, after all.

That was the original thought behind copying the hard drives and bringing them home. But the more Caroline Thurn listens to Zoran Petrovic's insufferable torrent of words, the constant flow of noise aimed at promoting himself, making himself seem more interesting, emphasizing his importance, sharing his experiences and moving himself higher up the hierarchy, the bigger the knot of anger grows in her chest. The man Thurn had spent her nights focused on just one week earlier is as obsessed with himself as he is full of disgust for the society which gave him his chances in life. No matter how humble Petrovic tries to make himself appear, he is actually ruthlessly arrogant toward his countrymen and -women, all toiling away so that people like him can sail through life with the least possible resistance.

Injustice, Thurn thinks. She hates it. She knows how it feels when it strikes.

And the task force leader's initial long shot has evolved into increasingly manic behavior. She starts to methodically write down the clues Petrovic throws around during conversations in his car and in restaurants. Nothing is enough to send him down on its own merit, but if they cross-reference Petrovic's insinuations with real events that autumn, Thurn is increasingly convinced that they'll find something.

She hears his confident tone in her ears, it fills her consciousness, and she wonders what he will sound like when she is finally in front of him, her service weapon drawn and an arrest warrant in hand, pushing him into her car on the way to Bergsgatan and remand prison.

Much more pathetic, she guesses.

62

It's a cool, crisp night. The scent of moss and pine in the air. In the glow of Ezra's flashlight, Sami Farhan and Niklas Nordgren go through the equipment. They check that the ladders can be easily extended and secured. They count the number of mailbags, feel the ropes, open the toolbox to make sure everything is there and then put it into one of the mailbags along with the crowbars and the saw. All of this happens in silence, and Ezra shines his flashlight wherever Sami points.

Nordgren and Sami arrived at roughly the same time. It's ten days since they last saw one another, in Hjorthagen. Nordgren had pulled on his balaclava at the very moment he arrived, he doesn't want Sami's friend Ezra to be able to identify him.

Sami has told him that the police helicopter isn't in Myttinge, but Nordgren takes that information in his stride. He's counting on problems arising, and that's easy enough to handle. They can't do the job if they don't have the police helicopters under control. It's that simple. All they can do is keep working and hope for the best.

Nordgren continues to go through the equipment, paying particular attention to his own items. He has already prepared the cut-up Coca-Cola cans with silver tape packages at the bottom. The packages are full of neodymium magnets. He has prepared six cans, but he hopes he'll need to use only one of them.

He also has four U-channels, similar to an upside-down train track, cut into short pieces. They're heavier and more cumbersome, which is why the number is smaller. He's also hoping to use only one of them. He goes through the explosive putty and the detonators and worries about moisture.

"I should test one," he says, mostly to himself.

Sami has no objections. They're miles from the nearest built-up area.

Nordgren gets to work. It takes him only a few minutes to discover that the long detonation cable isn't with the detonators and the battery.

"Which damn cable?" Ezra asks, holding his hands up in the air.

It's the first thing he has said since the two key players arrived. He knows his place. Nordgren has his balaclava pulled down over his face, and though Ezra has worn one like it many times before, it still commands respect.

Sami, who had been testing the headlamps, turns around.

"The cable," says Nordgren.

"I took everything that was there!" Ezra shouts. "Do you think I'm some fucking—"

"The long cable's missing. It's fifty feet long."

There's no doubt in Nordgren's mind. He knows he packed it.

"I mean, shit, I don't know . . ." Ezra begins, but he quickly falls silent.

"What the hell!" Sami says, glancing at his watch.

It's quarter to two.

"We've got to have it," Nordgren says. "Without that long cable, we can't blow out the reinforced glass on the sixth floor."

Sami walks over to the rest of the equipment. He feverishly rifles among the ropes and bags, hoping to find the cable.

But it isn't there.

"Shit, Ezra!" he hisses.

Ezra Ray looks deeply unhappy.

63

In the apartment in Norrtälje, Michel Maloof places the food on the kitchen table. He had gone into the McDonald's alone while Petrovic and Kluger waited outside. Three large Big Mac meals with Coke Zero. Extra salt. He sits down and starts eating before it gets cold. Halfway through his burger, he realizes that the others aren't planning on joining him.

He gets up from the table and goes into the bedroom. They're busy checking the weapons. Petrovic and the American have taken apart the machine guns and handguns and laid out all of the parts on two sheets.

It turns out that Kluger is as much a perfectionist as the tall Yugoslavian, and every single bullet has to be checked before it can be pushed back into the magazine.

"I could do this blindfolded," the former marine says in his broad Southern accent, adding, "I have done it blindfolded."

"Right." Maloof nods. "The burgers are getting cold?"

"That's fine," Kluger replies.

"I might have a few fries later?" Petrovic says, to show goodwill.

"No, no," Maloof says. "Or maybe . . . can I have your burger?"

"You're insane," Petrovic decides.

"So it's OK?" Maloof asks.

"Totally fine." Petrovic returns to his machine gun parts.

The realization that Petrovic and the American are like two big children playing with Legos strikes Maloof as he sits back down at the table and tries to stop the lettuce from falling out of the burger when he lifts it from its cardboard carton.

Back in the bedroom, Kluger makes the exact same remark.

"He's like a little kid," the American says to Petrovic. "I mean, who eats McDonald's?"

64

Sami grabs a large branch from the ground and swings it down onto a rock. Splinters fly. But he doesn't say a word. The helicopter isn't where it's meant to be. The detonation cable is missing. He's also worried that the ladders might be too short.

They're "extension ladders," or at least that was what the kid at Bauhaus had called them. One is thirty-six feet long, with three twelve-foot sections, and the other is twenty-four, three eight-foot sections. You unscrew the plastic clips, pull out the two collapsed sections and then screw it back together again.

The longer of the two ladders will be lowered through the glass roof down to the balcony on the fifth floor. They'll then use the shorter ladder to climb up to the sixth floor and blow a hole in the reinforced glass. But Sami isn't convinced that thirty-six feet will really reach all the way to the balcony from the roof.

Not that there were any longer ladders suitable for being strapped onto a helicopter.

It had to be enough.

He moves in circles around all their things. Loop after loop, and Nordgren starts to get annoyed. He does the math in his head. To Lidingö and back can't take any more than forty-five minutes. They'll be able to get the cable here before the helicopter lands. He's sure it must be lying exactly where he left it.

Water has worked its way into Nordgren's left shoe through a small hole. Suddenly, he feels exhausted, but he knows his weariness will vanish the minute it's time to get going. Since Ezra still isn't back, Nordgren pulls off his balaclava for a moment. His hair is damp.

Sami's phone starts to ring and both men jump. The silence in the woods is so compact, the breeze so faint, that it's not even making the treetops whisper; to them, the phone sounds like it could wake half of Östermalm.

It's five past two in the morning.

Sami glances at the display. It's Team 3. Myttinge.

He takes a deep breath before he answers.

"Yeah?"

"The police helicopter just landed."

Västberga, Marieberg and Norsborg have all called in. Everything seems fine.

"Time for Michel to do something at last," Sami says.

He calls Maloof in Norrtälje. It's the first time they've spoken since Hjorthagen.

"Morning, morning," he says.

"Good morning," Maloof replies.

"All green," Sami says. "Time to go."

"Right, right," says Maloof, hanging up.

65

Team 3 consists of two nervous teenagers lacking in experience, if not criminal records. They have been lying low in the woods in Myttinge for some time now, waiting for the police helicopter to return to its base. They have no idea how much is at stake; no idea that without their input, months of planning will have been in vain. They saw that the hangar was empty and then started playing strategy games on their phones.

But not on the phone Sami had given them.

When they hear the sound of thudding rotor blades in the distance, long before the helicopter's blinking warning lights appear in the dark night sky, they're not even sure it really is the police helicopter at first.

A few minutes later, they hear the sound of the chopper landing on its dolly, followed by the noise of its being rolled into the hangar. Five minutes after that, the pilots leave the area. They lock the huge iron gate with a chain and padlock, then drive away in the car that has been parked outside the fence.

That's when Team 3 lets Sami know that the helicopter is back.

And then they wait for the green light.

When the phone rings and Sami shouts that it's time, they feel like they've been waiting a long time.

One of the boys carries the two black toolboxes, the other takes the bolt cutters. They move quickly through the trees, involuntarily squatting as they run, as though that will make them less visible. But there's no one around to see them, nothing but a startled hare or two. The police helicopter base, still considered temporary after six years of use, has been left abandoned and alone in the deep forests of Värmdö.

The boys cross the road. The first uses the bolt cutters to smash the surveillance camera on a post opposite the gates, then he moves on to the chain and the lock. At first, he tries to cut the padlock, but it's impossible, the shackle is too thick. He tries the chain instead. That proves easier. After just a few attempts, he manages. When he pulls the chain through the steel fence, the noise is ear splitting.

The boy runs back onto the road to keep a lookout while his friend, carrying the black toolboxes, opens the gates and moves into the area. The hangar has two doors, and the boy decides to prepare the boxes in front of the farthest one. He sets them down on the ground and opens the lids.

Inside each box is a rock and a dummy car alarm that Niklas Nordgren bought from Teknikmagasinet in Fältöversten.

The dummy alarms consist of a battery-powered bulb for sticking onto the dashboard of a car. Their red blinking lights are meant to trick car thieves into thinking that the vehicle is alarmed. The black toolboxes are plastic, bought online, and they weigh almost nothing. The stones are just ordinary rocks that Nordgren found in the woods, but without them, a strong breeze would be all it took to tip the boxes over.

The boy switches on the two fake alarms and then sticks them to the boxes. Afterward, he places one of the dummy bombs outside each door into the hangar, takes a few steps toward the gate and turns around.

From a distance, the red blinking lights look ominous, and the black boxes are hard to make out; they're perfect.

"Let's go," he says to his friend, and they start walking along the road.

There's a bus stop about a mile away.

After a hundred or so yards, the first boy hurls the bolt cutters into the woods. They land so softly they don't make a sound.

66

When Michel Maloof, Zoran Petrovic and Jack Kluger pull the door to the apartment in Norrtälje closed behind them, they leave very few traces of themselves, other than the uneaten remains of their McDonald's meal. Petrovic has promised to make sure someone goes over to get rid of "every last bit of DNA" the following morning.

The men go down the stairs without talking, and Maloof grabs the door so that it swings shut quietly behind them. The street is deserted.

They take Zoran Petrovic's car, the dark blue BMW. The moon, which was shining brightly a few hours earlier, is currently hidden behind a cloud. Just an hour earlier, Petrovic had asked the pilot whether the moonlight made much difference to night flying.

"Makes it easier to see, but it also means you're easier to spot," came his reply.

Petrovic chose to interpret that as meaning Kluger was indifferent to whether the dawn was light or dark.

The American climbs into the front seat next to Petrovic, and Maloof chooses to jump in the back with the weapons. Not because he doesn't trust Kluger, but just because it's a bad idea to let any old stranger sit behind you with a loaded gun.

Petrovic has filled the trunk with cans of helicopter fuel. They'll pick up everything else down in Stora Skuggan.

For once, Zoran Petrovic is quiet as the car slowly carries them out of the small town. Back in the apartment, the American's aftershave hadn't been much more than a faint scent of musk, but in the confined space of the car, the smell is stronger. Maloof cracks open the window to let in some fresh air.

"It's to the right here, yeah?" Petrovic asks.

Maloof glances around. "Yeah, yeah."

They turn off onto Kustvägen. From there, it takes less than two minutes to reach the helicopter hangar in Roslagen. They park, leaving the weapons in the backseat, and all three men go over to check that everything is as it should be. There are no other cars anywhere to be seen, the hangar is bathed in darkness, and the stillness is absolute. The pines and firs down by the lake are their only breathless audience.

The American walks over to the hangar door and studies it skeptically.

"These things are solid," he says in his nasal English. "You can't pick these. This needs to be blown open."

"Right, right," Maloof agrees.

And then he laughs. It's comical. The door into the hangar is as secure as can be. They probably installed it on the recommendation of the insurance company, in some attempt to lower their premiums. Blowing it open would work, but the charge would also echo across the entire neighborhood.

Maloof takes out the long-bladed knife that he had been wearing in a holster beneath his coat. He goes over to the door.

"That'll never work," says the American, as though Maloof had been planning to attack the steel door with his blade.

But instead, he cuts a long slash into the canvas of the hangar, right next to the door. Since the hangar is made from fabric, he doesn't even have to exert himself. One more cut, and he's managed to create a flap that can be pushed to one side, and with a welcoming gesture and a grin, he invites Petrovic and the surprised pilot into the hangar.

Petrovic laughs.

"Smart of them to buy an expensive door."

Maloof's grin grows wider, and he follows them in.

The helicopter, a white Bell 206 JetRanger, is where it should be, at the end of its row, making it relatively easy to roll out.

So far, everything is just as Manne Lagerström had promised.

The American quickly inspects the machine. The hangar smells of gasoline and electronics, and the huge, empty helicopters are lined up in three rows. Maloof can't help but liken them to bees. It's as though they've flown in to rest for the night, and come dawn they'll wake up again, their heavy, drooping rotor blades suddenly starting to spin, panels lighting up and engines roaring.

Kluger walks around the helicopter, occasionally raising his hand to the metal body. He climbs up and inspects the rotor blades and the mechanics. Maloof and Petrovic leave him to it and head back out to carry in the weapons and petrol cans from the car. When they return, the pilot has finished his checks. Everything is as it should be, the tank only partially filled so that they can fly with a heavy load, and he gives them the thumbs-up. They manage to maneuver the helicopter out of the hangar using the small tractor. The wheels on the dolly move smoothly over the flat ground, possibly because Manne gave them an extra oiling ahead of tonight's events.

The white helicopter glistens in the moonlight. Kluger starts the engine, and the rotor blades slowly come to life. A low whirring, rising to a controlled roar. After ten or so seconds of picking up speed, he can no longer see them; they're just one great big spinning disc above the body of the helicopter.

"OK!" Petrovic shouts over the roar of the helicopter once they've loaded the weapons. "See you in a few hours, hopefully."

"Right, right," Maloof shouts back.

Kluger is already in his seat. He's wearing ear protectors but no headphones. He isn't planning to turn on the communications system during their flight. His feet are on the pedals and his hands on the levers. Petrovic has bought a pair of goggles, but Kluger doesn't need them. In his experience, they're more trouble than they're worth.

Maloof takes his seat next to the American. The two bowl-shaped seats behind them are empty for now.

A second later, they lift off. The wind from the rotor blades tears at Petrovic's clothes, and he watches the enormous white bumblebee fly away.

He turns around and rushes back to the car.

It's almost five in the morning.

67

The dark blue BMW is factory fresh, and the engine more powerful than the car Zoran Petrovic usually drives. He borrowed the vehicle direct from the reseller, a friend of a friend who owed him a favor or two. Petrovic's part in the events of that early morning isn't over yet.

He doesn't have much time. He needs to make it from Norrtälje to Skärholmen in fifty minutes, and he's going flat out. When they first talked about it, Maloof had said it was too tight, that they would need to find someone else, but Petrovic had insisted. He could do it.

Driving down the empty highway at 120 miles an hour that bright September night, the steering steady, Petrovic feels pure joy. The car isn't swaying in the slightest, the engine nothing but a low whirr, and he turns on the radio. He needs music for this. "Run This Town," by Jay-Z and Rihanna. The radio stations have been playing it all summer. He turns up the volume.

And that's when he notices it.

The blue lights loom up in his rearview mirror. He has no idea where the police car has come from, he hasn't overtaken any, but there's no doubt it's him they're after. There aren't any other cars on the road.

The goggles the helicopter pilot recently turned down are lying on the seat next to Petrovic. He realizes that he probably has traces of gunpowder on his clothes and his hands from checking the weapons earlier. And he also knows that if he doesn't turn up at the agreed meeting point in time, there'll be trouble.

He stares into the rearview mirror.

He still hasn't slowed down. In fact, according to the speedometer, he is now doing 140 miles an hour.

The police are gaining on him. He won't be able to lose them on the highway. But turning off now?

Petrovic doesn't even know where he is.

68

Since Ezra Ray returned with the cable for the detonators, not much has been said in the woods out in Stora Skuggan. He had found the cable lying beneath a plastic bag full of empty bottles.

At regular intervals, Sami walks over to the open field where the helicopter will land and squints up at the sky. He knows he will be able to hear it before he can see it, but he can't sit still. The grass is damp with dew, and he can already feel the adrenaline building. It's lying in wait to start pumping around his body in the next half an hour or so. Ideally, he would like to go for a quick run around the field, but he decides not to.

Nordgren has managed to find a stump that is more comfortable than the rock he was sitting on earlier. His weariness has vanished, but he doesn't feel either nervous or expectant. It's hard to explain. He can spend weeks and months planning something that, from the very beginning, is a real challenge; where every problem that he solves leaves him with a deep sense of satisfaction. But when the time finally comes, all that's left is his desire to get it done. Nothing else.

"You're not sleeping, are you?" Ezra asks from his rock a few yards away.

It's a joke.

"No chance," Nordgren replies quietly.

It's two minutes past five when Sami's phone rings. He is halfway back to the woods and he knows Nordgren will have heard it. Maloof's voice is drowned out by the sound of the engine. Sami can't hear what he's saying, but from the context, it's clear why he is calling.

They're on their way.

A minute later, and the silence over Frescati and Stora Skuggan is broken.

It's no more than a low whirring sound at first, way in the distance, but it completely possesses them.

Niklas Nordgren gets up and stands perfectly still.

Sami and Ezra, who had been going to bring the equipment to the field, stop where they are.

Listening.

Allowing the sound of the helicopter to grow louder.

It's as though someone had turned the volume far above what the speakers can handle.

And, as though on command, Sami and Ezra drop the equipment and run with Nordgren into the dark field. They stop. They had measured out the triangle an hour or so earlier. They turn on the torches.

The helicopter comes in low. The sound is deafening, but Sami experiences it as pure joy. Euphoria. The white machine seems to almost glide in above the treetops, toward where they're standing.

Slowly, the pilot attempts to find the right position above the three lights. For a few seconds, the helicopter is completely still, hanging freely in the air, but then he lowers the machine to the ground. The wind makes the trees rustle and the bushes lie flat.

Sami and Ezra pull on their balaclavas.

Neither plans to let the pilot see their faces.

Jack Kluger lands, kills the engine and the rotor blades come to a halt. Maloof jumps out of the helicopter. He hugs Nordgren and Sami, but they don't say much to one another. There'll be time for that later.

Each of them is aware that the clock has started ticking. It's not unlikely that someone has seen or heard the helicopter, either on the way down from Norrtälje or on a radar screen somewhere.

While Maloof, Nordgren and Ezra run into the woods to grab the equipment and load it on board, Jack Kluger moves around the helicopter, showing Sami the minimal storage space. There'll barely be room for a single mailbag. They'll have to use the main cabin instead.

Maloof and Nordgren fasten the ladders to the landing skids using cable ties. It's much easier than they had thought it would be, the short ladder isn't too short and the long ladder not too long. While they do that, Sami and Ezra load the rest of the gear into the cabin.

When the helicopter takes off a few minutes later, things are cramped. They plan to abandon a lot of what they brought with them in Västberga, leaving room for the bags of money.

Nordgren and Sami are in the seats behind Kluger and Maloof. The pounding inside the cabin is loud and rhythmic. It's almost ten past five in the morning when they feel the power of the liftoff and the helicopter swings up into the air. The movement feels at once incredibly light and unbelievably heavy.

Kluger puts the machine into a sharp turn, and the dark contours of the woods by the university are heading straight toward them from one side until he straightens up again. Beneath their feet, the silent black expanse of Haga Park spreads out. To the north, Solna glitters like a small town, and to the south, the Wenner-Gren Center towers over the buildings around it, a reminder that Stockholm is a low-lying city. The red and white lights of the cars on Uppsalavägen are like drops of water rolling along a viaduct.

Sami, Maloof and Nordgren struggle into their bulletproof vests in silence, pulling on black plastic masks on top of their balaclavas. Before they climbed on board, both had taped up any openings in their clothes, around their gloves and shoes, to make sure they don't leave any DNA behind.

Nordgren pulls on his cap. The equipment makes them less mobile, but they have no idea what might be awaiting them inside the building. The explosives are a risk. That's the reason they're wearing headlamps. If the electricity cuts out for any reason, they'll need lights of their own to be able to move freely.

Kluger turns across the water. At high speed, and flying low, he follows the line of the highway south, past the Essinge Islands, where the beautiful houses are bathed in darkness at the top of the rocks, cars parked tightly along the narrow streets. The cloud cover breaks, the winds are strong at that height this morning. But lower down, it's no more than a few miles per hour.

Nordgren checks the explosives, cables, batteries and soda cans in his backpack once more. He has the detonators in one of the pockets on his vest.

Sami checks his gun.

Maloof glances at his watch. They have plenty of time, the question is whether they're moving too quickly. Will Zoran Petrovic make it? Should he ask him to send a text once he arrives, just to stay on the safe side? Maloof isn't sure. And then his thoughts drift to Alexandra Svensson, who would be shocked if she could see him right now, in his black balaclava. He doesn't feel guilty at not having told her everything about himself; leaving out certain details isn't the same as lying. He has two different lives, and he wonders whether they could merge into one. Could Alexandra, he wonders as thin veils of cloud sweep by like anxious ghosts outside the helicopter, become a permanent part of his life? Could he imagine her sitting in the kitchen at his mom and dad's house in Fittja, actually enjoying herself there? He hopes so. If everything goes to plan over the next hour or so, he'll be able to be more open about himself in the future, once the money is clean and life is simpler. Maloof nods imperceptibly. That's what he has been longing for, to make life more simple.

They float through the sky. From time to time, the helicopter lurches suddenly, and it comes as a surprise every time. An unexpected gust as they're landing would flip this little steel bubble, Sami thinks. He knows it won't happen, he's gone through the statistics, flying a helicopter is relatively safe. But the sudden lurches mean he can't relax; it feels as though they're at the end of a rubber band that someone keeps erratically pulling on.

His thoughts turn to John, to how much he would be laughing through the pockets of air that occasionally make them bounce sideways.

Sami doesn't fantasize about what will be awaiting them when they arrive. He knows what he has to do, from the second the helicopter lands on the roof in Västberga until the moment they climb into the cars that will take them away from Norsborg. His own run-throughs and preparations over the past week have been so frequent and intense that, in a way, it almost feels as though he has done this before, like the robbery has already taken place.

Instead, as he stares down at the lights on the highway, the headlights rushing toward Södertälje like a string of white pearls, his thoughts are on his two families; his parents and siblings, Karin and the boys. Deep down, he knows that he can't win over both of them. What he will be able to tell his brothers tomorrow would win back their respect and recognition, but it's also the very same thing that could cause Karin to pack up the kids and leave him.

It's a catch-22. If he can never tell anyone where the money came from, then how will his brothers ever know that it was more than just words, more than empty promises? And if he tells the truth, if the rumors about who was responsible for this robbery spread across town, then how will he explain to Karin that he had no choice, for their sake?

The helicopter suddenly veers to the right, and Sami falls to one side. It's the wake-up call he needs. He empties his mind. Ignore all that, all those thoughts and speculations. He's here now, and it's time to get to work.

69

Zoran Petrovic veers off from the highway. He drives down the exit ramp at just over ninety miles an hour. In the rearview mirror, he can see that the police car has moved considerably closer. Petrovic turns off the radio and hears the police siren.

He doesn't have a plan.

He's improvising.

The exit takes him onto a small country road leading into a forest. He slams on the brakes just before he reaches a crossroads and throws himself out of the BMW. The police car is still several hundred feet away, and the sound of its sudden braking cuts through the darkness.

Petrovic runs around the car to the edge of the road. He unbuckles his belt, unbuttons his trousers and drops them to the ground, along with his underwear. As the police pull up behind him, he squats down.

He's not pretending. He loudly tries to take a real shit.

The police jump out of their car. One of them is holding a flashlight, and he shines it straight at the crouching Yugoslavian.

"What the hell are you playing at?" the police officer shouts.

But when they see what Petrovic is doing, they keep their distance.

"I've got such a fucking stomachache," Petrovic whines pathetically. "I panicked. I had to."

"You can't just sit here and . . ."

"What a damn creep," says the other.

"You'll have to find a real toilet," the first police officer says firmly.

"I'm lactose intolerant," Petrovic moans, still not getting up.

"Did you hear what I said?" the first officer asks, in a considerably gruffer tone this time. "This is disorderly conduct. You could go to prison for this."

It's a threat the police are sure will work and, with a despairing sigh, more like a howl, Petrovic reluctantly stands up.

"There's a toilet at the Statoil station," the police officer's colleague says nonchalantly, trying to be just helpful enough.

"Shit," Petrovic whines. "How far's that? I don't know if I—"

"Get going!" the first officer says. "Right now. And make sure you stick to the damn speed limit, even if you do have a stomachache."

Petrovic has no intention of tempting fate. He buttons his trousers as he moves around the car, and climbs in behind the wheel before the police officers have time to change their minds. He drives off. In the rearview mirror, he can see them standing there.

They're probably finding the whole incident hilarious.

The minute they are out of sight, Petrovic puts his foot down again, back up to ninety miles an hour. His cell phone flashes in the seat next to him. A message from ZLATAN JR. One of his many names for Michel Maloof. Without lifting his foot from the accelerator, he grabs the phone from the seat to read the message.

70

They're approaching from the north.

The helicopter's rotor blades cut a path through the calm air.

The rhythmic pounding of the engine shatters the silence.

Two hundred and fifty feet below them, the black water races past at sixty miles an hour, as do the huge, forest-covered islands where the occasional light reveals a cluster of houses or a farm. Tonight, the outlines of the islands look like ominous gray Rorschach inkblots.

Inside the helicopter, the four silent, black-clad men are strapped into their seats. Each of them is completely still, staring straight ahead, lost in himself and his thoughts.

Down on the ground, the lights of the cars and streetlamps glitter, illuminated facades and bulbs that have been burning all night in the low office buildings along the edge of the highway. But the four men don't see any of that. Their eyes are fixed straight ahead.

The brightest light ahead of the helicopter's curved windshield is shining up from the roof of the G4S cash depot in Västberga. It's like a beacon lighting up the building, like a revelation.

From this point on in the robbers' lives, there will always be a before and an after these few seconds, this morning of September 23.

Sami's grip tightens around the machine gun in his lap.

Nordgren closes his eyes for a moment.

Maloof catches a flash of stars through a quick gap in the clouds.

That's a good sign.

*   *   *

Kluger gets into position directly above the building. He allows the helicopter to sink slowly but deliberately through the air.

They land feather-light on the roof. Kluger turns to Maloof with a grin and then nods.

It's almost a quarter past five in the morning; the journey took just as long as planned.

Everyone knows what he needs to do. Each has his own role.

They have to work quickly now.

Maloof is first out of the helicopter. Nordgren stays inside and begins to pass the equipment out to him.

Sami grabs the handle of the heavy sledgehammer and jumps out of the cabin. As he runs toward the glowing, pyramid-shaped skylight, Nordgren climbs out of the helicopter and helps Maloof unfasten the ladders from the helicopter's landing skids. They work in time with the dull thudding of the rotor blades. And just as they finish and carry the ladders away, Kluger lifts off.

The white helicopter pulls up into the dark night sky. The wind from the rotor blades tears at the mailbags full of equipment still lying on the roof.

Sami has made it to the skylight.

He lowers the heavy end of the sledgehammer to the roof and gets a good grip on the wooden handle. Then he gets ready. Bends his knees; finds a low, stable position. He raises the sledgehammer and, in one fluid motion, swings it in an arc above his head. He can feel the weight of it in every inch of his body, can feel the power of the movement take over and help him follow through.

The hammer crashes down in the middle of one of the square, three-foot-wide windows. The vibration travels up the handle and into Sami's hands. It couldn't have been more perfect.

He stares at the glass.

There doesn't seem to be a scratch on it.

71

The night has been relatively uneventful so far. Kalle Dahlström, the duty officer on shift at the police force's regional communication center, has barely had anything to do. Tonight's night shift is his second of the week, the time sheet has him down for three in a row followed by one day off before he goes back to ordinary hours. The phones are quiet and his colleague Sofi Rosander is sleeping on the uncomfortable couch that some sadistic person brought in to stop the staff from taking naps. When she wakes up, it'll be with a back that feels like it's been welded straight.

Kalle is playing Tetris on his phone. He's secretly proud of how good he is, but he won't share his high score. Despite the hours, weeks and days he has spent with those blocks and squares, he's still an amateur compared with the real pros.

When one of the phones suddenly starts to ring, Dahlström jumps. He answers by pressing a button in front of him. He doesn't even need to look up from his smartphone.

It's 5:14. The man on the other end of the line is a security guard, and he's speaking in broken, almost incomprehensible Swedish.

Eventually, Dahlström manages to work out that he's talking about a robbery on a cash service in Västberga.

"Secure transit robbery?" he replies; he isn't surprised.

Secure transit vehicles were the new banks. Six out of every ten robberies these days had something to do with guards either carrying or transporting cash. All that surprises Dahlström is the time. Who could be out collecting money at this time of night?

"It's the G4S cash depot," the guard says down the line. "They came in a helicopter."

Dahlström looks up from the blocks and squares. He stares blankly at his computer's blue home screen as though it might give him the answers, and then he asks the guard to repeat what he just said.

"It's a helicopter," the guard insists.

"A helicopter?" says Dahlström.

"It's taken off again. It's hovering above now."

Dahlström can't believe what he's hearing. A helicopter attacking a cash depot in Västberga? He knows the area, the Söderort district station is on Västberga Gårdsväg, less than a quarter of a mile from the secure transport company's offices. He's been to the station himself, as recently as a month ago.

"Are you sure about this?" he asks.

"Are you stupid?" the guard replies.

Sofi Rosander has woken up on the sofa. She's heard the conversation, their phone calls play automatically over the loudspeaker.

"We need to call someone," she whispers.

"Stay on the line," Dahlström orders the guard, ending the call.

"We need to raise the alarm," Sofi Rosander repeats. "And call the district commissioner."

"I can't ring Caisa fucking Ekblad and wake her up," Dahlström protests, terrified by the thought. "I'll call Månsson instead. He's in charge of Söderort. It's his problem."

It takes a while for Dag Månsson to answer. He sounds muddled, newly woken and annoyed. Dahlström introduces himself and repeats the information that has just come in. Månsson reacts with the same degree of surprise.

"The cash depot in Västberga? But it's right next to the station?" he says.

Dahlström has to repeat the information several times before Månsson finally understands that the robbers have landed a helicopter on the roof of G4S.

"I'm on my way in," he says. "I'll call the commissioner en route. You raise the alarm."

72

The helicopter is in the air, hovering just to the right of the building, far enough away not to hinder the three men working on the roof.

Maloof had run over to Sami when he realized something wasn't right. Together, they squat down and study the pane of glass close up. Thanks to the lights below, they can see a small crack, thin but long.

Maloof knows that it could have been there before, but he decides not to mention that.

"Keep going, keep going," he says instead, returning to Nordgren, who has started to screw together the ladders.

The longer of the two seems inconceivably long, but it does need to reach all the way to the fifth floor.

"Let's move everything over to the window," he says to Nordgren.

It's more a type of therapy than anything else. They need to keep themselves busy while Sami lets the sledgehammer do its job.

Sami strikes the glass. He strikes it again. The movement reminds him of a condemned prisoner in a chain gang in some film from the early sixties. Every time the sledgehammer hits the window, it makes the same dull thud, the same anticlimax, and after the fifth or seventh or eleventh strike, once Nordgren and Maloof have moved all the bags, ropes, ladders, tools and explosives over to the window, his patience starts to wear thin.

Maloof had planned on them being out of there in quarter of an hour. Fifteen minutes. It can't take any longer than that.

Three of those fifteen minutes have already passed, and they haven't even managed to smash the window.

"I'll blow it open," Nordgren says quietly to Maloof, who nods.

Nordgren bends down to prepare a charge, but as he does so, they finally hear the sound of the hammer breaking the glass into thousands of tiny pieces.

With Nordgren's help, Maloof lifts one end of the longer ladder above his head and they raise it vertically in the air. Next, they carefully lower it through the hole in the skylight. The balcony on the fifth floor is directly below them, little more than a ledge.

Slowly, they lower the ladder down through the building. It has to be long enough.

Afterward, Michel Maloof will look back at those few moments and think of them as having been the longest of the morning. If the ladder is too short, it's all over. They won't have any choice but to wave back the helicopter and leave.

Foot by foot, the ladder disappears through the hole in the broken window. With just six inches of the full thirty-six feet to spare, it hits the floor.

Maloof leans forward and looks down.

"I think it'll work," he says.

Getting the ladder into place took twenty-five seconds.

It felt more like twenty-five minutes.

Nordgren grabs the shorter ladder and swings it onto his right shoulder. He grabs the bag of explosives in his other hand.

"You holding?" he asks Maloof.

He starts climbing without waiting for an answer.

Maloof holds on to the ladder as tightly as he can. It shakes. Nordgren is only halfway down when it starts to bend as though it were made of bamboo.

But it doesn't collapse.

Maloof asks Sami to hold it while he grabs as much as he can and then sets off as the second man. Sami climbs down last of all, the Kalashnikov hanging from a strap around his neck.

73

"Do you think you could turn down the radio a bit?" Claude Tavernier asks as diplomatically as he can, though he already knows the answer will be a long, difficult telling off.

Ann-Marie always has the radio on when she's working. She manages to find channels on frequencies no one else even knew existed. Right now, she's enjoying Swedish hits from the sixties, nonstop without any ads. Of the fourteen people working this shift, five have brought their own headphones to avoid Ann-Marie's canned tunes, but the others have been forced to endure vintage Swedish hits for hours now.

They've made it through the night without any conflict so far, but, as usual, patience starts to wear thin as dawn approaches. Tavernier has a theory that it's linked to the bad air, and he has raised the problem with management. Every night shift is the same. Tonight, on top of the usual workload, they've also had to handle two additional secure transports from Panaxia. The smaller company hasn't had the capacity since its move the week before.

It means the tempo is higher than usual.

After being received and registered down in the vault, the cash is sent up to Counting through the internal tube system. On the sixth floor, the staff don't just have to count and package up the money, they also have to weed out any notes that are too old or damaged to return to general circulation. Once that's done, they register the deposits and send everything back down to the vault.

The room is big and gently U-shaped, which means that the people working at one end can't see those working at the other. Also meaning, in theory, that it is possible to keep your distance from Ann-Marie and her radio, but Tavernier still has to ask her to turn down the volume. Like always. And, as usual, Ann-Marie, who has both been on the local union board and has held the position of shop steward, explains precisely which rights she has.

One of these rights is to listen to music.

Tonight, Claude Tavernier has much less patience than usual. He doesn't quite know why. But it's the reason he raises his voice and interrupts Ann-Marie before she even has time to start protesting.

"Just turn it down, Ann-Marie," he barks. "Or I'll do it."

Ann-Marie is so taken aback by his change in attitude that she reaches out and turns down the volume on the old radio. It's not her device, it belongs to the company.

As the languorous strings grow quiet, they all hear it.

The sound coming from outside.

Colleagues elbow workmates wearing headphones so that they can hear it for themselves.

"What the hell's that?" someone asks loudly.

Counting, on the sixth floor, has no windows. But it's obvious that the clear thudding sound none of them can identify is coming from outside.

"That's not the air-conditioning, is it?"

"We'll have to ask the big boss what we should do," Ann-Marie says, dripping with irony, as though to point out how dumbstruck Claude Tavernier looks, standing in the middle of the room with all eyes on him.

Like many who have driven a secure transport vehicle or worked for a company dealing in them, Tavernier has personal experience of being robbed. That's why his first thought is that it must be a robbery. It's an automatic assumption. But six floors up, in one of Stockholm's most secure depots, with a police station just a stone's throw from the entrance, Tavernier brushes off the thought. It seems so unlikely.

"Keep working," he says. "I'll go and check."

"What a hero," Ann-Marie mumbles.

A low giggle can be heard as Tavernier leaves the room.

He comes out into a corridor, the elevators and stairs to his right. He turns the other way, to the left, and passes a couple of locked doors that he opens with his key card. He's heading for the break room, where there is a window out onto the atrium. His plan is to take a quick look at the lower floors, to see whether anyone down there has noticed the noise.

But as he steps into the break room, the first thing he sees is two black-clad men climbing down a ladder from the roof with bags on their backs.

It takes a few seconds for Tavernier to process what he is seeing.

He runs back to his department, but not so fast that he doesn't have time to make sure that every door he opens is locked properly behind him.

His leadership qualities are about to be put to the test. It's time for him to prove that he's capable, that he's strong.

When he reaches his department, everyone falls silent and turns toward him. The man that has just stepped through the door isn't the same one who left a few minutes earlier. Tavernier's pale face and wide eyes reveal that something serious has happened, he doesn't need to ask for their attention. From Ann-Marie's radio, a deep male voice is singing quietly.

"Secure the cash," Claude Tavernier says.

No one protests or asks any questions, not even Ann-Marie. Time after time over the years, they've practiced this very drill. It's a case of moving the bundles of notes to the lockable, bar-covered cages in the middle of the room as quickly as possible. There's probably over 100 million kronor in Counting that morning. Most of it in 500-kroner notes, but also in lower denominations.

Tavernier makes a point of moving as slowly as he can. Adrenaline is pumping through his veins, and he would rather be running between stations, making sure that everyone is doing his or her job quickly and effectively. But he knows that if he shows any sign of panic, it will spread through the room like an echo.

He moves over to his desk and tries to find the number for Skövde. His instructions are crystal clear. There are procedures, a well-thought-out plan that he is expected to follow. Every fourth month, Palle Lindahl, the G4S security chief, stages a run-through with all the company's middle managers.

The first thing to do in situations like this is to call the alarm center in Skövde.

But Skövde changed its number a few weeks earlier, and Tavernier can't find the piece of paper with the new details. He knows it's on his desk somewhere, and while his staff assiduously and silently continues to secure the money, Claude Tavernier feels the panic rising. He has only one job to do, one call to make, but he doesn't seem to be able to manage even that.

He resists the urge to tear the drawers from his desk and throw them to the floor. Eventually, he is forced to accept that the number for Skövde isn't where it's meant to be. He picks up the phone and calls down to Valter, on the ground floor.

"Valter?" he says. "Claude up in Cash. There are people in the building."

He doesn't want to say too much, because all around him, the others have their ears pricked. He strains to speak without any hint of his French accent.

"Reported," Valter replies. "I've already called Skövde."

Tavernier nods. He breathes out. That's better. Skövde has already been informed. No one can blame him for not having done it.

74

5:19 a.m.

It's just turned twenty past five in the morning when County Police Commissioner Caisa Ekblad is woken by the angry sound of the phone. She is no stranger to being woken in the middle of the night, and when she picks up, her voice is clear and steady, as though she had been sitting by the phone waiting for the call. Only last spring, Caisa Ekblad was Dag Månsson's colleague; he was one of the district chiefs behind her nomination.

"We've got an unusual alert," Månsson says.

He's panting into the phone. He is just leaving home, on the way down the stairs in his building.

"A possible robbery ongoing in Västberga. We've got reports of a helicopter landing on the G4S cash depot roof."

"A helicopter?" Ekblad repeats.

"The building's practically next door to the police station."

Månsson has reached the garage, and he climbs into his car.

"The robbers arrived in a helicopter?" Ekblad repeats. She doesn't want any misunderstandings.

"Apparently. This is no ordinary alarm."

"I'll call Olsson," the county police commissioner says, instinctively sensing that robbers in helicopters aren't something that should be handled by the local police force.

"Do it," Månsson agrees.

"I'll call you again as soon as I can," Ekblad says.

"Same."

Månsson ends the call as he pulls out onto the Essingeleden highway.

* * *

The relationship between the chief commissioner for Stockholm County and the national police commissioner operated as the circumstances demanded. They kept their distance from one another. Two female police officers in a male-dominated environment, two careerists surrounded by bureaucrats, two experienced officers now in primarily administrative roles, the women did actually have quite a lot to learn from one another. But Ekblad's and Olsson's fields of power weren't compatible. It was more a case of personal chemistry than it was of women competing more with one another than with the men on the force.

"Shit," is the national police commissioner's first reaction.

The county commissioner notices the complete lack of surprise in Therese Olsson's tone; she detects only anger.

"You knew about this?" she asks.

"This is ours, Caisa," Olsson says, dodging the question. "We'll take it from here. Ask your people to cut off the exits. Get a couple of patrol cars out there, with the lights on, and we'll take care of the rest."

"Sorry, but I don't know . . . This is happening now, and it's happening practically on the doorstep of Söderort station. It'll probably be quicker if we carry on than if you try to take over."

"We've been working on this for a month, Caisa. It's too big for you."

"A month?" the county commissioner exclaims, sounding surprised. "Without informing me?"

Olsson is silent for a moment, and then she says: "It had nothing to do with you."

Ekblad explodes. With suppressed rage, and with a level of clarity she would usually reserve for talking to a five-year-old, she explains that a robbery being planned in the Stockholm area is very much to do with the Stockholm County commissioner. If Olsson can't understand that, then perhaps the Police Authority should be made aware at the next meeting that its commissioner is illiterate.

"Caisa, I—" Olsson begins.

But Ekblad ends the call without listening to Olsson's excuses. She is still in bed, but she angrily tears back the covers and heads into the bathroom. That's when she hears her cell phone ring, followed shortly afterward by the house phone. She doesn't answer. By the time she makes a quick trip to the bathroom and heads down to the garage, the worst of her anger has abated.

She calls Månsson for an update from the car. He confirms what the guard reported; the robbers are still in the building. He has set up a liaison unit in a police van by the Statoil gas station opposite G4S.

"We've already got enough people here. Should we go in?" Månsson asks.

It's a good question.

The display on her phone flashes, indicating an incoming call. Ekblad realizes she has to take it.

"Hold off," she replies.

It's Therese Olsson.

"We made a mistake, Caisa," Olsson immediately says. "We misjudged the situation. Of course we should have kept you informed. But it is what it is, and we can't afford to lose any more time. You know Caroline Thurn, don't you? With the Criminal Investigation Department? She's been working on this for a month or so, she knows who's in the building in Västberga. She has the best chance of being able to handle this."

Ekblad sighs.

"OK," she replies, resigned. "I was just talking to Dag Månsson. He's set up a liaison unit outside."

"Then I'll ask Thurn to get in touch with Månsson and the people at the scene."

Ekblad sighs again. She goes back to Månsson to tell him the bad news.

75

5:21 a.m.

The buzzing of her cell phone is transmitted through the thick cushions in the alcove. Caroline Thurn can't hear anything, but she can feel the vibrations. She pulls off her headphones, Zoran Petrovic's droning stops and she glances down at the display. It's the national police commissioner, Therese Olsson.

Thurn feels her adrenaline levels spike as she answers.

"Good morning," she says.

"They pushed it back a week," she hears Therese Olsson's dogged voice say. "It's happening as we speak."

Thurn understands immediately. She can still hear the echo of Petrovic's voice in her ears.

The fifteenth of September. That was why he slipped up. That was why he planted that particular date several times. It was the only mistake he made.

Only, it wasn't a mistake.

He had tricked them.

"The situation is ongoing," Olsson repeats. "Get out to G4S in Västberga. Call me from the car."

Caroline Thurn is on her way out.

"Wait!" she shouts down the line.

"What?"

"Is our helicopter airborne?" Thurn asks as she opens the door into the stairwell.

The silence on the other end tells her everything she needs to know.

"Get it in the air!" Thurn shouts at her boss. "Now!"

76

It went better than he expected.

On the way from Frescati to Västberga, there had been two moments when he'd had to blink, concentrate and fight back the sense of panic he could feel welling, ready to spread through his body as quickly and easily as a drop of blood in a glass of water.

Both times had worked.

Since then, everything has been calm.

After dropping off the robbers and the equipment, Jack Kluger takes the helicopter up to a high altitude again. Bands of thin clouds float across the sky, their edges sharply defined by the moonlight. Far below him, to the northwest, the Essingen Islands and southern Alvik glitter at the far edge of the dark waters of Lake Mälaren. To the northeast, he can see the Liljeholmen industrial area and the deserted office buildings that have been plastered with brightly lit company logos.

Kluger has no goal other than to save fuel. They have agreed to be back on the roof in ten to fifteen minutes, and though he set off with less than a full tank, that gives him good margins.

He lowers the helicopter slightly when he spots the first police car. Its flashing blue lights seem to glide forward over the ground.

Just as Maloof and Sami predicted, the car is approaching from the station on Västberga Gårdsväg. It swings up onto Västberga Allé, followed closely by another car. Kluger watches them from the heavens, two blue will-o'-the-wisps in an otherwise black night. When the first car suddenly skids, spins sideways and comes to a stop, Kluger knows why. Petrovic had told him about the chains, about the caltrops. The

American watches the second car slow down, but he can't tell whether its tires have also been ripped to shreds.

Just then, he spots a string of blue lights approaching on the highway from Stockholm. They'll take the exit by Midsommarkransen and drive straight into the chains stretched across the road.

Once nine minutes have passed since the drop-off, Kluger allows the helicopter to sink farther, meaning he is now hovering right alongside the building. The chains with the caltrops have delayed the police, but judging by the stream of new cars and blue lights flickering in the darkness, they've dealt with the problem. The cars are coming from the north, from the south. He's lost count. They're keeping their distance from the building, and it seems to Kluger as though they're forming some kind of base over by the gas station on the hill, three hundred or so feet away from the entrance to the building.

He feels comfortable in the helicopter, behind the controls. He can't understand why he was so nervous about it now. It's like riding a bike. He hasn't forgotten a thing; in fact, he's forgotten too little. Flying with the dark sky as a backdrop, it's as though he never left Afghanistan.

And then he notices the sinking feeling his stomach.

He blinks it away. Once. Once more.

He doesn't want to remember.

He flies a loop around the building, just for something to do.

He feels a vague sense of unease that the police will open fire. After almost two years in Sweden, he knows that weapons and force are the exception, but he's still an easy target. That's why he's keeping close to the building. He assumes they won't dare shoot if there's a risk of him crashing into the cash depot.

The next time he glances at his watch, it's 5:23. Jack Kluger feels relieved. It'll soon be over. He peers down at the roof and expects to catch sight of them any moment now. He's aware that they said ten to fifteen minutes, and it hasn't even been ten yet, but he just wants to get away. The pulsing blue lights on the ground are making him nervous, but it's toward the horizon that he keeps glancing anxiously.

If he catches sight of another helicopter, he doesn't know what he'll do. Landing on the roof to pick up the robbers would be pointless if that happened. He'd never be able to take off again. The police helicopter would make sure of that. Nothing is stopping him from simply flying off. He decides that if he sees anything coming toward him in the sky, he'll have to make a run for it.

77

It's exactly twenty-three minutes past five when Caroline Thurn pulls out of the garage on Väpnargatan in her Volvo. A white layer of frost covers the ground on Strandvägen, and as she drives toward the red lights on Hamngatan, she grabs her phone, pushes the white headphone into her ear and dials Berggren's number.

He answers immediately.

"They shifted it back a week."

She doesn't need to be any clearer than that.

"Where are you?" he asks.

"It wasn't Bromma, it was Västberga."

"Where are you?" he asks for a second time.

"The situation's ongoing. County police are involved. Local are outside the building with the lights flashing."

"Where the hell are you, Caroline?" Berggren shouts.

By now, Thurn has made it to the Gallerian shopping center, and she turns left.

"Excuse me," she says into the earpiece.

She comes close to hitting a homeless woman pulling a shopping cart across a crosswalk.

"I'm on the way," she says. "To Västberga. Five, ten minutes. Might make it before it's all over."

"What the hell're you going to do there, Caroline?"

She doesn't have a good answer to that, she's just obeying orders.

"Get hold of Hertz, Mats," she says. "Tell him to get in touch with the military."

Berggren doesn't know what to say. The military? The robbery is ongoing? Had Bromma never been the target, or did the plans change?

"The military?" he repeats.

"They wanted to sabotage the police helicopters," Thurn says as she passes city hall. "I don't know if they stuck to their original plan, but . . . the military has helicopters out in Berga, doesn't it? Or up at the Air Combat Training School in Uppsala?"

"Uppsala? I have no idea . . ."

"Ask Hertz to requisition the military helicopters. Make sure they get airborne."

Thurn ends the call before her colleague has time to protest. Norr Mälarstrand is narrow, and she's driving at almost sixty miles an hour. If she passes any newspaper delivery boys on bikes, or retirees out walking their dogs, she's going to have difficulty avoiding them. Her fingertips are on the wheel, ready to make the maneuver that could save a life.

But when she reaches Rålambshovsparken, she still hasn't seen another soul.

And in her head, she can hear Petrovic saying that he has something big planned for the fifteenth of September.

That bastard.

Caroline Thurn has made it onto the highway when her phone rings. Olsson again. She accepts the call by pressing the button on her earpiece's microphone, whose white cable is hanging next to her face. There still aren't many cars around.

"Where the hell are you?" asks Therese Olsson.

"Arriving in Västberga in four minutes."

"What the hell are you doing there? You should be here."

"You said to . . ." but she doesn't finish the sentence.

Olsson has forgotten asking her to go out to the cash depot.

"I'm no use in Kungsholmen," Thurn says instead. "But I need to talk to our helicopter pilot. Can you get someone to patch the call through to my cell? And I want to talk to whoever's in charge out in Västberga."

Olsson takes a few seconds to think.

"OK," she says, and hangs up to avoid wasting any more time.

Thurn can see the exit for Västberga when the phone rings again. She glances at the time. Only eight minutes have passed since she left home.

"Thurn," she says into the microphone.

"Hello?"

"This is Caroline Thurn. Who is this?"

"Jakob. The pilot. I . . . We're on the way to Myttinge."

"We've got an ongoing robbery," Thurn explains. "There are reports of a helicopter, a Bell Jet . . . being used to . . ."

"A JetRanger," the pilot corrects her. "A 206. We know, we heard about it last week."

Thurn doesn't know whether she should feel pleased or annoyed. She is on the line with an unknown person who knew about the robbery a week ago. Is this a case of another damn leak from police headquarters, or is the pilot one of those who was on standby in Solna last week?

She makes an irritated mental note.

"If I understand correctly," she says, "the robbery is happening right now. So you need to hurry."

"We've got the coordinates," the pilot answers. His voice sounds like a young boy's. "But this isn't Bromma?"

"Västberga."

The pilot takes a moment to think.

"Good," he says. "That's better. We'll fly over the park in Årsta. We'll be in the air in ten minutes."

Thurn checks the time. It's 5:31. The helicopters will be in the air by twenty to six.

"If they're still inside when you arrive, you need to stop them from taking off," Thurn tells him, slowing down to turn into the industrial area via Västberga Allé. "You shouldn't intervene. If they still manage to take off, just follow them and let us know where they land."

"Intervene?" the pilot repeats with a brief laugh. "Do you think we'll be flying some kind of assault helicopter?"

"Did you understand the instructions?"

The pilot mumbles a yes as a new call flashes up on Thurn's display.

"Report back once you're in the air," she says, switching her conversation partner.

"Månsson." Thurn suddenly hears a deep, calm voice in her ear. It doesn't tell her anything about the police officer's decision-making abilities, of course, but it still sounds reassuring.

"Task Force Leader Caroline Thurn," she says. "Give me an update."

"Well, nothing's happening right now. Maybe that's why the helicopter flew off?"

"It's gone?"

Thurn is confused. She had always assumed that the robbers were planning to get away in the helicopter.

"We can still hear it," says Dag Månsson, "but we can't see it. Wait . . . is that you?"

At that very moment, Thurn catches sight of the police van parked by the gas station, and she ends the call, leaving the earpiece in her ear.

She parks up next to the van and opens the door.

"Where's Månsson?" she asks as she climbs out of the car.

A tall, well-built officer in uniform jumps out of the van and comes forward to meet her.

"Dag Månsson," he introduces himself, shaking Thurn's hand.

"Have you requested backup?" she asks.

There is a sea of blinking lights outside the G4S depot, but Thurn can see only ordinary patrol cars, no specialists.

"Backup?" Månsson asks. "What do you mean?"

"Are the riot squad on the way? Did National confirm?"

"I don't know anything about that," Månsson replies in his deep voice.

"OK, make sure you check," Thurn says.

"We haven't had time," Månsson mutters, sounding annoyed. "We were clearing crap from the access roads so you'd be able to make it over here with your wheels intact."

78

Everything has been carried down from the roof to the balcony on the fifth floor, and Nordgren is busy setting up the ladder to the floor above. He leans it against the reinforced glass, but he can barely get any angle, the balcony is too shallow.

Still, up he climbs. He has one of the explosive frames in his hand. Balanced on the ladder, he fixes the frame to the glass, fills it with explosives, pushes in the detonator capsule and attaches the long detonation cable.

Once Maloof and Sami see that Nordgren has everything in place, they start to climb the long ladder back up to the roof. Nordgren has made it down to the balcony, but he holds the ladder steady for the others before he makes the ascent himself.

They won't need much of a charge to break the glass, but considering the shards will rain down onto the balcony on the fifth floor, the three of them have no choice but to climb out of the way.

Back up on the roof, Nordgren gets to work with his cable and the motorbike battery. As a result, he doesn't notice what Sami has already seen.

Down on the street, there is a police van and a sea of cars with flashing blue lights. They're already here. Sami decides to take no notice of it. There's no other way to handle it.

A second later, the explosion cuts through the atrium.

"Quick now," says Nordgren.

He's already on his way back down the long ladder.

79

"What was that, Claude?"

Everyone in Counting hears the explosion, and Ann-Marie isn't the only one to look questioningly at Tavernier.

But when nothing happens after the first blast, they return to bundling and locking the notes into the cages in the middle of the room.

Everyone but Ann-Marie. She is staring expectantly at Claude Tavernier, demanding an answer.

"What was that?"

"I don't know," says Tavernier.

He dials the number for the guardroom on the second floor, and Valter answers immediately. The guard is following the unfolding events on his CCTV monitors.

"Have the police arrived?" Tavernier asks.

Valter doesn't know. But he does have around eighty video cameras watching over the majority of areas inside the building, and he tells Tavernier what he knows. That a helicopter landed on the roof, that the robbers have smashed a window in the skylight. He can't see where they are right now, and he hasn't heard any explosions from where he is on the second floor.

Valter falls silent, as though he is deliberating with himself, but then he says:

"They're heavily armed. But the police will probably be getting here any moment," he adds, in an attempt to dampen the drama.

Tavernier hangs up.

"The police will be here soon," he tells Ann-Marie, something that has an immediate calming effect on her.

The fear in her wide eyes seems to lessen slightly.

"They got in through the roof, didn't they?" she asks.

Tavernier nods. It's something everyone working at G4S in Väst-berga has discussed. The new information spreads across the room. They knew it. That damn glass skylight is like a beacon for all the coun-try's would-be criminals at night.

They get back to work.

"Anyone who's finished, come over here," Tavernier says.

He is already standing in the area of the room that could be de-scribed as the center. The so-called safety position where they're meant to gather to wait for the police or guards. All in line with the instructions of Security Chief Palle Lindahl, instructions that he took from one of the international conferences G4S holds for its security chiefs every year. At these events, the combined experiences of over a hundred different countries come together. Stay in the room until help arrives, that's the message. Don't start running around a building full of armed criminals. They'll be searching the corridors and won't appreci-ate any surprises in the shape of confused staff members trying to find a way out.

Everyone knows the drill.

One by one, they finish their work and move over to Tavernier and Ann-Marie, who are already standing in position.

All that's left now is to wait until it's over.

It seems obvious to Tavernier that the robbers will be making their way toward the vault on the second floor.

80

The hole in the reinforced glass is big enough for Nordgren to use the crowbar to break an opening they can get in through.

On the other side is a room that seems to be used as some kind of storage area, but right now it's empty. The door is open, meaning they are now wall-to-wall with Counting.

Maloof points to the fire door they were expecting. Nordgren goes over and studies the frame. The door is on a metal runner, meaning it can automatically move to one side if the fire alarm sounds. At the very top right, tucked in beneath the ceiling, he spots the cable controlling the door. He doesn't have any wire cutters with him, but a powerful tug is all it takes to pull it from its connection. Then they just need to push the door to the side. It moves smoothly in its tracks, revealing a steel-clad security door behind it.

It's the last barrier between them and the money.

Nordgren pulls a Coca-Cola can from his backpack. It's been cut in the middle, filled with explosives and a magnet has been attached to the bottom. He pushes the detonation capsule into the explosive putty and fixes the can to the door, an inch beneath the handle. With one hand, he gestures for Sami and Maloof to go back into the storeroom by the reinforced glass. The concave base of the can will direct the explosion inward and away. It's something Nordgren has done many times before.

He deliberately chooses a smaller charge. He doesn't know how much it will take, and he doesn't know what's on the other side of the door. Where the money is located, where the workstations are.

Nordgren clamps the long detonation cable onto the capsule and joins Maloof and Sami in the storeroom. He moves quickly and confidently. He touches the cable to the poles of the battery, the charge explodes, and he runs back out to the door.

There's barely a scratch on it.

Nordgren nods. He knows what he needs to do. He applies a new charge in the same place. He tries to stop himself from feeling any stress, doesn't doubt for a moment that he'll manage, works methodically. He's back in the storeroom with the others in less than thirty seconds, and the next charge goes off.

This explosion is considerably more powerful than the last. The smell of burned gunpowder fills the room when the three go in to see whether it worked. The smoke and dust quickly settle.

The door is still barely damaged.

"What the hell are you doing?" Sami whispers.

81

They hear the next explosion at almost the exact moment the last bundle of notes is locked in the cage. The sound makes them jump; it's louder than before, it seems closer.

"We can't just stand here, Claude," Ann-Marie whispers.

It's unclear whether she is whispering so that the robbers won't hear her, or because she doesn't want to worry her colleagues.

"The instructions are clear," Tavernier replies unnecessarily formally.

"We can't just stand here," she repeats, shaking her head.

"Can someone turn off that damn radio?" Tavernier snaps.

He doesn't see who does it, but a few seconds later the device finally falls silent.

"Don't worry," he says aloud. "When the robbers make it into the vault, they'll realize it's pointless."

But just before Tavernier has time to continue, they hear the third blast, and it's worse than those before it.

"Shit," he swears.

"It's the security door!"

The voice comes from someone standing by the bend in the room, and they can see what Tavernier can't.

"Everyone stay here," Tavernier orders.

82

If things had been different and they were sitting around a kitchen table, talking about this, Sami Farhan's frustration would have known no bounds. He would have gotten up, moved around the table and talked nonstop. Gesturing wildly, he would have reminded the others what he had been through, stories he'd heard about cautiousness and a lack of decisiveness, and he would have pointed to Niklas Nordgren and said, "Fuck whatever's on the other side of the door, just blow the damn thing open."

But not now.

Not now that they're on the sixth floor of the cash depot, staring helplessly at the steel-clad security door as their helicopter hovers overhead.

Now Sami says nothing. He trusts Niklas Nordgren because he has to trust him, and he assumes that Nordgren knows better than anyone what needs to be done.

"OK," says the explosives expert. "Third time's lucky. Take cover."

He says it quietly. Without any hesitation, without apologizing. And while Sami and Maloof resolutely return to the storeroom, Nordgren pulls out an explosive frame rather than another can. He fixes the frame to the door, and this time he primes it differently. He knows there's a risk he'll take out half the wall with it. He knows there's a risk that the money on the other side will be buried by plaster and dust and splinters.

Not to mention what might happen to the people working there.

But he has no other option. Though he hasn't looked at his watch since they got onto the sixth floor, he knows they're running out of time. Every stage has taken longer than it should have. This has to work now.

83

Tavernier quickly goes over to inspect the steel door. It's the emergency exit out to the atrium, and even from a distance he can see that there's a dent in it, right beneath the handle, as though someone had taken a battering ram to it from the other side.

He takes out his phone and calls Valter.

"Can you see them?"

"No. But they must be up with you somewhere, they haven't appeared on any of the cameras by the elevators or the stairs."

"They're trying to blow their way in here," says Tavernier.

He doesn't have time to say any more.

The third blast is more powerful than those that came before it, and it feels like the walls are about to come crashing down. Plaster, splinters and dust swirl through the air, and Ann-Marie starts screaming. No one tries to stop her.

Tavernier has had enough.

"Follow me!" he shouts, breaking into a run.

He is still holding his phone to his ear, and he rushes over to the opposite door, toward the stairwell.

Finally, he has become the leader he's always wanted to be. They follow him, all of them, without any hesitation. The moment they make it into the stairwell, his phone loses the signal, but Tavernier continues—the stairs will take them down to the security doors outside the vault—and the others follow.

I'll create a new secure position, he thinks. Because real leaders make smart decisions in difficult situations.

84

This time, it takes a while for the dust to settle.

Maloof's ears are ringing when he steps out of the storeroom. The relief he feels when he sees the battered door is indescribable. The gap is more than wide enough. Nordgren is already moving past him with one of the crowbars. He grabs the other.

With the larger of the two crowbars, they manage to force the door open. It falls into Counting with a thud.

Sami already has his gun raised, and he enters the room ahead of the others. He scrapes his hand on the half-destroyed wall on his way in.

He doesn't expect there to be any staff left in the room, the bank world always instructs its employees to evacuate the premises as soon as they can. But nothing is guaranteed.

With his machine gun at hip level, he searches the room. It's empty.

Maloof is close behind him. He glances at his watch. They've already taken over five minutes, and they still haven't seen the money.

He starts the angle grinder. He does it by hand. It's gasoline driven, so it's a bit like starting an outboard motor or a lawnmower from the sixties. The engine starts with a loud roar. He moves over to the cages where the notes have been stashed and uses the grinder to cut the locks. A shower of sparks cascades beautifully to the floor. The smell of two-stroke gas fills the room.

Nordgren realizes that the staff has managed to lock everything in the cages. Yet more proof of how long it took them to get in. He banishes the thought. He doesn't want to think about how many police officers are currently waiting outside.

As Maloof cuts open the cages, Nordgren and Sami fetch the mailbags.

The money is bundled up in red plastic boxes. They search for the 500-kronor notes and throw the boxes containing the 100- and 20-kronor notes to the floor.

Maloof moves on to the next cage. He puts down the angle grinder without turning it off, and it spins on the floor as though it had a life of its own. He tests the cage door. It won't open. He grabs the angle grinder and cuts through the last bit.

The second cage contains the larger denominations.

They get to work.

As soon as one bag is full, they drag it out to the next room, into the storeroom by the reinforced glass window, and then throw it down to the balcony on the fifth floor.

All this takes time.

Each of them knows that they can't spend much longer inside the building, but they continue anyway. They've been in a rush since they first stepped out of the helicopter, but they now know that they're in an extreme rush. Once it looks like there's no more room for mailbags on the little balcony on the fifth floor, they decide that they're done.

85

5:35 a.m.

Task Force Leader Caroline Thurn climbs into the police van serving as the liaison center parked outside the Statoil station directly opposite the G4S cash depot. The station is on a slight elevation, which means it has a good view of its surroundings. The blue flashing lights from the patrol cars in the distance lend a cinematic quality to the scene. The sound of the robbers' helicopter adds to that. Thurn had spotted it earlier, but it now seems to have disappeared into the dark night sky.

She has two options: either send people into the building immediately, risking shots being fired and a possible hostage situation, or wait until the robbers are back in their helicopter and attempting to make their getaway. She has a few more minutes to make her decision.

There are two uniformed police officers sitting in the front of the van, and several other people in the back. One of them is in plain-clothes, and he has a laptop computer open in front of him. On the screen, Thurn catches sight of the green, pixelated images typical of live CCTV cameras.

"Who is that?" Thurn asks the nearest police officer.

"No idea."

"What's a plainclothes officer doing here?"

"Ask Månsson," the officer suggests, referring her to the commanding officer.

The officer crouches back into the front seat. Thurn moves toward the back of the van and the stranger with the computer. The man seems to be in his early middle age, and he has a ruddy complexion and thick glasses.

"I'm Caroline Thurn," she introduces herself. "I'm taking over command out here. Who are you?"

The man looks up at the tall police inspector and nods.

"Palle Lindahl," he replies. "G4S security chief."

Lindahl pulls out a business card and hands it to Thurn.

"You got here very quickly," Thurn comments.

"I live just over there," Lindahl replies.

He points out of the window and then continues:

"The manager in Counting, Claude Tavernier, raised the alarm with the on-duty guard. That was"—Lindahl checks the time on his phone—"twenty minutes ago. The guard called Skövde, which is where we have our control center. Skövde called me, as they're meant to. I pulled on some trousers and . . . walked over. You lot were already here."

Thurn nods. "Is there a risk of a hostage situation?"

That's her most pressing concern.

"There's no need to speculate," the security chief replies, turning his computer so that she can see the screen.

On it, two men dressed in black are standing in front of what look like tall, bar-covered cages. They are lifting boxes out of the cages and then dumping bundles of notes into fabric bags. One of the men has an automatic weapon, probably a Kalashnikov, hanging from a strap over his shoulder.

"We have over eighty CCTV cameras in the building," Security Chief Lindahl explains, "I can bring them all up on screen."

"Impressive." Thurn nods approvingly. "But sadly that doesn't help."

"The cameras aren't meant to prevent crimes," Palle Lindahl replies, sounding offended. "No number of cameras or vaults will keep skilled criminals away for particularly long. Our reasoning is that the perimeter security should stand up to attack for fifteen minutes. That should be enough time."

"Enough time for what?" the inspector asks.

"Enough time for the police to get here. That fifteen minutes has passed, and you're here. I can open and lock the doors and elevators throughout the entire building from my computer. You have a lot of people here. I can lead you up to the robbers, if you want."

Thurn nods thoughtfully and peers out the police van window.

The many uniformed officers are standing outside their blue-twinkling cars, talking to one another in small groups. The reason none of them seem to be hurrying, or expecting orders of any kind, is that none of these officers have been trained for a situation like this. These were men and women who could chase down vandals and muggers, who could keep drunks away from public places, overpower men who abused their wives in apartments in the southern suburbs and in the best case also hit the target during their annual shooting exam. But they had no experience tackling international organized crime.

Ordering these men and women to storm the cash depot would be extremely risky.

And with civilians inside the building over the road, it would be a risk in which lives would be at stake.

Thurn is staring at the computer screen, struck by how calmly the robbers seem to be working. She watches them methodically fill their mailbags with cash. When one sack is full, they swing it up onto their shoulders or drag it across the floor and out of the room. Since they're coming and going, all dressed alike, it's difficult to tell how many of them there are. Four, she would guess, but it could just as easily be three or five.

"Where are they?" she asks. "In the vault?"

"No, no," says Lindahl. "No one gets into the vault. That's where the big money is. No, they're up on the sixth floor. We call it Cash. Counting. It's where we send the notes to be counted. Then they're sent back down to the vault. We never have more than a few hundred million up there."

"A few hundred million?" Thurn repeats, amazed.

"Right now, we have over a billion in the building," Lindahl points out, to put those hundreds of millions in context.

"And there's no one else there?" Thurn asks, nodding toward the screen.

"The room should be manned . . ." Lindahl eventually replies. "We have a dozen or so people working in Cash at this time of day. And their orders are to stay put if something happens. But I can't see them. I don't actually know . . ."

"So even with your eighty CCTV cameras, you can't tell whether your staff are in harm's way?"

Palle Lindahl shakes his head. "No," he says. "I can't."

"No," Thurn says.

"But what I can say, and unequivocally," the security chief continues, without any attempt to hide his sense of wronged irritation, "is that if you storm that building and arrest the robbers, our staff—wherever they are—will be much better off."

The headphone in Thurn's ear starts to ring, and she presses the button on the cable around her neck. The pilots have finally taken off, she thinks.

But it isn't the young helicopter pilot's voice she hears in her ear, it's Mats Berggren's.

"I just spoke to Hertz," he says. "There won't be any helicopters from Uppsala or Berga."

"There aren't any?"

"Hertz is at Police HQ. I don't know what's happening, but the message from the military authorities is that we'll have to handle this ourselves."

"Politics."

"They've promised to watch the radar. They can see everything in the air, they say. Apparently they've already seen our robbers' helicopter a few times. Both when it took off and when it got to Västberga."

"Politicians," Thurn repeats.

"Hasn't our helicopter taken off?" Berggren asks.

"No," Thurn says, glancing at her watch. "But the pilots should have made it to Myttinge by now."

"The Task Force is getting ready," Berggren tells her.

"Getting ready?" Thurn is dismissive. "By the time they get here, there won't be anyone left."

But then the inspector spots something that puts her in a better mood. Two riot vans are approaching the gas station. The robbers' white helicopter has also just dropped down toward the roof. It's hovering just above the cash depot now. There's no doubt about it: the pilot has also seen the riot vans.

Thurn nods to herself.

These are the type of officers she's willing to send into the building.

"Finally," she says in the direction of the frustrated security chief.

86

The riot vans drive up to the gas station and come to a halt next to Thurn. An enormous police officer climbs out of one of them, he has to be over six and a half feet tall, with a crew cut and shoulders like a bodybuilder. He's the commanding officer.

"Who's in charge here?" he barks.

Thurn points to herself. The man nods uninterestedly and glances over to the building and the helicopter hovering above it.

"You want us to take him down?" he asks.

"Take him down?"

"We can shoot the bastard down," the uniformed officer says with a confident nod.

Thurn looks up at the helicopter. The beefed-up policeman is insane, she thinks. Shooting down the helicopter while it's hovering above the roof could cause it to explode and fall onto a building full of people. What is he thinking? But before Thurn has time to say anything, Palle Lindahl sticks his head out of the police van.

"The robbers seem to be on the move," he shouts.

He has his laptop in one hand, prepared to prove his words by showing them the images from the CCTV cameras.

Thurn turns to the riot squad leader.

"Storm the building," she says to him. "Now. Get them before it's too late."

It's time for Palle Lindahl to prove that being able to open doors from his computer wasn't just talk.

The riot squad leader is already striding back toward his van. Thurn glances at her watch. Why hasn't the helicopter pilot called?

87

Jack Kluger is breathing too quickly. He's hyperventilating. And because his body isn't getting enough oxygen, his hands are shaking. He's been through this before. Many times. He knows he needs to calm down. He needs to breathe more deeply, draw air into his lungs.

But it's impossible.

Nothing is happening. The green light from his watch is glowing fiercely on his wrist. Almost thirty minutes have now passed. Thirty minutes. Something must have happened. How long should he wait, how long should he just sit in position above the roof, waiting for them? Would it be better to just leave?

He has no way of communicating with the robbers inside.

What are they waiting for?

And right then, the fuel-warning light starts to blink. In the darkness inside the helicopter, the red light pulses with unrelenting arrogance. The countdown is serious now. The light's blinking matches the pounding of the blood in Kluger's temples. Beneath him, on the dark ground, the flashing blue lights of the police cars cast long, licking beams of light onto the cash depot, which lies heavy and calm. The building's powerful brick walls and dimly lit windows give no indication of anything in particular going on inside.

In the bright glow of the light on the roof, Jack Kluger is at no risk of making a mistake. He gently tilts the helicopter forward a fraction and stares down at the ladder that is still sticking up through the broken window.

No movement, no shadows, nothing.

The roof is empty.

The red fuel-warning light illuminates his face. His blue eyes reflect the blue light from the police cars over by the gas station. It's getting more and more crowded down there, new cars keep arriving all the time.

The helicopter pilot doesn't notice that he's sweating. He is no longer thinking about his breathing being too quick or too shallow.

Suddenly, something new happens down by the Statoil station. Kluger spots it out of the corner of his eye, and he turns the stick to the right so that the helicopter twists in the air. He sees the two riot vans arrive.

Having done small jobs for Balik in Södertälje for over a year now, Jack Kluger knows that riot vans are a bad sign. They're full of the kind of police officers he remembers from Texas. People who aren't afraid of firing a weapon, people who don't care.

Again and again, Kluger stares toward the southern horizon. He expects to see the police helicopter approaching at any moment, and he makes up his mind: If it appears, it's over. He'll fly away.

But maybe that has to happen sooner.

They took off from Norrtälje with less than a full tank of fuel to avoid being overweight. He realizes now that that was a mistake. The indicator has been at the bottom for a minute or two now.

He swears loudly.

His breathing is quick.

One more minute, he thinks. Then I'm off.

88

5:39 a.m.

Jakob Walker is behind the wheel.

He's sticking to forty miles an hour, he doesn't dare go any faster through the dense forests of Värmdö. He also doesn't want to admit how tired he is. They landed at two, managed to get a couple of hours' sleep and then the call came in.

The car's headlights cast a bluish glow onto the pines and spruce. They pass low, rocky outcrops and suddenly appearing fields. Jakob has driven between the station and the hangar hundreds of times before, but at night he's always surprised by the many tight bends.

"Maybe we could go a bit faster?" says Larsson.

Jakob turns his head. He has never really got to know Conny Larsson. They're too different. Larsson is a quiet, solitary man in his sixties, from the far north of the country, while Jakob was born and bred in Stockholm.

"Better to make it there in one piece than end up with an elk through the window," he says.

As expected, Larsson doesn't reply.

Last week, they had been stationed at the National Task Force base in Solna, taking the helicopter up into the air once an hour despite the fact that absolutely nothing was happening. Jakob has never done military service, but he imagines that his night in the army-like police department is as close as he'll ever get. They had been given a quick briefing about the robbers' plans the night before; how a helicopter would land on the roof of the Panaxia cash depot in Bromma and then, in all likelihood, be used again for the getaway.

The night had been an emotional roller coaster. The mood in the briefing room was tense, serious, and it had felt as though all the men with the powerful jawlines around him were preparing for war.

The task was, and still is, Jakob assumes, to obstruct or possibly pursue a Bell JetRanger helicopter. He knows the model well. The 206 was the first in the series, a type of helicopter originally developed for the Americans and then successfully marketed to the civilian population once the US Air Force changed its mind and decided not to order any.

Both the Swedish military and police had used the model, or variants of it, anyway. It was actually a JetRanger II in which Jakob had taken his helicopter pilot's license. These days, they tended to fly the ordinary Airbus Eurocopter. To an outsider, the only visible difference was the encased fantail, Eurocoptor's pride and joy, for which it held the global patent.

In the distance, they finally spot the lights illuminating the hangar at Myttinge, and Jakob steps on the accelerator for the last quarter mile. Conny Larsson sighs. What he means by that remains to be seen.

Last week, they had discussed the risk that the robbers might open fire and came to the conclusion that if they hovered above the robbers' helicopter, only an idiot would risk bringing down a police chopper on top of himself.

And, as Jakob understands it, the robbers are far from idiots.

He pulls up by the fence in the darkness, a short walk from the entrance. They climb out into the dark night and move quickly toward the gate. With just a few yards to go, and Jakob already fumbling with the key for the padlock, Larsson shouts. A second later, Jakob spots the same thing.

On the other side of the fence, just outside the doors into the hangar, there are two square, black boxes with blinking red lights on top of them.

Bombs.

"Stop, for God's sake!" Larsson shouts.

But Jakob is already still. "What the hell are those?"

The two on-duty pilots stare at the bombs. It feels so strange, to be in such a familiar place, radiating a sense of peaceful stillness, and to be staring at something straight out of an American action film.

"This was what they meant," Larsson says as he slowly backs away from the fence.

"What?"

"It's why we were moved to Solna last week. It's a way of making sure we can't get into the air. Those damn things are probably on a timer. They'll go off any moment."

The pilots continue backing up toward the car.

"What the hell do we do?"

89

"Are you in the air?"

Thurn is standing next to the gas station with Dag Månsson and the G4S security chief, Palle Lindahl. The riot vans are making their way toward the cash depot. For the first time since she got into the car that morning, Thurn feels in control. In just a couple of minutes, the riot squad will storm the building and the helicopter from Myttinge will arrive to block the robbers' getaway.

But that isn't what Jakob Walker has to tell her.

"We're not in the air, we're still on the ground," the pilot says into Thurn's earpiece.

Thurn is listening, but she doesn't understand. "Could you repeat that?"

"There are two bombs outside the doors into the hangar," the helicopter pilot continues. "We don't know how they've been constructed. We're waiting by the gates until help arrives."

"Bombs?" Thurn says. "Is it—"

"My colleague is just calling it in to Control," Jakob interrupts, glancing at Larsson, who, sure enough, has the control center on the line. "They'll have to send someone who knows how to handle this. We need to wait until the danger is over. If it happens quickly, maybe we can—"

Thurn rips the headphone from her ear and starts running. Straight over the grass toward the riot vans and the G4S depot. Her hands cut through the air like knives, her long legs pound the ground. She runs quickly.

She shouts out as the riot vans draw closer and closer to the building.

"Abort! The buildings might be booby-trapped!"

90

Nordgren is climbing the longer of the two ladders, up toward the roof. He's carrying a thick rope that loops back down to the balcony on the fifth floor. The first thing he sees when he steps out into the dark dawn is the sea of blinking blue lights on the ground below.

The second thing he sees is the helicopter hovering above him.

It feels like hours have passed since he was sitting in it.

He starts pulling on the rope. Maloof has hooked one of the full mailbags to it. Nordgren backs up, backs up, backs up. It's not quite as heavy as he expected. When he stops to catch his breath, he turns around to check where he is.

He's an inch from the edge of the roof.

No time to get scared or to think about that now.

With the mailbag acting as a counterweight, he moves back over to the broken window and quickly hauls it up the last part of the way.

Behind him, the helicopter lands.

While Maloof holds the ladder, Sami climbs up to the roof to help Nordgren with the bags. Maloof stays behind on the balcony on the fifth floor, fastening a couple of bags at a time to the rope, to make things go more quickly. He feels exposed on the tiny ledge. He knows that the police could storm the building at any moment, if they aren't already inside. He's visible from every floor below, and the ladder is his only escape route, making him an even easier target.

He glances at his watch.

The fifteen minutes they had planned have turned into thirty.

It can't take any longer. He decides to leave the last few bags they still haven't managed to haul up and starts climbing.

Up on the roof, Sami runs over to the helicopter to throw the money into the cabin. When he opens the door, he's met by a furious pilot.

Jack Kluger is shouting loud enough to overpower the sound of the engine.

"You said fifteen minutes! Where the hell have you been? We're out of juice!"

The fuel warning is still blinking away with its ominous red light.

91

If the robbers had placed bombs outside the helicopter hangar in Myttinge, the chances of their having done the same at the cash depot in Västberga were high. And Caroline Thurn didn't want to be responsible for ordering a police officer to open a door that then exploded in his or her face.

Shouting and gesturing wildly, she manages to get the riot squad to stop before they make it to the entrance. The enormous commanding officer climbs out of the first van. He's wearing a bulletproof vest and a helmet, and he is furious. He strides toward Thurn and stops dead right in front of her. He's standing so close that he is actually looking down at her. The muscles in his neck are taut.

"It's probably best if you back off," he hisses. "We're going in now."

The sound of the helicopter hovering directly overhead is now so loud that they have to raise their voices.

"It might be booby-trapped!" Thurn shouts.

She imagines she can smell gasoline. It could be coming from anywhere: the helicopter, the riot vans, the gas station.

The heavily armed commanding officer looks suspicious, and then he turns to look at the entrance. One floor up, in the CCTV room, the guards are sitting in front of screens showing the same images that Palle Lindahl has on his laptop. Could they have missed someone planting bombs in the building?

"Booby-trapped?" the aggressive officer repeats, sounding like he doesn't believe it. "I can't see anything."

"We have reason to believe so."

"You do? Meaning we shouldn't go in?" he asks, sounding incredibly disappointed.

"We need to make sure that—"

But before Thurn has time to finish her sentence, the sound of the helicopter becomes deafening, and a second later they see it lift off.

"They're leaving!" Thurn shouts, feeling the panic rise. "They're getting away."

Two police officers carrying rocket launchers throw themselves out of the van. They run onto the grass, squat down with the weapons on their shoulders, and point them up at the helicopter.

The commanding officer stares at Thurn. "Give the order!" he hisses.

Thurn looks up at the helicopter.

"The order!" the riot squad leader barks. "Give me the order!"

Other than the robbers, she has no idea who is inside the helicopter. Is the pilot being forced, or is he complicit in the robbery? Do they have hostages on board?

"Give the order!" the officer screams at her. His face is red, a vein bulging on his neck.

Thurn stares at the two officers squatting down with their weapons ready. Then she looks up into the air and realizes it's already too late, the helicopter has made it too far.

"Shit!" the officer shouts as he realizes the same thing, and he starts running back toward his vehicle, closely followed by the two men who had been on their knees on the grass.

"Follow them!" Thurn shouts to the riot squad leader, and she starts running in the opposite direction, back toward her car up by the Statoil station.

As she's halfway there, her phone rings. She answers the call without slowing down.

"Caroline? Caroline?" Berggren shouts into her ear. "It's me. Hertz got in touch. The military says they have two fighter jets in the air, roughly where you are."

Thurn tries to gather her thoughts.

"The robbers just flew off," she shouts. "I've got a riot van following them. Could you make sure I can keep in touch with the van, Mats? Fighter jets? How would they help?"

"I don't know," Berggren replies. "Could they shoot down the helicopter?"

Thurn has made it to the parking lot. Without knowing who is on board, she can't even think about shooting down the helicopter. Could the answer be in Lindahl's CCTV cameras? Did any of the cameras capture who went on board?

"Give me a minute," she pants down the line.

"What should I say to the jets?"

"Tell them to stand by," Thurn replies. "Stand by."

She runs over to the police van, but before she manages to speak to Lindahl, Berggren calls back.

"Counterorders, Caroline," he says.

"What does that mean?"

"Olsson found out about the fighter planes. It's illegal."

"What's illegal?"

"The military's not allowed to get involved in police activity. There's a law . . . Olsson gave the counterorder. The planes have gone back to their original course."

"Politicians," Thorn says with a snort, but she feels a certain relief at not having to take responsibility for a Swedish combat fighter attacking a private helicopter within the capital's airspace.

"Is the helicopter showing up on any radars?" she asks.

"Not even when it took off," says Berggren. "The military's looking. Us too. No one can see a thing."

"They're flying too low."

"Exactly. They're flying too low. But surely that means the riot squad should be able to see them from the highway?"

Thurn nods. Berggren is right. Since the robbers aren't only choosing to fly low, but also have probably turned off all communication equipment, they'll have no choice but to stick to well-lit roads for navigation. Thurn can see daylight approaching on the horizon, but it's no more than a thin line against the dark sky. From her own experience, she knows that through the thick windowpanes of a helicopter, the world seems even darker.

"Let me talk to the riot squad," she says to Berggren. "Patch me through. Maybe I can help them."

92

5:35 a.m.

Tor Stenson yawns and runs his hand over his stubble.

The night shift was always long and boring. His had started at midnight, as usual, when the intensity of the newsroom is at its worst. Deliveries to the printers have begun, and the next day's paper is starting to take shape. People run down corridors, phones ring, articles are added and taken away, and discussions about the front-page headlines, kickers and puff boxes reach frantic levels. Tor Stenson has nothing to do with any of that. He is one of the younger members of the staff, and is employed by one of the recruitment companies owned by the paper. There has been a freeze on any new reporters in the newsroom since 2001; its current employees enjoy job security, but things are different for the people hired by the recruitment company. Though Stenson's work focuses on the Web—in the tabloid world, everyone under the age of thirty-five is an online guru—he never knows whether his job will exist from one month to the next.

Stenson always begins his shift by exchanging a few words with his colleagues on their way home. Is there any Hollywood gossip to follow up on? He goes through their competitor's site. Do they have anything he's missed? All around him, the newsroom empties out, and after an hour or so the rows of desks in the open-plan room fall quiet.

When the phone rings, it's already after five thirty. Stenson jumps. In the early hours, the flow of news is minimal, meaning the call is unexpected.

"Stenson," he answers

It's someone calling in a tip from the police command center.

What he has to say is incredible. Sensational, even.

Stenson's pulse picks up as he listens. Robbers in a helicopter. Breaking into a cash depot through the roof. And making their getaway—with an unimaginable sum of money—in the same helicopter.

Stenson immediately knows that this is front-page news. He can feel his heart pounding in his chest. This is his chance to bag that permanent position.

"Pictures?" he asks. "Do you have any pictures?"

The police officer gives him the number of the guard who called in the robbery from Västberga.

"Shit," Stenson swears to himself as he dials the guard's number and waits for the call to go through. "Shit."

He swears aloud, though he doesn't know why.

Yes, the guard has taken pictures of the white helicopter lifting off from the roof of the G4S building and disappearing into the black night sky. Deep down, Stenson is celebrating, but he tries to sound as indifferent as he can when the guard begins to negotiate on price.

It's 5:48 when Tor Stenson uploads the first fuzzy images to the website. He quickly checks whether the paper's rivals have done the same, but he can't see anything yet.

After that, Stenson calls the paper's news editor at home, waking him up. Stenson repeats his name a few times to begin with, making sure the editor is perfectly clear about exactly who has broken the story. And then he tells him about the helicopter.

The news editor mumbles something, hangs up and then calls the deputy editor, who reluctantly calls and wakes the editor in chief.

"Were you asleep?" the deputy asks.

"I never fucking sleep," the editor in chief slurs, clearly emerging from some kind of pleasant dream. "I'm the editor of a tabloid. I don't get paid to sleep."

The deputy quickly explains what has happened.

"A helicopter robbery?" the editor in chief sums up, already sitting on the edge of his bed, pulling on his underwear. "Is there a more concise way of saying that? Whatever, doesn't matter, we'll see. I'm on my way in. Send people out to Västberga to interview the police at the scene. Are there any hostages?"

The deputy has no idea about hostages, but the Web editor Tor Stenson, the one who got ahold of the pictures they now have online, claims the witness heard pops coming from inside the building.

"Pops? What the hell does that mean? Were the robbers making popcorn?" the editor in chief hisses, grabbing a half-stale cinnamon bun from a plate in the kitchen and heading for the door. "We need details!"

93

5:47 a.m.

The fuel-warning light continues to blink. It's all Kluger can see, all that exists in that moment; the red light fills the dark cabin like a constant, fateful reminder that they'll soon run out of fuel.

"Where the hell were you?" he shouts as he angles the rotor blades forward a few degrees, allowing the metal bubble to cut through the air, away from the glowing glass pyramid on top of the building at Västberga Allé 11. "We said fifteen minutes?! It's been . . . thirty-four. This isn't going to fucking work!"

The sweat is running down his forehead, and the drops that don't get caught on his eyebrows roll down into his eyes. He tries to blink them away. No one can hear him, the loud thudding of the machine is overpowering everything else, and they can't communicate using their headsets, because they have chosen not to put them on. All nonessential electronics have been switched off. They don't want to be caught on the military or police radars. They're flying dark, with a red blinking warning light constantly reminding them of reality.

"Fucking idiots!" Kluger shouts again, though no one hears him.

Maloof is in the seat behind Jack Kluger. He leans forward with his eyes closed. Waiting for the explosion. He tries to tell himself that if the police had been given orders to shoot them down, it would have already happened by now. But still, he's waiting for the rocket. The sound of the blast, followed by the sensation of falling. Weightlessness. Emptiness.

But there is no blast, there is no explosion. Maloof slowly sits upright. He opens his eyes. Nordgren is half-lying across the seat next to him. Diagonally in front, he can see the outline of Sami's face beneath the anonymizing polyester of his balaclava. The blood is still pounding in Maloof's neck, but the stillness around him comes suddenly. Is it over? He looks out the window. The sky is grayish black, he's flying.

Is it over?

Niklas Nordgren is on his stomach on top of one of the mailbags. He had thrown himself into the helicopter, onto the seat behind the pilot and next to Michel Maloof. The way he landed means he can see out through the window in the door, and down on the ground a swarm of swirling blue lights continues to search for opportunities. There are several dozen emergency vehicles on Västberga Allé and Vretensborgsvägen, gathered in three distinct groups.

It looks like a still life, Nordgren thinks, as though someone had placed the cars there to create drama in an otherwise sleepy business park.

Along the streets crisscrossing the Västberga industrial area, the sharp white light of the streetlamps is painted like street crossings on the ground. The six-lane highway alongside it is still relatively empty. And with each second that passes, the helicopter takes them farther and farther away from the looming tower and its glowing glass pyramid on the roof.

It's over, Nordgren thinks, but he still can't take it in. He can feel the cold metal of the ladders beneath his palms, in the arches of his feet, but his muscle memory is clearer than his other senses.

Did we do it?

We did it, he thinks.

Despite the stubborn blinking light, Kluger carries out the planned diversionary maneuver. He makes it shorter, tighter, saving them just

over a minute. His powerful jaw muscles seem to be chewing something, possibly a piece of gum that has long since lost its taste. Not
once, despite his cursing, has he given his three passengers as much as
a glance.

He cuts across the park in Årsta. They're barely a hundred and fifty
feet off the ground, and each of them gasps when Stockholm's southern neighborhoods suddenly loom up in the distance, the illuminated
Globe Arena—an enormous, abandoned golf ball—a clear navigation
point in the foreground. Right beside it, Kluger spots the rows of red
buses in Gullmarsplan. Waiting for the first departure of the morning. He takes in the proud arc of the Johanneshov Bridge, allowing the
cars to roll dramatically down toward the gaping mouth of the South
Way Tunnel, and higher up, to the left, the huge hospital complex like
a cluster of dark, gloomy blocks. He puts the helicopter into a sharp
right turn and the bright city lights disappear from view. Along the
road toward Älvsjö, all that is beneath them is forest.

Sami is next to Kluger, and is staring out the window. The sky is still
dark. It'll be another half an hour before daylight starts to reveal the
thin strips of cloud that are currently no more than gray shadows high
in the sky, but Sami can already make out a faint glow on the horizon.
The helicopter sweeps across the treetops. The Gömmaren nature reserve sweeps by beneath them in dark silence; a spellbound world of
trees, paths and thickets hiding wild animals and abandoned cars.

Sami turns on his phone. It has been off since before they went into
the building. He calls Team 2 at the gravel pit in Norsborg, but he can't
hear a thing, the roar of the helicopter drowns out any sound from his
phone. He glances at the display. The call seems to have gone through.

"Turn on the lights!" he shouts.

He can't hear whether anyone answers. He ends the call and tries
again.

"Turn on the lights!"

If the team on the ground doesn't turn on the headlights, it'll be impossible for the helicopter to land in Norsborg. The gravel pit might be big, but the forest around it is dense.

"Turn on the lights!" he shouts.

Now that he has given the instructions three times, he feels satisfied. They've been waiting for his call, and he knows it went through. That's enough.

Sami unbuckles his seat belt and turns around. Maloof is diagonally behind him. He nods, pulls his balaclava up over his nose, scratches his beard and grins.

Sami turns again and glances at Niklas Nordgren. His black balaclava doesn't reveal any expression, but he nods too.

Sami turns back to face forward.

He can no longer hear the noise of the rotor blades.

They did it.

They did it.

Thoughts of how his brothers will react when he throws the bundles of cash at them fill his mind. Payback. He can already feel people's eyes on him in town, everyone knowing that he has fulfilled his promises. He can just see them coming over to say hello without looking him in the eye as he's eating a meal at some fancy restaurant. And Karin. She's in front of him, with John clinging onto one leg and the baby on her hip at the other side. He won't need to say a word. Their eyes will meet and she will know it's all over. He's the man who kept his word.

Jack Kluger is flying low, no more than 100 or 120 feet above the treetops. He assumes they have six or seven minutes of fuel left. As the forest comes to an end and the water begins, the blinking fuel light is replaced by a steady red glow. He flies straight above the treetops on the south side of Lake Alby and continues north, toward the glittering lights of the E4 road.

94

5:51 a.m.

Detective Chief Inspector Caroline Thurn drives out of the industrial area in Västberga, leaving the sea of blue flashing lights behind her. She isn't responsible for the fact that Central Command seems to have directed all the patrol cars in the county to G4S. Thurn's initial order not to shoot at the helicopter has now become the official line—meaning that the only thing the fifty or so frustrated and slightly bored officers at the scene have done is to stand and watch as the robbers lifted off and flew away.

Thurn is still experiencing an adrenaline rush when she reaches the entrance ramp to the highway. She brakes and hesitates. She still hasn't heard from the riot squad and has to guess where the helicopter might be heading.

The question is whether she should go north or head south on the E20. There are plenty of exits and on-ramps around Västberga, so whatever she decides, she can quickly change her mind.

No Swedish police officers have experience chasing helicopters at night. But after all the years Caroline Thurn has spent hunting robbers, she has developed a keen sense of intuition. And the minute her hands grip the wheel as hard as she can, swinging up the on-ramp heading north, back into Stockholm, her intuition tells her that it's too late. It's just a vague feeling, she hasn't even formulated the thought, but there's no ignoring the emptiness burning in her stomach.

She hears a ringing sound in her ear, and accepts the call.

"Thurn?" It's Berggren. "I have Olsson here. She wants to talk to you."

Before she has time to protest, the national police commissioner's voice comes on the line.

"Have we lost them, Caroline?"

At first, she doesn't reply.

"We've got a riot squad chasing them," she eventually says.

The line is silent.

"Is that a flying riot squad, Caroline?"

Thurn hates sarcasm. She passes the turnoff to Årsta and blindly continues along the Essingeleden. The helicopter full of robbers could just as easily be heading south, toward Södertälje.

"Caroline, I have Ekblad ringing me every third minute. The papers have already published pictures of the helicopter, and it's not just our own damn broadcasters we've got camped out there in Västberga, we've got people from all over the world. *Der Spiegel*, the BBC. We're not going to get away from this one, Caroline. It reeks of official statements and press conferences."

Thurn dislikes press conferences even more than sarcasm. The traffic into Stockholm is still sparse, but in just a few hours' time it'll be at a standstill.

"Ekblad will explain that the police made a unique effort, as always," Olsson continues, "which is something people should remember when we need increased funding for the police force in general and Stockholm in particular in the next budget. You know the script."

Thurn isn't listening. She isn't stupid. She knows that Olsson is asking her to prepare for the inevitable questions. How much they knew in advance, why they didn't manage to stop it.

"Caroline?"

Berggren is back on the line. Olsson falls silent. She can hear him too.

"I have the riot squad leader on the line. Want to take it?"

A second later, the call with Olsson has been ended and reality fills Caroline's ears.

"Thurn here," she says when she hears the static of the riot van's communication equipment. "Give me an update."

"We've lost it."

The detective swings into the right lane and pulls in behind a slow truck with Estonian plates. She passes the exit for Gröndal.

"What happened?" she asks.

"We were following it toward Årsta," the voice replies. "Then it turned across the park. We couldn't follow, so we lost it."

"Which direction did it turn?"

"South. Down toward Älvsjö."

Thurn nods. She swings back into the left-hand lane and steps on the accelerator. It isn't far to the next exit. But as she reaches ninety miles an hour and her knuckles turn white, she can't fool herself any longer.

It's over.

"Caroline? Are you still there?" Therese Olsson's voice has reappeared in her ear. "What's happening?"

95

Kluger holds up a finger.

They are less than one minute away from the first meeting place, he signals. He has a GPS unit in his hand.

Sami brushes his fantasies to one side. He turns around. Nordgren and Maloof have already managed to tie the mailbags to the rope. There are five bags in total, but there's no way of knowing how much money they grabbed. Didn't they haul more than five bags out of Counting?

Sami doesn't have time to think any further than that before the pilot slows down and allows the helicopter to move even closer to the ground. They are now flying lower than the treetops around them, across the north end of Lake Alby. Along Masmovägen, running parallel to the beach, there is a row of simple wooden cottages. Summer houses to some, something to be torn down to others.

Zoran Petrovic had docked the boat by the jetty, as agreed, a few days earlier.

It wasn't a particularly spectacular vehicle. A typical metal archipelago motorboat with a cabin at the front, big enough to hide ten or so mailbags full of money. The two outboard motors at the stern would be able to keep anyone following them at a distance, if necessary. Going at a speed of ten knots, no more, you passed through two narrow straits, first beneath the Botkyrkaleden Bridge and then beneath the E20, and that would bring you out in the Vårbyfjärden Strait. From there, you could either choose to go northward, toward Stockholm, or turn south, toward Södertälje. It would all depend on the movements of the police.

Maloof opens the side door of the helicopter, and the cold wind forces its way into the cabin. The helicopter is hovering directly above the boat.

Together, Nordgren and Maloof lower the mailbags with the rope they just used on the roof in Västberga. Once they are sure that the first has landed in the middle of boat, they let go and allow the remainder of the money to fall from the heavens.

Before Maloof has even closed the cabin door, the boat has pushed off from the jetty and started its journey north. Kluger quickly guides the helicopter higher, and they continue toward Norsborg.

96

It's barely two minutes from Lake Alby to the gravel pit in Norsborg. They are still flying low, and now the American is checking his GPS every ten or so seconds. Sami, sitting next to him, doesn't need to ask about the red light.

After about a minute, they spot the lights of the cars. They're arranged in a triangle, just like the flashlights at the takeoff site in Stora Skuggan a few hours earlier.

Sami points and the American nods.

The landing happens quickly, without any drama.

Ezra comes running from one of the cars with a couple of gas cans. He puts them down next to the helicopter, whose engine has just been turned off, and Sami then runs back to the car with him.

They drive away without saying goodbye to anyone.

Nordgren quickly hugs Maloof. The feeling of having succeeded has started to creep through his body, no matter how much he tries to fight it. He isn't back in Lidingö yet, he's still not out of the woods.

But he's close.

He runs over to the car where Jonas Wallmark, one of his childhood friends, is waiting. It's not the first time Wallmark has been the driver in this kind of situation.

Maloof and Kluger are left alone by the helicopter. The American is busy refueling from one of the cans, and he nods. He's calmer now.

"It felt good to be up in the air again," he says.

Maloof nods. He doesn't know what the pilot means, but he doesn't care. When Kluger lifts off in the white helicopter a few minutes later, disappearing toward a horizon that is slowly turning blue, Maloof knows he will never see or hear of the man again.

He goes over to the lone car left at the gravel pit in Norsborg. He glances at his watch. It's just turned six. They're almost half an hour behind schedule. He'll probably get stuck in the morning traffic heading for Södertälje.

He opens the passenger's side door of the BMW and climbs in.

The shock renders him speechless.

Petrovic is sitting behind the wheel.

"But . . ." Maloof stammers. "What the hell . . . are you doing here?"

"You texted me and told me to come."

Petrovic had been confused when he got the message after tricking the police to the north of Täby.

Up until that point, the plan had been for him to drive the boat and the money.

"Texted?" Maloof asks. He can't believe this is happening. "Wait . . . so who the hell's driving the boat?"

Petrovic looks at him. At first, he doesn't seem to understand. "What?"

"If you're here, who's driving the boat?" Maloof repeats. "Someone drove off with the money. If it wasn't you . . . ?"

SEPTEMBER 23–25

97

Stenson's ordinary working hours ended one hour after the first publication, the one he alone was responsible for: images of the white helicopter lifting off from the roof in Västberga. By seven, people had started pouring into the office, and Stenson knew he should have gone home after a long night. But it was impossible. There was a sense in the air that something historic had happened, and this was his story, even if the paper's head start over its main competitor had narrowed. The tabloids, morning papers and Swedish public media were all at the scene out in Västberga, along with a huge number of foreign correspondents—all starved of any internationally interesting news from the Scandinavian backwater where they had been stationed. The scene at the crossroads of Västberga Allé and Vretensborgsvägen was chaotic, and a press conference had been scheduled at police HQ in Kungsholmen for later that day.

Stenson darted between the desks with very little to do, following the foreign coverage of the robbery with the rest of his colleagues. Their European colleagues from the closest time zones were already broadcasting the news by eight, but it took a few hours before the Americans woke up.

On CBS, the focus was on the fact that no one had been hurt. There was talk of the heist being like something from a Hollywood movie, and when they described the skillful robbers, they used an image of Tom Cruise in an action sequence of some kind.

On CNN, they concluded that reality, yet again, had exceeded fiction.

The online headlines from the English papers were, in typical fashion, all humorous plays on words:

"Chopper Heist Is Swede-ly Done," wrote the *Sun*. "It was a heist that would have caught the imagination of any Hollywood producer," wrote the *Times*. "But not even Danny Ocean—despite having three George Clooney films to play with—thought of using a helicopter."

The coverage seemed much more focused on reviewing the robbers' methods, drawing parallels to the world of film, than it was on reporting a crime.

Stenson knew that he wouldn't be invited to the press conference at police headquarters after lunch; he was just a temp from the recruitment company. But at eleven thirty, the paper's star reporter—who had won out and been awarded the prestigious job of covering the robbery by the deputy editor—came over to his desk.

"You can come along if you want, Stenson," he said. "You were first, after all."

Tor Stenson nodded. His pride swelled like a sponge in a bathtub.

98

The American airlines would have been out of the question. With Sami Farhan's criminal record, the obligatory tourist visa applications made it impossible for him to fly via the United States.

Both Air France and British Airways flew from Arlanda to the Dominican Republic, via Paris and London respectively. But the flights also left at six thirty in the morning, and such tight margins weren't acceptable. If everything had gone according to plan, they were meant to have landed in Norsborg at five thirty. Having only an hour to make it up to Arlanda after that would have been too tight.

That left Swiss Air as the only viable alternative. The first leg left at ten in the morning, and he would land—after a change in Zurich, and thanks to the time difference—in Punta Cana early the same evening.

When Sami climbed out of the car at Arlanda and walked into the international terminal, heading for the check-in desks, he felt as though a huge spotlight on the ceiling were following his every move through the departure hall. It seemed to him that everyone was staring, that the police officers talking outside the 7-Eleven were getting ready to pounce.

By the time he handed over his passport to collect his ticket, he could barely talk, his mouth was as dry as sand, and he pulled at the neckband of his T-shirt so hard that it stretched. A few minutes later, standing in the line for Security, his legs were trembling so much that he was shaking all over.

It wasn't even seven in the morning yet.

Just over an hour earlier, he had been standing on a rooftop in Västberga, about to climb into a helicopter.

He could barely believe it when they let him through Security, and when he sat down to wait by the still-empty gate, he couldn't shake the feeling that it was all just a trap. They were giving him false hope, they wouldn't let him leave the country.

During the brief moments when Sami failed to keep up his cautious nervousness, two opposing feelings rose inside him:

The first was a bubbling feeling of joy, something like letting go of a small plastic ball you've been pressing to the bottom of the bath.

They had done it. Shit, they had actually managed to do it.

The second feeling was one of paralyzing anxiety when he thought about Karin and the boys back home on Högbergsgatan.

He closed his eyes and suddenly found himself in Vitabergsparken. It was spring, and the air smelled like grass; Karin was walking alongside him, right by his side, he could make out the scent of her shampoo, she was holding John's hand. The boy was wearing a denim jacket and a pair of what had once been white Converse, laughing his cackling little laugh when a huge dog suddenly approached them. The dog was white and shaggy and as big as the stroller Sami was pushing ahead of him up the hill. John ran forward, toward the dog, and he hugged it, clinging to its neck. Karin followed him, squatted down and stroked its nose and head. Sami knew she wanted him to take the baby out of the stroller, but he hesitated. He didn't like dogs. And so Karin got to her feet, picked up the baby and let his tiny hand, no bigger than a tablespoon, stroke the dog's white fur, so he could see how soft it was.

Suddenly, between him and his family, a crack appeared in the ground. It ran along the path, the gravel falling into the dark opening, and the pang in his heart was followed by a sinking feeling of melancholy that he knew all too well.

Sami stood on one side, looking at them—Karin and the kids next to the huge white dog—on the other. Suddenly, Karin jumped onto the dog's back, lifted the boys up in front of her and then the dog ran away, away from the perilous opening, up the hill. Sami shouted, he shouted again, but no one could hear him.

His heart was pounding like two bass drums, his veins ready to burst in his temples, the tears streaming down his cheeks, and then he woke with a start. He couldn't have been asleep for more than a few seconds, but he glanced suspiciously around the room. Everything looked the same as before.

Almost two hours passed before it was finally time to board the plane. To Sami, it felt like an eternity. But afterward, he would look back and remember it as no more than a few seconds. Even as he walked down the windowless tunnel between the terminal and the plane, he couldn't believe it was true.

They had done it.

By the time he sat down in his seat and fastened his belt, his anxiety had sucked the last of his strength out of him. He fell asleep with his mouth open before the plane even made it onto the runway.

99

The big room that had been put at their disposal for the press conference was far too small. At the very front, standing next to temporary screens bearing the police emblem, were the day's key figures: the police spokesman, Christer Ade, and behind him, Task Force Leader Caroline Thurn from the National Criminal Police. County Police Commissioner Caisa Ekblad and the National Police Commissioner, Therese Olsson, were also present. Each looked surprised at the size of the assembled media in front of them.

Christer Ade waved his arms and shouted out the rules of conduct in both Swedish and English. As a rule, journalists were terrible at taking orders, and it took almost ten minutes just to get the people and the cameras into the right places and for them to stop talking.

The many languages being spoken in the room gave everyone the sense that the world's eyes, that early afternoon of September 23, 2009, were focused on police headquarters in Kungsholmen. It felt like the oxygen was going to run out even before the questions began, and Ade asked someone from the BBC to open the windows and let in some fresh air. But when the sounds of the city came rushing in to the media's assembled microphones, tape recorders and cell phones, they were quickly closed again. The journalists would rather suffocate than not do their job.

Once the noise levels in the room had fallen low enough that Ade thought he could make himself heard, he loudly cleared his throat and began by outlining what had happened. Nothing he said was news to those in the room:

"The robbery was well organized, well planned and technically well equipped. All in all, that may lead to a number of different hypotheses about who was involved, and during this afternoon and evening—"

"Have any arrests been made?" the reporter from *Aftonbladet*, Sweden's biggest tabloid, impatiently interrupted him, waving a yellow microphone in the air.

Ade realized that there was no point continuing his prepared statement. He answered *Aftonbladet's* question with the particular kind of authority that can only be learned in media training courses.

"No. We have questioned a number of people, the type we usually question in situations like this, but . . . no. At present, no one is being held in custody for the robbery in Västberga."

"Martin Hogan, *New York Times*. How much did they steal?" The correspondent's broad American accent caused everyone else to turn around.

He had neither a tape recorder nor a microphone. Instead, he was holding a small notepad and a pen in his hand, as though it were still the 1980s.

Ade switched to English.

"According to G4S, the robbers have stolen a 'large but unconfirmed sum' of money. We don't know any more than that at present."

"Why didn't the police storm the building?" a columnist from Sweden's leading newspaper, *Dagens Nyheter*, wanted to know. The paper's news reporter, standing next to her, was irritated at not having thought of the question himself.

Christer Ade glanced at the national police commissioner, who shook her head almost imperceptibly. And yet Ade took a step to one side, as though to indicate that it was time for someone who had been directly involved to answer the question. County Commissioner Caisa Ekblad cleared her throat.

"There were indications that the robbers were heavily armed," she said in English. "We may be dealing with individuals with military training and equipment here. We wanted to wait for the right resources."

Her words made the room explode with excitement.

"Were they mercenaries?" the *Washington Post* reporter shouted.

"There are reports of helicopters exploding. Can you confirm that?" a representative from the French channel TF1 asked. "We know the police cars were stopped by the chains across the access roads!"

Therese Olsson took a step forward. There was something so authoritative in her movements that the room immediately fell silent. She replied first in Swedish and then in very good English.

"We are defining this robbery as an extraordinary event. This means that police forces from across the county are working on the case. The police chief from the Norrmalm district was the commanding officer this morning, working alongside two operation heads, one in Västberga and one in Arninge. The operation is now working alongside us and the serious, organized crime unit. Which means that we are on high alert across the country."

They loved it.

Caroline Thurn was standing in the shadows, right behind County Commissioner Ekblad, and realized that she would make it through the press conference unscathed. Neither Olsson nor Ekblad could hand over to Thurn at this point; it would make it look like they were shirking their responsibilities.

From her ringside seat, Thurn could feel that the atmosphere in the room was different than usual. Not just because of the number of journalists and nationalities. The questions were being asked in a very different tone, and there was a very different sense of expectation and intensity. At first, she assumed it was just because of how spectacular the robbery had been. Pictures of the helicopter taking off were already plastered across the Internet. No one had been hurt, they had gone in through the roof; this was the type of raid people loved.

But after listening to the commissioners for a while, and realizing that none of the reporters asked any follow-up questions about the course of action the police would be taking, she became doubtful.

A team from Japan and another from Taiwan pointed their cameras at Therese Olsson and asked, in unison, how likely it was that the robbers had left the country.

"We're watching our borders and airspace closely," Olsson replied, sounding very reassuring.

But since the police had no idea who had carried out the raid—not even Zoran Petrovic's involvement was a given—keeping an eye on the country's airspace wouldn't help, Thurn thought.

The Japanese reporter seemed satisfied, however, and didn't follow up with the obvious objection.

In that moment, it dawned on Thurn why this particular press conference was different. What she had already felt in the corridors of the police station over the past few weeks, a reluctant admiration for the robbers' planning and professionalism, was now shaping the questions and attitudes of the assembled media. Ordinarily, the press would be trying to find a scapegoat, or else they would direct their interest toward the victims. The staff at the cash depot had undeniably gone through a deeply unpleasant morning, but no one had been physically hurt, no one had been subjected to a concrete threat.

These journalists, photographers and cameramen, Thurn realized, were here to create heroes.

In a few days' time, in a week or a month, the fact that the police had known about the robbery in advance would come out, she thought. It wasn't hard to imagine what the headlines would be like when that happened: "Police Force Knew Everything, Robbers Escaped." She discreetly glanced around the room. The bright eyes, the loud voices. This, she thought, was just the beginning.

Tor Stenson cleared his throat. The press conference was coming to an end, and so were his chances. He needed to ask a question, something none of the other journalists had thought of, and he had to make sure it was caught on film. There was a job at stake. It had been a long night, morning and day, and weariness washed over him in waves. But suddenly, the question came to him.

Stenson pushed forward a few feet and waved the tabloid's microphone in the air. Therese Olsson nodded.

"My name is Tor Stenson," he said, "and I was first to publish the images of the robbers' helicopter this morning. My question is, where were the police helicopters during the robbery?"

He could see from Olsson's face that she knew the answer but didn't want to say it. He glanced at the cameras around the room. They were rolling. Stenson breathed out. The job had to be his now. He waited for her answer.

100

Mats Berggren wasn't frustrated, he was furious. Unlike Caroline Thurn and the other policemen and -women in the conference room, Berggren couldn't hide what he was feeling. He was neither a diplomat nor a politician; in that moment he was just a fat, annoyed police officer who, for reasons unknown, was being forbidden from hauling in an unquestionably guilty robber.

"This is completely insane!" he repeated. "Everything the Serbs told us happened exactly like they said it would. What is there to think about, surely we just need to bring Petrovic in?"

The late-afternoon sun was low in the sky, shining in through the windows out onto Bergsgatan. The light brutally revealed ancient coffee rings and fresher grease marks on the rectangular table. Those unlucky enough to be sitting with their backs to the corridor had no choice but to squint, as the high windows had no curtains. Breathing heavily, Berggren turned to Caroline Thurn, who was sitting a few seats away.

"Right, Caroline?" he said.

"Mats is right," Thurn replied, since her loyalty in that room was to her partner. But she also added: "It's just a question of when we do it."

After the press conference, Thurn had been mentally exhausted, despite having been able to keep to the background. She hated attention almost as much as she disliked meetings. Like this one. Being cooped up in a room with four walls and a couple of windows, discussing what needed to be done, was the polar opposite of going out and actually doing it. All she could do was bite her lip and keep going, her specialty. She was painfully aware of the play that was going on right now. The people around the table were positioning themselves. They were strengthening their brand and making sure to keep a line of retreat open by bringing up their reservations and concerns. Which they could later remind everyone of, if and when it was necessary. The hundreds of microphones belonging to the Swedish and foreign media would continue to be pointed at every police officer who happened to walk by outside, and they would be a constant reminder that no one could escape. This was a police operation in which, sooner or later, all those involved would have to explain how and why they had acted like they had. The media would love uncovering the constant battle between the county and national police forces, Thurn thought.

Berggren continued his moaning; he wanted to bring Petrovic in, and Thurn felt a certain sympathy for his desire to actually get out there and do something. But it wasn't time yet.

Prosecutor Lars Hertz was standing at the front of the room, next to a huge whiteboard. He was wearing light, well-ironed clothes, something that distinguished him from the crumpled, ashen police officers around the table. He had taken command of the meeting, and he loved the role. His blue eyes shone. The board next to him was covered with notes. Names, dates and arrows drawn in both red and green marker. Though they would use the special cleaner to rub it all out at the end of the day, faint traces of the ink would be left behind.

Berggren got up. He paced back and forth along one wall of the room, making everyone else nervous. His breathing was strained.

"Maybe you should sit down, Mats," Thurn said. "Even though I do understand your frustration."

It was still Wednesday, September 23. The day had been drawn out and endless since the alarm was first raised at a quarter past five that morning. Thurn had stopped off at her apartment to take a shower and change her clothes earlier in the day, and she had since tied her unruly ponytail up into a soft bun that sat low on the nape of her neck.

During the morning, it would have been quicker to count the Stockholm police officers who weren't working on the robbery in Västberga than the other way around. Representatives from practically every department and unit within the National Criminal Police force were gathered around the meeting table in police headquarters. Since the national police commissioner had been forced to stay at the Ministry of Justice, explaining to various ministers why hundreds of police officers outside G4S had stood by while the robbers flew away with their loot, Hertz was leading the meeting.

"But we know who he is," Berggren whined stubbornly, though he did as Thurn told him and sat down.

Even early on that morning, the evidence they had been collecting ahead of the fifteenth—among it the recordings of Zoran Petrovic—had been revisited. Her colleagues may not have known quite how much Thurn had been listening to the tapes, but it was clear to each of them that she knew the material better than anyone else. She was also the only one to know with certainty that there were no direct references to the helicopter heist.

Hertz talked about Serbia, terrorist organizations and criminal networks in Europe.

"Which fucking network? We know who he is," Berggren interrupted for the third or fourth time.

"If we bring in Petrovic now," Hertz said, "then everyone else we want to talk to will disappear within a few hours. That's how it works. And we don't want to make it that easy for them."

The police officers around the table would have nodded in agreement if Hertz hadn't been so inexperienced.

"He's probably right," Thurn eventually said.

"If we have the name of the main suspect before twelve hours have even passed," Hertz continued with a conciliatory smile, "then I suggest we keep working on this for another twelve. Maybe that way we'll find them all?"

The meeting ended and people disappeared in different directions. There were mountains of leads to work through. Back in Thurn's office, she and Berggren continued to rifle through the material from the earlier surveillance operation. They focused on the huge number of names and people Zoran Petrovic had been in contact with.

They produced two separate lists. The first was of known criminals, and the second of those without criminal records. But all the damn nicknames and code words made the lists difficult. There were over a hundred people in each.

Their work wasn't made any easier by the constant interruptions by people from other departments who wanted to discuss their findings. Thurn was considered some kind of expert on Petrovic by that point. She wanted nothing more than to fob them off and finish working on the lists, but as usual she couldn't be rude. She patiently made time for every single person who stuck his or her head in the door to ask for help.

But eventually, midway through a monologue by a young colleague from the Suspect Profile Group, Thurn got up from her desk, grabbed the thin jacket that had been hanging over the back of her chair, and left the office. She just left. Enough desk work now. It was after eight, and darkness had fallen over Kungsholmen.

101

"How was the conference?"

Annika Skott shouted from the hallway, and Niklas Nordgren heard the outer door close a moment later. Then she noticed the smell.

"Hey . . . what are you doing?" she shouted.

A few seconds later, she came into the kitchen and found Nordgren by the stove. The huge pot bubbling away smelled incredible, garlic and bay leaves. It was just after seven in the evening, but the sun was still shining in through the window.

"We finished around lunch, and I didn't think there was much point going back to work," he explained. "So I stopped off at Östermalmshallen and bought some lamb."

He said nothing about having walked most of the way home to Lidingö from Östermalm, a distance of over six miles. Which, in turn, was just a fifth of the total he had walked that day.

The endorphins were refusing to leave his body, he couldn't stop smiling. In his attempts to go back to being the ordinary Niklas Nordgren, the calm and slightly sulky man who liked to keep himself busy, the exact opposite had emerged. He felt even more wound up than he had that morning.

"That smells incredible," said Annika. "God, I'm hungry. I'm just going to get changed. Then you can tell me everything."

She disappeared into the bedroom, as always, to take off her tax adviser clothing and put on something more comfortable.

Nordgren continued to stir the pot.

It was going to be tough to tell her about the conference he'd told her he was attending when, in fact, he had actually been sleeping the days away in a too-short bed on Runmarö. He wasn't a good liar to begin with, but a conference of hundreds of electricians would—as Nordgren imagined it—be an unbearably boring story.

But the real problem was that his body was still singing.

That was how it felt. As though his muscles, synapses and connective tissues were celebrating in secret.

They had done it.

102

Thurn took the elevator down to the garage, and as she climbed into her car she knew she wouldn't be going home.

She still wasn't sure. In her new-smelling Volvo, she could no longer avoid the questions that had been bothering her all day. How could someone who had planned a robbery involving at least twenty people, requiring thousands of hours of careful planning, manage not to give anything away for an entire month? Especially someone like Petrovic, who had said plenty of other revealing things, suggesting he hadn't been aware of the microphones until, perhaps, the end.

How could her colleagues in police headquarters be so sure that this previously unknown man was the brains behind the spectacular helicopter heist?

It didn't add up.

She turned left onto Scheelegatan, drove over the Barnhus Bridge and then took another left.

Zoran Petrovic lived no more than five minutes from police head-quarters.

Caroline Thurn had never seen him in person, but she knew where he lived. When she parked her car outside his door, it was almost eight thirty in the evening.

She had to see him.

She wouldn't know until she saw him.

She had spent so many nights with him, with that incessant voice in her ears, that self-confident tone, the way he placed himself at the center of the universe. She couldn't help the fact that she was equal parts impressed and annoyed with him. But she had to supplement everything she knew with a real person's gaze, movements and presence. It was the only way to be sure.

After half an hour, a young woman came out of the building, and Thurn took the opportunity to sneak in. She climbed the stairs to Petrovic's apartment and rang the bell, not quite knowing what she would say if he answered. But there was no one home, and when she picked the lock and went in, she didn't see anything that gave her a particular feeling either way.

With a sigh, she returned to the street and waited on the sidewalk.

He appeared just after ten, walking down Upplandsgatan in a short, thin jacket. She spotted him from a distance and immediately knew it was him. Tall and slender as a flagpole. She took a step out into the middle of the sidewalk just as he was about to reach the door, and he had no choice but to stop.

"Sorry," she said, "but you don't know what time it is, do you?"

Zoran Petrovic glanced at her with a wry smile. Thurn allowed him to look her up and down, to value and judge her. There was a certain timidity to him, she thought, but for a few seconds he brushed that to one side, stood up straight and went onto autopilot.

"Not too late for a drink," he replied.

She must have passed his first appraisal, but she couldn't sense any concrete conviction behind his invite. Despite the mocking smile, which she assumed was meant to pique her interest, he seemed more tired than anything.

She smiled.

"Thanks," she said. "But I don't think so."

She looked him deep in the eye, utterly indifferent to whether he had misunderstood her.

"OK," he replied, with a certain sense of relief. "That's fine. It's been a long day, but there'll be others. Do you live around here?"

She smiled. Studied him. The uncertain flash in his eyes when she replied with a laugh: "I work nearby."

And then she turned and walked away.

She felt better.

She was sure.

It was him.

103

Work in police headquarters was complicated on Thursday, September 24, by the sheer number of crime scenes that had to be examined. The forensic resources they had at their disposal simply weren't enough.

To begin with, they had to go through the robbers' entry route into the cash depot in Västberga. From the roof to the balcony on the fifth floor, and then up to Counting on the sixth. The helicopter had been found early on Wednesday, and along with it a good deal of abandoned equipment that could yield traces of DNA. By lunch, a pair of gloves and a balaclava had been found in a trash can by a bus stop a few miles away from the launch site on Värmdö. These had been sent for analysis along with the two bomb devices that had been placed outside the hangar.

The investigations of the various crime scenes were taking place more or less simultaneously, which meant that on Thursday morning, neither the prosecution authority nor the National Criminal Police had a good overview of what was actually known or expected. Paradoxically, information was also leaking out of police headquarters like a surging spring river. The Swedish media seemed to be completely up to date with the investigation, and by afternoon, Hertz realized that it was quicker to read the online version of the evening papers than it was to wait for internal updates.

The content was identical.

On the morning of Friday, September 25, Detective Chief Inspector Caroline Thurn was called into a meeting at the prosecution authority on Fleminggatan. Since the walls of police headquarters seemed to have ears, they had given up holding meetings there.

Therese Olsson was already waiting when Thurn arrived, as were Berggren and a couple of other colleagues. There was a tangible sense of excitement in the room. Traces of blood had been found at G4S during the previous day. And not in just one place, but several, most clearly by the damaged door into the cash depot. As the computers in the basement raced to find a clear match in the extensive Swedish crime register, bets were currently being made.

Names from the investigation flew through the room.

"One hundred on Zoran Petrovic."

"I'll bet two hundred," said Berggren.

"Three fifty on Michel Maloof," said the youngster from the Suspect Profile Group.

Maloof was one of hundreds of names in Thurn and Berggren's list of criminals who had been in contact with Petrovic during August.

Thurn didn't take part in the betting. It wasn't how she thought police work should be done.

They spent a few minutes discussing their surveillance options and how the day could best be spent, but everyone fell silent when the phone on Hertz's desk started to ring. Breathlessly, they stared at the prosecutor as he listened tensely, noted something down and then nodded.

He hung up and said: "Sami Farhan?"

It was a question.

"Sami Farhan?" Caroline Thurn repeated, astonished. "That's the middle brother."

"You know who he is?" Hertz asked. He sounded surprised.

But Prosecutor Lars Hertz was the only person in the room with no idea who the Farhan brothers were.

"Farhan?" said Therese Olsson. "But . . . he doesn't have anything to do with Zoran Petrovic, does he?"

"He's not mentioned in the investigation reports or on the tapes," Berggren confirmed. "He's not on our lists."

"Who is Farhan?" Hertz asked in frustration.

"Do you remember the robbery at the National Museum?" Berggren replied. "The art heist? Just before Christmas a few years ago?"

"That was Sami Farhan and his brothers. Among others," said Thurn.

"But there's no mention of him anywhere in our investigation," said Hertz.

Berggren got up.

"OK," he said. "Let's go and pick up Farhan."

"No," said Hertz.

"No?"

"No."

Berggren looked dismayed.

"I want to find the money first," said Hertz.

The room was silent.

"I want to find the money, then we can haul them all in. Without the cash, the media will lynch us."

"It's too late," said Berggren.

"I'm afraid you'll never find the money, Lars." Thurn backed up her colleague. "I agree with Mats that it's better to drop that thought."

"Twenty-four hours," Hertz insisted. "Let's give ourselves twenty-four hours. If we haven't gotten anywhere by tomorrow morning, we'll go and pick up Farhan and Petrovic and his entire damn address book. OK?"

"Is that a promise?" asked Berggren.

"That's a promise," Hertz replied.

"I'd like to bring in Petrovic personally," said Caroline.

Thurn's colleagues turned to look at her, but no one asked why. They all knew the answer would be polite but insignificant.

104

Michel Maloof had spent Wednesday with Zoran Petrovic, trying to find out exactly what had happened. True to character, he had brushed his anger, disappointment and surprise to one side, and he worked methodically. Who had sent the text message to Petrovic's phone during the early hours of the morning? How could Maloof's number have been used without his knowledge? Who was behind the wheel of the boat, and where had it gone? Where was the leak, who had tricked them?

But when evening came around and he was still none the wiser— other than finding out that if someone knew his phone number, it was fairly easy to use the cellular network to make it appear on Petrovic's display—Maloof was overwhelmed by a weariness that caused him to sleep through the night and well into Thursday.

When he woke, it was late afternoon, and he felt completely crushed.

They had done it, that was sure.

But the money was gone.

Sami and Nordgren still didn't have a clue. In their respective worlds, everything was as it should be, and Västberga was still the perfect job. The thought of telling them made Maloof feel even more desperate. He knew what Sami would say; he would point to Petrovic and blame him. It was the simplest explanation, but only if you hadn't seen the surprise in the Yugoslavian's eyes when he realized what had happened that morning.

Whoever had screwed them over had also screwed over Petrovic.

At eight that evening, Maloof called Alexandra Svensson. He couldn't bear being alone any longer. He needed the full attention of a sympathetic woman, warm skin for the night ahead.

But Alexandra didn't answer. Her phone rang, but there was no answering machine linked to the number, there never had been. He tried several times that evening, all without success. Something might have happened to her, but he didn't have the energy to worry about it. Thoughts of the money, the boat and the phones were still spinning through his mind, and he didn't have room for anything else. He fell asleep just after midnight, and dreamed he was flying low through the air.

On Friday, the first thing Maloof did was to call Alexandra Svensson, before he had even climbed out of bed. By eight o'clock, when she still hadn't answered, he was starting to get seriously worried. He decided to find out what had happened. He knew she lived in Hammarby Sjöstad, but he couldn't remember the exact address. Maloof had never been to her sublet sublet, but she had told him where it was.

Or had she? He usually remembered addresses.

After a cup of black coffee, he called G4S and asked the switchboard if he could speak with the head of HR. He was told that Ingela Planström wouldn't be in before nine, and so at nine on the dot he called back.

"Planström," she answered.

"I'm calling about Alexandra Svensson's father," Maloof said. "It's of the utmost importance that we get hold of Alexandra as soon as possible, but she isn't answering her phone. Do you have an address where we can reach her?"

"Her father?" said the head of HR, sounding nervous. "Is he ill? Just a moment . . . Here. Sickla Kanalgata Six."

"Thanks so much," said Maloof, hanging up.

Just over twenty minutes later, he climbed out of his Seat in Hammarby Sjöstad. There was an intercom in the doorway to Sickla Kanalgata 6, and he pressed the buzzer. He heard a rustling over the speaker, but before he had time to say anything, the door buzzed open, and

Maloof stepped inside. There was a list of residents in the entrance hall, and Alexandra's apartment was on the second floor. He ran up the stairs and knocked.

A young woman Maloof had never seen before opened the door, a slim blond in jeans and a T-shirt.

"Oh," he said, surprised. "I didn't know . . . I'm looking for Alexandra?"

"Yeah?" the woman in the doorway said.

"Alexandra Svensson?" Maloof clarified.

"Yeah. That's me."

"No . . . but . . . the other Alexandra Svensson," said Maloof. "Who lives here."

Alexandra Svensson stared at him. She shook her head, not understanding what he meant.

"I live here. I'm Alexandra Svensson. What do you mean?"

105

There are over one hundred thousand islands in the Stockholm archipelago, and just as many capes and bays.

Lena Hall had spent the summers of her childhood on the island of Utö, and was so used to the archipelago that she would never underestimate the rocks that weren't marked on the nautical charts. She had learned to sail before she was ten, chugged around in a small dinghy with a five-horsepower outboard motor, fishing for perch in the streams and pike in the reeds by the time she was twelve. Now she was behind the wheel of a motorboat, moving southward through Hårsfjärden at a speed of thirty knots. The morning of Friday, September 25, was cold, and the water lay still and calm. The boat's metal hull cut through the water like a knife through warm butter, and the wind in her hair was cold as ice. Autumn had arrived.

Lena slowed down as she approached land, and she headed along the coast.

It was one of these bays, she just wasn't sure which. She always got them confused. He had forbidden her from putting up any markers.

She pulled out a small pair of binoculars, but before she had time to raise them to her eyes, she spotted movement on the island.

A black dog.

It was standing on a rock, its paws in the water, looking out to sea. Lena slowed down again and set a course toward the rocky beach and the dog. When she focused, she spotted two more dogs at the very edge of the woods. She smiled, and knew she had found the right place.

As she slowly drifted toward land, the dogs caught sight of her, and all eight gathered around the boat as she dragged it up onto the pebbles. The old man and his walking stick didn't appear before Lena had jumped ashore. She was in the process of unloading the mailbags when, suddenly, he was behind her.

"In your element, I see," he commented.

"You had no idea, did you?" she said. "Every summer vacation in the archipelago. Not that far from here, actually."

He shook his head. He hadn't known.

During the seventies, he had been head over heels in love with the woman who would much later become Lena Hall's mother. When Lena's biological father vanished from the scene a decade or so ago, it had been natural for him to offer what help he could. From a distance, of course.

And now she had helped him.

Lena disappeared into the cramped cabin of the boat and returned with the last of the bags. She threw it over the railing.

"How much is in there?" he asked, peering at the haul without any interest.

"No idea," she said. "Haven't counted it, I just took what was mine."

"You can move it up into the woods," he told her. "I'll take care of it from there."

She did as he said. It took her less than five minutes, occasionally tripping over a black dog that wanted to help out.

Once she was finished, she couldn't help but ask.

"What about Michel?"

Lena would miss Michel, she had grown to like him. She wouldn't miss Alexandra Svensson, however. She could just imagine Alexandra's disappointment on Tuesday, when she didn't turn up for the usual class at Friskis & Svettis. She would never have to listen to Alexandra Svensson's long stories about her job or her loneliness again.

"Michel Maloof's a good boy," the old man replied.

Lena smiled, she agreed.

"I meant with the money," she said. "Is he going to get any?"

"We'll have to see how it goes," the old man replied.

Lena nodded, not knowing whether he was just saying what he thought she wanted to hear. She pushed the boat back off the shore and jumped on board before it drifted out of the bay. Once it had moved deep enough, she lowered the motor.

It took the old man almost an hour to move the five mailbags up to the house. He used a wheelbarrow, but thick tree roots had grown over the path and sharp stones stuck up at each side, threatening to burst its tire. On top of that, he had a bad back. The dogs, as always, hoped it was a game, and they got in his way several times, making him stop and set down the wheelbarrow to wave them away.

People foraging for berries and mushrooms usually came close to his cottage only a couple of times a year, but it wasn't worth the risk. He would sort and store the money in his earth cellar. He pulled the money from the bags and sorted it into plastic sacks according to denomination. Then he piled the plastic bags on top of one another in the small cardboard boxes he unfolded as he needed them. Finally, he stacked his new boxes on top of the old ones, and once he had done four bags, he stretched, sighed deeply, and decided that was enough.

He took the fifth bag into the cottage with him, setting it down next to the boots by the inner door.

It was eleven o'clock, which meant it was time for a cup of coffee. But as he moved to fill the machine with water, he noticed a crack in the pot. He ran his finger over the glass, but he couldn't feel anything. Still, he could see it clearly.

He filled the machine with water and measured the coffee into the filter, but his eyes were fixed on the crack the entire time. It had happened before. He had no idea where the cracks came from, but the exact same thing had happened a few years earlier. He had paid no notice to it at the time, but the pot had later broken, sending scalding hot coffee pouring onto the worktop and burning his thigh.

He would have to go into Handen to buy a new one.

He hated taking the bus into Handen. He sighed and decided he could do it next week.

Acknowledgments

First and foremost, I'd like to say a huge thanks to Niclas Salomonsson. It's as simple as this: without Niclas, there wouldn't be a book. I'd also like to thank everyone else who has worked on this project at Salomonsson Agency; no one named, no one forgotten. Then there are you few who have read the various versions of the manuscript and, through your ideas and opinions, made the novel better. For that, aside from Niclas, I'd especially like to thank Helena, Ulrika and Daniel. A special thanks to Love and Ina too. Just to be on the safe side.

Alongside court transcripts and interviews, a number of authors and journalists have made this plunge into 2009 and the events leading up to the helicopter heist, culminating on that dramatic night in September, much easier. The huge amount of journalism connected to both the robbery and the trial provided me with a real sense of the time line, the gossip and the facts. In particular, I'd like to mention Sveriges Radio and P3 Dokumentär, where Anton Berg did such fantastic work and enabled both the staff at G4S and task force leader Hans Knutsen-Öy of the National Criminal Police to have their say. Håkan Lahger's careful, well-written book *Helikopterpiloten* also made my job much easier.

But above all, of course, I'd like to thank Goran Bojovic, Charbel Charro, Safa Kadhum and Mikael Södergran for having endured hours and days with me, my notepad and my thousands of questions.

About the Author

Jonas Bonnier is a screenwriter and journalist as well as a novelist. He was the CEO & President of the Bonnier Group from 2008 to 2014. Bonnier lives with his wife and two children in Miami.

Alice Menzies holds a master of arts in Translation Theory and Practice from University College London, specializing in the Scandinavian languages. She lives in London.